P10

MURDER BY THE BOOK

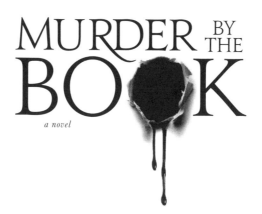

a novel

MURDER BY THE BOOK

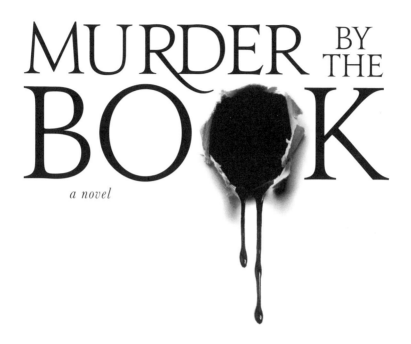

a novel

BETSY BRANNON GREEN

Covenant Communications, Inc.

Cover images: *Old Book* © Steve Cole; Courtsey of Getty Images. *Bullet Holes* © Caspar Benson; Courtsey of Getty Images. *Dripping Blood* © Renee Lee; Courtsey of iStock Photo.

Cover design copyrighted 2009 by Covenant Communications, Inc.

Published by Covenant Communications, Inc.
American Fork, Utah

Printed in The United States
First Printing: October 2009

15 14 13 12 11 10 09   10 9 8 7 6 5 4 3 2 1

ISBN-13: 978-1-59811-938-1
ISBN-10: 1-59811-938-9

To Curt, Julie, James, Amanda, and Will
Five of the most amazing people I know
(who just happen to be my brothers and sisters)

ACKNOWLEDGMENTS

As always I am thankful for the support I receive from my husband and children. When I was young I dreamed of having a large, busy, happy family, and my life now is proof that dreams do come true. Every day is an adventure, and I wouldn't trade places with anyone else in the world.

Another huge blessing in my life is my wonderful editor, Kirk Shaw. I cannot possibly say enough good things about him and all the other talented, dedicated, and genuinely nice people at Covenant. They consistently publish some of the best fiction in the LDS market and I'm honored to have my name listed among their authors.

And finally, thanks to all my readers. Without you, none of this would be possible!

CHAPTER ONE

THE DAY STARTED OUT WITH a speeding ticket and ended with a murder. The ticket was only a minor inconvenience, because the issuing officer was my ex-husband, Cade Burrell. He just pulled me over so he could try to finagle a date. He was wasting his time, because I didn't agree to go out with him, and I have no intention of paying that ticket. The murder was another matter entirely.

My name is Kennedy Killingsworth, and I live in the town of Midway, Georgia—home to four thousand people who don't have anyplace better to go. I've never been able to get a satisfactory answer to why the town is called Midway. It's not halfway between anywhere as far as I can tell—unless you count despair and hopelessness.

Midway is so small that if you blinked during your drive through town, you'd miss it. And until a few weeks ago, if you kept your eyes open, all you'd have seen was a blur of broken glass, drooped awnings, and peeling paint. For as long as I can remember, Main Street has been pitted with potholes and lined by abandoned buildings. The only interesting thing about Midway is a stop sign that used to hang from the branch of an oak tree at the intersection of Main and First. But that was replaced years ago with an ordinary, stuck-in-the-ground sign. My father said it was done in the name of progress. If that was the goal, the new sign was a failure.

I have two sisters—both older—one father, and one mother. My parents live in the farmhouse that has been in the family for generations. I've always resented those original Killingsworths. If they'd had just a little foresight, they would have pushed on past Midway and settled a mere fifty miles farther south on the Gulf Coast. Then my parents would own valuable beachfront property instead of a few acres of mediocre farmland.

My father is a quiet man who delivers mail for a living, tinkers with old cars as a hobby, and fishes when he needs time away from my mother.

Mother is an enthusiastic Christian and a consummate homemaker. She believes that true happiness can be achieved only through heavenly sanctioned matrimony followed, after a respectable passage of time, by pregnancy and childbirth. Both my sisters are married, so she constantly harps on my single status. She tries alternately to set me up with eligible bachelors or reunite me with my ex-husband so I can join the ranks of motherhood. She already has four grandkids, and you'd think she'd be satisfied, but apparently in her circle, grandchildren are like stocks and bonds—the more you have, the more respect you command.

When I received the aforementioned speeding ticket, I was on my way to the Midway Library, where I am the director, cataloger, purchaser, custodian, and owner of almost every book on the shelves. I've been obsessed with books all my life. I blame this mostly on the fact that I live in the dullest spot on earth, and during my uneventful childhood I found escape from paralyzing boredom through the written word. My mother didn't understand my need for books, but she allowed it. However, when my collection surpassed five hundred she said she had reached her tolerance limit and demanded that they leave her house.

So I built some shelves in my grandpa's old barn and lined each volume up according to the Dewey decimal system. Friends and neighbors came by to borrow my books, and I checked them out in a spiral notebook.

For several years I did a respectable business, and shortly after I graduated from the local junior college, the mayor of Midway came in to look around. Mayor Cook, who runs a towing business in addition to his civic responsibilities, said he was impressed with what I'd been able to accomplish and offered to give me the use of an empty trailer near the public pool where I could set up a real library for the town.

He went on to explain that once the library was established, the county would be required to pay my salary and the monthly rent for the trailer. The mayor owned the empty trailer and was probably more interested in collecting rent than promoting literacy in Midway, but I didn't care. Finally we were going to have a real library, and I was going to be the director. I thought I'd died and gone to heaven.

The Midway City Library has since expanded into two trailers, and my dream is to someday boast five trailers like our more prosperous neighbors to the south. Their trailers are arranged in a star-shaped design. We're a T at the moment, but I've spent hours thinking of how to add trailers in eye-catching ways.

I arrived at the Midway City Library fifteen minutes late, thanks to Cade, and found Miss Ida Jean Baxley waiting. She's my mother's next-door neighbor and one of the most irritating people on the face of the earth.

"I thought the library hours were ten to five on Mondays," Miss Ida Jean whined the minute I got out of my truck. She has a perpetual string of saliva between her lips that moves up and down as she speaks but never seems to break. Since childhood I've been morbidly fascinated by this phenomenon.

"You're correct about the hours, Miss Ida Jean," I returned in my fake-nice voice. "I was delayed by car trouble." I figured this wasn't a complete lie since I *had* been driving, and Cade *definitely* qualified as trouble.

"If you were still married to Cade, you wouldn't have to worry about car trouble," Miss Ida Jean lectured senselessly. "Every woman needs a man to help her handle things like that."

"I've got a father who can take care of car repairs," I replied.

Miss Ida Jean just couldn't let it go. "Your father is a saint, and of course he'll help you with anything, but I know it breaks your mother's heart to have a divorce in the family."

I wasn't brave enough to tell her exactly what I thought about this remark, but I muttered a few choice words under my breath.

"I've never believed in divorce." Miss Ida Jean continued her sermon. "*What God has joined together, let no man put asunder!* That's from the Bible," she added, as if my divorced state had rendered me stupid as well as immoral.

I gritted my teeth and turned on the lights. "Yes, ma'am."

Her beady little eyes brightened. "So are you and Cade going to get back together?"

This illustrates a nasty nuance of Southern etiquette. It is perfectly acceptable for Miss Ida Jean to ask me such a personal, painful question. But if I were to ask Miss Ida Jean how her son Robby was enjoying his extended stay in the state penitentiary, that would be a gross breach of good manners. My mother blames the injustice on the fact that Miss Ida Jean is elderly, but I can't accept that. Rude is rude no matter how old you are.

Of course I didn't say any of this to Miss Ida Jean (since I value my life, and my mother would have killed me for an etiquette infraction of this magnitude). I just smiled and said, "Cade and I will always be friends." I'll admit that by now my voice was a little more fake and a little less nice. Cade's betrayal had been very public and fairly recent. I could still barely force myself to think about it—let alone discuss it.

"Well, you know the old saying: 'boys will be boys,'" Miss Ida Jean said. "We women are often called upon to overlook their frailties and weaknesses."

"Yes, ma'am," I managed again, although I strongly disagreed. Cade was a full-grown man—not a boy—when he made his marriage vows, and I believed he was under the same obligation as me to keep them.

Because of his job as a sheriff's deputy, Cade had always worked odd hours. Consequently, I didn't think a thing about it when he called that infamous night and said he'd be late. My sister Reagan (who lives almost an hour away in Macon) was in town, and my other sister, Madison (unfortunately she lives nearby in Albany) came up with the idea for the three of us to go see a movie at the local drive-in. (Yes, such places do still exist—in fact, in Midway it's our only cinematic option.)

By the time we got there, the movie had already started. Madison had a new car and didn't want to risk running into something by driving up and down the rows in the dark, so we parked in the very back. The couple beside us was already heavily involved in a semi-dressed wrestling match. What we could see in the dim light was much more interesting than the movie on the screen, and we were avidly watching when I recognized the intertwined couple. Cade had dated Missy Lamar all through high school. Missy moved away for a while but was home now, and apparently the two of them were having a private reunion.

From that point on, my marriage was over. Honestly, I might have been able to get past the infidelity—but knowing my sisters had seen my husband with another woman was too much.

"I heard that Missy moved to Nashville," Miss Ida Jean continued as if I should be relieved. "So you won't have to worry about her distracting Cade again."

After Miss Ida Jean's insensitive remark, I knew I was within my rights to mention her jailbird son. But I love my mother, who loves her standing in the community, so instead I pasted on my most professional smile and said, "What can I help you with today?"

Unfortunately, Miss Ida Jean had several things that required my attention. She stayed at the library for nearly an hour, making me look for various inspirational fiction books that I don't have. Then she left empty-handed. It seems like the least she could do was check out a lousy magazine, since the only way I'll ever qualify for another trailer is by increasing my circulation.

It was a nice day in early March, but by noon the double trailer was feeling stuffy, so I opened the windows. This was an involved process that required an old broom handle and two bricks. Once I had a cross-breeze going, I got out my lunch, which consisted of a day-old bag of boiled peanuts and a Pepsi. While I was eating, the UPS man arrived with a box full of used books I'd bought on eBay.

I put aside the peanuts and opened the box with all the anticipation of Christmas and my birthday combined. But before I could start cataloging the new books, I was interrupted twice. First by Enid Ford, who was looking for a book on birthday party ideas. The second interruption was Mabel Osgood, an English teacher at the local high school. She was returning a stack of classical fiction books she had borrowed to help the seniors in her class complete the required reading.

"Thanks, Kennedy," Miss Mabel said as she stacked the paperbacks on the counter by the door.

"You're welcome," I replied. "I hope they were helpful to you."

Miss Mabel sighed. "The kids didn't read them, if that's what you mean. It's nearly impossible to get them to appreciate the great authors. But I feel that by checking the books out I fulfilled my obligation to my students."

I commiserated with Miss Mabel about the literary shortcomings of the rising generation until she left for a parent–teacher conference. Then I finished cataloging my new books and arranged them on the Recent Acquisitions shelf.

Once my new books were displayed to full advantage, I finished my lunch and was contemplating a run to the Quick Mart down the street for a Snickers bar when the library door opened. I looked up to see a tall man and a sturdy-looking little girl standing in what I affectionately call "the lobby."

The man was a walking explanation of why Southern stereotypes exist. His deeply tanned skin resembled sun-hardened leather, indicating that he'd worked outside most of his life. He was wearing fairly clean coveralls and held a ragged baseball cap in his callused hands. I couldn't see his neck from my vantage point, but I would have bet every dime I owned that it was red.

He nudged the child forward and said, "Girl's got a report due tomorrow on Abraham Lincoln."

For some reason, people equate *librarian* with "homework specialist."

The man gave the girl another, less-gentle shove and said, "I'm not too good with writing, so you'll need to help her."

I re-pasted the fake smile on that I usually reserve for Miss Ida Jean and said, "I'd be glad to." While I led the way over to the library's biographical section, I covertly checked my watch. The library was supposed to close in exactly fifteen minutes.

"My name is Ms. Killingsworth," I continued with artificial cheerfulness.

"I'm Foster Scoggins, and this here is Heaven," the man reciprocated around a cheekful of chewing tobacco.

Heaven appeared to be about seven, and if the layer of dirt on her skin were cleaned away, she might have been pretty. In an effort to be child-friendly (which is not one of my strong points), I bent down so that our eyes were on the same level and asked, "Was there something particular about President Lincoln that you'd like to research?"

Heaven shrugged as if she couldn't care less.

"It don't matter what," Mr. Scoggins contributed. "Just as long as she has something to turn in to her teacher tomorrow. Otherwise she's going to have to stay in the first grade a third time."

The inclusion of the word *third* to assess the number of completed years of *first grade* was mind-boggling. Wondering if it was truly possible to fail the first grade more than once, I stood straight and removed an illustrated version of Abraham Lincoln's life called *Who Was Abraham Lincoln?* After putting it on the small table in the middle of the room, I suggested, "Why don't we try this?"

Heaven blew a bubble that momentarily obliterated her face from my view and then popped it with a grimy finger. I watched in horror as she peeled the pieces of gum from her dirty face and rammed them back into her mouth.

Working hard to control a shudder, I opened the book. "Did you bring paper?" I asked.

"We're out." Mr. Scoggins spit tobacco juice out the open window, and when he turned back to face me, a brown dribble was settling itself into the whisker stubble on his chin.

Thankful for the opportunity to look away, I walked to my desk and removed a few pieces of loose-leaf paper from a drawer. I selected some pencils from the cup full of writing utensils and returned to the table. I put them in front of Heaven, pulled out a chair, and said, "Why don't you sit here so you can write more easily."

Heaven just smacked her gum.

"She can't write," Mr. Scoggins said.

As if on cue, Heaven lifted her right hand. It was loosely wrapped in filthy gauze.

"She cut it with a knife," Mr. Scoggins continued. "All the way to the bone. Doc said another inch and she'd have lost her thumb."

I'm not usually squeamish, but I'll admit that this description of the child's injury made me light-headed. So I sat in the chair I had offered to Heaven. I pulled the paper into place and began to write. It took me five minutes to succinctly summarize the life of Abraham Lincoln. I handed the paper to Heaven and stood in what I hoped they would recognize as my please-don't-waste-any-more-of-my-time manner.

Mr. Scoggins didn't take the hint. He gave the library a visual once-over and then asked, "You got books on rabbits?"

I walked about a foot to my right and studied the nonfiction section of the Midway Library. "No, sir." I tried to sound regretful. "I've got beavers and gophers, but no rabbits."

"I love rabbit," Heaven confided, and I was pleased by the friendly overture.

I leaned toward her. "I've heard they make good pets."

"We eat 'em," she informed me, and I'm positive I saw a gleam of malice in her eyes.

Feeling light-headed again, I held on to the back of the chair.

"I'll take the book on gophers," Mr. Scoggins said. "They taste about the same."

I'm proud that I didn't know the flavor of either animal. After I had carried the book on gophers to the checkout counter, it came as no surprise to find that Mr. Scoggins did not have a library card. I handed him an application and suggested that he fill it out in Heaven's name. "A library card is a good thing for students to have."

Mr. Scoggins reviewed the form carefully. "This don't cost nothing, does it?"

"No," I assured him. "The library card is free. But if you fail to return the book by the due date, there will be a fine."

He nodded. "I wouldn't mind having a card myself—since you got books on gophers and such."

Two new library card applicants would look good on my monthly report, so I felt a little more congenial. I gave Mr. Scoggins a second application, and after sending one more brown stream of tobacco spit out of the window, he sat down at the table and began to write.

During this tedious process, Heaven walked around my tiny library, pulling books from the shelves and then sticking them back in the wrong places. When she saw me watching her, I thought she'd be ashamed or at least stop this inexcusable behavior. But instead, she removed two more books and dropped them on the floor, effectively proving her name a misnomer and strengthening my resolve to remain childless.

Finally Mr. Scoggins completed both applications, and I prepared temporary library cards for him and Heaven. "Your permanent ones will come in the mail," I said.

Mr. Scoggins nodded and picked up the gopher book. Then he stepped out onto the trailer's small front stoop. "Come on, girl!" he hollered over his shoulder at Heaven.

Instead of joining Mr. Scoggins, Heaven walked up to me and placed a book about goats on the counter. "Would you like to check out this book?" I asked.

She smacked her dirty gum and nodded.

Against my better judgment, I stamped the checkout slip. "You have to bring both books back in two weeks," I instructed her firmly. However, when the door closed behind them, I figured I'd seen the last of the Scogginses and the part of my nonfiction section that was now in their possession. Fortunately we don't have a lot of requests for books on gophers or goats, so neither book would be greatly missed. And never let it be said that I haven't done my part toward wiping out illiteracy in Midway.

I picked up the paperbacks Miss Mabel had returned and walked toward the classic fiction section. I was placing the books on the shelf when a folded piece of notebook paper fell out of a well-worn copy of *The Old Man and the Sea.* Scrawled across the top of the paper was one pencil-written sentence. It said, "If boring books could kill you, I'd be dead."

I shook my head as I considered the words written by one of Miss Mabel's students. In this visual world of electronics and technology, it seemed that children could no longer appreciate the beauty of the written word. I loved *The Old Man and the Sea,* and the words written on the paper made me sad.

I crumpled the piece of paper and walked up to the garbage can by my desk. As I passed the window, I glanced outside and saw Mr. Scoggins and Heaven climbing into a pickup truck that was in worse need of a paint job than mine. I threw away the paper, stepped back from the window, and didn't give that old truck another thought. Until they found the body, that is.

Since we were not yet equipped with computers, I placed the application forms Mr. Scoggins had filled out into an envelope and addressed it to the main branch of the Dougherty County Library System. I left the envelope on my desk with the intention of mailing it first thing the next morning.

Belatedly I began my closing time routine, which was further delayed by two phone calls. The first was from my mother asking if I'd like to come to dinner. My mother's motives are much the same as Miss Ida Jean's. She wants to know when I'm going to forgive Cade for his "misconduct." Her methods, however, are more subtle. She uses food and guilt to lure me home for a lecture on the sanctity of marriage.

The second phone call was from my oldest sister, Madison, asking me to babysit. Unlike my mother and Miss Ida Jean, Madison is in no hurry for me to resolve my marital difficulties, since until my divorce, she had created the biggest scandal in Killingsworth family history by marrying a Mormon. To make it worse, she converted. But the upside for my mother is that Mormons believe in having lots of kids. Madison has produced three of my mother's four grandchildren, and she's pregnant again—hence her need for a babysitter. She and her husband, Jared, were scheduled to attend childbirth classes that evening. I figured they ought to know all the important stuff about birthing babies this fourth time around, so I didn't feel guilty when I said that I had plans.

Thanks to the Scogginses' visit and the phone calls, it was ten minutes after five o'clock when I finally locked the door and turned the sign in the window to CLOSED. I did a quick walk-through to make sure my little library was in order, straightening the books Heaven had disturbed as I went. When I passed the table in the center of the room, I saw the report about Abraham Lincoln that I had so patiently written out for Heaven Scoggins on the floor.

I frowned at the single sheet of paper. I suspected Heaven had left the report on purpose and knew it would serve the little beast right if I let her fail the assignment. Then I thought about Mr. Scoggins. He had driven her all the way in to town and asked for my help. But honestly what tipped the scales in Heaven's favor was the thought of the first-grade teachers at Midway Elementary having to keep the child for another year. Surely it was time for the second grade teachers to have their turn.

So I went to the desk and opened the envelope that contained the library card applications. I scanned the form until I found a phone number. I called it but got no answer, and, not surprisingly, there was no voice mail. Again I considered taking the wise approach—tossing the report in the trash. I was sure Heaven didn't care. But Mr. Scoggins had gone to the trouble to bring the child to the library, and it seemed a shame to let a perfectly good report go to waste. So I decided to deliver the report to Heaven (which proves that I'm not as sensible as I pretend to be).

The address listed on the application was Scoggins Salvage Yard. There were only a few places around Midway that I had not visited at least once during my twenty-four years of life. The Scoggins Salvage Yard was one of them. I knew my father had gotten parts for his old cars from them on occasion, and I knew exactly where it was located—off County Road 34 just before Mr. Bateman's gas station. The salvage yard was not on my way home, but a trip there to deliver Heaven's paper could be considered "plans for the evening"—just in case my mother or sister tried to pin me down as to exactly why I couldn't babysit.

So I put the applications back into the envelope, locked the library, and headed out to my 1972 Chevy Cheyenne C10. It's orange with white side panels and the original factory air conditioner (which still cools occasionally). As I said, it could use a paint job (and some bodywork too, for that matter), but it runs pretty good most of the time. My mother hates it. She says driving a truck is unladylike. But I love my truck, and I've never cared all that much for being a lady.

To better appreciate the mild spring weather, I left my windows down as I drove. Once I got out of town, I admired all the farmland, freshly tilled and ready for planting. I passed the Feed and Seed store, crossed over the railroad tracks, and when I got to Bateman's Quick Mart, I knew I'd gone too far. I was turning around when Mr. Bateman flagged me down. He's a dental patient of my uncle Forest's and therefore considers himself a friend of the family.

"How's your folks?" he asked.

"Fine," I answered through my open window. Then I gunned my engine, hoping to convey that I was in a hurry, since Mr. Bateman has a tendency to be long-winded.

"Where you headed?"

"Scoggins Salvage Yard," I said. "I must have missed the turnoff."

"The turnoff's easy to miss. Them Scogginses never cut their grass, so it's grown all over the road. Just go back about a quarter mile, and if you look real close, you'll see it on your right."

"Yes, sir," I replied. "And thanks." I eased off the brake, and the truck rolled forward. Mr. Bateman walked along with me.

"Something wrong with your truck?" he asked. "Is that why you're going to the salvage yard—to get a part?"

"There's nothing wrong with my truck, and I don't need parts," I assured him as I pressed the gas pedal gently. "I have library business with Mr. Scoggins."

"Well, I'll be." Mr. Bateman scratched his head as he moved into a trot to keep up pace. "This truck is a fine piece of machinery. If you ever want to sell it, I'm sure I could find a buyer."

What Mr. Bateman meant was, "It's a shame to waste a manly truck like this on a girl." But he was much too polite to actually say so.

"I'll sure let you know," I promised—which I wouldn't: either want to sell *or* tell Mr. Bateman if I did.

I pushed the gas harder, and he couldn't keep up with the truck. He stopped, leaned forward with his hands on his knees, and hollered after me, "You be careful going up to the salvage yard! The road is full of potholes that could damage your tires."

I waved in response and left Mr. Bateman in a cloud of dust. Then I followed his directions, turning off County Road 34 a quarter mile down onto an overgrown gravel road lined with trees. The woods eventually gave way to the acreage owned by the Scoggins family, and a sorrier piece of real estate you'd be hard pressed to find. The open space was dotted with dilapidated buildings, intersected by dirt paths and littered with tires in various sizes. Toward the center of the property were two houses right beside each other. Both were made of unpainted, weathered wood and had tin roofs.

I parked my truck in front of the closest house. No human came out to acknowledge my presence, but a pack of dogs swarmed around me as soon as my feet touched the packed dirt. I jumped back up on the running board of my truck and pulled the door mostly closed to protect myself. Then I tried some basic dog commands like "Heel!" and "Stay!" The dogs were unimpressed and continued their aggressive snarling.

I was just about to stoop to yelling "Help!" when a man wearing grease-slathered overalls rounded the corner of the building. At first I was too distracted by the dogs to notice much about the man. But after he corralled the dogs in a pen beside the house, I realized that he was kind of cute.

The fabric of the T-shirt he was wearing stretched nicely over his well-defined shoulder muscles. His dark hair was cut short, and his eyes were an interesting hazel. There was a little lump at the bridge of his nose indicating that it had been broken at least once, and a tiny chip was missing from a front tooth. Like my truck, he had battle scars that gave him character.

I was just about to apologize for staring so rudely when he astonished me by saying, "Hey, Kennedy."

After I got over the surprise of hearing my name on his sensuously full lips, I studied him more closely. Then a smile spread across my face. "Luke Scoggins. Miss Springer's third grade."

He nodded. "I was in the sixth grade with you too—Miss Dunaway."

I was embarrassed and tried to cover my complete lack of memory with a quick nod. "Oh yes, Miss Dunaway."

I didn't fool him. "I went to high school with you too, until I dropped out."

"I . . . well . . ." I stammered, looking for a way out of the situation. Finding none, I settled on, "I'm sorry."

He walked over to my truck, and soon I was looking right down into his greenish-brown eyes. "Sorry that I dropped out or sorry that you don't remember seeing me after the third grade?"

"Both," I admitted.

He waved at my truck. "You need a part?"

With a nervous laugh I reached for the report on Abraham Lincoln. I wasn't sure what relation the Mr. Scoggins I'd met earlier was to Luke, so I worded my explanation cautiously. "Heaven was in the library earlier, and she left this. It's due tomorrow."

Luke rubbed his hand ineffectually on his dirty overalls before reaching out to claim the report. "My uncle's not home right now, but I'll be sure he gets this. Heaven's got enough bad grades. She sure doesn't need to miss an assignment."

"Glad I could be of service." And I was. Suddenly I felt all civic-minded and kindhearted and oddly feminine.

It was a little awkward, standing by my truck in the salvage yard talking to someone whom—while intriguing—I barely knew. If I'd run into any other former schoolmate at this point, they would probably have invited me into their home or suggested we go get some dinner. But Luke wasn't dressed for a trip into town, and obviously he couldn't ask me into his hovel to discuss old times that I didn't remember. So we were at an impasse.

Finally I said, "Have you been working here since, well, since you left high school?" I could have kicked myself for bringing up his educational failure again.

He seemed amused by my discomfort. "No, after I dropped out, I joined the Marines. I just got home a few days ago."

My eyes skimmed his short hair and green T-shirt. "I guess that's why I haven't seen you around town."

His grin widened. "I guess. Or maybe you did see me and just forgot."

Determined not to be flustered by his good looks and teasing attitude, I asked, "And now you're joining the family business?"

He glanced at his dirty hands. "Only for a few weeks. I'll be leaving in April to attend the summer semester at Purdue University."

I stared at him, stupefied.

"It's in Indiana," he provided.

"You're going to college?" I hoped I didn't sound as surprised as I felt.

"Yeah, while I was in Iraq, my commanding officer convinced me to take some online classes, and it turns out I'm smart." He stuck his hands in his overall pockets. "I was as surprised as everybody else."

"What's your major?"

"Engineering."

Suddenly my associate's degree from the local junior college didn't seem so impressive. "I guess you *are* smart!"

He shrugged as if it didn't matter much. "Being an engineer beats working in the salvage business."

"I'll say." Awkwardness returned, as if we'd used up everything we had in common. So I slid down into the seat of my truck as gracefully as possible. Since my window was open I was now just inches from Luke's face. "I guess I'll be heading back into town. Good luck with school and all."

"Thanks." Then he lifted up the report. "I'll give this to Heaven."

Something about the way he looked at me made me want to blush for the first time in years.

"I gotta tell you," he said softly. "I never thought I'd see *you* here."

"Life is full of surprises." I meant it as a joke, but the words sounded bitter even to my own ears.

He nodded solemnly as I started the truck. "Maybe we can get together sometime," he said.

"Sure," I agreed, although I didn't think we would. To say that Luke and I didn't move in the same social circles was an understatement. But I was wrong. I saw quite a bit of Luke Scoggins over the next few days.

As I drove away, I glanced in my rearview mirror. Luke was still standing there, watching me check him out one last time.

He smiled and waved. Definitely cute.

CHAPTER TWO

Since neither man nor woman can live by books alone, and since my library salary is laughable, I'm also the resident manager of one of Midway's few thriving businesses—the Midway Store and Save. Mr. Sheffield, the owner, pays me two hundred dollars a month for collecting rent and unlocking the occasional storage unit for customers who've lost their keys. But more importantly, he lets me live in the apartment over the office for free.

I think it's a great deal, but Mother is adamantly opposed to the arrangement. She says it's not a respectable living arrangement for a single woman.

The job offer came right after the incident at the drive-in. Since the house Cade and I were living in belonged to his parents, I couldn't very well kick him out. So I moved out, and the only other choice I had besides living over the storage office was to move in with my parents. I think my mother would have liked having the chance to console me and then direct me back to my husband, where she thinks I belong. But what I needed was peace and space. Those are two things in short supply at my parents' house. So in spite of my mother's objections, I took the job and the apartment.

My apartment is nothing to brag about—just four small rooms. A set of wooden stairs leads from the ground up to my front door so I don't have to go through the office to get inside. But there's also a set of stairs inside the office that leads up to the apartment. I rarely use them, but they're handy during rainstorms, and I love having options.

Because of a trip to the grocery store to replenish my supply of Pepsi and a stop at the dry cleaners to pick up most of my limited wardrobe, it was dark by the time I parked my truck in front of the Midway Store and Save sign. It was no small feat carrying my clothes and two boxes of canned drinks up the outside stairs all at once. But I managed. After unlocking my door, I stepped inside and turned on the ceiling fan to get the stale air moving.

I had time to open a fresh Pepsi and take one sip before the phone rang. I figured it would be my mother, and I was right.

"Kennedy?" She let her voice rise up on the end like this was a question—as if she expected someone else to answer the phone in my apartment. "Where have you been? I've been calling for an hour. Madison said you had plans this evening, but you never said a word to me about it. Was it a date? When are you going to get a cell phone? What did you have for dinner? You eat way too much junk food. I've got chicken and dumplings. Why don't you come over?"

Since it would take more energy than I possessed to figure out which questions she really wanted me to answer and which ones were just filler, I simply said, "I've already eaten, but thanks." I didn't even try to cover my yawn. "And I'm tired, so I think I'll go to bed early."

My mother ignored this. "Ida Jean said you were late opening the library this morning."

"Only a few minutes. Cade stopped me for speeding."

Instead of being offended in my behalf as seemed appropriate, my mother laughed.

"You think it's funny that Cade gave me a ticket?" I demanded.

"That's how men are," my mother said in defense of her former son-in-law. "When they want your attention, they aggravate. You know, like pulling your pigtails in grade school."

"It's time for Cade to grow up," I muttered.

"Wives have to be patient. All husbands make mistakes," she responded, as if *all* husbands slept with old girlfriends in drive-ins. Before I could come up with a clever retort, she switched to a new topic. "I saw that handsome, rich, and very single Drake Langston today. He spoke at the Ladies' Auxiliary meeting. He told us all about his plans to help finance the addition of a family center to the Baptist church."

I rolled my eyes. To my mother the next best thing to my reconciling with Cade would be for me to forge a new relationship with Drake Langston. He was a real estate developer from Atlanta who was buying up land in and around Midway. He was planning two housing developments—one north of town and one south. Affordable yet attractive homes would, he claimed, attract young professionals willing to commute to work in Albany, thereby putting Midway on the map. I was understandably skeptical. No one else had been able to make anything of Midway in over a hundred years. But my mother trusted Drake Langston almost as much as she trusted her preacher, which put him in very important company. So I knew better than to cast aspersions.

"You won't believe what Drake's planning for downtown!" Mother continued. "It's going to be so modern and impressive."

Not words to charm a girl who still missed the stop sign hanging from the tree limb. "Yes, well."

"The preacher and his wife are going to sell the land they own out north of town to Drake. He's offered them an incredible amount—well above the market value. With some of the proceeds, they're going to take a trip to the Holy Land."

My Pepsi was getting warm, and I cast around for a way to end the conversation quickly.

"Drake is buying land from several of the ladies in the auxiliary, and they will be so rich! I wish we had some useless acreage we could sell."

"Hmmm." Getting desperate now, my eyes settled on the dry cleaning I had draped over a chair. "Well, I've got to finish my laundry."

No self-respecting housewife would argue the importance of well-done laundry, so my mother said, "Oh, I'll let you go, then."

I hung up the phone, turned off the lights, and went to bed. And as I closed my eyes, I pictured Luke Scoggins the way he'd looked in my rearview mirror that afternoon and fell asleep with a smile on my face.

* * *

I slept through my alarm the next morning and was therefore behind schedule before my day ever began. I took a quick shower and rushed to the library. I was ten minutes late and figured that Miss Ida Jean would be waiting on me, but this time it was only the mayor's wife who was inconvenienced by my tardiness.

Francie Cook was dressed in one of her trademark jogging suits. She owned one in every color imaginable with an impressive collection of cute little tennis shoes to match. Obsessed with her appearance, she tanned constantly and ran—a lot. And according to the local gossip mill, she'd had plastic surgeries, dental reconstructions, and dermabrasion as well. If you ask me, it was a huge waste of the mayor's money. Francie is still unattractive, and the skin around her eyes has been pulled so tight that she always looks startled.

Francie was at the library that morning to perform the monthly extermination treatment—something which the county library system required in all its facilities. At the Midway Library, the extermination treatment consisted of Francie making a quick rotation of the two trailers with a can of Raid. I suspected that the bill the mayor submitted to the county for pest control was considerably higher than the actual cost of the bug spray. But then I suppose Francie's time was worth something. And you can't really blame the man for trying to make a few extra dollars. All those matching jogging ensembles can't be cheap.

I unlocked the library door for Francie and waited while she sprayed. Two minutes later she was finished and on her way. At that point I settled down at my desk and selected a banana Moon Pie from the stash I kept in a bottom drawer. Then I opened a Pepsi and was halfway through my breakfast when the phone rang.

"You were late again," my mother said by way of greeting. "I called at ten o'clock."

"Guilty," I mumbled around the banana-flavored cookie-cake. "But I wasn't late exactly. I just couldn't come inside when I first got here because Francie was doing the monthly extermination treatment."

This remark deflected my mother's attention away from my tendency to be tardy. "That Francie Cook," she said wistfully. "She has the most amazing willpower."

Mother was a few pounds overweight and admired anyone who kept fit.

"She didn't eat a bite at the Ladies' Auxiliary meeting yesterday. Then I saw her jogging past the house last night while I was sitting on the porch eating apple pie with homemade ice cream."

I felt an unusual sympathy for my mother, who felt such a need to be perfect. "Self-denial and exercise can be taken too far," I assured her. "And Francie is living proof of that. She looks like a squashed raisin with wide eyes. I'd rather have you just the way you are."

"You don't think I need to lose a few pounds?"

"Not an ounce."

"Well, then I guess I won't worry about it." Ordinarily my mother does not value my opinions, so I knew she wasn't really serious about losing weight.

"I don't want to keep you from your duties," she continued as if she really had any consideration for my time, "but I wanted to see if you could come with me to the funeral home tomorrow night."

There are few things I dislike more than going to the funeral home, but in the South when somebody you know dies, it's inescapable. And since my mother works part-time for her brother, who is the only dentist within a hundred miles, she knows *everybody* who dies. So I just asked, "What time?"

"The arrangements haven't been made yet, but I'm assuming six at Shady Grove Memorial."

I yawned and then out of morbid curiosity I asked, "Who died?"

"It was a patient—nobody you know," my mother replied as I pushed open the window I could reach from my desk. "Truthfully," she continued, "he wasn't exactly a patient. But last summer he had a toothache, and Uncle Forest did the extraction, so of course I feel obligated to attend the viewing."

"Of course," I agreed as if this actually made sense.

"His name is Foster Scoggins."

"Foster Scoggins?" I repeated, nearly choking on Moon Pie. My eyes moved of their own accord to the library card application on my desk. "The same Foster Scoggins who runs the salvage yard off Highway 34 and is related to Luke Scoggins and a little girl named Heaven?"

"How many Foster Scogginses can there be?" she asked. "Of course it's that same Foster. Heaven is his grand-niece. Luke's father, Parnell, is Foster's brother. Your father buys parts from them sometimes."

I put my Moon Pie aside, no longer hungry. Mr. Scoggins had been alive and checking out books on gophers and goats just yesterday, and now he was dead. It was unsettling, and I knew the loss would be quite a blow to Heaven, who didn't seem to have much going for her in the first place.

Softly I said, "Foster Scoggins was in the library yesterday afternoon."

"Well, isn't that an odd coincidence?" Mother remarked.

"Very odd," I agreed. Then I asked, "How did he die?"

"I thought I told you." I could picture my mother frowning. "He killed himself."

Now I was stunned. "Foster Scoggins committed suicide?"

"Just last night," she confirmed.

"I can't believe it."

"It is quite shocking," Mother agreed. "Everybody in town is talking about it."

Now *that* I could believe.

"Not only did he kill himself," my mother continued, "but he decided to end his life because he was involved in a scandalous relationship with a mysterious woman. And when she broke it off, Foster couldn't bear to live anymore."

I hated to sound interested, but I was. "How scandalous was the relationship, and what makes the woman mysterious?"

"Scandalous because Foster kept the whole sordid affair secret although they were apparently meeting regularly at motels in Albany. And the woman is mysterious because no one knows her identity." My mother's voice had dropped to a whisper as if repeating gossip quietly was less spiteful. "Foster wasn't the most pleasant fellow, and it's hard to believe that he had a friend of any kind—let alone a *female* friend."

I pictured Foster Scoggins as I had seen him at the library on the previous afternoon and had to agree that he didn't seem like a ladies' man.

"And what makes it worse," my mother added, "is that Foster wasn't saved at the time of his death. The preacher has gone out to the salvage yard several times to try and bring the Scogginses into the fold, but Foster always ran him off. The preacher finally gave up after Foster fired buckshot at him."

My affinity for the late Mr. Scoggins grew stronger. I, too, was estranged from the faithful fold and resented the constant attempts by everyone in town to get me to come back. Not that I would ever shoot at anyone—especially the preacher—but I did understand the motivation.

"If they didn't want to come to church the preacher should have left them alone."

"Like I said, Brother Jackson quit trying to save Foster after the shooting incident," my mother replied in a disapproving tone. "And I'll bet Foster is mighty sorry he didn't take advantage of the preacher's efforts now that he's dead by his own hand with a soul black as soot."

I had no comeback for this since I was morally opposed to suicide and the state of my own soul was questionable.

"Anyway," Mother went on, "it's an awful mess, and I feel sorry for the surviving Scogginses. They've had so much tragedy already."

Before I could ask what other tragedies had befallen the Scoggins family, my mother had moved on.

"So come by the house right after you lock up the library tomorrow. I'll have dinner ready, and once you've eaten a decent meal, you can take me to the funeral home. Since we aren't close to the family, we won't stay long. We'll just pay our respects and be on our way."

Arguing with my mother is an exercise in futility, so I agreed, and we concluded our conversation.

After we hung up, my eyes strayed to the envelope on my desk. I opened it and pulled the library card applications out. There was certainly no reason to mail Foster's in now.

And I might not have given the matter another thought if Miss Eugenia Atkins hadn't walked in at that moment. Miss Eugenia is a part-time volunteer at the Haggerty Public Library. Haggerty is Midway's neighbor, nine miles to the west, and their library facilities were almost as bad as ours until a wealthy benefactor paid to have a new building constructed. Conscious of their good fortune and the need to share, the Haggerty Library frequently gives us books.

Miss Eugenia carried her miniature dog, Lady, in a basket on her arm like Dorothy in *The Wizard of Oz*. Her white hair was pulled back in a careless bun, and she was wearing a turquoise dress covered with large black dots. Her knee-high hose were rolled down to expose a multitude of intersecting varicose veins, and her red sandals looked at least a size too small.

"Hellooooo!" she called out to me. "I've got a box of books for you in the trunk of my car."

I greeted her warmly—mostly because I like her and partly because I was glad to get the books. While I lugged in the box, Miss Eugenia settled in the chair behind my desk and put her dog basket on the floor beside her feet. I offered her a Moon Pie, and she selected a double-decker chocolate. Then I retrieved my partially eaten banana-flavored pie and sat on the box of books so we could talk while we ate.

Miss Eugenia looked around my two-trailer library and said, "I sure do miss the days when we had a small library like this in Haggerty."

I was understandably shocked. "But the new library in Haggerty is the envy of all the librarians in the surrounding towns—especially me!"

Miss Eugenia laughed. "Progress has its downsides. As nice as our new library is, we had to give things up when we moved in. For instance, the old library was so small that any one of us could run it alone. Now we need a certain number of employees and volunteers there before we can unlock the doors. Naturally this creates disagreements and scheduling conflicts."

"Naturally."

"And back in the old days, if I saw a tattered book on the shelves, I just threw it away. Now there's a whole discard process involving a meeting of the library board and making a circulation check and deciding whether the book should be replaced." Miss Eugenia shook her head. "I find all the red tape exhausting."

I remained unconvinced. "I think I could deal with the complications involved in having a new building."

Miss Eugenia shook her head. "Be careful what you wish for. Newer and bigger is not always better, I promise you. For instance, we could never sit at the front desk at the new Haggerty Library and enjoy a traditional Southern snack like this. Not anymore."

"I would miss my snacks," I acknowledged, although secretly I considered that a small price to pay for a beautiful brick building full of new books.

"And I can't even bring Lady into the new library." Miss Eugenia pointed at the basket where the little dog was sleeping. "I tried to pass her off as a seeing-eye dog—but they said I had to get a permit."

"Lady is always welcome here." I crumpled my Moon Pie wrapper, feeling better about my modest establishment.

"And how is Madison?" Miss Eugenia asked. For some reason that has never been fully explained to me, Miss Eugenia is a staunch Methodist who attends church with the Mormons. When Madison married Jared, it was the scandal of the century (well, of the decade, anyway). But Miss Eugenia's weekly worship with a Mormon congregation didn't seem to raise an eyebrow. I told you old folks in the South can get away with anything. It's the young people who bear all the scrutiny.

Anyway, because of her weekly association with the Mormons, Miss Eugenia knows my sister Madison, her husband Jared, and all their horrible children.

"She's fine and says she's ready to have the new baby," I replied. "Although for the life of me, I don't know why. The longer she can keep it inside where we don't have to hear it, the better."

Miss Eugenia smiled. "Madison and Jared are loving parents. They're just lenient, and as a result, their children are a bit spoiled."

I snorted at this. "Madison and Jared are beyond lenient, and their children are *awful*. They don't believe in spanking under any circumstances. I remind Madison that we got spanked every day of our childhood, and we turned out okay—but she won't listen."

Miss Eugenia laughed. "I'm a believer in 'spare the rod, spoil the child' to a point."

"I'm not advocating child abuse!" I assured her. "Although you'd think so to hear the way my sisters carry on when the subject comes up at Sunday dinner. I just think children should be taught that they can't always do what they want to. Case in point, last Sunday I was minding my own business, reading the funny papers after one of my mother's delicious fried chicken dinners. Major, who just turned six, came over and demanded that I give the comics to him. I said he could read them when I finished, and he promptly hauled off and kicked me in the shin."

Miss Eugenia frowned in disapproval. "Well, that was certainly unacceptable behavior. What did you do?"

"Well, one of the few verses in the Bible that I believe in firmly is the one about an eye for an eye," I prefaced. "So I kicked him back."

Miss Eugenia shook her head. "I don't think that's what the Lord had in mind."

I decided not to debate Bible interpretations with someone who was well versed in both Methodist and Mormon dogma. "Anyway, little Major ran and told his mother and, more importantly, *my* mother. A big commotion followed, and I eventually left unrepentant and with everyone mad at me. Now that she knows I'm a brutal child-kicker, my mother probably wouldn't invite me to Sunday dinner ever again. Except that she's afraid I'll become malnourished."

"Try to be patient with your nieces and nephews," Miss Eugenia said. "One day you might actually grow to love them."

I doubted that, but I smiled and said, "Maybe."

"And I'm sure you'll always be welcome to dinner at your mother's house."

I nodded. "In fact, I'm invited tomorrow night. Although the meal is just a bribe so I'll go with her to the funeral home to view Foster Scoggins."

Miss Eugenia frowned again. "Poor Foster. His death came as quite a shock."

"Mother says the whole town is talking about it."

Miss Eugenia didn't condemn the residents of Midway for their interest. "I haven't been able to think about much of anything else myself. It's not every day someone commits suicide. Strange business carrying on an illicit affair with an unidentified woman while his family was completely unaware."

I nodded, although I didn't find this so strange. After all, Cade had an affair, and I never would have suspected a thing if I hadn't been an eyewitness.

"And then killing himself when the girlfriend broke off their relationship," Miss Eugenia continued.

Because of the circumstances surrounding Foster's death, I would have been anxious to continue the discussion even if I hadn't met the man personally the day before. But considering my recent contact, I felt a connection with Foster Scoggins—almost possessiveness. So I leaned forward and asked, "Did you know him?"

Miss Eugenia nodded. "I more than *knew* Foster. Like most everyone else in this county, I've spent a good portion of my life discussing him and the other Scogginses. They are just that kind of people. In the days before TV, they provided most of the entertainment around here."

I had to smile at this remark even though it seemed a little disrespectful to the newly deceased. "What did they do?"

"Oh, it would take a week to tell you everything that happened with that family, but I can give you a few highlights. When I was a child, a previous generation of Scogginses—which would be Foster's grandparents—made and sold moonshine. They had customers from all over the county, and almost every weekend they had a shoot-out with either the police or one of their competitors. That gave the preachers plenty of topics for their Sunday sermons and provided us with interesting conversations for dinner after church."

"I can just imagine," I murmured. "Although it's hard to picture Foster as a child—with grandparents!"

"I know Foster probably seemed old to you, but he was only about sixty, which is almost young enough to be my son."

This remark did change my perspective, but it didn't make Foster seem younger. It just made me realize how truly ancient Miss Eugenia was. But rather than share this new insight, I said, "Foster was definitely too young to die. Now tell me more about the Scogginses."

Miss Eugenia was only too happy to comply. "Foster's father went to the same high school I did, but he was a couple of years ahead of me and didn't attend much. He married a timid little woman from Brunswick, and she died of emphysema when Parnell and Foster were toddlers. After prohibition ended, the demand for moonshine was reduced, so the Scogginses started the salvage yard, and making illegal whiskey became more of a hobby. Foster never married, and Parnell waited until later in life to find a wife, but the extra time didn't help him make a good choice. Parnell's wife was named Olive, and she was slovenly and promiscuous . . ."

Judging from Miss Eugenia's facial expression, she considered this a particularly bad combination.

"Olive had apparently gotten the impression that the Scogginses were rich. After they were married, Parnell moved her into one of those shacks at the salvage yard, and, well, Olive realized her mistake. She held out for a few years, but she left Parnell shortly after their second son was born."

Her second son was Luke, and he was the baby she left behind. "How could she just go off and leave her sons?"

Miss Eugenia shrugged. "It happens all the time. Especially with those Scogginses."

I thought about all the dilapidated buildings made of rusty metal that I had seen out at the salvage yard when I had delivered Heaven's paper. "Do they still make moonshine?"

"Their moonshine days ended about twenty years ago when Parnell wrecked their delivery truck out on Highway 34. From what they said, it was quite a sight—tons of twisted metal drenched with gallons of illegal booze." Miss Eugenia shook her head. "I sure would have liked to have seen it."

"Foster's brother survived the wreck?" I prompted, anxious to hear more about Luke's father.

"Barely," Miss Eugenia confirmed. "He was in the hospital for weeks with a spinal injury. He should have gone to jail, but because he was hurt, the judge gave him probation and took away his driver's license—not that it was necessary. He's been in a wheelchair ever since. Poor Foster had to do the best he could to raise Parnell's boys, take care of an invalid brother, and run the salvage yard."

This information did change my opinion of Foster. Now, instead of perceiving him as just a grumpy, unkempt old man, I also saw him as the backbone of a troubled family.

"Anyway," Miss Eugenia continued, "after seeing what his brother went through in his marriage, Foster didn't have any use for women. That's why I can't believe he had a secret girlfriend."

"People get lonely," I offered as a possible explanation. "Maybe he finally decided to give feminine companionship a try."

Miss Eugenia shook her head. "I'll never believe he had a girlfriend."

I thought about the way Foster Scoggins looked when he was in the library the day before. Dirty overalls, dusty boots, tobacco juice nestled in the stubble on his chin. And I decided Miss Eugenia was right. Foster might have had redeeming qualities, but he wasn't a ladies' man. "Maybe the police were wrong about the girlfriend?"

Miss Eugenia nodded. "That's a logical deduction. But Eula Mae Maddox at the Midway post office plays with my bridge club occasionally, so I stopped by to speak to her on my way into town. Eula Mae said over the past few weeks Foster has gotten several little pink envelopes with no return address. Yesterday he picked up his mail around noon. Eula Mae remembers because she had just finished eating her tuna salad sandwich. She said Foster opened the pink envelope right there at the counter in the post office."

"It was the letter from his girlfriend saying she was breaking off their relationship?" I guessed.

"I assume so. Eula Mae said he looked real upset when he finished reading it." Miss Eugenia shook her head. "It's hard enough to imagine Foster with a secret girlfriend, but I have the most trouble with the idea that he killed himself over her. Foster was no stranger to disappointment. I can't believe that he got a letter from this woman ending their relationship of a few weeks and was so devastated that a few hours later he drove himself out past the landfill and jumped down onto some of those high-voltage coils at the electrical relay plant."

This was new information. I figured Foster had just swallowed some pills or something. "Is that how he died?"

Miss Eugenia nodded. "He shorted out the relay plant, causing power outages up and down the highway."

I shuddered. "Poor Mr. Scoggins. When I saw him yesterday I never would have guessed that he was about to kill himself."

Miss Eugenia looked surprised. "You saw Foster yesterday?"

I nodded. "He came into the library to help Heaven with a report for school." My eyes moved to what was left of my nonfiction section. "He checked out a book on gophers and applied for a library card."

I showed Miss Eugenia the applications, and she frowned. "What time was this?"

"I was getting ready to close, about five o'clock."

"That was only a couple of hours before he died," Miss Eugenia said. "Did he seem upset?"

I shrugged. "Not to me."

"If he was about to kill himself, it seems like Foster would have been displaying some signs of anxiety." She tapped the application in her hand. "And it's odd that he took the time to fill this out if he had already planned to end his life."

"But if he didn't kill himself," I thought aloud, "then . . ." The full implications of what Miss Eugenia was suggesting finally occurred to me. "Are you saying that Foster Scoggins was *murdered*?"

"It's possible," she murmured.

I didn't contradict her, but neither did I take her seriously. Nothing that interesting ever happened in Midway.

Still frowning, Miss Eugenia continued. "My sister says I look for trouble where there is none—but truth is, when I look for trouble I usually find some! I'm a pretty good judge of character, and I don't think Foster was the suicide type. If he had a girlfriend and she dumped him, I can see him becoming a recluse. But Foster was a private person, and killing himself is so dramatic and public and—well, not Foster's dull, unimaginative style."

I could barely breathe. "So you *do* think it was murder."

"Something is not right," Miss Eugenia confirmed. "And just because Foster was receiving letters in pink envelopes doesn't mean he had a girlfriend."

"What other explanation could there be?"

"They could have been sent by the murderer to cover the crime," Miss Eugenia hypothesized.

It was strange just hearing words like *murderer* and *crime* spoken in regards to Midway and the possibility that they had actually happened . . . Well, it was just too much.

"And you should take this library application to the police," she told me.

I'd heard that Miss Eugenia had been instrumental in helping the Haggerty police solve several crimes over the past few years, so I took her advice seriously. But the police in Midway meant the county sheriff—which meant Cade. Calling him was out of the question. I was formulating a plan to *mail* the application to the sheriff when Miss Eugenia continued.

"Even if there was no foul play involved in Foster's death, you were one of the last people to see him alive." She returned the application to me. "That means you can give them insight into his frame of mind. Promise you'll call."

"Why don't you call?" I suggested bravely. "You know much more about this kind of thing."

Miss Eugenia shook her head. "I talked to the sheriff this morning and asked him to take a closer look at Foster's death. But while some people appreciate my aptitude for crime solving, others feel threatened by it. The sheriff falls into the threatened category."

I couldn't imagine Sheriff Bonham feeling threatened by anyone, especially an eighty-year-old lady. But, as usual, I kept this opinion to myself.

"But the sheriff might listen to you." Miss Eugenia stood and collected her dog basket. "Well, I guess I'd better get back to Haggerty. I have a hot date with an old lawyer."

I smiled. "I think *hot* and *old* are contradictory terms."

Miss Eugenia laughed. "You young people don't have a monopoly on love, and life doesn't end at thirty."

"I certainly hope not, since I'm not thirty yet and don't have a love in my life," I said as I walked her to the door.

Miss Eugenia was instantly sympathetic. "Things will work out for you in time."

I assumed she meant that I'd eventually cave in to all the pressure and remarry Cade, so I just nodded vaguely.

"And please let me know what the sheriff has to say about Foster."

After Miss Eugenia left, I returned to my desk and stared at the application Foster Scoggins had filled out shortly before he died. I felt guilty, like I'd let him down. Was there something I should have noticed or something I could have done to prevent the tragedy? I couldn't bring Mr. Scoggins back to life, but if there was even a chance that someone had killed him, surely I had an obligation to help expose them.

So I did something I'd sworn never to do again. I called my ex-husband at the sheriff's department. I had braced myself for the inevitable emotional reaction to Cade's voice, but the sheriff himself answered instead, and I relaxed.

"Cade's in Albany, Kennedy," the sheriff informed me. "I'll get him to call you as soon as he gets back."

I considered telling the sheriff about Miss Eugenia's Foster-murder theory and presenting as evidence the library card application, but I decided to wait for Cade. He was trying to get back on my good side and would be more likely to listen. So I said thank you and hung up the phone.

The rest of the day was unusually busy, which looks good on my monthly report and makes the time fly by. Everyone who came in wanted to talk about Foster Scoggins and his scandalous affair and his grand finale at the electrical relay plant. Unlike my conversation with Miss Eugenia, this seemed like plain old gossip, and I was thoroughly tired of it by closing time.

The sun was beginning to set, and I was ushering a homeschooler and her four children out the library door when the phone rang.

"Midway Library," I answered a little breathlessly.

"Kennedy," Cade said, and my heart pounded (proving that I'm not as immune to him as I pretend to be). It's not that I want him back—but I would like for things to be like they were before I knew that he's lower than a roach. There is some bliss in ignorance and a lot of loneliness in knowledge.

I cleared my throat and said in my most businesslike tone, "Thanks for returning my call."

"Did you change your mind about going out to dinner with me?" he asked hopefully.

I bit back all the responses that came to my mind since I wanted his cooperation. "No, I've already eaten dinner." I popped the last bite of a Snickers bar into my mouth and crumpled up the wrapper. "But I do need to talk with you for a few minutes."

Now he sounded ecstatic. "My shift ends at eight. I'll come by your place right after work, and we can talk."

I may not be as immune as I pretend to be, but I'm not stupid either. "No, that's not good for me." I checked my watch. "When I leave here, I'll come down to the sheriff's office. We can talk there." I didn't give him a chance to argue, just hanging up the phone.

Five minutes later I polished off my last Pepsi and tossed the can into the garbage. Then I went through my closing time routine. Once all was secure, I placed Foster's library card application into an envelope and walked outside. It was another perfect spring night, cool and not too humid. I took several deep breaths of gardenia-scented air, climbed into my old truck, and headed toward town.

CHAPTER THREE

When I reached Main Street, I saw indications of the progress Drake Langston had promised at my mother's Ladies Auxiliary Meeting. Several dump trucks and a concrete mixer lined Main Street. There was also an industrial-sized salvage bin and a huge stack of lumber on an empty lot in front of the Midway office of the Dougherty County Sheriff's Department. Accepting the possibility that Drake Langston might not be all talk, I parked my truck and climbed out. Cade met me at the door with a cold Pepsi in his hand.

I accepted the drink with a grudging, "Thanks."

He gave me one of the grins that had been melting hearts since elementary school. "The sheriff said I could leave a little early. We could stop by Jack's for a sandwich and then go to the Blockbuster on Highway 76 and get a movie . . ."

I held up my hand. "I told you I'm not hungry and this isn't a personal visit. It's business."

His face fell. To keep from feeling sorry for him, I remembered how he'd looked that night at the drive-in, showcased in the window of his Rodeo and wrapped in Missy Lamar's arms.

I opened the Pepsi, took a sip, and then pointed at an empty office to our left. "Can we talk in here?"

Cade stepped into the office and flipped on the light. He propped himself on the edge of the desk and waited until I was seated. Then he asked, "What's so all-fired important?"

"It's possible that Foster Scoggins was murdered."

At this pronouncement Cade burst out laughing. I wasn't expecting him to embrace the theory with open arms, but I didn't think he'd find it ridiculous. I waited impatiently until the laughing fit passed. The fact that he obviously wanted to control his mirth but couldn't made it even worse.

Finally he took a couple of deep breaths and managed, "Who in the world would want to kill old Foster?"

"That's the question you folks at the sheriff's department need to be asking yourselves," I replied with stiff lips.

Cade was still amused but no longer hysterical. He leaned forward, and I could see a smear of dried toothpaste near the corner of his mouth. If he'd brushed his teeth in honor of my visit, he must truly have had high hopes.

"And why have we got to ask ourselves anything about Foster Scoggins?"

I removed the application from the envelope and spread it out on the desk. "Because he came to the library yesterday and filled out this."

Cade read the application, and then his eyebrows rose. "Foster wrote that?"

"Just a couple hours before he supposedly killed himself over a mysterious woman nobody has ever met."

"I have to admit I'm surprised." Cade squinted at the application, and for a moment I thought he was taking me seriously. He dispelled this notion by saying, "I didn't know Foster could write, and I'm pretty sure he couldn't read. So why would he want a library card?"

I gave him a look of annoyance. "The important question is why was he filling out applications and checking out a book on gophers if he was about to kill himself?" Cade didn't seem to be making the connection, so I decided to use Miss Eugenia's clout to support my theory. "Miss Eugenia Atkins came by the library today. She thought this whole 'suicide' was fishy, and she has had a lot of experience with crime, so you shouldn't be laughing."

Cade wasn't impressed by Miss Eugenia's credentials. "Sheriff Jones in Haggerty says that Miss Eugenia and her crime-solving tendencies are a pain. And maybe Foster wasn't planning to kill himself when he came to the library. Maybe that desperate idea came to him later."

I narrowed my eyes at him. "Miss Eugenia talked to Eula Mae at the post office. She said Foster read the break-up note at lunchtime. So if the letter upset him to the point of suicide, you'd think he'd have shown some signs of anxiety while he was in the library."

"Maybe he thought he could live with it but then changed his mind."

"The whole thing seems strange. You have to admit that it's hard to imagine Foster Scoggins with a girlfriend. He was so, well, not attractive."

Cade leaned closer. "To you he might have looked like a grouchy, sloppy—"

"Dirty," I supplied.

Cade frowned at me. "—old man. But to a woman near his own age, he might have been attractive."

I decided to give in a little. "Although incomprehensible to me, we'll assume for the time being that Foster Scoggins did have a girlfriend. But I'm not convinced that he killed himself over her. I presume the sheriff's office is in possession of those letters she's been sending weekly according to Eula Mae?"

He glanced at the door to be sure no one was listening. Then he whispered, "You can't tell a soul . . ."

I crossed my heart in the age-old gesture of silence until death.

Reassured, Cade continued. "We found four of them in Foster's truck. They were signed *Mary* and postmarked Albany. The first one dated back almost a month ago."

"Love letters?"

He nodded. "Recounting the nights they spent together at motels."

I didn't even try to disguise my revulsion.

"Except for the one he received yesterday telling him she didn't love him after all and never wanted to see him again." Cade shook his head in commiseration with poor Foster. "If that's not the coldest thing I've ever heard. Breaking up in a letter."

"I presume you're having the letters checked for fingerprints?"

Cade made a face. "That hasn't been mentioned yet, but I guess I could ask the sheriff."

"I certainly think you should," I encouraged him. "If you can get fingerprints for this mysterious girlfriend, you can identify her. And if you can talk to her, you might be able to learn more about Foster's state of mind."

"Okay," he agreed, "I'll ask the sheriff. But he's not going to be interested in going to a lot of trouble over a suicide, so I'm not making any promises."

"You seem so sure it was suicide. Did Foster leave a note?" I asked.

"Foster could barely write," Cade hedged, and I felt he was holding out on me.

I tapped on the library card application again. "Evidence to the contrary."

Cade chose this time to nitpick. "I don't know if what you have can be considered *evidence* of any kind."

I ignored this. "Was there a note?"

"Sort of," Cade admitted. "He had scribbled something on a piece of paper. It was addressed to Heaven, and he was apologizing for being a failure and asking her to forgive him."

"He didn't specifically say he intended to kill himself?"

"No, but it's not hard to make the connection since it was in his truck, which was parked right beside the relay plant where he jumped onto the high-voltage coils."

I couldn't really argue with this, so instead I asked, "After Foster left the library, where did he go? He had Heaven with him, so he must have taken her somewhere."

"He took her home," Cade responded. "The housekeeper that comes in a couple of times a week was there, and Heaven stayed with her."

"So he brought Heaven to the library, took her home, and then drove out to the electrical plant and fried himself?"

"I guess," Cade replied with a shrug.

"I'm telling you something isn't right with this picture," I insisted.

Cade's reluctance was obvious, and if he hadn't owed me big-time, he probably would have refused to help. "I'm not saying there's anything to your murder theory, but I guess I can ask Luke Scoggins a few more questions."

"What about Foster's brother? He might know something."

"Parnell? Nah, he's sick and in a nursing home," Cade said dismissively. "Luke's my best source for information."

"So you'll talk to him?"

"Yeah." Cade pointed at my evidence. "And I'll show this to the sheriff." Then he glanced up with a hopeful smile. "Now, what about that movie?"

I was about to refuse him again when a voice spoke from behind us. "Excuse me, I'm looking for Sheriff Bonham."

I turned to see a face I had previously seen only on television. Drake Langston, who had come to save Midway from another hundred years of obscurity, was standing in the doorway to the office Cade had commandeered for our discussion.

I'd watched Mr. Langston handle himself well during the news interviews and heard his praises sung endlessly by my mother and other ladies in town. Since I didn't think it was possible for anyone to live up to all the hype, I expected the man to be a disappointment, but I was wrong.

Drake Langston was not particularly tall, but he had a commanding presence. I stood and noted his expensive suit with the silk tie loosened casually at his neck. Then I let my gaze drift over his handsome features—warm brown eyes framed by stylish spectacles, light blond hair, a sprinkle of freckles across his sunburned nose, and the straightest and whitest teeth I'd ever seen. A little sigh escaped my lips. He was perfect. The twenty-four-carat gold, tailored-clothes, Ivy League–education kind of perfect.

"I'm Drake," he said, although introduction was unnecessary. He held out his hand to me, and I couldn't help but notice how beautiful his fingers were—long and strong and manicured.

I reached for Drake's hand, but Cade stepped between us, and there was a definite edge to his voice when he said, "I'm Deputy Burrell, and this is my wife, Kennedy."

I leaned around Cade and took the hand of the famous Drake Langston. "Ex-wife," I corrected. "Kennedy Killingsworth."

Drake clasped my palm in his and shook it firmly. "Nice to meet you, Kennedy." It was as if Cade had ceased to exist.

Before I could respond, the sheriff walked in. He looked around the room and said, "Is something going on I need to know about?"

"No, sir," Cade responded. His angry face was still angled toward Drake. "Kennedy came by to talk about Foster Scoggins's death, and I'm not sure what Mr. Langston wants."

If the sheriff noticed the edge to Cade's voice, he didn't acknowledge it. Instead he turned and addressed the most important person in the room. "What can I do for you, Mr. Langston?"

Drake waved toward me. "Kennedy was here before me."

The sheriff was a tall black man in his sixties, with zero tolerance for nonsense. I'd always been a little intimidated by him, and when he turned his skeptical gaze to me, my confidence shriveled. I didn't want to state my case in front of Drake Langston, since there was a good chance that the conversation would end with my humiliation. So I politely pointed to Drake. "I don't mind waiting."

Drake shook his head. "Ladies first."

"Please," I insisted.

The sheriff sighed in exasperation. "Will somebody just say something?"

Afraid if I didn't speak now, I'd forever have to hold my peace, I cleared my throat and began. "Foster Scoggins came into the library yesterday afternoon about five o'clock. He had Heaven with him, and they were asking for my help with a school assignment."

I paused to gauge his reaction, and the sheriff rolled his finger, indicating I should continue.

"Mr. Scoggins didn't have a library card but said he wanted to get one, since he likes books about goats and rabbits."

In my peripheral vision I saw Cade roll his eyes.

I handed the sheriff the library card application. "He filled this out less than two hours before he died.

The sheriff looked at the application with a frown. "I didn't know Foster could write."

I was gritting my teeth in frustration when Cade said, "Kennedy thinks somebody killed Foster."

The sheriff's eyebrows jumped up. "Why would anyone do that?"

I tried not to cringe under his piercing gaze. "I don't know, but the whole idea of him committing suicide over a woman is suspicious to me. Foster Scoggins was old and unkempt and chewed tobacco." I couldn't control a grimace of distaste. "It's hard to believe any woman found him attractive. But assuming this Mary person does exist, she should be located and questioned. And I'm not even sure he wrote what you're calling his suicide note . . ."

Cade winced, and I regretted my words. So much for crossing my heart.

I decided to finish quickly. "I just think the sheriff department's conclusion that Mr. Scoggins committed suicide was premature and that the case should be investigated a little more thoroughly."

The sheriff turned his scowl to Cade. "I won't ask how Kennedy gained access to police information, but we've been looking for a way to verify Foster's handwriting on," he turned his eyes to me, "what we're calling a suicide note. Since Foster operated almost totally on a cash basis and rarely signed anything—even his name—we were having trouble coming up with a verified handwriting sample for comparison." He shook the application. "Thank you very much for providing one."

This was not my intention, obviously, and I was about to despair.

Then the sheriff continued. "However, based on the concerns you've raised, I'm willing to authorize a limited investigation into Foster's death. It'll be under Cade's direction," he stipulated. "And, Kennedy, I'm going to ask you to help since you're the one opening this particular can of worms." He gave Cade what he thought was a covert wink. Apparently he didn't really think my concerns had merit but had decided to humor me—and at the same time force me to spend time with Cade, thus advancing his deputy's attempts to patch up our broken marriage.

My options were limited, so I had to take whatever help I could get. But as I nodded in agreement, I resolved to prove myself to them. I would solve this crime, and then we'd see who was winking at whom.

"Find out about the alleged girlfriend," Sheriff Bonham was telling Cade while I fumed about his patronizing attitude. "Wrap your investigation up before the funeral, which is scheduled for Friday afternoon. And don't upset the family."

Cade nodded. "Yes, sir."

I would have preferred that they postpone the funeral until all the questions had been answered but decided to be satisfied with the sheriff's modest concession.

Sheriff Bonham turned to Drake Langston. "Your turn."

Drake smiled, showing that even busy, important, rich men can be patient. "I just need to get a couple parking permits signed."

The sheriff scrawled his signature on the permits and waved toward me. "I hope you won't let this little discussion concern you about the safety of our town, Mr. Langston. We haven't had a murder here in the hundred years our town has been in existence."

Drake smiled at the sheriff. "I'm not concerned in the least."

After the sheriff walked out of the office, Drake turned his gorgeous smile to me. "So you run the town's library?"

I could see Cade was seething as I nodded. "Yes."

"Then you're on my list of people to talk with." His brown eyes made me feel like I was the most interesting person in the world.

"About what?" I asked a little breathlessly.

"We're planning some major renovations to the downtown area—you might have noticed."

This was a silly statement, but Drake was nice and cute, so I let it slide. "I noticed."

"We're in the process of trying to rent the retail spaces and a big concern for potential vendors is the amount of traffic that we'll be able to generate."

I could see why this was a concern for potential vendors. Main Street was just a way to get from one place to another—not a destination in and of itself. I stared at his hair and wondered if it was as silky as it looked.

I forced myself to concentrate on Drake's words as he continued. "I believe that a nice new library, strategically placed downtown, would be a draw for town residents and outsiders alike."

"A new library?" I repeated, knowing I sounded like an imbecile.

He nodded. "It's one of my favorite tricks to improve a downtown area. It doesn't cost much, because there are numerous literacy programs that offer grants, and I've got an experienced staff back in Atlanta who are already hard at work lining up the financing. We'll also get corporate sponsors to donate materials, furniture, etc. We take a lot of 'before' pictures. Then when the library is finished, we do a little film—kind of like those makeover shows. The local TV stations will snap it up, and we might even get some national coverage. It's good PR for the sponsors and will give Midway some much-needed positive publicity."

All my dreams of a library made of geometrically arranged trailers disappeared in an instant. Not only were we going to have a new library—we were going to be on television. "I don't know what to say." It was true.

He was smiling again. "Say you'll help me make this dream library into a reality."

I nodded, almost hypnotized. "I'll do anything I can to help you."

"Do you have time for me to show you what I have in mind? It will only take a few minutes."

Cade walked over to Drake. "Kennedy and I were talking before you interrupted."

I'd never had men fight over me before, and I'll admit I was tempted to see what happened next, but good sense prevailed. I stepped between them and addressed Cade first.

"We're finished talking, and you have a phone call to make." I mouthed *Luke Scoggins*. Then I turned to Drake. "I'd love to hear more about your plans for the new library."

Drake put a hand on my elbow and gently led me into the sheriff department's small lobby.

"I'll call you later," Cade called out as he trailed after us.

Drake flashed Cade a condescending smile and pushed open the door. When he returned his brown-eyed gaze to me, I pinched myself to be sure I wasn't having a really wonderful dream. "After you," he said.

I didn't even give Cade a backward glance as I walked out with Drake.

Once we were on the sidewalk, he said, "Your ex-husband seems kind of possessive."

I shrugged. "We haven't been divorced very long, and Cade's finding the adjustment difficult."

"And how are you adjusting?"

"Better than Cade."

Drake nodded but didn't probe. "How long have you lived here in Midway?"

"My entire life," I admitted.

"Are you, by any chance, related to an Iris Killingsworth who is a member of the Ladies Auxiliary at the Baptist church?"

I nodded. "She's my mother."

Drake smiled. "You look a lot like her."

I was pleasantly surprised. My mother and sisters are beautiful, pageant-winning girlie-girls. I've always been a tomboy, and most people say I look more like my father.

My happiness turned to alarm when Drake said, "Your mother has told me quite a bit about your family."

I was wondering what my mother had divulged when he stopped in front of a deserted building that at one time had been a branch of the First

National Bank. Once the folks at First National's headquarters realized that nobody in Midway had any money, they closed the branch, and the building had been empty ever since.

"Here's the spot I have picked out for the library," Drake announced.

I'm not sure what I expected when he said he wanted to move the library downtown. I guess I thought I'd be given a little office space between two paying customers on one of the retail blocks. And don't get me wrong—I would have been happy with that. But when I looked through the cracked windows into what was potentially the best building in downtown Midway, I was speechless, awestruck, spellbound.

"It's wonderful!" I was already picturing the rows of bookshelves inside the ample space.

"An architectural firm that I've used before on projects like this is working on a proposal for the renovation," he informed me. "I'll have a construction crew in here tomorrow to do basic repairs. Once we have an architectural plan approved, we can get started on the changes."

"So soon?" I whispered. Usually everything in Midway happened at a maddeningly slow pace.

He smiled. "The sooner the better."

I pressed my face against the dirty glass of the old bank's window and peered inside. The hardwood floors were scuffed and worse for wear, but with a little buffing and waxing they would be beautiful. There were some holes in the plaster walls, and all of the windows were broken, but those were fairly easy fixes. Mostly it just needed a good cleaning.

"It's so big," I said, wondering how we'd fill the massive space.

"We plan for the library to be a commanding presence in town. Main Street will be the first impression many potential homebuyers will get of Midway. We want to send them the right message, and a big library says, 'We care about education! Bring your children here!'"

Up to this point I had figured Main Street's message to passersby had been "Run for your lives!" But I kept this to myself.

He pulled some keys from his pocket and unlocked the bank's front door. Then he took my hand and pulled me into the dark, empty building. Fractured moonlight streamed through the big, broken windows and reflected off his blond hair, creating almost a halo effect. He pointed toward a far corner. "I was thinking this would make a good children's section."

I was again tempted to pinch myself to be sure I wasn't dreaming.

He turned his finger toward the back wall. "And I'd like to have an atrium built there to house rare books and historical artifacts."

"We don't have any," I told him. "Rare books or artifacts."

This didn't bother Drake in the least. "I think you'll be surprised by how quickly your collection will grow once you have a place to display it." His soft, warm fingers tightened around mine, and I followed him across the open space. "The architect is coming tomorrow. I'm sure he'll want to get your input on the layout and design. Would you join us for lunch to go over the plans he's drawn up?"

I nodded mutely. To my knowledge I'd never met an architect in my life, and now one wanted to hear my opinions. Amazing.

"We'll have to work hard and fast so that everything will be ready by the time the computers arrive."

"Computers?" This time I did pinch myself. I wasn't dreaming.

"Microsoft is donating twenty. Five will be for administrative use, and the other fifteen will be for patrons. You'll be networked to the rest of the county library system, and they will provide your high-speed Internet," he continued.

Not just Internet, but *high-speed*. If the bruise from my original pinch hadn't been throbbing, I would have pinched myself again.

"Will noon tomorrow be convenient?" He was standing close and he smelled great—like woods and moss and maple syrup.

"For what?"

"For lunch with the architect," he reminded me. "I thought we'd eat at the Back Porch."

We wouldn't have any choice since the Back Porch was the only real restaurant in town. "Noon tomorrow at the Back Porch will be perfect," I assured him.

He glanced around the large room that would soon house the Midway Library. "This is going to be a showplace."

"A dream come true." For the first time the thought of progress didn't upset me. "I don't know how we can ever thank you."

"No thanks necessary." He was now standing very close, and his voice was almost a whisper. "This is what I love to do—make something from nothing."

I couldn't seem to stop staring. "I think it's wonderful."

"You seem pretty wonderful yourself," he said softly.

His presence was intoxicating, and I leaned forward. He reached out and cupped my chin in his hands. I was waiting expectantly for the kiss of my life when a scrabbling sound from the back startled us apart.

"Sounds like we're not the only visitors here tonight," Drake remarked good-naturedly.

"Probably a rat," I predicted. There was a crunching sound—like a shoe grinding broken glass into old hardwood—and I wondered if it was a *big* rat. The one I used to be married to. Then there was silence, but the romantic mood was broken, and I knew Drake wasn't going to kiss me. At least not that night.

"I'll walk you to your car," he said.

We went out through the front entrance, and after Drake locked the door, I led him to my truck. And for the first time, I wished that I drove something sleek and black and elegant instead of my old truck. I tried to open the door, and it stuck. Drake reached over me and gave it a firm tug. The door swung open, and I thanked him.

He gave me another one of those million-dollar smiles. "You're very welcome." Then with a little wave, he turned and hurried away.

CHAPTER FOUR

I TOOK THE LONG WAY home to my apartment to give myself time to think. While I drove through the back roads of Midway, my mind was still reeling with all of Drake's plans. We were going to have a real library with shelves and furniture and computers. I thought about my collection of books. For a single person it was an impressive accomplishment, but for a fancy library like the one Drake described, my collection would be shabby and inadequate. I was ashamed of my books and then felt guilty for the disloyal thoughts.

Once we had our nice new library full of nice, new books, maybe I'd get the chance to be magnanimous. Like Miss Eugenia and the Haggerty Library, I could donate my old, embarrassing books to a less-fortunate town. This thought pleased me until another, grimmer idea came to my mind.

When Drake got this new library going, would he want to hire a *real* librarian? I had an associate degree from the junior college, but it was in business and not library science. My mother was always badgering me to go ahead and get a bachelor's degree, and for once I regretted not listening to her. I laughed bitterly at myself. That would be my luck. I'd help Drake Langston get a nice new library set up and lose my job in the process.

I was so concerned about losing my position as director of the Midway Library that by the time I got back to my apartment, I had forgotten all about Foster Scoggins and the possibility that he had been murdered. But a phone call from Miss Eugenia reminded me.

"So did you take the application to the sheriff?" she asked as soon as I answered the phone.

"Yes, ma'am. I gave him the application, and he agreed to let Cade conduct a quiet investigation as long as I help him and we wrap it up before the funeral, which is scheduled for Friday."

Since Miss Eugenia had started all this anyway, I didn't feel *too* bad about telling her that I'd learned about Scoggins's Mary. It was vital to our investigation, after all.

"Hmmm," Miss Eugenia replied, "that doesn't give us much time. At least we don't have to solve the case by Friday—we just have to come up with some compelling evidence that it was murder."

"How compelling does our evidence have to be?" I asked.

"If we can find this mystery woman, Mary, or if we can come up with a motive for Foster's murder—either one should be enough to start a full-fledged investigation."

I wanted to laugh at these lofty goals, but I could tell by the tone of her voice that she wasn't kidding. "And how will we get this evidence?"

"Deputy Burrell is our best bet, so maybe it's a good thing that the sheriff insisted you work with him."

Assuming that Miss Eugenia, like everyone else, wanted me to get back with Cade, I said, "I'll work with him, but I won't marry him again."

"I'm just trying to solve a murder here," Miss Eugenia assured me.

I can't say I believed her completely, but I didn't want to discuss it anymore, so I just said, "Cade promised he'd go talk to Luke Scoggins again tonight."

"That's a good place to start," Miss Eugenia said.

"I feel so inadequate to conduct a murder investigation," I admitted.

"The deputy will be conducting it—not you," Miss Eugenia pointed out. "You'll just be recording the data. You need to get a notebook—something small and nonthreatening. Then whenever you and the deputy are investigating, take very careful notes of everything. Write down where you go, what you see, and transcribe every interview."

"So I can tell you later?"

"I will be interested to hear," Miss Eugenia admitted, "but mostly the notes are for you. You'll never be able to remember who said what unless you write their comments down at the time. And it's amazing how things that appear to have no connection can turn into clues when you look at them right."

"I'll get a notebook," I promised.

"Call me in the morning to let me know what the deputy finds out from Luke Scoggins."

Miss Eugenia wasn't the type of person you argue with, so I just said, "Okay."

After we ended our call, I found a mostly empty notebook and tore out the used pages. Then I made a detailed list of everything I knew about Foster Scoggins and his death. I wrote about the library application and the cut on Heaven's hand and the dubious theory that Foster had a girlfriend. Finally I wrote Murder Book on the front, since I knew it would annoy Cade.

Then I took a long, hot shower. I had just stepped out and wrapped a thick towel around me when I heard someone banging on my door.

I checked the clock with a frown. It was almost ten o'clock, which was *way* past the polite hour to visit folks uninvited. "Who is it?" I hollered as I padded across the living room.

"It's me," Cade replied through the door. "Let me in!"

I opened the door a crack and hissed, "I will not! It's late, and I'm not dressed." Tucking the towel more firmly around me, I added, "It wouldn't be proper."

"You weren't worried about being proper when you were hugging in the dark with that Drake Langston character."

"You followed me!" I accused. "You were in the back of the new library spying on us!"

"I was not!" he denied, but not very convincingly. "Although who could blame me if I was? Somebody's got to watch out for you if you don't have more sense than to go off with a stranger."

I ignored this ridiculous comment. "Did you come here in the middle of the night to complain about the time I spent with Drake Langston?"

"No," he said a little sulkily, "I stopped by on my way home from the Scoggins salvage yard to tell you what Luke had to say about his uncle."

If I'd been wearing more than a towel, I would have opened the door. "Well, what did he say?"

I heard Cade exhale heavily. "He said he doesn't think Foster killed himself."

I was so excited that I did open the door but just a little. "I told you!"

His eyes dipped to the edge of the towel, and when he raised them up to mine again, his pupils were fixed and dilated.

I yanked the towel toward my chin—madder than I'd been since that night at the drive-in. How dare he act all tender and loving when he was the one who had ruined everything?

"We're divorced!" I reminded him. "Now tell me what else Luke said."

Cade walked to the edge of the porch and faced away from me. He reached up and ran a hand through his hair. "He gave us what might be motive for murder." Cade turned back and stared at what he could see of my face through the crack in the door. "You know your boyfriend Drake Langston has plans to build two housing developments around town—one to the south and one to the north?"

I nodded. Everyone knew that. "He's not my boyfriend."

"Well, apparently it's an all-or-nothing deal, and the Scoggins Salvage Yard sits right in the middle of the northern development."

I opened the door a little farther, my mouth dry and heart pounding. "Let me guess. Foster refused to sell."

Cade nodded. "He was adamant about holding on to his twenty acres of squalor. Langston had made two counter offers—increasing the purchase price each time—without success. Langston was applying plenty of pressure, but Foster wasn't budging."

"You think someone killed him because he wouldn't sell?"

Cade shrugged. "*If* someone killed him, that's the obvious motive. With Foster out of the way, the decision to sell or not will be made by his brother, Parnell."

"Luke's father," I clarified. "The one in a nursing home?"

"Yeah, and Luke said his father would never be able to work in the salvage yard again and didn't care that much about keeping the land."

"So once the decision was up to Parnell, a deal could be struck."

"Yeah. Probably pretty quickly, too."

"This is great!" I couldn't contain my enthusiasm even though it required that I praise Cade. "Now we just need to make up a list of everyone who would have benefited from the sale of the salvage yard, and we'll have our suspects."

"Everyone in Midway would benefit," Cade pointed out. "Or at least most everyone. Even you—since you're getting a new library out of the deal."

"I didn't kill Foster," I assured him.

Cade rolled his eyes. "Of course you didn't. I'm just pointing out that there are plenty of people who would benefit besides the landowners. And no one would benefit from the sale *more* than Drake Langston himself."

This was a sobering and unwelcome thought. "Drake wouldn't kill an old man to make a sale." At least I was fairly sure he wouldn't. "He might resort to badgering or even legal harassment. But there are hundreds of towns just like Midway all over the Southeast. If he couldn't strike a deal with Foster, he would have just moved on to another needy community."

"He's already spent money and time here. He wouldn't want to lose that investment to an ignorant salvage yard owner," Cade insisted. "He stays on the suspect list."

"Okay." It was an easy concession. I knew Drake wasn't a murderer, but Cade could keep him under suspicion if that made him feel better. "Don't you think you should tell the sheriff that you have a motive for murder so he can postpone the funeral?"

"I'll talk with him about it," Cade responded noncommittally.

"So what's next?"

"Sheriff Bonham told me to fax copies of the library card application and the suicide note to the FBI in Atlanta for a handwriting comparison. While we wait for those results, we'll be compiling the suspect list and conducting some low-key interviews."

I could barely contain my exhilaration. I, Kennedy Killingsworth, was part of a murder investigation. For anyone that would be exciting. But for someone who had lived her entire life in Midway, Georgia—it was, well, *life-changing*!

I was so happy I could have hugged Cade, but he still had that longing look in his eyes, so I stayed safely inside my apartment. "Why don't you come by the library tomorrow morning, and we can work on the suspect list."

He nodded. "I'll come by around ten."

"Okay." Then I felt required to add, "Thanks, Cade. For taking me seriously."

For a few seconds the words hung between us.

Finally he said, "You're welcome. And I can see why that Langston guy is so interested in you. You're looking really great lately."

I wasn't sure how to respond. I'd lost a few pounds—thanks to the grief he'd caused me. And I'd gotten a haircut—a short, tuck-behind-the-ears style that he'd always argued against when we were married. Eventually I settled on, "Thanks again."

"I guess it would be a waste of breath to ask you to stay away from Drake Langston until we figure out what happened to Foster?"

I nodded. "It would be a waste of breath. Drake's going to help us get a new library, and besides, if he's guilty, I'll find that out quicker by spending time with him than by avoiding him."

Cade took a step toward the stairs and then turned back. "Be careful, Kennedy. You don't know him. No matter how rich and charming he seems, he might not have your best interests at heart."

It was tempting to point out that I'd known Cade all my life, and my heart hadn't been safe with him either, but since he was helping me with Foster's murder investigation, I just nodded. "I'll be careful."

As he turned to leave, I saw his eyes make one last sweep across the top of my towel. Then he hurried down the steps and was gone. I closed the door and leaned my head against the cool wood. I heard Cade gun the engine in his patrol car, and I was overcome with loneliness. I refused to consider the possibility that I actually missed Cade. But I did miss my old life, and in my weakened state I longed for the arms of a man I knew I couldn't trust.

I opened the door, but thankfully he was already gone. (Which proves that God watches over me even if I don't deserve it. Resuming a romantic relationship with Cade would be a monumental mistake.)

So I picked up my Murder Book and wrote down everything Cade had told me, including his suspicions about Drake Langston.

CHAPTER FIVE

My alarm went off at seven o'clock on Wednesday morning. I hit the snooze and promptly fell back asleep. Fortunately the sound of someone pounding on my door at 7:15 reawakened me. It was one of the storage unit renters who wanted to pay his monthly fee. I took his check, reminded him there was a slot in the office door downstairs for just such a payment emergency, and then closed the door. Thinking that I should ask Mr. Sheffield for a raise, I went to the kitchen and ate a granola bar for breakfast.

I looked up Miss Eugenia's number in the phone book and placed the call. She answered on the second ring.

"I hope I'm not calling too early," I apologized, in case I'd awakened her.

"Nonsense," Miss Eugenia said. "Old people don't sleep much. Now what did Luke Scoggins have to say about Foster?"

I gave her a quick rundown of everything Cade had told me. As I was wrapping up my report, I said, "And they found what they are calling a suicide note in Foster's truck, but it was very vague and might have been something else entirely. Apparently the sheriff has his own doubts about the note too, because he told Cade to fax a copy of it and the library card application to Atlanta so the handwriting can be compared and analyzed."

"Suicide note?" Miss Eugenia repeated. "I didn't know Foster left a note."

I felt bad for breaking my heart-crossed promise again, but it was too late now. So I further divulged, "It said he was sorry and hoped Heaven could forgive him."

"Hmmm. We'll have to figure that out. But it's good that the sheriff had the letter and the application sent off to a handwriting expert."

I always prefer to hear the bad news first, so I said, "Actually he's just using the application to prove that Foster did write the note and thereby confirm his death as a suicide. But," I paused for a deep breath, "Luke Scoggins gave Cade what might be a motive for Foster's murder."

"A motive is exactly what we need."

"I'm sure you've heard of Drake Langston and how he's giving Midway a makeover," I began.

"Of course I've heard of Drake Langston," she replied. "And I'm glad he's making over Midway. Goodness knows somebody needs to."

I told her about the improvements Drake was planning—including the new library. Then I said, "Drake is also buying up a lot of land around town to build two housing developments that he hopes he can fill with professional people willing to commute from Albany. He's offering good prices, and a lot of folks stand to make a lot of money. But according to Foster's nephew, it's an all-or-nothing deal. And Foster was refusing to sell the land he owns."

"That's what I call a motive. Good work."

It wasn't exactly my work—it was Cade's. But he had gone to talk to Luke at my request, so I didn't correct her. "What do we do now?"

"That's something we should discuss in person. Why don't you come over?"

"Now?"

"As soon as you can get here. I'm heading next door to eat breakfast with my neighbors the Iversons. Mark Iverson is an important secret agent with the FBI, and he could be very helpful to us in solving this murder. That is, if we can convince him to get involved. He usually likes to stay out of this sort of thing, but maybe he'll give us some advice at least."

The inclusion of an FBI agent made the whole thing seem even more exciting and so official. So I agreed to go right over.

"And I'll ask my lawyer friend to come by too," Miss Eugenia added, "to make sure we keep the investigation legal."

A lawyer and an FBI agent. This was now a bona fide investigation and I was part of it.

"No need to thank me," Miss Eugenia continued as if I'd spoken. "I love a good murder mystery." Then she gave me directions to her house.

"I'll be there in fifteen minutes."

"Don't drive too fast," she warned. "Our police chief is notorious for setting speed traps to boost his operating budget."

I laughed. "I'll be careful."

Just as I hung up, my mother called. Under most circumstances this would be a bad thing. But since I needed someone to watch the library for me while I went to lunch with Drake Langston, I considered it divine intervention.

"Good morning!" she greeted me cheerfully.

"Morning."

"The viewing tonight is from six to eight," she informed me. "They're expecting a big crowd, so I'd like to get there early. Can you pick me up at 5:45?"

Wild horses couldn't have kept me away. "Of course."

"I'll be glad when the funeral is over tomorrow so this town can go back to discussing something besides poor Foster and his embarrassing death."

"Are you sure the funeral is tomorrow?" I asked, hoping that Cade had convinced the sheriff to postpone the funeral. It seemed best to keep the body—what was left of it, anyway—out of the ground until all questions of foul play were settled.

Mother misunderstood the reason for my question. "It's kind of you to be willing to go to the funeral too, Kennedy, but since we weren't close to the family, an appearance at the viewing tonight will be sufficient."

I wasn't worried in the least about fulfilling our social obligations—my mother worried about that enough for our entire family. "Agreed."

Then all I had to do was mention that I had a lunch date with Drake, and my mother nearly begged to watch the library for me. "I'm sure Uncle Forest won't mind if I leave the dental office early."

And I was able to get off the phone with her by saying that I needed to iron my black dress so I could wear it to the funeral home that evening. I've never understood why my wearing wrinkled clothing reflects badly on my mother, but she insists that it does.

The next order of business was to call Cade. I tried the office first, since calling him at home—the one we used to share—seemed uncomfortably personal. But as my luck would have it, he was off duty. So I called the familiar number. I could imagine the old slimline phone on the nightstand by what used to be our bed ringing insistently. Cade would growl and reach over to grab it. I stopped imagining before I had to consider whether or not he was alone.

"Burrell," he mumbled.

I took childish pleasure in knowing I'd woken him up. "It's Kennedy."

I heard the sheets rustling and figured he was sitting up on the edge of the bed. "Hey."

"My mother said Foster Scoggins's funeral is still scheduled for tomorrow. How can you bury him when he might be the victim of a murder?"

Cade cleared his throat. "The sheriff didn't want to upset the family until we had proof. He said he should have preliminary results on the handwriting samples back from Atlanta by this afternoon. If they say the suicide note wasn't written by Foster, we'll ask the family to delay the funeral long enough to do an autopsy."

"Okay." I decided I had no choice but to be satisfied with this. "I guess I'll see you at ten."

I heard him yawn. "Ten."

I hung up the phone and dressed quickly for my appointment with Miss Eugenia. I drove fast until I reached Haggerty. Then I made sure to stay just below the speed limit. Haggerty is the antithesis of Midway. Set up around a well-maintained town square, it fairly screams Southern charm. It is a few miles closer to Albany and therefore has benefited from commuters without any help from Drake Langston. The small businesses in Haggerty are booming, and the real estate market is competitive. All of us Midway folks look at Haggerty with respect and a little bit of envy.

The town square makes navigation easy. I followed Maple Street past the Haggerty police station, admired the new library, and ended up a few blocks down at the address Miss Eugenia had given me. Her house was an older home, covered in white clapboard shingles and surrounded by a profusion of flowers, shrubs, and blooming trees that would put a botanical garden to shame.

As I parked at the curb, Miss Eugenia stepped from the house next door and waved for me to join her. I crossed the neighbor's yard and noted the stark difference. While Miss Eugenia's yard looked like something out of *Southern Living*, the neighbor's yard was browner than green and could barely qualify as grass since it was so full of weeds. There were some flowers planted in beds along the house, but they looked like they didn't have long to live.

"I see you found us," Miss Eugenia said as she walked down the steps to greet me.

Miss Eugenia turned and led me through the front door of the house. The large entryway was dominated by a round antique table which accommodated an arrangement of fresh yellow roses. To the left was an old-fashioned parlor complete with a baby grand piano. To the right was a cozier family room furnished with overstuffed, modern pieces that were obviously chosen for comfort.

"This house is beautiful," I mumbled as we walked through the parlor into a dining room full of more antiques.

"It is nice. Kate had contemporary furniture when she moved to Haggerty. She sold it to my sister, who likes to think she's modern." Miss Eugenia rolled her eyes. Then she reached out a hand and stroked the silky finish of the old table. "I found this set for Kate at an estate sale. We got a few pieces at flea markets, and some things are reproductions."

I was amazed. "The Iversons are very fortunate to have you as their neighbor."

Miss Eugenia nodded. "I remind them of that every day."

We passed into a large kitchen, where the Iverson family was gathered around the table. Mark Iverson stood as we walked in, drawing my attention to him. He was tall and handsome with short dark hair and brown eyes.

"Everyone, this is Kennedy," Miss Eugenia introduced. "She's helping the sheriff in Midway on a murder case, and she's here to get my advice."

This was a gross overstatement of the facts, but I didn't correct her.

Miss Eugenia pointed to each family member in turn. "This is Mark. He's very high up in the FBI."

"I'm not high up," Mark corrected.

"Mark is the bishop for the local Mormons, which is like being their preacher," Miss Eugenia elaborated. "So he knows your sister, Madison, and her family well."

I saw Mark Iverson flinch. He knew Madison and her horde of monsters, all right.

Miss Eugenia pointed with pride at a blond-haired girl. "This is Emily, and she's five."

Emily raised a hand in greeting, and I smiled at her.

Miss Eugenia turned to a boy who was a miniature copy of his father. "Charles is almost four, and he's named after my late husband."

"Hey, Charles," I said.

He stuck his fingers in his mouth and mumbled something unintelligible.

Miss Eugenia's attention moved to the woman with dark blond hair and green eyes. "And of course, this is Kate."

"Welcome," Kate said. "Would you like some pancakes?"

"No, thank you." My eyes were riveted on the tiny baby she was holding. Swaddled in a light blue blanket, his skin was the color of well-creamed coffee. His black hair looked as soft as duck's down, and suddenly my hands were itching to touch him.

"This is our foster baby," Emily explained. "We call him Jake, but that's not his real name. His adoption mother gets to pick that out."

Miss Eugenia walked over to a kitchen cabinet and removed a plate. "Are you sure you aren't hungry?" she asked me while placing several pancakes on her plate.

"I'm sure." I couldn't drag my eyes away from the baby.

"Do you want to hold him?" Emily offered. "Mama will let you."

I sat down in the chair beside Kate. "I'd love to."

The baby was transferred, and I had to work hard to control a whimper. I've held babies before but never had a reaction even close to the one I felt when I held the little foster baby "Jake." Maybe it was because he hadn't found the place where he belonged yet. I felt that way myself. I guess we were kindred spirits.

"How long do you get to keep him?" I asked, savoring the soft weight of him against my arms.

"It varies," Kate replied. "Sometimes they only stay a few days. The longest we've had one is three weeks."

"Kate and Mark are just a layover between the birth mother and the adoptive parents," Miss Eugenia explained. "The length of time they keep the babies depends on how long it takes to work out the legalities."

"Isn't it hard to give them up when they have to go?" I asked.

"I was worried about that at first," Kate admitted, "but it hasn't been a problem. From the beginning I understand that I'm just babysitting for the real mother. And I've found I'm more attached to the idea of a baby in the house than the individual baby. It's hard to explain."

I nodded, but I didn't understand. How could anyone bring this baby into their home and then let him go? Just the thought brought tears uncharacteristically to my eyes. I stroked Jake's little cheek. He opened his eyes, and I swear he smiled right at me.

"He likes you," Emily said.

I thought my heart would break.

"Emily, why don't you and Charles go out and play on the swing set," Miss Eugenia suggested. "The adults need to talk about important things for a few minutes."

Emily nodded. "Come on, Charles."

"Stay where we can see you," Kate admonished.

"We will," Emily called over her shoulder as she pulled her brother through the back door.

I noticed that Kate's eyes trailed along with her children, keeping them constantly in her line of vision. And once they were settled on the swings, she angled her chair toward the window so she could continue to supervise them.

Miss Eugenia generously doused her pancakes with Log Cabin syrup. Then she said, "Kennedy, why don't you tell Kate and Mark about Foster's murder."

Kate's eyes temporarily left the children playing in the backyard. "I thought that man in Midway killed himself."

"That's because it's currently classified as a suicide," I explained.

"Currently," Mark repeated. "I presume that means you have doubts about how he died?"

"Yes," I confirmed.

"Remind me about the circumstances," Kate said.

"Are you familiar with the Scoggins Salvage Yard?" I asked.

Kate shook her head. "Never heard of it."

Mark shook his head.

"Mark is many wonderful things, but he's not handy with car repairs," Miss Eugenia said. "And he's even worse with yard work."

I recalled the dead lawn and bedraggled flower beds.

Mark shrugged. "I have a brown thumb."

Kate glanced at little Jake. "And I'd rather play with babies than fight weeds and bugs."

Miss Eugenia waved a fork. "I've offered my services, but they won't let me take over their yard."

I saw Kate and Mark exchange a glance.

"It would be too much for you," Kate said.

"And your yard wouldn't look as good if ours wasn't such a terrible comparison," Mark added.

Miss Eugenia hooted with laughter. "You don't need to sabotage your yard to make mine look good."

At this point a man arrived at the front door. Miss Eugenia introduced him as Whit Owens, her lawyer friend, and I realized he was her hot date from the night before. He was attractive—for an old man. Tall with wavy white hair and a pleasant smile.

He shook my hand, declined Kate's offer of pancakes, and sat down.

Mark turned to Miss Eugenia. "Is Winston coming?"

"I'm here," the Haggerty police chief said from the back doorway.

"Pancakes?" Kate offered.

He held up a Styrofoam coffee cup. "I grabbed breakfast at Hardees on my way in." He looked at me. "You're Cade Burrell's wife?"

"Ex-wife," I corrected.

He frowned. "You're divorced? The way he talks, I thought he was crazy about you."

"Unfortunately he isn't crazy about me *exclusively*," I said with the intention of putting the subject to rest permanently. I was successful.

Chief Jones mumbled, "Sorry," and took a seat at the table.

Mark folded his hands together and asked, "So what makes you think Foster Scoggins was killed?"

I reluctantly passed the baby to Kate and took my Murder Book out of my purse. I opened to the first page and then, with Miss Eugenia's frequent assistance, gave them our case in a nutshell.

"I'm convinced that the girlfriend was fabricated by the murderer to make a suicide seem plausible—but it was a miscalculation," Miss Eugenia said when I had finished. "If they had chosen financial problems or a terminal disease, *that* would have been believable. Even if they had tried to show that Foster had gone crazy. But a *girlfriend*? I'd sooner believe he was the Boston Strangler."

Chief Jones frowned. "Well, I wouldn't have believed that. I don't think Foster's ever been out of Dougherty County let alone to Boston."

Miss Eugenia rolled her eyes, and I pressed on quickly.

Kate encouraged us with a smile every now and then, but her focus was on the baby and her children outside. Mr. Owens listened with care, obviously looking for legal issues. Chief Jones seemed openly skeptical, but Mark Iverson was attentive. He asked several pertinent questions, and by the end Miss Eugenia was beaming.

"You should be honored that Mark is interested in our case," she told me. "Usually when I tell him I have suspicions of foul play, he tries to keep me from getting involved."

"I definitely don't want you to get involved in this either," Mark was quick to say. "And I don't want Kennedy to get *more* involved than she already is. But if a murder has been committed, I'd like for the responsible party to be brought to justice. And if Kennedy can point the Midway sheriff's department in the right direction, I see no harm in that."

"I think you ladies need to mind your own business," Chief Jones said—just in case we couldn't tell how he felt by the scowl on his face.

Mark ignored this and said, "Mention to Deputy Burrell that I am willing to help with the investigation. I can arrange to have the deceased's truck checked over by an FBI forensic team or check the suicide note for fingerprints—anything."

Whit Owens cleared his throat and said, "Just be sure that everything you do is run through the sheriff's department so that it's official. Otherwise evidence collected might not be admissible in court."

Mark nodded. "Of course we'd have to go through the sheriff."

"I'll tell Cade about it when I meet with him later this morning," I promised. "We're going to make up a suspect list, which will probably start out as the entire population of Midway. For once I'm glad we have so few residents."

Miss Eugenia chuckled.

"Why is everyone in Midway a suspect?" Kate wanted to know.

"Have you heard about Drake Langston, the real estate developer from Atlanta?" I asked.

She nodded. "I've seen him on TV a few times. He's building some houses near Midway?"

"That and more," I confirmed. "He's buying land from several residents, and some stand to gain substantially from the deal. In addition to that, he's refurbishing the downtown area, and from what I hear, it's going to be spectacular. He's fixing up rental space for retailers and putting in new sidewalks and planting trees. He's also promised to build a family center for the Baptist church and convert the old First National Bank building into the new Midway Library."

I paused for a breath.

"And how does this relate to Foster Scoggins?" Whit Owens asked.

I felt a blush rise in my cheeks. I'd gotten so carried away talking about Drake I'd forgotten I was there to discuss the murder. "Foster Scoggins owned twenty acres of land right in the middle of one of the housing developments Drake wants to build. It was an all-or-nothing deal—"

"And ornery old Foster didn't want to sell," Miss Eugenia interjected. "So he had placed the whole deal—houses, downtown, family center, and library—at risk. Which is probably why somebody killed him."

"It hasn't been established that Foster Scoggins *was* killed," Chief Jones said.

"It's been established as far as I'm concerned," Miss Eugenia countered. "I'm just waiting for the Midway sheriff's department to come to the same conclusion."

This drew Kate into the conversation. "It's hard to believe anyone would kill an old man over land or money or a new library."

Mark frowned. "People kill for much less every day."

"But not in Midway," Kate clarified. "Not here."

"If there was a murder," Chief Jones prefaced, "it might not be anyone from Midway. Drake Langston would be my suspect."

I didn't know if this conclusion—which was identical to Cade's—was a police reaction, a male reaction, or just an effort to accuse someone from outside the immediate area. But I was getting tired of these unfounded accusations against Drake.

"Mr. Langston will be on the suspect list and needs to be investigated thoroughly," I assured them. "He has some time and effort and money invested in the Midway project, but he's extremely rich, so if this deal fell through, I don't think it would impact him significantly. He'd just go on to another town in need of new development."

Chief Jones narrowed his eyes at me. "It sounds like you know this Langston fellow pretty well."

I refused to be cowed and looked him straight in the eyes. "I don't know him well, but I don't think he's a murderer."

"So the guilty party is from Midway?" Kate sounded dismayed.

Miss Eugenia nodded. "That's the likely explanation, but we'll keep an open mind while we investigate."

Chief Jones groaned. "Why can't you just let the sheriff do the investigating?"

"I'd be glad to," Miss Eugenia claimed, "if he *would* investigate!"

"If there's an investigation, it must be carried out by Sheriff Bonham in Midway," Mark concurred. "Kennedy is only helping Deputy Burrell to collect evidence so the sheriff can make an educated decision."

"Humph," Miss Eugenia replied. "Unless we prod him along, Sheriff Bonham will ignore the possibility that Foster was killed, since he thinks that route would be better for the town and progress."

"It would be better for the murderer, too," I added, trying not to sound disrespectful.

"Yes," Miss Eugenia agreed. "So, Kennedy, you keep pushing Deputy Burrell."

I nodded but without enthusiasm.

Miss Eugenia nodded. "And Mark could check Foster's phone records."

"I can if the sheriff asks me to," Mark amended.

"Once you come up with your suspect list, you can narrow it by checking alibis," Mark suggested. "Start by interviewing people who had the most to gain. Watch for their reactions when they hear Mr. Scoggins's name. Look around their home and see if there's evidence of recent spending."

I took notes furiously. "As in money they didn't have yet but were expecting to get from the land sale?"

"Exactly," Mark confirmed. "People who have spent money before their chickens have hatched, so to speak, would have been particularly desperate if it looked like the whole deal was going to fall through."

I covertly checked my watch. If I didn't leave soon, I was going to be seriously late opening the library. So I stood. "Well, I need to go, but I appreciate your time and advice."

Miss Eugenia smiled at the assemblage. "Yes, this is a good group to have on your side during a murder investigation."

Chief Jones murmured something under his breath, but I couldn't understand him, which I thought was just as well.

"Call me this evening and tell me what you and the deputy have been able to accomplish," Miss Eugenia commanded. "By then I may have more suggestions for you."

"Yes, ma'am." Then I said good-bye to everyone, and after one last longing look at Baby Jake, I moved toward the front door.

Mark stood up and followed me. When we stepped out onto the porch, he prefaced his remarks by saying, "Miss Eugenia is a wonderful person, but she does have a tendency to get involved in dangerous situations. She was in the hospital a few months ago because a man she was 'investigating' drugged her."

I was shocked to hear this. "That's awful!"

"That's the kind of risk you take when you go after murderers," Mark stated firmly. "So if you want to help the sheriff's department, I think that's fine. But make sure you stay in the background and never question a suspect alone."

I nodded, still shaken.

Mark seemed satisfied that his warning had been effective. "Well, then, it was nice to meet you, and good luck with this case."

I waved and walked down the front steps, crossed the Iversons' poor excuse for a lawn, and climbed into my truck. After making use of a neighbor's driveway to turn around, I headed back through Haggerty's town square.

When I saw the old train station, now converted into a restaurant, I remembered my upcoming lunch with Drake. My eyes skidded left and landed on Miss Corrine's dress shop. Miss Corrine's is known for high quality, high fashion, and high prices. I mentally calculated the amount in my checking account and decided that I could afford to at least look at the clearance rack.

I had a little fit of nerves as I approached the door to the dress store. My mother and sisters have great taste and can find a bargain anywhere. But no matter how much I pay for clothes, I always feel unsure of my choices and rarely wear anything with confidence. And pushy sales clerks are torture.

But providence was smiling on me that day. Miss Corrine was attending a funeral in North Carolina and had left her establishment in the questionably capable hands of a teenage relative. This took care of my high-pressure-sales concerns, and as it turned out, the store sitter had taste and patience. So I walked out of Miss Corrine's thirty minutes later with a new dress that was professional yet flirty. I would have loved to run by Edith's Shoe Emporium on the corner for a new pair of shoes and a purse, but I had neither the time nor any available funds.

CHAPTER SIX

ON THE WAY BACK INTO Midway I stopped by my apartment to change into my new dress even though I knew it was going to make me late. To save a little time, I took my cosmetic bag with me and applied makeup while driving down the road. I figured the risk of getting a ticket for reckless driving was minimal since Cade was at the library waiting for me.

By the time I arrived it was ten-thirty. Cade was not only waiting, but he had also opened the library and was conducting business in my behalf. One of my regulars, Miss Phoebe Smitherman—who loves to talk about her health problems and the difficulty of adjusting to the death of her husband (which took place over twenty years ago)—was leaving when I walked in. I nodded in greeting but did not ask how she was feeling.

I glanced around as I headed toward Cade, who was ensconced behind my desk. My EASY READER section was in shambles—a sure sign that a mother with preschoolers had stopped by. And based on the stack of biographies on the counter, I presumed that Miss Mabel from the high school had called needing more books for her senior English class.

Cade had paid a high price for his decision to help me out, and I knew I owed him at least a little gratitude. "Thanks for opening the library," I said casually. "And I'm sorry you had to deal with Miss Phoebe."

He looked me over from head to toe but didn't comment on my new dress. "At least she doesn't require much in the comment department," he said. "All I had to do was listen to her. Now Miss Ida Jean is another story."

"Miss Ida Jean has been here already too?"

"She was waiting at the door when I arrived at 9:55. She wanted to check out a book on boils in case she ever gets one," Cade replied with a little shudder. "But you don't have one."

"I never have whatever book Miss Ida Jean wants. I think she keeps track of my inventory and purposely requests things she knows are unavailable just so she can complain." I sighed. "You should have just made her wait until I got here."

"I was afraid if the library didn't open on time, she might report you to the mayor and you'd lose your job—right when it's about to get interesting with the new library and all."

I couldn't bear to thank him again so I directed my comment toward my most faithful and most annoying patron. "Miss Ida Jean is a pain."

"But the library *is* supposed to open at ten," he countered. Punctuality was one of Cade's few virtues.

"Now you sound like my mother."

"Sometimes maybe you should listen to her."

I was not going to be lectured on proper behavior by Cade Burrell. So I said, "We'd better make use of this patron-free time to discuss Foster's murder."

"Death," he corrected.

I waved a hand in dismissal. "Whatever."

I led the way to the middle of the small library, and we settled down at the same table where I had prepared Heaven's report on Abraham Lincoln just two days before. The same table where Foster Scoggins had applied for a library card that he'd never get the chance to use. My resolve strengthened, and I pulled out my Murder Book.

"What's that?" Cade asked with a frown.

"Miss Eugenia suggested that I use a notebook to keep track of everything related to Foster's murder."

His frown deepened. "Death."

"Yes, well, 'Death Book' doesn't sound nearly as dramatic."

He smirked in disrespect for my notebook. "I guess it doesn't matter what you call it." He leaned back in his chair and announced, "I asked Serene to request a list of everyone who had agreed to sell property from Langston's company."

His casual reference to the young and very attractive receptionist employed by the sheriff's department was mildly suspicious. Since I was no longer his wife, I didn't have the right to question his relationship with the girl, but unfortunately a legal severance does not end the pain caused by a marriage gone bad.

"There are fourteen people who were offered money in exchange for land they own in or near Midway," Cade continued. "A couple of these folks own a lot of land and stand to make almost a million dollars each. Others only owned a few acres, but Langston is offering top dollar, so even people without much land will make some good money."

I stared at his list with hungry eyes. "I'd like a copy of your list."

He pulled a duplicate from underneath. "I expected that."

I put the list into my Murder Book and then turned to a fresh page so I could take notes as we discussed our suspects.

"This list," Cade said, pointing at his copy, "is only a good starting place. There are many other people who would benefit either in increased business, sales of building materials, jobs, etc."

"We've got to start somewhere," I agreed. "I think we need to interview all the landowners first and find out if they have an alibi for Monday night. Once we've done that, we can add to our list of suspects."

Cade didn't object to this plan, so I glanced over the list. I noticed that Mr. Bateman, who owned the gas station near the salvage yard, stood to make almost a million dollars on the sale. As my mother had told me, the Baptist preacher and his wife would also come out of the deal with a hefty amount since they owned the largest parcel Drake was purchasing.

"I think we can check the preacher and his wife off the list," I said. "And Mr. Bateman, too. He's harmless."

Cade gave me a bland look. "That shows how much you know about police work. You can't discount anyone at the beginning of an investigation. In fact, the more innocent they seem, the more suspicious I am."

This was a side of Cade I'd never seen. I kind of liked it.

"Even though the Lebows don't have much land, they will make almost three hundred thousand dollars," I remarked.

"And since they are both laid off from the tire plant, that money will keep them from losing their house and give them the money they need to train for other careers."

"That's what I call incentive," I murmured.

"Incentive is not the same as motive," Cade pointed out. Then he folded his list and put it in his pocket. "You realize that we are going to have to tread carefully with these interviews," he continued. "We can't accuse the preacher or other town leaders of murder without proof."

I rolled my eyes. "I wasn't planning to ask them outright if they killed Foster. We'll just make small talk, discuss what's going on in their lives and find out where they were at the time Foster died. All very subtle."

"Very."

"Once you check out alibis, we can zero in on the people who don't have good ones."

"Subtly."

"Very."

"If you're with me when I make these visits, they won't seem too official," he slipped in slyly. "So maybe people won't be on their guard. What time are you free this afternoon?"

"I've got a lunch appointment with Drake Langston and an architect from Atlanta." Just saying the word *architect* made my heart beat a little faster. "My mother is leaving Uncle Forest's office early to man the library while I'm gone. I'll see if she can stay here for the rest of the day."

Cade's eyes skimmed my new dress again, and this time he frowned. "Just come by the sheriff's office when you're through with lunch."

He stood, and I felt a little bad. But I wasn't exactly *using* him to further my own cause. After all, as a deputy sheriff he was partially responsible for the safety of Midway's citizens and the arrest of criminals. So really I was helping him do his job. But I knew he wouldn't be giving Foster's death any time at all if he didn't want to please me. I mentally returned to that night at the drive-in, and all my guilt evaporated. He owed me.

My mother arrived at eleven-thirty and was very pleased with my appearance. "Is that a new outfit?"

I turned in a quick circle so she could get the full effect. "I got it at Corrine's when I was in Haggerty this morning."

"You should shop there more often," my mother decided.

I smoothed the fabric of the dress. "I just might."

"I spoke to Miss Ida Jean when I was leaving to come here," Mother continued, "and she said Cade opened the library for you this morning."

"He did," I confirmed. "I'm helping him on a case. That's why I had to go to Haggerty. So Cade covered the library until I could get back."

"I don't know about you getting involved in police work," Mother said with a frown. "But the more time you spend with Cade, the better, so you can work out your differences."

I wanted to say "—like the fact that Cade couldn't tell the *difference* between *fidelity* and *infidelity*?" But since she was there to help me and I needed to extend the length of my favor, I kept my thoughts to myself. "Cade needs me to come by the sheriff's office after lunch. Can you stay a couple of extra hours?"

My mother considered this for a few minutes and then said, "I can give you until four o'clock, but then I've really got to get home. Otherwise I won't be able to have dinner ready before it's time for us to go to the funeral home."

"Four will be great," I assured her.

My mother had tended the library before, so she was familiar with my basic book check-out system, but I gave her a quick review.

At the end of my refresher course, she said, "I think I can handle it, dear. You hurry on to the Back Porch so you won't be late."

Unaccountably nervous about a lunch date that was strictly business, I gave my mother a quick hug and walked out to my truck.

I arrived in town at eleven-fifty and found that thanks to the construction vehicles lining one entire side of Main Street, all of the Back Porch's limited parking was already taken. So I parked in front of the sheriff's department in the space reserved for DEPUTY—since that meant Cade and goodness knows what belonged to him *should* belong to me.

I was out of my truck and just about to cross the street when the parking spot's true owner pulled up in front of me.

"I can move my truck," I offered halfheartedly.

He gave me a lazy smile and let his eyes drift over my new outfit again. "That's okay," he said. "I'll park in the back."

"Thanks." I didn't like to be put in the position of having to express gratitude to Cade, and that seemed to have been happening a lot lately.

"Purple looks great on you," he continued, his voice taking on a sultry tone. "It changes the color of your eyes."

My eyes are gray, and they do tend to reflect whatever shade I'm wearing, but I wasn't going to stand in the middle of Main Street discussing my eye color with Cade. So I said, "I'd better get over to the Back Porch."

"I'll see you after your business lunch." He eased his car around the corner toward the back of the sheriff's office. I looked both ways before crossing the street and climbed the restaurant's stairs. Drake was there, waiting for me.

Today he was dressed in a gorgeous olive green suit. His tie was a floral print with dashes of lavender. He touched it and said, "We match."

I was more pleased than ever with my new dress. "We do," I agreed.

He placed his hand on the small of my back and drew me forward. I thought he was going to embrace me, but he was only directing me toward our table—the restaurant's best by a front window, where another man was already seated. Papers and blueprints were spread on the table's wooden surface, so I assumed that the meeting was already underway. As Drake pulled a chair out for me, he introduced the architect.

"Kennedy Killingsworth, this is Morris Pugh."

Mr. Pugh was about Drake's age and even more handsome. He could have been a model for *GQ* or the star of a Diet Coke commercial. "Nice to meet you, Kennedy."

Despite his perfection, I wasn't attracted to him. Maybe there was such a thing as being too perfect. "Likewise."

"Let's order our food first," Drake proposed as one of the Back Porch waitresses rushed up, nearly beside herself at the opportunity to serve the important visitors.

"What's good?" Mr. Pugh asked her.

"Our special today is chicken fried steak with new potatoes and field peas," the waitress recited nervously.

I saw both men flinch at these fat-ridden, though delicious, options. So I said, "The grilled chicken salad is great." Then I told the waitress, "That's what I'll have, with ranch dressing on the side."

She scribbled my order and turned back to the men.

"Sounds good to me," Drake handed her his menu. "I'll have the same."

"Me too," Morris said.

The waitress scurried off to place our orders, and Drake said, "I know you're anxious to see the layout of the library."

"I am," I confirmed.

He nodded at Morris. "Go ahead and show her the inspiration piece."

Morris lifted a huge framed print that had been leaning against the wall under the window. It was a Monet—I could tell that much. The frame itself probably cost a thousand dollars. I squinted to read the inscription on the little gold plaque. The Artist's Garden at Vetheuil, 1881.

"It is exquisite," I managed when I was able to get some air into my lungs. And even that extravagant praise fell short of what the print deserved. The major colors were greens with gold and a deep orange splashed in. A set of gray stone steps and a dark blue sky added contrast.

Morris smiled. "I'm glad you like it."

"It's a personal gift from me to the city of Midway," Drake explained. "I thought you could hang it over the circulation desk to set the mood for people when they first come in."

"It's very calming," I agreed. "It might even help us keep patrons quiet."

His smile expanded into a tasteful little laugh.

Then Morris put the print aside and pulled out a series of architectural drawings. I stared in amazement, wondering if a building of such beauty and grandeur could truly exist in Midway.

"The plans are in three stages," Morris explained. "The first is the renovation stage where we will take the space we have and make it usable. The other two stages are for future expansion if that ever becomes possible. Stage two involves adding an atrium and stage three is an addition taking in the building to the immediate right."

I stared at the three-stage plans in amazement. Drake gave a whole new meaning to "thinking positive."

"But today we will be concentrating only on stage one," Morris was saying. "I've chosen the gold color from the print for the walls. It's bright yet bold. Dramatic yet tasteful."

"Exactly," I agreed as if I knew the first thing about picking paint colors.

"We'll use a creamy eggshell on the baseboards and crown molding. For the furniture upholstery and drapes we'll choose coordinating fabrics."

"What do you think?" Drake asked.

I shuffled through the drawings of stage one. "I think our library is going to be incredible. No one will ever want to leave. Which, if you'd met some of our patrons, you'd realize is a bad thing."

Drake laughed again and turned to Morris. "Didn't I tell you she was witty?"

Ordinarily I would scoff at such a comment. But since Drake said it, I decided to consider it a compliment.

Morris nodded. "You mentioned it more than once."

Our salads arrived, so I passed the drawings back to Drake. During the transfer, our fingers touched, and I felt a shock of awareness. Drake was polished and professional and wealthy. Different than any man I'd ever associated with before. I was anxious to get to know him better—and afraid at the same time. Drake Langston was definitely out of my league, and the last thing I needed to do was fall in love with another man who couldn't commit to me.

While we ate, Morris asked me, "So do the plans for stage one meet your approval?"

"They surpass any hopes I've ever had for the Midway Library," I replied honestly.

"Then our consultation is over," Drake declared. "The mayor told me that Kennedy, as the library's director, was authorized to make all decisions on the renovations. So we'll proceed with stage one of this plan."

I was astonished and relieved. Apparently Mayor Cook had a great deal more confidence in me than I'd realized, and maybe my job wasn't in danger after all. "So when do we start?"

"Since Morris has come up with such a fine plan, I anticipated your approval and have a crew at the library right now," Drake replied. "They are making general repairs like replacing the windows and patching the plaster. Now that we've chosen our paint color, I need to notify them so it can be ordered. If you have time after lunch, we could walk over there."

"I'll make time," I said. Foster Scoggins was already dead, and Cade could be patient.

"Good." Morris stacked the architectural drawings and put them back into his briefcase. "Now we can enjoy our salads."

I did enjoy my salad and the company and the whole experience. In fact, I was disappointed when Drake finally asked for the check.

Drake gave the waitress a large bill and told her to keep the change. She stared after him in adoration as we left the Back Porch and walked the short distance to the new library. We approached the entrance where jazz music and sheetrock dust drifted from the open door toward Main Street. I counted eight men hard at work when we stepped inside. Only one stopped working and walked over for Drake to introduce him.

"This is Sloan," Drake said.

Sloan was tall with high cheekbones and long black hair that hinted at a Native American ancestry. He walked with a swagger that *more* than hinted of male arrogance. The hand he extended toward me belonged to a craftsman— an artist—and his fingers were warm as they curled around mine.

"Nice to meet you," he said as his eyes did a quick examination of me from head to toe. The slow smile that spread across his face told me he liked what he saw.

"I'm Kennedy," I managed to say.

"Sloan is the best in the business," Drake told her. "He can do anything from drywall to carpentry to electrical wiring. I have to pay him a fortune to keep someone else from stealing him away from me."

I glanced at Sloan and he raised an eyebrow as if challenging me to think more of him now that I knew he made a lot of money.

"Sloan runs my top crew." Drake waved his hand to include the other men. "They work hard and their skills are top-notch. We're very lucky that they are temporarily available to work on this project. Once we get the land purchase issues settled, they'll be transferred to one of the housing developments."

I was impressed by the way Drake treated Sloan and his construction crew. He seemed to respect their contribution to his dream, even if he was the rich boss and they were his employees. And I was pleased that Drake had mentioned the land purchase situation since that would make it easier for me to bring it up again later.

"Kennedy has chosen the paint colors," Drake continued.

Morris pulled two paint color discs from his pocket and handed them to Sloan. "Goldenrod with glossy Antique Linen for the trim."

Sloan nodded in approval. "Excellent choices. I'll order them now, and we should be able to start painting in the morning. By then all the windows will have been replaced, and we'll have a new lock on the door to keep sight-seers out."

I was too mesmerized by his startlingly blue eyes to say anything so I just nodded.

"This job is top priority," Drake said. "Work as much overtime as you need."

Sloan nodded. "You're the boss."

I doubted that anyone ever forgot that, in spite of Drake's pleasant, friendly manner.

"If you have questions about anything, you can call me or Morris." Drake looked over at me. "Unless you'd like them to deal directly with you, since you have the final say anyway."

I glanced back at Sloan, and our eyes locked for a few heart-stopping seconds. "You are welcome to call me," I said a little breathlessly. "But I'm not always easy to reach."

"It's not always easy to reach Drake either," Sloan remarked, and I felt stupid. Of course the great Drake Langston was much more in demand than I was.

"I just meant that I don't have a cell phone," I explained quickly.

Sloan pulled a little black notebook out of his pocket and flipped it open. "Give me your numbers," he told me. "If I can't get you, I'll try Drake or Morris."

I gave Sloan my home number and the one at the library. I watched as he recorded both in his little black book and wondered how many other women's numbers were already there.

Drake turned back to Sloan. "That's settled, then. Call if you need us." He put a hand on my elbow and steered me toward the entrance.

I didn't want to leave the library. I could have stayed for hours, watching the progress and Sloan. But rebelling against Drake Langston was unthinkable, so I allowed him to lead me outside. Once we were on the sidewalk, Morris said he needed to get back to Atlanta. Polite farewells were exchanged, and soon Drake and I were alone.

"Well, I guess you need to get to work," he said.

"I do."

"You might want to consider closing up the old library this week," Drake suggested. "That way you can supervise the renovations here full-time."

I glanced into the future library and saw Sloan watching me. He winked, and a blush warmed my cheeks. "That sounds fine."

Drake started down the street, and I kept pace beside him. "I'd be glad to send some guys over to pack up the books and transfer them here."

I thought about my little two-trailer library and the books that lined my few shelves. "My books will be swallowed up in all that space in our new library."

Drake laughed. "We've applied for a grant to buy new books. By the time the library is finished, your shelves won't be empty."

It was almost too much to comprehend. And to think that just a few weeks ago, nobody in Midway had ever heard of Drake Langston. The future had been grim. Now everything was different. Better.

"I'll make Friday the last day of operation for the old library," I said.

"A crew will meet you there at eight o'clock on Saturday morning to pack up the books and make the transfer."

That was way before my usual workday started, so I made a mental note to set my alarm. "I'll be there. Thanks." Then remembering my obligation to find out more about Foster Scoggins and his unpleasant as well as untimely death, I asked, "How soon do you think you'll have the land purchase problems resolved so you can begin building houses?"

Drake didn't look nervous or upset by the question. "It shouldn't take more than a week or so."

"I understand that Foster Scoggins was the only landowner unwilling to make a deal," I ventured bravely.

Drake nodded. "Mr. Scoggins was a stubborn man, but I had to respect his right to keep his land."

"I guess that's not an issue anymore."

Drake frowned. "No. I've already talked to the surviving brother, and he's willing to sell. So we should be able to move forward quickly."

If there was any guile in Drake, I couldn't detect it. "I was afraid you'd have to wait for Mr. Scoggins's will to be probated and things like that."

"No, they had it set up like a partnership, so at Foster's death, his brother Parnell became the sole owner."

When we reached my truck, he pulled a business card out of his wallet and jotted an additional number across the bottom before passing it to me. "Here are the numbers you can use to reach me. I almost always have my cell with me."

I accepted his card and tucked it safely into my purse. Then I ripped an unused page from the daily organizer my mother had optimistically given me at Christmas and scribbled my parents' number across the blank lines. I handed it to Drake and said, "If you need to get in touch with me, just call my mother. She can always track me down."

Drake smiled and waved as I climbed into my truck. I waited until he had driven away in his Lexus before going into the sheriff's department. I'm not exactly sure why I didn't want him to know that I was spending my afternoon with Cade, but for some reason I didn't.

Cade was standing right inside the door when I walked in. I had the feeling that he'd kept an eye on me throughout my lunch and library tour. I shook my head at him. "You need to get a life."

"I had a life," he returned. "I'm trying to get it back."

I knew I should set him straight and assure him that there was no way I was ever going back. But I decided that this was not the time or the place for a continuation of this never-ending discussion. So I let the remark pass.

"We can talk in my office," he suggested.

So I followed him past the receptionist's desk, where the lovely Serene sat filing her nails. She gave me a brief nod as we moved down a hallway and into Cade's small office. Once there, he closed the door and said, "The sheriff got a call from Mark Iverson, an FBI agent in Albany. He said the FBI is interested in making sure Foster's death gets investigated. He offered to send a forensic team over to look at Foster's truck, but the sheriff declined."

I felt a little guilty for not warning Cade that this offer was coming and felt frustrated with the sheriff. "Why would Sheriff Bonham decline help?"

"Because he doesn't believe old Foster was murdered, and he doesn't want the FBI messing around in his business."

I did my best to hide my disappointment.

Cade pulled out the list of landowners and pointed to the first names. "I thought we'd start with Brother Jackson and Miss Zelda."

I groaned. "This better not get me in trouble with my mother."

"Just make sure nobody sees the title of that notebook," he suggested, pointing at my Murder Book. "And remember: subtle."

CHAPTER SEVEN

CADE AND I MANAGED TO visit eight of the fourteen people on our list of suspects before I had to get back to the library, and his interviews gave *subtlety* a whole new meaning. It seemed as if he just wanted people to see us together—like we were making social calls as a couple. Since Cade was determined to sip coffee and make small talk, I was left the task of working in comments about Drake Langston and the land deals he was offering. And to find out where people were on Monday night when Foster died.

While listening to Mrs. Castleberry tell us how the land money was going to make it possible for her to send her grandson to law school, Cade actually tried to take my hand into his, which earned him a scathing look. We saw no signs of recent spending other than the wish-list kind. Everyone sang Drake's praises, and most showed varying signs of resentment when we mentioned Foster and his refusal to sell the salvage yard. Three had good alibis. The rest did not.

When we finished our conversation with Mr. Bateman, which had consisted almost entirely of a detailed description of his plans for this year's vegetable garden, I was frustrated and angry.

As we walked behind the gas station, where our vehicles were parked, Cade cheerfully asked, "Where do you want to go next?"

I put my hands on my hips and said, "I don't know about you, but I've got to get to the library and relieve my mother. I guess you could go discuss boils with Miss Ida Jean or the weather with the clerk at the Jiffy Mart."

He frowned. "What do you mean by that?"

"I mean that you weren't taking these interviews seriously. You barely asked anything about Drake Langston and never mentioned Foster Scoggins once! It was more like a date than an investigation."

He had the decency to look ashamed. "I told you we had to tread lightly with the people in town."

"You were treading so lightly you might as well not have even walked there at all!"

"I was just trying to get a feel for them—see if they reacted with any anxiety about being questioned about the land sale deal."

I rolled my eyes. "I was the only one who asked any questions about that."

"It was better that way—less official."

I'd had it with him and was grateful I'd insisted on driving separately. "Thanks for nothing," I told him and stalked to my truck.

My mother takes meal-cooking very seriously, and I knew I had to be back on time. So I exceeded the speed limit all the way to the library, almost daring Cade to chase me down and give me a ticket. I made it with five minutes to spare and no police escort.

"How were things while I was gone?" I asked breathlessly.

"Fine—hardly anyone stopped by all afternoon."

I didn't tell her that this did not constitute "fine." No circulation meant an unimpressive report to the county library department. Then I remembered that I now had Drake Langston as a fairy-godfather, and the report suddenly didn't seem as important anymore.

"Tell me all about your lunch date," Mother requested.

"It was strictly business," I reminded her. "We just picked out a color scheme and layout for the new library."

My mother reached over and tucked a lock of hair behind my ear. "A pretty girl like you can take a man's mind off business."

I couldn't help but think of how Cade seemed to be concentrating really well on Missy Lamar at that drive-in.

I wondered if Mother had read my mind when she said, "How was Cade?"

"Fine. He said to tell you hey."

"You should have invited him over to dinner tonight."

"The time I spent with Cade was business too," I said firmly. "You're welcome to invite Cade over to dinner any time you want—but if he comes, I won't. We're divorced. We don't socialize together."

Mother stood. "I didn't mean to upset you. I'd better get home and finish dinner."

Overcoming my annoyance, I gave her a quick hug. "Thank you for helping me."

"What are mothers for?" She started for the door and then turned. "Promise me you'll change into your black dress for the viewing tonight. And you did iron it, didn't you?"

I assured my mother that I had ironed my black dress and I would wear it. Relieved, she left. Once she was gone, I made up a sign saying that this location of the Midway Library would be closing on Friday, and the library would reopen at its new location downtown as soon as possible. I felt nostalgic as I taped the note on the little diamond-shaped window on the front door. I remembered how I'd felt the day I moved my books into the old trailer. It had seemed like such a step forward. Now the trailer had served its purpose and would be relegated to something . . . less. My books—which had at one time constituted the entire Midway Library—would now be competing with newer, nicer books for patrons' attention.

With somewhat dampened spirits, I began packing up the books that had particular sentimental value. These consisted mostly of the first books I ever bought—the beginning of the library in Midway—and the task absorbed me to the point that I forgot about the time. When I finally checked my watch, it was almost five-thirty. I rushed through my closing routine and headed home.

I changed into my black dress, ran a brush through my hair, and touched up my makeup before walking back out the door. I was standing on the top step of the porch to my apartment when I remembered that I would see Luke Scoggins at the viewing. So I went back inside and kicked off my sensible black pumps. Then I skimmed my toenails with dark red polish and put on my most recent footwear purchase—a pair of flirty sandals. I'd bought them to cheer myself up the day I got word that my divorce was final.

I was prepared for my mother's wrath, since I was too late to eat dinner, but figured she'd forgiven me for worse. What I didn't anticipate was Miss Ida Jean, who always seemed to be watering her front lawn whenever I visited my parents. Like a buzzard zeroing in on a day-old carcass, she met me on the driveway.

Pointing a bony finger, she said, "You got your haircut."

I looked away so I wouldn't have to see Miss Ida Jean's permanent spit string. "Yes." Cade loved long hair, and I'd gained a certain amount of satisfaction from cutting it off. "It's something I've wanted to do for a long time."

"It looks better. The cut got rid of all those dead ends and gave it a little body." Miss Ida Jean had an uncanny ability to turn even a compliment into an insult.

There were so many responses I wanted to make, but I was short on time and didn't want to end up in a pine box beside Foster Scoggins, so I just nodded and murmured something insincere.

Miss Ida Jean's cousin pulled up at that moment, ending my torture. She dropped her hose and hurried to the car. I walked over and turned off the water that would otherwise be left to pool wastefully in Miss Ida Jean's yard. Then I headed to my parents' porch, where my mother was waiting for me. She, too, was wearing a black dress. However, she also had on wrist-length gloves and was clutching a starched white handkerchief in her hand. I presumed this was a precaution against overwhelming grief.

She kept her eyes averted as we walked to my truck.

"I'm sorry about dinner," I apologized.

She nodded stiffly. "You can eat when we get back, although the roast will be dry and the creamed potatoes crusty." She paused to compose herself—the thought of ruined food more painful than the need to visit the funeral home. "But it's better than nothing."

"I was planning to get here in time to eat, but when I met with Drake he told me to close the old library on Friday, so I started packing books and lost track of the time."

Mother perked up a little. "You're going to be moving into the new library soon?"

I nodded. "He already has a crew making repairs, and he wants me to be available at the new location to make decisions about paint and furniture and things like that."

"Oh, Kennedy, it's wonderful that you're working so closely with Drake!" my mother said, and I knew she was already planning to announce this fact to all her friends. "And I can hardly wait for him to start on the family center at the church. He's amazing."

I had to agree. "He is that."

"And speaking of the church," Mother said as we climbed in the car. "Brother Jackson said you and Cade came by to see him today. He said it was wonderful to see the two of you together again."

"We're not together, Mother," I reminded her. "We were just asking questions about Drake and the land they're selling him."

"Why?"

"I told you I was helping Cade with a case," I reminded her. Then I bravely added, "We're looking into Foster Scoggins's death."

Mother frowned. "What about Foster's death?"

"We're not sure he killed himself." I quickly outlined our concerns and Miss Eugenia's desire to have the matter turned into a full-blown police investigation.

By the end of this monologue, my mother was working her nicely starched hankie into a wad of wrinkled linen. "Good heavens, Kennedy.

Poor old Foster is dead, regardless of the circumstances, and we should just let him rest in peace."

"I wouldn't rest in peace if I'd been murdered and the responsible party was never brought to justice. I'd go haunt a house or something."

My mother shook her head in despair. "Leave it alone, Kennedy, please. And I'm surprised at Miss Eugenia for encouraging this nonsense. A murder in Midway—the very idea!" She sat quietly for a few seconds, and then a new thought occurred to her. She turned and fixed me with narrowed eyes. "Swear on your father's life that you won't question people at the funeral home, trying to find evidence to support Miss Eugenia's murder theory."

That had been my plan, and I was disappointed. But I wouldn't risk my father's life under any circumstances, so reluctantly I agreed.

"You've got to stop reading so many mystery novels. They're giving you strange ideas. And you've got to start eating something besides Moon Pies," she added as I pulled into the mortuary parking lot. "High blood sugar might be contributing to these crazy notions. And you look like a skeleton!"

Just for the record, I do not look like a skeleton, and I do, occasionally, eat something besides Moon Pies.

The first person we saw when we got out of the truck at the funeral home was Miss Ida Jean, who scolded me for not inviting her to ride with us, thereby saving her cousin from making an unnecessary trip. Apparently I was supposed to read her mind.

My mother, whom Miss Ida Jean held blameless, apologized for my lapse of manners and assured the old crone it wouldn't happen again. Then she invited her to ride home with us. I told you in the South young people are always at fault.

Cade was the second person I saw, and I was beginning to wonder if God hated me until I spotted Luke Scoggins standing near the closed coffin in the mortuary's crowded viewing room. My grandmother used to say that some people clean up nicely, and such was the case with Luke. In a dark suit with a crisp white shirt, he was more than cute. He was adorable.

On the other side of the coffin was an older man sitting in a wheel-chair. He looked a lot like Foster, so I guessed this was Luke's father, Parnell. Apparently he had been released from the nursing home long enough to attend the funeral. His head had drooped forward onto his chest, and he appeared to be asleep. I didn't know if this was a sign of his ill health or if it was just past his regular bedtime. But one thing was sure—Parnell hadn't cleaned up nearly as well as Luke.

Cade was standing at the door to the viewing room speaking to a little group of guests. He wore his uniform and was acting all official. I skirted neatly past him and walked up to Luke. I introduced my mother and Miss Ida Jean, who had attached herself to our respect-paying party. We expressed our sympathy for his loss, and Luke politely thanked us for coming. Then my mother and Miss Ida Jean moved down to try to wake Parnell.

I waited until they were out of hearing range before leaning close to Luke and whispering, "I'll stay here with you for a few minutes if you don't mind. They are driving me crazy."

Luke smiled. "I'd be glad to have the company, but people will probably talk if they see us together at my uncle's funeral."

Luke was right. Standing together at the funeral of a close relative was tantamount to announcing a pre-engagement.

"They'll talk about me no matter where I stand," I assured him.

"I heard you and Burrell got divorced." It wasn't uncommon for men to refer to other men by only their last names, but something in Luke's tone alerted me that he was not a big fan of my ex-husband.

"Did you hear why?"

He nodded. "The guy's a jerk."

I can't explain how nice it was to finally hear someone place blame where it was due instead of treating me like I was the one in the wrong for refusing to overlook public adultery. Tears actually stung my eyes (and I never cry).

"I thought life was perfect for girls like you," Luke continued.

I shook my head. "Not hardly."

The Baptist preacher and his wife walked up at that moment. Once they had delivered their condolences to Luke, they turned to me. "Hello, Kennedy," Brother Jackson said with a meaningful glance at Luke. After seeing me with Cade just a few hours before, I'm sure he was totally confused.

"Hello," I returned cheerfully, offering no explanation for my presence at Luke's side.

"Luke, we'd love to have you at church with us on Sunday," Miss Zelda, the preacher's wife, invited—apparently feeling bold now that Foster and his antipreaching guns were no longer a threat.

"I appreciate that very much," Luke replied.

Miss Zelda turned to me. "We'd love to have you too, Kennedy."

I leaned a little closer to Luke, giving the impression of intimacy that didn't exist. "Thanks. We'll try to make it."

I saw the amusement in Luke's eyes as he played along. "Yes, if we can."

Finally Brother Jackson and Miss Zelda moved on, looking perplexed, and I took un-Christian pleasure from their bewilderment.

I stood supportively beside Luke while he greeted a steady stream of guests. Whenever someone would speak to me, I smiled and nodded. Then, like the Jacksons, they'd walk away mystified. It was the most fun I'd had in weeks.

My only regret was that I'd promised my mother—at the risk of my father's life—that while at the funeral home I wouldn't discuss the possibility that Foster was murdered. There were several things I was dying to ask Luke, and it seemed like a wasted opportunity.

When we were alone again, I asked, "Where's Heaven?"

He frowned. "The Georgia Department of Human Resources has her. I applied for temporary custody with family court, but they denied me."

I knew that Foster's death would be a blow for the child, but I hadn't realized her situation was quite that dire. "That's a shame."

He shrugged. "They didn't think I was qualified to be a parent—especially of a child like Heaven."

A funeral home was close enough to a church so I couldn't lie, but I did try to state my opinion as nicely as possible. "Heaven did seem a little willful when she was in the library."

"She's completely unmanageable," Luke said. "She's always in trouble at school, and Uncle Foster was at family court almost weekly trying to keep custody himself. But as bad as she is, I feel sorry for the kid, and I'd try to raise her if the courts would let me."

"What about her parents? Can they get custody?"

"My brother didn't even know he had a daughter until a couple of years ago when the mother dropped Heaven off at the salvage yard on her way to California to become a movie star. He drives a tractor trailer truck and is gone for months at a time, so I doubt the courts would give him custody."

I raised an eyebrow. "And the mother?"

Luke shrugged. "Nobody knows where she is. DHR said they'd try to find Heaven a foster family, but that's going to be hard because of her behavior problems."

I felt bad for Heaven. After all, she was just a kid. "I'd take her if I could, but there's no one less qualified than me."

Luke smiled and said, "I bet you'll make a great mother someday. But you should start out with a nice little baby and not a hardened child like Heaven."

His words warmed me all the way from the top of my head to the tips of my freshly polished toes. I was thinking how fortunate it was that we were in a viewing room with dim lighting to hide my blush when Luke said, "Don't look now, but your ex-husband is coming this way."

I frowned. Cade had apparently noticed that I was acting like a member of the much-maligned Scoggins family and intended to put a stop to the charade. I dug the heels of my cute sandals into the thin carpet. He could try.

When Cade arrived at our position beside the coffin, he did indeed look unhappy. But since he was trying to win me back, he focused most of his angry glare at Luke. "Scoggins."

"Burrell," Luke replied in terse greeting.

Then Cade said to me, "Your mother is ready to leave."

I was going to argue until he added, "If you're not too busy consoling folks."

Luke stiffened, and I knew I had to keep the situation from escalating. Even my mother might not forgive me for causing a scene at the funeral home.

"I'm ready to go," I said, putting my hand on Cade's arm to propel him away. Once I had separated the men by a few feet, I turned back to Luke. "I hope I'll see you again soon."

He grinned. "We've sort of promised to attend church together on Sunday."

I laughed and played along with the joke. "It's a date."

Luke kept his eyes on me during my entire walk to the exit, and I'm pretty sure he noticed my toenails.

As we worked our way through the crowd of mourners in the lobby, Cade whispered, "Since when did you and Luke Scoggins become buddies?"

"Since our divorce it's none of your business who my buddies are."

He stopped and turned to face me. I could see that he wanted to say more about Luke, and I dared him with my eyes. I hoped he'd give me a chance to have it out with him once and for all. I wanted to succinctly express how much he had hurt and humiliated me. And if I did it in front of all the people at the funeral home, he could experience some of the humiliation he'd subjected me to. But after a few awkward seconds, Cade just shrugged and the moment passed.

I said, "Call me when you find out about the handwriting analysis." Then I found my mother and Miss Ida Jean standing by the door, and together we left the funeral home.

During the short ride home, I expected to be interrogated about Luke, but fortunately for me, Mother had spoken to a disgruntled dental patient during the viewing. The patient was having trouble with a tooth my uncle had crowned and wanted Uncle Forest to redo the crown for free. Mother was so incensed by this that she didn't even mention Luke.

"Forest crowned that tooth ten years ago," she ranted. "There's no such thing as a ten-year guarantee on dental work, and the fact that she's having trouble now doesn't mean Forest didn't crown the tooth right. It could just be that she doesn't floss regularly."

"Good dental hygiene is very important," Miss Ida Jean agreed. "Do you have any books on tooth flossing at the library, Kennedy?"

"No, ma'am, I'm sure we don't," I answered. "But when we start ordering books for the new library, I'll get one."

"I heard you're dating Drake Langston now," Miss Ida Jean continued. "Are you trying to make Cade jealous?"

"I'm not trying to make Cade jealous," I assured Miss Ida Jean. "And I'm not dating Drake Langston. I just had a business lunch with him and an architect from Atlanta to discuss the new library."

Miss Ida Jean nodded. "That's what I figured. I mean, why would someone like Drake Langston be interested in you?"

I didn't even bother to respond to this as I pulled my truck into my parents' driveway. I smiled when I saw that the light was on in my father's workshop. I was anxious to talk with him and even more anxious to get away from Miss Ida Jean. So I climbed out of the truck, said good evening to the annoying neighbor, and headed across the lawn.

"I think I'll speak to Daddy," I told my mother.

She frowned. "Don't stay in there long. I'm going to reheat your dinner."

I nodded and kept walking.

As I mentioned earlier, my father is a postal worker, but—contrary to the stereotype—he's the most mild-mannered, least-likely-to-go-"postal" man I've ever met. He loves to tinker with old cars and has had one in the workshop for as long as I can remember. He can't afford antiques but gains satisfaction from taking something old and tired and returning it to a shade of its former glory. Since he makes a few dollars on the resale of the cars he repairs, my mother permits this hobby. If I ever make it rich, I'm going to buy him an old T-bird that he could fix up and keep. If ever . . .

He looked up when I walked in and gave me a big smile. "How's my baby girl?"

I kissed his least-grimy cheek and propped myself on the edge of his tool cabinet. "I've been worse," I replied.

"Did you enjoy your visit to the funeral home?"

"It wasn't as boring as I'd expected." I anticipated his need for a lug wrench and handed it to him. "If Foster Scoggins hadn't died in a scandalous way, you'd have had to pay people to come to his viewing. As it was, there was standing room only."

"I'm sad I missed it," he lied.

"You are not," I challenged him mildly.

"I never have been able to understand why we have viewings. Once I'm dead, the last thing I want is for my friends and family to come stare at my corpse."

"The casket was closed, so there wasn't much actual *viewing* going on," I told him. Then a thought occurred to me. "Have you ever seen a body that's been electrocuted?"

"No, and I hope I never do," he said. "Hand me that roll of tape."

I passed the electrical tape to him and asked as casually as I could, "Do you know Luke Scoggins?"

"I've met all the Scogginses at one time or another when I've been out at the salvage yard buying parts. But I haven't seen Luke since he was a teenager," Daddy said. "He was kind of a troublemaker as I recall."

"He's been in the Marines, but he's home now, and he's going to college at Purdue in a few weeks. That's in Indiana."

"Is it, now?"

"And he's pretty cute."

My father looked up from the engine he was rebuilding. "I wouldn't know about that."

I laughed. "And speaking of cute, I met Drake Langston today—and would you like to guess what he's going to do with the old bank building on Main Street?"

"I wouldn't like to guess."

"He's going to move the library there after he completely renovates it and installs twenty computers donated by Bill Gates himself."

Daddy lifted an eyebrow. "Bill Gates?"

"Well, Microsoft anyway," I amended slightly. "What do you think?"

"I think it's downright peculiar. A few months ago, none of us had ever heard of this Langston character. Now he's in Midway promising to build houses and add a family center onto the Baptist church and move the library to the old bank building. I can't make myself trust the fellow—too much money, too much change, too fast."

My father knew how to cut right to the heart of things. "It is a little hard to comprehend. And I'm afraid that once he gets a nice modern library, he'll want an older, more qualified director."

Daddy shrugged. "If that happens, you'll find a new job. Maybe it's time for you to leave Midway and try your luck somewhere else."

I was surprised and touched by his comment. I was surprised because my father had never given any indication that he thought I should leave the town where I'd been raised. And I was touched since we both knew that if my mother heard he'd made such a suggestion, he'd be in the doghouse for weeks. My mother likes for her children to live nearby—the easier to keep all of us under her thumb.

I cleared my throat and then announced, "Foster Scoggins came into the library yesterday—just a couple of hours before he died."

Daddy's frown deepened. "Foster never seemed like the book-reading sort to me."

"Well, he checked out a book on gophers and took the time to apply for a library card, even though he was supposedly in a deep state of depression because some girlfriend no one has ever seen dumped him. Then, according to our sheriff's department, he dropped Heaven off at the salvage yard and drove to the relay station on Highway 72. There he threw himself on some high-voltage coils, ending his life in a dramatic and unpleasant way."

My father set aside his tools and gave me his full attention. "Now why do I get the feeling that you don't think it happened like that?"

"I've been talking to Miss Eugenia Atkins, and we don't think Mr. Scoggins killed himself," I admitted. "Or at least we think his death should be investigated a little more thoroughly. I've given the library application to Cade and Sheriff Bonham. They sent it along to Atlanta with what they think is a suicide note they found in Foster's truck to have it analyzed by an expert. And in the meantime, Cade and I are interviewing people who stood to gain a lot of money by selling land to Drake."

"You and Cade?" Daddy confirmed.

I grimaced. "Yeah, the sheriff made our working together a requirement."

"And why would someone kill old Foster?"

"Because he didn't want to sell his land to Drake Langston for the housing development they plan to build north of town. Apparently it was an all-or-nothing deal. If one person refused, no one got to be a millionaire."

"You think someone in town wanted the money bad enough to kill Foster?"

I nodded. "It's possible."

"If someone did commit a murder and if you're going around asking questions about it, you could be putting yourself in some serious danger."

This thought had occurred to me quite a few times, but I was trying to ignore it. "Are you saying I should stop?"

Daddy shook his head. "No, I'm saying that before you leave here tonight, you'd better get my .45 out of the glove compartment of my truck and keep it with you at all times. Loaded."

I reached over and kissed him again, and this time I disregarded the engine grime. "Thank you, Daddy."

"You be careful," he admonished. "Now get in there and let your mother feed you. She's been looking forward to the opportunity all day."

I had put off the inevitable long enough, so I trudged inside and sat at the kitchen table while my mother fussed over me. She buttered my roll, salted my roast, and added more ice to my tea. I picked at the food on my plate until I couldn't stand it anymore.

"I've got to get home," I announced abruptly.

"But you've hardly eaten a thing," she objected. "And I have a peach cobbler for dessert."

My mother's cobblers are legendary, but her kitchen was beginning to stifle me. So I stood and moved toward the door. "Cade is supposed to call, and I don't want to miss it." I knew this would appease my mother, and it did.

"Well, okay. But let me wrap up some cobbler for you to take home."

Now *that* was a compromise I could live with. So I took the container of cobbler my mother prepared for me and stopped by my father's truck to get his handgun. Armed in more ways than one, I drove back to my apartment.

The first thing I did when I got into my little home above the storage company office was check my answering machine, but there were no messages from Cade or Drake Langston or Sloan or anyone else. Disappointed, I peeled off my black dress and kicked my sandals into the closet. Then I washed a fork and sat on the couch to eat cobbler while watching the local news. At ten o'clock I was up to date on current events, including the next day's forecast, and full of peach cobbler. After stowing the leftovers in the refrigerator for breakfast, I took a quick shower and had just put on my pajamas when I heard the phone ringing.

I grabbed it in delicious anticipation.

"Sorry to call so late," Cade said a little stiffly, and I knew he was still mad.

I decided to be gracious. "It's okay."

"We got a preliminary report back on the handwriting comparison," he continued. "There's an eighty percent chance that the application and note were written by the same person."

"So what does that mean?"

"It means that Foster wrote the suicide note, and you provided us the positive proof since you saw him fill out that application," Cade replied. "In addition to Foster's prints, there were a couple of partial prints and some smears on the letter, but nothing that we can use for identification. So our investigation is over."

"We can't end the investigation now! That note was vague and could have been written about something completely different."

"Kennedy . . ."

"And we have a motive—remember?" I asked, sounding desperate even to my own ears.

"We came up with a reasonable motive but no corroborating evidence," Cade pointed out. "So Foster will be buried tomorrow, and that will be the end of it."

I didn't want the most exciting thing that had ever happened in Midway to be buried—literally. So I asked, "What if the family decided to postpone the funeral and asked that the investigation continue?"

"Why would they do that?"

I searched for an answer and came up with, "Maybe they don't agree with the cause of death and want an autopsy?"

"Anyone who saw what's left of Foster knows he was electrocuted," Cade assured me.

I was losing patience. "But what if he was already dead when he hit the high-voltage coils?"

Cade didn't answer immediately, and I was encouraged. Finally he said, "This isn't a game for us to guess around with. We have to consider the family's feelings."

"I am considering the family," I replied. "They'd feel terrible if they allow Foster's murderer to go free!"

Again Cade was quiet, so I pressed on.

"Luke told you he didn't believe his uncle killed himself, so he might be willing to request a postponement."

This time Cade responded quickly, and his tone was almost sneering. "You know *Luke* so well you can predict what he'll do?"

I refused to be goaded. "Maybe."

"You should stay away from Luke Scoggins," Cade advised irritably. "He's got a police record."

I knew his "record" couldn't be too bad since he'd been in the Marines. But I just said, "We've discussed this already. My friendship with Luke is none of your business."

After a few seconds of petulant silence, Cade said, "If you can get the family to postpone the funeral and request an autopsy, I think the sheriff will go along."

This was as much as I could hope for. "I'll be in touch."

I ended my call with Cade and tried to decide what to do. The answer was pretty obvious. I had to call Miss Eugenia.

It was well past the polite hour to call people—especially little old ladies—but she had told me that she didn't sleep much, and since our murder case was going to be buried along with Foster the next day, I felt it qualified as an emergency.

Miss Eugenia answered on the third ring and promised that she had been awake. Since I had enough on my conscience already, I chose to believe her. I summarized my conversation with Cade and then asked, "So what do you think?"

"There's only one sensible course of action," she replied. "You have to call Luke Scoggins right now. Have him meet you somewhere and convince him to postpone that funeral!"

In most parts of the country this would be perfectly acceptable, but in small Southern towns, women who call men without invitation—especially late at night—are still considered forward. I had hoped she would volunteer to meet with Luke, and I told her so.

"I couldn't possibly do that," Miss Eugenia replied. "I have a neighbor who watches every move I make. If I were to leave my house this late at night, she'd call most of Haggerty, including Police Chief Jones, and within half an hour the whole county would be looking for me. Eventually they'd find me, and when police and sheriff vehicles surrounded us . . . well, it wouldn't make for a very good interview with Luke Scoggins."

"No," I had to concede. "But I barely know him and just feel awkward calling, especially so late."

"Ordinarily I would agree with you, but we are talking about a murder here."

I surrendered without further resistance. "I'll call him."

"Meet him in a public place that stays open twenty-four hours, like the truck stop out on Highway 17."

My mother would die a thousand deaths if she found out I'd met a man who had a police record at a truck stop in the middle of the night, but I feared Miss Eugenia more than my mother at the moment. "Okay."

"And while you're talking to Luke, see if he'll let you look through his uncle's things."

"For what?"

"Letters from Drake Langston offering to buy his land or receipts from the motels where he supposedly stayed with his girlfriend," Miss Eugenia listed. "Anything."

"I'll ask him."

"And it would be a good idea if we could look over those letters the girl-friend supposedly sent. You could ask Luke to get copies from the sheriff."

"We're asking enough of Luke. I can probably get copies of the letters from Cade."

"Either way. Call me when you get back to tell me what Luke said," she commanded. "No matter how late it is."

I ended my call with Miss Eugenia and looked up Scoggins Salvage Yard in the phone book. As I dialed the number, I was half hoping that no one would answer, but seconds later Luke's voice said, "Hello."

"Hey, Luke," I replied a little breathlessly. "It's me, Kennedy."

"Are you calling to say you can't make it to church with me on Sunday?"

I smiled. "No, although I don't plan to attend church on Sunday or any other day."

He laughed. "So why did you call?"

"I know this is bad timing, but I'd like to talk with you. Could we meet? I won't take much of your time but it could be important."

"My time is cheap and plentiful, so I can meet you whenever it's convenient for however long you want to talk."

I appreciated his willingness and tested his honesty by asking, "How about the Flying J out on Highway 17 in fifteen minutes?"

I sensed his hesitation. "Tonight?"

"It's important," I confirmed and tried not to think about the lectures my mother was going to give me on the subject of ladylike behavior if she ever found out about this.

"I'll be there," he promised.

CHAPTER EIGHT

I CALCULATED THE TIME I had available to improve my appearance before my meeting with Luke. It would take me a good six minutes to get to the Flying J, and since I had issued the invitation, it would be beyond rude to show up late. So that gave me about seven minutes to get ready, leaving a couple of minutes for getting to and from the car.

In an effort to save time through multitasking, I held my hair dryer in one hand and my toothbrush in the other—ignoring the dangers of using an electrical appliance near water. I figured since Foster had just electrocuted himself, the odds of it happening again in Midway were in my favor.

Once my hair was mostly dry and my teeth mostly brushed, I yanked off my pajamas and put on the cleanest pair of blue jeans I could find. I took the sweater my mother had given me for Christmas from the gift bag where it had been since the holidays and pulled it over my head. It was pink, a color I would never have picked out for myself, but it fit well, and my options were limited. I ran a comb through my hair and applied a little mascara. As a final touch, I put on the cute sandals Luke had admired earlier at the funeral home. I glanced at the mirror as I rushed by, and considering the time restrictions, I thought I looked pretty good.

I arrived at the Flying J with one minute to spare, but Luke was already inside the restaurant. He had chosen a booth near the window, and as I walked over to join him, I noted that he was dressed casually in jeans and a T-shirt. My bright-pink, brand-new sweater made me feel overdressed, and I was beginning to regret my clothing choice. Then I saw the appreciative look in his eyes, and from that point on I didn't mind.

I slipped into the bench across from him and began by apologizing for the late hour and out-of-the-blue invitation.

He smiled and said, "No problem. I usually stay up late, and it was time for a midnight snack, anyway."

Now I felt guilty since my invitation came with ulterior motives.

The waitress arrived and took our orders. Luke chose an oatmeal muffin from the "heart-healthy" section of the menu and a glass of skim milk. I virtuously did the same.

After the waitress left, I said, "You're snacking light."

He grinned. "Actually, I'm snacking *again*. I'd just finished a big bowl of Fruit Loops when you called, but I couldn't resist the chance to see you again."

I had a mixed reaction to this announcement. I love Fruit Loops, and I liked having something in common with Luke. However, I felt even guiltier since I'd lured him to the truck stop under somewhat false pretenses, and I knew I had to set the record straight. I was trying to think of a way to confess without hurting his feelings or losing his cooperation.

Then he said, "I know this isn't just a social visit, Kennedy. For as much fun as we had at my uncle's viewing, there has to be a good reason for us to be here." He waved to encompass the truck stop restaurant. "What do you want?"

Some people might have been offended by such a frank question, but I was tremendously relieved. Much of polite Southern conversation involves inconsequential small talk and what my mother calls "little white lies." It was refreshing to speak with someone who didn't beat around the bush. Someone who could handle the truth.

Before I answered, the waitress returned with our muffins and milk. As Luke lifted his glass, I noticed his hands. They were impeccably clean. I had the feeling that he'd made a point to eradicate any salvage-yard grime before coming to meet me, and I got a little quivery feeling in my stomach. Then I saw that there were several small cuts on his fingers.

Luke followed the direction of my gaze and glanced down at the scratches. "It comes with the territory," he said. "Hazards of working at the salvage yard."

I nodded, took a deep sip of my own milk, and said, "That brings me to what I wanted to talk to you about. It's possible that your uncle was murdered by someone who stood to gain from the sale of the salvage yard."

Luke didn't look shocked. "That thought occurred to me, but I dismissed it pretty fast. The only thing more ridiculous than Uncle Foster killing himself is the possibility that a murderer is running lose in Midway."

"It does seem crazy," I agreed. "But as long as questions still exist, the investigation should continue."

"What questions do you have?"

I listed the reasons Miss Eugenia and I had come up with, beginning with our doubts about the mysterious girlfriend and ending with the library card application filled out just a couple of hours before Foster died.

"But Uncle Foster left a suicide note," Luke pointed out.

"There was a note, but it wasn't necessarily written by your uncle." I was clinging to that twenty percent room for error. In case the handwriting expert in Atlanta was correct, I added, "Or if he did write it, it was pretty vague, so he may have written it for some other purpose."

Luke frowned. "Like what?"

I felt like I was making some headway and didn't want to get derailed, so I waved this aside. "I don't know. The important thing is that the police continue their investigation."

Luke frowned. "You said when my uncle came into the library the day he died he applied for a library card?"

I nodded. "Just a few hours before, well, the electric relay station."

Luke ignored this insensitive reminder of his uncle's gruesome death. "Can I see the application?"

I wished I'd kept a copy and apologized for this oversight. "I don't have it, I'm sorry." Then I decided to blame it on Cade. Goodness knows he deserved it. "The sheriff's department confiscated the application before I had time to make a copy. But I'm sure they'll make one for you if you ask them to."

Luke shrugged. "It's not that important. I was just curious."

I pressed on quickly to distract him from the application. If he asked the sheriff for a copy, he'd probably also find out that a handwriting analysis had been done and that I had essentially shot the investigation in its hypothetical foot.

"When I heard your uncle had died, I was surprised since he'd just been in the library. Then Miss Eugenia from Haggerty came in."

Luke nodded. "I know Miss Eugenia."

I hoped he also knew about her penchant for sniffing out unsolved crimes. "She pointed out all the things about your uncle's death that were suspicious. Then she convinced me to take the application to the sheriff's department and request that they investigate."

"And they agreed?"

I didn't want to explain that the sheriff had tried to help Cade's hopeless efforts to remarry me by assigning us to work on the case together. So I just said, "Sort of. And even though we haven't come up with any evidence to prove it yet, I can't get rid of the feeling that your uncle did not kill himself."

"Uncle Foster didn't love life all that much, but he wasn't the suicide type either," Luke agreed. "I don't think that would have ever occurred to him as a valid option."

I was encouraged. "And the whole story about the girlfriend seems far-fetched. Miss Eugenia thinks the murderer made it up to cover the crime, and I agree with her."

"And sent the letters for weeks in advance?"

I nodded. "Premeditated."

Luke broke off a piece of muffin and studied it carefully. "The only place Uncle Foster really went, besides into town to pick up his mail, was to car auctions, and it's hard to imagine him finding a woman to strike up a relationship with there. But strange things happen."

I tried not to let this very true statement deter me. "Cade said you didn't notice any signs that your uncle had a girlfriend—like secretive behavior, mysterious phone calls, or unexplained absences?"

Luke shook his head. "Nothing like that. Uncle Foster was a little distracted lately, but I think that's because he was worried about the salvage yard."

"Business has been bad?" I guessed.

"No, we've had plenty of customers—too many, actually. With the economy like it is, everyone is looking to patch up the cars they have rather than buy new ones. But for years Uncle Foster has counted on my dad to do the books, order supplies, file the tax returns—all the financial stuff. Until a few weeks ago, my father's been able to live comfortably at home with regular nursing care. But then he took a turn for the worse and had to be put in the nursing home."

"Do they know what's wrong with him?"

"He's been in a confused state lately, which his doctor thinks might be the beginnings of Alzheimer's, and that was hard on Uncle Foster."

"So things were busy at the salvage yard, your father was sick and couldn't handle any of his regular duties for the business, and Drake Langston was pressuring him to sell. That sounds like your uncle was under a lot of stress."

Luke nodded. "And you wonder how he'd find time to work in a girlfriend."

I beamed at him. "Very good point."

He smiled back. "Thanks."

"In fact, it's possible he was in fear for his life."

Luke frowned. "Uncle Foster wasn't easily intimidated, and he didn't fear anything—except for the IRS. He was terrified of them." Luke fixed me with a penetrating gaze. "You really think someone killed Uncle Foster?"

"At first when Miss Eugenia mentioned the possibility that he was killed, I liked the idea of a murder in Midway—just for the excitement factor," I admitted honestly. "But I've had a lot of time to think about it since then, and I really don't think he killed himself. I realize that's just my opinion, but if we can encourage the sheriff's department to continue the investigation, I hope we'll find some real proof."

Luke didn't look completely convinced, but he asked, "So what do you want me to do?"

This was going to be easier than I had dared to hope. "Three things: first, ask your father to postpone the funeral."

Luke frowned. "How long?"

"Just a few days."

"Delaying the funeral isn't a big deal," Luke said. "What next?"

"Will you request an autopsy on behalf of your family?"

"And why do we want an autopsy?"

"Miss Eugenia thinks your uncle was dead before he was electrocuted. If she's right, an autopsy should prove that."

"Okay," Luke agreed, but he didn't look happy. "What else?"

"I need to look around your uncle's house."

"So *you're* working the case?" He sounded both surprised and impressed.

"Well, not officially, but Miss Eugenia thinks if we leave it to Sheriff Bonham, he'll ignore any evidence and bury your uncle, effectively ending all chances of finding the murderer. So I'm assisting Cade with a subtle investigation."

At the mention of my ex-husband, Luke's friendly expression darkened. "I'll help you in any way I can."

"Do you have access to your uncle's personal financial information?"

He raised an eyebrow. "You mean the old shoebox where he kept receipts and bills?"

I nodded. "If we can track what he spent and where, we might be able to confirm the existence of a girlfriend—or completely eliminate the possibility."

"You're welcome to look through the shoebox, but I doubt you'll find anything. Uncle Foster totally operated on a cash basis. If he had bought any gifts for a girlfriend or paid for motel rooms, there won't be a record."

This was disappointing, but I pasted on a brave smile. "I'd still like to try. And if I look around the house, maybe I'll notice something that no one else has—using a woman's perspective."

Luke smiled. "Fine with me."

"And maybe I could talk with your father about your uncle's financial situation."

"Like I said, he's been confused lately, so I don't what he can tell you, but he loves company, and I'm sure he'd be glad to have a beautiful lady visitor."

I couldn't help but blush.

"When do you want to do all this?"

I reviewed my schedule for Friday. I wanted to go to Haggerty and discuss the case with Miss Eugenia before opening the library at ten o'clock. I'd be there until five, packing up my old books in preparation for the move into town. I hated to schedule our next meeting during the dinner hour since he would probably think I was asking him on another date, but I didn't have an option. So I said, "How about five-thirty tomorrow evening? I'll bring pizza."

"Why don't I just cook for us instead," he suggested around a mouthful of muffin.

"You cook?"

He grinned. "I do."

"Well, aren't you just full of hidden talents."

"I didn't say that I cook well," he warned me.

I smiled. "I'll be the judge of that."

Having concluded my business, I turned the conversation to only moderately more pleasant subjects like his tours of duty in Iraq and the high-school days that we had both tried to forget. Since I'd invited Luke to the truck stop I intended to pay for our food. But when the waitress brought our check, Luke insisted, and I finally gave in, feeling more indebted to him than before.

He walked me to my truck and waved good-bye as I headed down Highway 17 toward home. While I drove, I went over our conversation in my mind. He had been polite and friendly and definitely helpful. I wondered if he'd been that nice during high school and I'd missed the opportunity to have a friend I could have really used back then.

There were a few other cars on Highway 17, so I didn't think anything about the vehicle behind me until I turned onto my shortcut, a dirt road between two cotton fields, and the car followed me. The road is rarely used during the day and almost never at night. So when the other car turned in behind me, all kinds of red flags went up in my mind. I made two more turns, both unnecessary, wanting to see what the car would do. It dropped back a little farther but followed me turn for turn. Positive now that I was being tailed, I reached over and took my father's gun from the glove compartment and wished I'd listened to my mother and purchased a cell phone.

Once I got onto the paved road where the Midway Store and Save is located, I studied the car behind me in my rearview mirror. It was a newer-model sedan in a dark color—either black or blue. The driver appeared to be the only occupant. I slowed down to see if he would pass me, but he hung back. With my heart pounding, I increased my speed and drove as fast as I dared to the storage complex.

I parked my truck close to the front of the building that housed the office and my apartment. Then with the gun clutched to my chest, I rushed to the closest door—the one that led to the office below my apartment. I unlocked it and went inside. Automatically I flipped on the lights and looked around. The room was dusty and empty, just like always.

I unlocked the interior door that led upstairs and climbed nervously. When I walked into the apartment, I saw my pajamas on the floor in front of the couch and my Pepsi on the coffee table, adding a new ring to the multitude already there. Everything seemed to be as I had left it. Picking up the cordless phone, I walked through the small apartment to confirm that there was no one hiding there—not in the bathroom or in the closet or under my bed. Then I double-checked the lock on the front door and put a chair in front of it for good measure.

I was feeling better and even wondered if the mysterious car had been a figment of my overactive imagination until I glanced out the window and saw the same dark sedan parked in front of the fruit and vegetable stand across the street.

Truly panicked now, I dialed Cade's home number. When he answered, I explained the situation, and he said he'd be right over. I paced across the short expanse of my living room while waiting for him to arrive.

Cade announced his approach with screeching tires and slinging gravel. I peeked out the window to watch him pull up. To my horror, the car across the street was gone. Now Cade would think I was crazy. Or worse—interested.

The phone rang. "The car is gone," I said miserably.

Cade didn't take the opportunity to chastise or ridicule me. "Where was it parked?"

I told him and then watched as he took out his high-powered flashlight and inspected the strip of road in front of the produce stand. Through the receiver of his cell phone, I could hear him breathing and his boots crunching on the loose gravel.

Finally he asked, "What make and model was the car?"

"Late-model generic sedan—maybe an Altima, probably a rental," I replied. If the car had been from the seventies or eighties, I could have probably nailed it exactly thanks to my father's hobby and the years I'd spent assisting him. But my father didn't work on late-model cars, and so my knowledge of more recent vehicles was limited. I didn't have to explain any of that to Cade. That was the advantage of talking to someone who knew me well.

"You're sure it wasn't a fancy new Lexus?" he asked, an obvious reference to Drake.

"It wasn't a Lexus, but it could have been a Malibu or a Camry. I was a little panicked."

"I'm coming up," he informed me and ended the call.

I met him at the door to my apartment, and I don't think I could have kept him from coming inside even if I'd wanted to, which I didn't. He gave my apartment a thorough once-over, similar to the one I'd already done, but since he was a sheriff's deputy, his search seemed more official. After checking the locks on the doors, he deemed everything secure.

"I'm sorry I dragged you out in the middle of the night for nothing."

"It wasn't for nothing," he replied. "Now we know your safe—even if the car did leave before I got here."

There is nothing he could have said that would have made me happier—except maybe "I have an identical twin and that's who you saw at the drive-in with Missy Lamar."

"Thanks for not doubting me," I told him.

Cade grinned. "You're a lot of annoying things, but not a liar."

I felt a tremor of happiness I thought was gone forever. And I was beginning to wonder if maybe I'd been wrong about a future with Cade.

Then he said, "That's why I'm glad this whole business with Foster Scoggins is over. Crime solving can be dangerous."

I narrowed my eyes at him. "First of all, the business with Foster isn't over. I talked to Luke, and he's going to postpone the funeral and request an autopsy."

The look of unhappy surprise on Cade's face was comical.

"And second, the fact that I was followed home tonight points toward murder, since I seem to be the only one investigating."

Cade sighed. "Well, if we're going to keep asking questions about Foster's death, you need to take extra safety precautions. The first thing you should do is buy a cell phone."

I couldn't argue with the prudence of this, but I knew a cell phone was not a financial possibility before my next paycheck from Mr. Sheffield. So I just nodded.

"And don't go off doing any investigating without me," he added, since I seemed agreeable to his dictates.

"I won't go off alone," I promised, carefully leaving the way open for me to investigate with Luke or Miss Eugenia or anyone else I chose. Then I asked, "Can I look at those letters Foster supposedly received from his girlfriend?"

He nodded warily. "We made copies that I guess I could let you look at. Although the sheriff probably won't like it."

"Is that a yes?"

"That's a yes, against my better judgment." He looked around the room, and I expected him to suggest that we make it a true all-nighter by ordering a pizza and watching a movie. I'm not sure what I would have said. Probably no, just out of habit. But I was feeling pretty generous toward him. After all, he had rushed out in the middle of the night to protect me. And more importantly, he didn't doubt the mysterious car's existence. And he'd even agreed to let me read Foster's letters at his own professional risk.

But surprisingly he didn't ask to stay. Instead he moved toward the door. "I'll bring the copies of the letters by the library tomorrow afternoon."

I followed him out onto my front porch, surprised (and, I'll admit, mildly insulted) that he hadn't even tried to stay. I thanked him again and watched as he ran cross the street and climbed into his car.

As he drove away, I smiled, happier than I'd been in months. I was involved in a real murder investigation, Midway was getting a new library, and even the idea of being followed was kind of exciting—especially since I had a gun and Cade to watch my back.

My euphoria was interrupted when the phone in my hand rang. It was Serene, the helpful receptionist at the sheriff's department.

"Hey, is Cade still there?" she asked. "He said he'd only be gone a few minutes."

All tenderness toward Cade evaporated and was replaced by empty anger. "He's on his way," I replied stiffly. Then I ended the call, walked inside, and locked my door.

* * *

I was changing back into my pajamas when the phone rang. I figured my mother had heard about my late-night rendezvous with Luke Scoggins at the Flying J, and I considered letting it ring, since I definitely wasn't up to a confrontation with her. But I was afraid she'd drive over if I didn't answer, and that would be worse. So I picked up the phone. It wasn't my mother. It was Miss Eugenia.

"You didn't call me," Miss Eugenia said the minute I answered. "I was worried sick about you!"

"I'm sorry," I apologized quickly. I told her first about my scare on the way home from the Flying J, since that was my excuse for not calling. Then I reported on my visit with Luke. I left out the most recent evidence that Cade is a faithless creep.

"Hmm," Miss Eugenia said when I was through. "If someone is following you, we must be on to something."

I noticed that she used the term *we*, although she'd sent me to the Flying J *alone*.

"Did Luke agree to help you search his uncle's things?"

"Yes, and Cade has agreed to let me look at the letters Foster's girlfriend supposedly wrote. He's bringing me copies tomorrow."

"If only the sheriff had allowed Mark's forensic team to search Foster's truck," Miss Eugenia murmured. "Maybe you can ask Luke to request that too—on behalf of the family. I don't see how the sheriff can refuse it, then."

I yawned. "I'll ask him."

"And can you come by my house in the morning? I'd like to look through your notebook and see what people said when you interviewed them."

"I have to be at the library by ten o'clock, but I guess I can come by earlier."

"Come about eight, and I'll feed you breakfast."

Hoping that breakfast might involve the Iversons and Baby Jake, I smiled and said, "I'll be there." Then I hung up the phone, climbed into bed, and slept fitfully until dawn.

CHAPTER NINE

It was almost a relief to get up with the sun on Friday, putting an end to my restless night. I took a quick shower and sipped my first Pepsi of the day. I was out of unworn Christmas gifts, so I put on a Midway Library T-shirt and my newest pair of blue jeans. When I looked in the mirror, I wasn't surprised to find that I had dark circles under my eyes. I did the best I could to disguise my exhaustion with cosmetics. Then I left my apartment and hurried out to my truck.

I drove fast in order to make it to Miss Eugenia's by eight, but remembered to reduce my speed when I reached the Haggerty city limits. I passed through the charming square and turned onto Maple Street just as I had the day before. I parked in front of Miss Eugenia's white, flower-framed house. As I followed the sidewalk toward her front door, my eyes drifted longingly toward the Iversons' house. My strong desire to see and hold Baby Jake again was surprising and unwelcome. I forced my attention back to the business at hand. I had a murder to solve.

My knock was answered by a petite woman whom I estimated to be in her sixties. Her clothes looked expensive, and her hair was cut in a stylish gray bob. She raised an inquiring eyebrow when she saw me on the porch.

"My name is Kennedy Killingsworth," I explained quickly. "And I'm here to see Miss Eugenia."

"I'm Eugenia's sister Annabelle," the small woman said. "Come right this way."

I stepped inside the house and closed the door behind me. Then I walked with Annabelle through a large but cluttered living room into the kitchen. Miss Eugenia was sitting on a red vinyl chair. Her left ankle was encased in an orthopedic boot and propped up on an identical chair.

"What happened to you?" I asked in lieu of the normal greetings.

Annabelle replied before Miss Eugenia had a chance. "While walking to the bathroom last night, she tripped over that little rat she calls a dog and sprained her ankle. She's lucky she didn't break her neck."

"It's not that bad," Miss Eugenia assured me. "Dr. Hinton stopped by this morning and said I just have to stay off of it for a few days."

"He *said* she was lucky she didn't break her neck," Annabelle corrected.

Miss Eugenia ignored her sister. "Have you had breakfast?" she asked me. "Annabelle lives in Albany so she brought bear claws from Marsh's Bakery."

I loved pastries from Marsh's, so I took a bear claw from the white bag. "Thanks."

"Have a seat." Miss Eugenia leaned forward and pointed at a chair across the table from her. "Kennedy is the director of the Midway Library," she added for her sister's benefit.

Annabelle's interest in me increased immediately. "My husband, Derrick Morgan, used to work at the main branch in Albany before he retired. Maybe you've heard of him?"

I hadn't, but as I sat down I nodded. "That name does sound familiar." It's just how things are done here in the Deep South.

Annabelle smiled and asked, "What brings you here so early in the morning? Library business?"

I shook my head. "I've come to report on the investigation into Foster Scoggins's murder."

"Murder?" Annabelle cried. "But old Foster committed suicide!"

"We have reason to believe otherwise," Miss Eugenia replied.

Annabelle's expression changed from surprise to anger. "Eugenia, you've started recruiting people in other towns to join your Merry Murder Club?"

Miss Eugenia gave her sister a dour look. "Of course I didn't recruit Kennedy, and there is no such thing as a merry murder—let alone a club by that name."

Now Annabelle looked relieved. "So you're not investigating a murder in Midway?"

"Of course we are," Miss Eugenia corrected her. "We're just not doing it frivolously as the word *club* implies. We're quite serious about solving crime."

Annabelle turned her eyes toward the ceiling. "Heaven help us!"

Miss Eugenia tapped one of her age-spotted hands impatiently on the tabletop. "Annabelle, if this conversation is going to upset you so much, why don't you go into my room and watch some TV?"

"That's probably a good idea," Annabelle muttered. "That way I won't have to worry about being called on to testify against the two of you when you get caught breaking and entering."

Miss Eugenia waited until Annabelle had made her exit. Then she turned back to me. "My sister is a frustrated comedian and a worrywart. Now, when are you and Luke going to search Foster's house?"

"I'm meeting him at the salvage yard at five-thirty tonight," I reported. "And Cade said he'd bring copies of Foster's love letters by the library this afternoon."

Miss Eugenia frowned. "I was planning to go with you to Foster's house, and I really need to read those letters. This sprained ankle is a big inconvenience. Maybe it wouldn't hurt me to take a quick trip to Midway."

"You definitely should follow the doctor's advice," I advised.

She sighed. "I suppose you're right." Then her face brightened. "Maybe you could get Deputy Burrell to make me a copy of them so I can study them at my leisure. It would help me keep my mind off my injury, and I might find a clue to the woman's identity."

Cade was already going out on a limb for me by letting me see the letters at all, so I knew I shouldn't ask for more. But I remembered Serene and her phone call the night before. I nodded. "I'll try."

The back door opened, and Mark Iverson walked in. I looked hopefully for Kate and the baby, but he was alone.

"When I told Mark you were coming over this morning, he wanted to come by and talk with you," Miss Eugenia explained.

Mark smiled at me. "I feel obligated to help, since you're the sister to a member of my congregation."

I doubted that any discussion involving Madison and her children could be pleasant, so I was glad when he moved on without waiting for me to comment.

"I've done a little checking," Mark continued. "I agree with you that the circumstances surrounding Foster Scoggins's death were suspicious."

Miss Eugenia looked delighted. "So the FBI is going to investigate?"

"At the moment, the sheriff's department has jurisdiction, and, as you know, they've already rejected a friendly offer of assistance from my office. So officially I can't do anything."

"What can you do unofficially?" I asked.

"I can give you advice and direction, which you will then pass on to Deputy Burrell," Mark replied.

"So basically you'll be directing their investigation through me?" I clarified.

Mark shrugged. "*Guiding* might be a better word."

"We need all the guidance and direction we can get," Miss Eugenia said for both of us. "Especially from one of the best agents in the FBI. So first, let me tell you where we are and then you can give us advice."

Mark looked a little annoyed but nodded for her to proceed.

"Kennedy and Deputy Burrell have compiled a suspect list," Miss Eugenia continued. "It comprises the landowners who are going to sell property and Mr. Langston himself. They interviewed some of these suspects yesterday."

"What we did yesterday could be more accurately described as friendly visits than interviews," I corrected. "Cade didn't do any serious questioning, and none of the people we talked to seem like suspects to me. However, I did take careful notes of everything we discussed." I tapped the cover of my Murder Book. "Just in case."

"That's not a bad approach," Mark said. "The more friendly the interviews seem, the less likely the suspects are to be on guard."

I had to accept the possibility that Cade's extremely casual interrogation approach had been intentional. And I didn't know how I felt about that.

"I recommend that you interview the rest of the people on your suspect list," Mark added.

I nodded. "We have more friendly visits planned for this afternoon."

Miss Eugenia reclaimed command of the conversation. "Kennedy talked to Foster's nephew, and he's going to ask for an autopsy."

"Good," Mark said.

"Let me know of anything else you want done, and I'm sure Luke will request it for you," I offered as though Luke and I were old friends.

"Just make sure you give him any new requests somewhere safer than the Flying J," Miss Eugenia said as if this meeting place had been my idea. "After being followed home last night, you need to be particularly careful."

Mark immediately became serious. "You were followed home from the Flying J? When?"

I explained my late-night meeting with Luke Scoggins and the car that followed me home. "Cade said he'd check into it, and I haven't noticed anyone following me since."

"I wish we could eliminate your involvement altogether," Mark said. "But until we can proceed without you, we'll have to guarantee your safety. Starting tonight I'll have a couple of my agents drive by your house a few times, and I'll ask the sheriff to have some of his deputies do the same."

"Do you really think that's necessary?" I asked.

"It's better to be safe than sorry," he replied.

I was reciting my address when Annabelle walked back in.

"Morning," she said to Mark. "Are you a part of the murder club too?"

"Murder club?" Mark repeated.

Miss Eugenia waved this aside. "Annabelle is just trying to be funny. Ignore her."

"Actually, I'm trying to do my sisterly duty to keep Eugenia off that ankle," Annabelle corrected. "Not that I get any appreciation for the fact that I've given up my day."

"So what did you give up?" Miss Eugenia demanded. "A few hours of puttering around your big old house with your husband?"

Annabelle turned to me in exasperation. "Eugenia doesn't understand the concept of 'happily married.'"

I wasn't sure I understood it either, so I just smiled.

"What other precautions should Kennedy take to ensure her safety?" Miss Eugenia asked Mark.

"Nighttime is when you're the most vulnerable," Mark replied. "But be cautious during the day, too. Keep your doors locked, notify your mother or someone else when you go places and when you expect to return, and always keep your cell phone charged and with you."

"I don't have a cell phone." I looked away from Mark quickly, afraid he'd be able to read the economic reason for this on my face.

Miss Eugenia looked appalled. "Oh, you have to have a cell phone! It's completely unsafe for any woman to be driving around without one—especially in that truck of yours."

Annabelle rolled her eyes. "It took years to convince Eugenia to get a cell phone, and now she's doing commercials."

Mark told me, "I agree that a cell phone is advisable as long as you're involved in what might be a murder case."

"When Derrick and I went to the Cayman Islands last month, we bought some cheap disposable cell phones so we wouldn't have to worry if we lost one of them," Annabelle said helpfully. "You could get one of those if you don't want one permanently."

I smiled even though I knew that until I received another paycheck, even a cheap cell phone was an impossibility. "Thanks for the information."

Miss Eugenia didn't seem impressed by Annabelle's kind advice. "Humph," she said. "Everyone knows you can get cheap disposable cell phones. Annabelle only mentioned the phones so she could tell you she went to the Cayman Islands."

Annabelle blushed crimson. "That's ridiculous. I'm only trying to help!"

Mark held up a hand to forestall an all-out battle. "Please, ladies!"

The sisters subdued themselves and settled for glaring at each other.

Mark extended a business card toward me. "This has all my numbers. Once you get a cell phone, call and let me know. In the meantime, how can I contact you?"

I recited my home number and my parents' number. Then I tucked Mark's card into my wallet. I smiled when I saw Drake's card already nestled there. If this trend continued, I'd soon have a whole collection of men's phone numbers.

"Don't hesitate to call me if you see that car again." Mark redirected my attention to more serious matters. "And keep me posted on any new developments with your investigation so I can look for ways to help."

"You don't know how lucky you are," Miss Eugenia told me. "Mark won't even *answer* my calls, and getting him involved in my cases has previously proved nearly impossible."

"I answer your calls," Mark claimed. "And I just want to get this settled before anyone gets hurt."

I stole a glance at my watch. "I can't begin to thank you all enough for your help, and I've really enjoyed going over things with you this morning, but if I don't hurry back to Midway, I'll be late opening the library on it's last day of operation."

"The Midway Library is closing?" Annabelle asked.

"Only the branch housed in the trailers," Miss Eugenia informed her with an air of importance. "Drake Langston is turning the old First National Bank building into a fabulous new library."

Annabelle turned to me with a smile. "Well, isn't that great news!"

"It is about the best news I've heard lately," I admitted. "But I'll have to let Miss Eugenia fill you in on it. I really do have to get back."

I said good-bye to Miss Eugenia in the kitchen. Annabelle and Mark Iverson walked me to the front door. I said good-bye to Annabelle on the porch, and Mark continued with me all the way to my truck. I expected that he was using the opportunity to reiterate safety measures, and I was right.

"I hate involving civilians in police business," he prefaced, "but since there doesn't seem to be any way around it, I want to be sure we do all that's necessary to keep you safe."

"And I appreciate that very much. I'll be careful."

Looking slightly reassured, he waved and then walked across Miss Eugenia's lawn toward his house. I took my time climbing into my truck and adjusting my mirrors, hoping to catch a glimpse of the Iversons' foster baby, but once again I was disappointed.

So I turned around and headed back for Midway.

I made it with minutes to spare and opened the library on time for once—and, of course, nobody was there to notice. I went through my opening routine and then started packing up the books I wanted to keep for my private collection. I had only been working for a few minutes when the phone on my desk rang. I expected it to be my mother, since I still hadn't faced the music for my late-night date with Luke. And I feared it might be Miss Ida Jean looking for another book I didn't have. But when I answered the phone with a fair amount of trepidation, Sloan the construction worker was on the other end of the line.

"Good morning," he said in his lazy, near-hypnotizing tone.

"Good morning," I managed, glad that no one was there to see how flustered he made me.

"We've got some paint on the wall, and I'd like to be sure it's what you want before we continue," Sloan said. "The time to make adjustments is now. So can you come by and look at it?"

"Sure," I agreed. "How soon?"

"The sooner, the better," Sloan replied.

"I'll have to see if my mother can come cover the library for me." I couldn't believe I was going to have to *initiate* a conversation that was almost certainly going to end in a lecture.

Sloan must have sensed my reluctance. "Why don't you just lock up and put a sign on the door that says you'll be back soon?"

"I never would have thought of that," I told him honestly.

He laughed. "Hurry on over. I'll be waiting for you."

I was too flustered to think of a response, so I just hung up the phone. I took a piece of paper from the circulation desk and was trying to compose my note for the door when the phone rang again. This time it was Drake Langston himself.

"Are you busy?" he asked.

"I was just about to put a note on the door explaining that the library is going to be closed for a little while," I told him a little breathlessly. "Sloan called. They've painted part of a wall at the library and want to be sure I like it before they continue."

"Perfect," he replied. "I've got some furniture options and fabric swatches that Morris overnighted to me, and I'd like you to look at them. I'm out at the housing development south of town. It will be a while before I can leave what I'm doing, but if you can come by here when you're through at the library, we can go ahead and place the order today."

"I should be able to be there within an hour."

After hanging up the phone, I amended my door sign to read BE BACK LATER instead of BE BACK SOON. I refurbished my makeup, locked the library door, and taped on the note explaining my temporary absence. Then I climbed in my truck and drove to town. More evidence of impending progress greeted me when I turned onto Main Street. A man with a jackhammer was breaking up the old sidewalks along one side of the road while his coworkers built frames for the new, wider sidewalks and the cement mixer waited in the wings. It was noisy and exciting, and I was thrilled to be a part of it.

There was a huge disposal bin blocking the sidewalk and the street in front of the old bank building. I parked behind it. Just as he had promised, Sloan was waiting for me. He stepped out of the future library and opened the truck door. Today his black hair was loose, just brushing his shoulders. He was wearing a tight blue T-shirt, snug enough to display all his muscles.

I stood on the running board, intending to jump down, but Sloan stepped up and put his hands on my waist. Then he lifted me gently to the ground. During this process I had an amazing view of the yellow flecks that highlight his very blue eyes and was so close to him that I briefly felt his breath on my cheek.

When he placed me on the sidewalk, I prayed that my legs would have the strength to hold me upright. Sloan smiled down at me, perfectly aware of the effect he was having. With an effort, I pulled myself together.

"I am capable of getting out of vehicles without assistance," I told him.

"But my way is much more fun," he replied, still smiling.

"Show me the paint," I told him firmly.

I followed Sloan inside, not expecting to see much progress in the old bank building. But the transformation was astonishing. The new front windows were installed and gorgeous. A crew was cleaning the wooden floors, new light fixtures were being hung, and the trim paint seemed to be finished. Anyone would have been impressed by what had been accomplished in so short a time.

Sloan led the way to the back of the new library where the children's section would eventually be housed. There he pointed to a wall with a large square section painted the yellow color we had chosen. The wall had a mixture of sunlight and shadow—making it perfect for color analysis. Sloan might be arrogant, but he was also beautiful and smart.

I studied the paint for a few minutes and then nodded. "It's perfect."

"Not too dark?" Sloan asked.

"No, Drake and I are going for dramatic."

Sloan shrugged a muscular shoulder. "Then we'll keep painting." He motioned to the crew standing behind him, and they immediately got to work.

"Thank you for having me come," I said. "It would have been a shame to paint the whole library and then decide the color was wrong."

Sloan's eyes were on my lips as he answered. "You're welcome."

"Well, I've got to meet Drake, so I'd better go." I started for the door.

Sloan didn't follow, but I felt his gaze on me as I walked. "Come back soon," he called after me.

Without responding, I hurried outside and climbed into my truck.

During the drive to the housing development south of town, I had a few minutes to consider my feelings. I barely knew Sloan, and didn't even really *like* him. So my shortness of breath and pounding heart were purely physical reactions based on his masculine charm and beauty. I thought I was above such superficiality and was disappointed in myself.

But that was as far as I got with my painful self-analysis. As soon as I turned the curve and saw the sprawling subdivision-in-progress, all other thoughts left my mind. I don't know what I expected. I guess just a few mounds of dirt and some for-sale signs. I was amazed to see that construction of smooth asphalt roads with pristine white curbs and neat little sidewalks had begun. A fancy brick sign identifying the neighborhood as LANGSTON LANDING was already in place by the gated entrance. Based on the number of lots that had been sectioned off, Drake was planning to build at least a hundred homes in this subdivision alone.

I turned into the main entrance and passed through the open gate. Several bulldozers were moving dirt around, and surveyors were marking lots. I spotted Drake standing near a cement truck. He waved me over, his blond hair glinting in the sunlight.

When I pulled up, Drake walked to my truck and leaned his arms inside the open window of my door.

"This is quite impressive," I understated.

"It will be a very nice place to live." He didn't try to disguise the pride in his voice.

"I didn't think all the land purchase deals were finalized."

"They aren't," he confirmed. "But they will be by the end of the week."

"Wasn't it a little risky to proceed with the development before you owned all the land?"

"There was never any doubt that it would happen—it was just a matter of when. And I don't like to wait until the last minute."

Drake had a pretty major financial investment in land he didn't own, and I felt a little wave of uncertainty. Surely Drake wouldn't kill an old man just to guarantee the sale.

I was about to ask another question, but he derailed me by saying, "Here are the swatches and furniture options." He handed me a FedEx envelope.

I pulled out five cards. Each card had a large material sample glued in the middle with four smaller, coordinating fabrics attached to the corners of the larger sample.

"What do you think?" he asked.

I studied each card in turn and finally put one on top. "I like them all," I said. "But I like these best."

He smiled. "Then those are the ones we'll use."

It was a lot of responsibility, and I hoped I had chosen the best option. When I voiced my concern, Drake said, "How can you miss? They're all perfect."

I couldn't argue with this. Then I studied the furniture collections I was to choose between. Finally I pointed at the one called Renaissance. "I think this one goes best with the Monet print."

Drake smiled. "I agree. It's all settled, then. I'll call our choices in to Morris. He'll order the furniture and have it shipped immediately." After he made his call, he said, "Do you have plans for tonight? I was thinking we could go to a restaurant in Albany. Not that I don't enjoy the cuisine at the Back Porch—but I have something special in mind."

While the search of Foster's house probably could have been postponed, I was unwilling to cancel my appointment with Luke, who had accommodated me even though I didn't deserve his help. So I had to sadly shake my head. "I'm sorry. I do have plans for tonight."

Drake didn't seem to mind being turned down by a lowly country girl. "Well, how about tomorrow night?"

"That sounds great," I accepted while wondering what in the world I'd wear on a real date with the great Drake Langston since I had completely exhausted my wardrobe and depleted my available cash.

"I'll pick you up around seven?"

I nodded. "I'll be looking forward to it."

When I got back to the library, I found a stack of books on the front steps, left by a patron who had come while I was gone. I took the books inside, checked them in, and then I called my sister Reagan, who lives in Macon. She's about my size and keeps up with the latest fashions. I explained the situation vaguely, emphasizing the date with Drake Langston and glancing over my lack of funds. Reagan enthusiastically agreed to loan me an appropriate outfit.

"Mother's been bugging me to visit anyway." Reagan didn't sound unhappy about this. "If you want," she continued, "I'll bring several options to Mother and Daddy's, and you can sort through them there."

I shuddered at the thought. Involving Mother in my clothing choice would make a stressful situation worse. "I hate to close the library again," I used as my excuse. "So would you mind stopping by the library instead? That way I can try on things in between patrons."

Reagan didn't object. "Sure, if that's better for you. I should be there around lunchtime. You want me to pick up some burgers?"

"Mother will want to feed you," I said. "Just bring the clothes to the library. I'll pick up something to eat later."

After ending my call with Reagan, I returned to my book sorting. A little before noon, Francie Cook came by. She said she'd just gotten word that the trailer would be available for rent again at the beginning of the next week.

"I didn't expect Drake to move quite so quickly." Francie's voice was almost reverent when she said Drake's name.

"He says the new library will be a draw for potential homebuyers," I explained. "It will tell them that we care about our children in Midway."

Francie nodded. "Drake has vision—unlike the rest of the folks in this town."

I thought about the farmland that was currently being divided into neat little lots for future houses. "Drake does see potential everywhere," I agreed. "So do you have someone to rent to?"

"Not yet, but I'm hopeful that I can find tenants quickly. We depend on the income. The towing business is unpredictable."

I looked at her and thought, *And plastic surgeries don't come cheap.*

"I want to take some pictures of the trailer to post up around town," Francie was continuing. "And I'd like to get it all taken care of this weekend, since I'm having outpatient surgery next week."

"Nothing serious, I hope," I said.

Francie looked uncertain for a few seconds and then pulled a folded piece of printer paper from her pocket. She extended it toward me, and I saw that it was a printout of several different noses. "I'm having a little work done on my face." She pointed at nose number three. "I picked this one. Do you think it will look the best?"

I hate doctors and needles and hospitals. So while I have some appearance deficiencies, I cannot even imagine having them surgically corrected. Besides, as I mentioned, Francie isn't ever going to be pretty, so a new nose would not be a significant improvement. However, it was not my place to lecture Francie on the wisdom of cosmetic surgery.

I nodded. "I think nose number three is a good choice."

She seemed relieved as she returned the picture to her pocket. "Well, I'll take some outside shots and then go make posters of the property."

I followed Francie out onto the porch, on the pretense of saying goodbye but mostly just to get some fresh air. Reagan pulled up just as Francie drove out. Reagan has one relatively well-behaved daughter named Dallas. Ordinarily I don't have much interest in children, but Baby Jake had changed me, and I was mildly disappointed to see that Dallas was not in the car.

"Did you lose your daughter?" I asked while Reagan climbed out.

"Chase was off today, so Dallas is at home with her dad." Reagan opened the backseat of her car and pulled out several outfits on hangers. She handed them to me. "Hold these while I get the rest."

"The rest?" I cried. "I only need something to wear on one date!"

Reagan laughed. "I know. But when I started looking through my closet, I found tons of clothes I can't wear thanks to baby fat left over from my pregnancy." She pointed at her midsection. "By the time I get back into shape, all this stuff will be out of style, so I decided to give them to you. Anything you can't use, you can pass on to the Goodwill."

I fingered the silky fabric of a beautiful blouse that reminded me of the Monet print Drake was using as his inspiration piece for the new library. "Are you sure? This stuff is all so nice."

Reagan laughed. "I'm sure. I'd rather buy new clothes than diet."

I studied my sister for a few seconds. She couldn't possibly be carrying more than a couple of extra pounds since Dallas's birth. She was very style-conscious, and it was possible that she was using me as an excuse to buy a new wardrobe. But I suspected she was just being generous.

"Try that on." She pointed at the blouse in my hand. "I bet it will look great with your eyes."

I stepped into my tiny storage room and changed shirts. The filmy blouse fit perfectly, and although it was something I never would have chosen for myself, wearing it made me feel sophisticated and stylish and maybe even able to hold my ground with the great Drake Langston.

I stepped back out into the library with my hands raised. "Ta da!"

I was unpleasantly surprised to see Cade standing beside Reagan. His eyebrows shot up, and my sister put her hand over her mouth in a useless attempt to prevent a giggle.

"Are you having a fashion show?" Cade asked.

I lowered my arms and shook my head. "No. Reagan brought me some hand-me-downs, and we're trying to figure out what fits."

"That shirt fits pretty good," Cade said appreciatively.

"Pretty good, indeed." Reagan gave me a teasing smile as she moved toward the door. "I'd better get over to Mother's before lunch gets cold." Reagan winked at me and left.

Once she was gone, Cade and I stood in awkward silence for a few seconds. Finally he held out a stack of papers. "Here are copies of those letters you wanted."

"Thanks," I forced myself to say. I pulled my Murder Book out of my purse and stuffed the letters inside.

His eyes drifted to the pile of clothes on the library table. "You want me to help you put this stuff in your truck?"

"No, I'm going to sort through it this afternoon in between customers. Reagan told me to give what I can't wear to Goodwill."

Cade shifted his weight from one foot to the other. "Luke Scoggins called this morning and talked to Sheriff Bonham. The family has postponed the funeral until an autopsy can be performed. The remains are headed to Albany in a county coroner van."

This was very good news, and I felt a rush of kind feelings toward Luke. "When will you have autopsy results?"

Cade examined a denim jacket decorated with lace and embroidery that Reagan had given me. "Preliminary report might be back on Monday. But even if we don't have the report, the funeral can be held on Tuesday. Once the autopsy's been done, they don't really need to keep the body—or what's left of it."

Things were moving more quickly than I had dared to hope. "That's good."

Cade put down Reagan's jacket and said casually, "I was thinking that we could work on our suspect list again tomorrow. We can interview folks throughout the day, and once we're done, we could catch a bite to eat."

"The interviewing part sounds good," I told him, "but I've got plans tomorrow night."

Cade's eyes strayed back to the array of expensive clothes. "With Drake Langston?"

I nodded.

"What kind of *plans*?" His tone was unpleasant.

I knew I wasn't under any obligation to explain, but I wanted to keep Cade at least somewhat cooperative, so I said, "We're just going out to eat."

Cade's expression darkened. "It seems like ever since you started asking questions about Foster's death, Drake Langston has taken a real interest in you."

"That's ridiculous," I replied.

"Be careful," he advised.

I thought about my father's gun and nodded. "I always am."

"I'll come by your apartment at ten o'clock tomorrow morning, and we can start making our visits."

"Just meet me here," I suggested. When dealing with Cade, it seemed wise to keep things as impersonal as possible. "I'll be packing up the library."

With a curt little nod, he ducked out the door and left.

Once Cade was gone, I opened a fresh Pepsi and scanned through the letters that had allegedly been written to Foster Scoggins by his mysterious girlfriend. They were all written in the same loopy, feminine script and were all signed by "Mary." And they did describe romantic assignations in the Albany area. There were no clues to Foster's murder that I could see. But since I was not the local murder expert, I called Miss Eugenia and read the letters to her.

"I didn't notice anything either," she admitted when I finished the last one. "But I think it will be better if I can actually see them."

I recognized this for what it was—a thinly disguised request for me to make another trip to Haggerty and deliver the letters to her.

"I'm meeting with Luke Scoggins as soon as I close the library," I reminded her, "but I can bring you a copy of the letters when we get finished."

"That would be fine," she said, accepting my offer to inconvenience myself.

I ended the call, ate my last Moon Pie, and went back to work.

After such a busy morning, the afternoon passed slowly. I had time to sort through all of the clothes Reagan had given me, and they fit with only a few exceptions. I looked back through my "keep" pile for an outfit to wear to my meeting with Luke. It had to be casual enough for a salvage yard but cute enough to impress an attractive ex-Marine. Finally I settled on a lacy tank top, a pair of jeans, and the denim jacket that Cade had admired during his visit earlier in the day. I hung my outfit for the evening over the chair behind the desk and transferred the rest of Reagan's donations to the Kennedy Killingsworth Charity Fund to the storage room.

My mother called just as I completed this process. She'd heard about my meeting with Luke the night before and demanded an explanation. Since Reagan was there, she didn't have much time to interrogate me, so I got off fairly easy. I listened to her lecture on proper, ladylike behavior—thankful she didn't know I'd been followed home from my late-night date at the Flying J by an unidentified car that mysteriously disappeared as soon as the police arrived.

Miss Ida Jean came into the library just before five and asked for a book on feng shui. Amazingly, I do have a book on this art of peaceful home décor, but I'd already packed it up and therefore had to refuse the request. I told Miss Ida Jean she could check the libraries in Haggerty and Albany, or she could wait until we were open for business in our new location in downtown Midway. She didn't leave happy, but at least she left.

After I got rid of Miss Ida Jean, I changed into the outfit I'd chosen for my non-date with Luke. I ran a brush through my hair and repaired my makeup. Then I hurried outside and drove north toward the Scoggins Salvage Yard.

I found the overgrown turnoff more easily this time. As I drove down the pitted gravel road, I felt a sense of sadness. The last time I'd been to the salvage yard, Foster was still alive. Now he was dead, possibly murdered.

And even though I'd never met him until two days before, Foster had become the center of my life.

When I reached the clearing, I saw Luke standing in front of one of the houses. He was wearing a pair of khaki pants and a blue dress shirt. I glanced down at my casual attire and realized that this time I was the one who was underdressed.

I parked my truck between the skeleton of an old Nova and a green Torino that my father would admire. Luke walked over and opened the door for me to climb out.

"You look nice," he said.

My eyes skimmed over his ensemble. "You too."

"I had to take my dad to the lawyer's office today to discuss how Uncle Foster's death will affect things."

Since I was there specifically to gather information that would help solve Foster's murder, I asked, "Like the sale of this land to Drake Langston?"

"Yes. I want to get all that settled before I leave for school."

The reminder that he was going to be leaving soon made me feel oddly bereft. I noted the empty dog pen and pointed at it. "What happened to the dogs?"

"I sold them to a man from Sipsey who hunts. Good dogs need to work, and that wasn't going to happen around here without Uncle Foster."

The empty pen became another grim reminder that a man was dead—his life cut short and now those dependent on him also paying the price. Heaven, the hunting dogs . . .

He interrupted my thoughts by saying, "Come on in. Dinner is ready."

Luke led me into the weathered-wood house behind him. The interior was surprisingly clean. The furnishings weren't modern, but they were wisely arranged in a cozy circle around the fireplace.

As if reading my mind, Luke said, "You didn't think a place where Scogginses live would be habitable?"

"I didn't expect too much from a bunch of bachelors," I replied carefully.

I knew I'd said the right thing when some of the tension left his shoulders. "Because of my dad's medical condition, the county provided nursing care and weekly housecleaning services—until he went into the nursing home, of course."

"Of course."

"Since then it's been up to me to keep things clean."

"It looks like you've been doing a pretty good job."

He smiled and gestured into the next room where I could see a small table. "Have a seat, and I'll get our dinner."

The table was covered with a blue cloth that still had creases on the folds, so I knew he had purchased it recently—probably right after I accepted his dinner invitation. The dishes were fragile-looking china in a faded floral pattern.

"These dishes belonged to my grandmother," Luke explained. "Nick's wife found them in the attic. She wanted to sell them on eBay, but Foster wouldn't let her."

"They're lovely," I said, and I could tell he was pleased. I was touched that he had gone to so much effort—buying a new tablecloth and getting out his grandmother's china.

The meal consisted of spaghetti, salad, and garlic bread. Nothing fancy but all delicious. "How did you learn to cook?" I asked as I twisted sauce-coated pasta onto my fork.

"I taught myself," he replied. "It was my first survival skill. I got tired of eating sandwiches, so I learned to cook."

"Very wise."

"And when I got tired of being dirty, I learned to wash my own clothes."

Unbidden memories of Luke from elementary school came to my mind—before he had become an intriguing ex-Marine. Back then he was an unkempt, smelly little hooligan. His clothes *were* often dirty. His hair was always too long and rarely even combed. He never had money for field trips, and no one came to watch him when we had programs. And he was frequently tardy.

I felt bad for unkind judgments I'd made about him then and wished I could go back and give that dirty little boy with uncombed hair a hug. Goodness knows he needed one.

"I'm sorry."

"Don't be," he replied. "My lack of parental involvement made me strong and independent. I don't envy those sniveling brats whose mothers ironed their clothes and cut their sandwiches into sissy triangles and tucked them into bed at night."

I laughed. "I'm guilty on all counts."

He smiled. "I know. But I don't hold it against you. You can't help it that you were a coddled little princess."

"I've tried to stop my mother from coddling—believe me," I told him. "But it's impossible!"

His expression turned soft and kind of dreamy. "Your mother seems nice."

"She is," I agreed, "in a smothery kind of way."

I expected him to laugh, but instead he said, "I think about my mother sometimes and wonder why she left. I mean, I understand why she left here." Luke waved to encompass the whole Scoggins compound. "What I can't understand is why she left Nick and me too. Why she didn't take us with her."

I remembered Miss Eugenia's unflattering opinion of Olive Scoggins. But I couldn't very well tell Luke that his mother was no good from the start. So I just said, "I don't understand that either."

"My plan was to find her and ask her," he said. "But social security notified my father about five years ago that she had died."

I hated to say I was sorry again, but it was the only thing that seemed appropriate. So I did.

He shrugged. "It's no big deal."

We ate in silence for a few minutes. Then I pointed at the spaghetti and said, "This is even better than my mother's, and that's something I don't say often."

He leaned closer. "It's from a jar—Mrs. Rosetta's Sicilian Recipe."

I was astonished. "No kidding? My mom spends hours on her special spaghetti sauce."

"Maybe you can buy her some Mrs. Rosetta's and save her a lot of time."

I shook my head. "I wouldn't want her to know there's spaghetti sauce better than hers—especially from a jar. And the last thing I want to do is free up more hours in her day to interfere in my life."

"I never realized that having a mother who cares could be a problem."

"If you only knew . . ."

He laughed. "Hurry and finish your dinner. I made dessert."

I raised an eyebrow. "You really can cook."

"Oh, yes," he assured me. "I can bake, broil, and even sauté if necessary."

I was impressed and didn't try to hide it. "Wow."

"Tonight I'm using one of my favorite dessert recipes—one that combines all the ingredients of strawberry shortcake in a bowl."

"It sounds delicious," I said as I put another serving of spaghetti on my plate.

While we finished eating, we discussed Luke's father and his recent decline in health. "He's always been confined to a wheelchair," Luke explained. "But for a long time he's been sound, mentally. It's been sad to see him go down so fast."

It was sad to me that everyone in Luke's life seemed to be either sick or dead or missing. "Is your brother coming home for the funeral?"

"Probably not," Luke replied. "He's in Wisconsin with a load of ball bearings."

"But if the funeral isn't until at least Tuesday, that gives him plenty of time to get here."

"But if he doesn't deliver the load, he doesn't get paid."

I was shocked that Luke's brother would put money ahead of their uncle, and it must have shown on my face.

"Uncle Foster was a hard man when we were growing up," Luke explained. "And Nick hasn't lived here for several years. I don't expect him to leave his load and buy a plane ticket he can't afford to come to a funeral for a man he didn't even like. I'm sorry the old man's dead, but I won't lay awake nights crying or anything."

I thought about my uncles. Between both sides of my family, I had four, and I loved them all dearly. My sympathy for Luke increased, and I asked, "How's Heaven?"

"Okay, I guess. Until they can find a foster home, she'll have to stay at a place called the Dougherty County Juvenile Facility."

"That sounds awful," I whispered.

"It's like a children's prison, which is no place for a kid like Heaven. She'll be a criminal in no time if she stays there for long."

"It seems like your brother would come home to see about Heaven, even if he doesn't care about your uncle."

Luke did look a little less indifferent when he replied this time. "Nick wasn't cut out to be a father. Heaven will probably be better off without him."

"Maybe it won't take them long to find a foster home for her."

"Maybe," he repeated, but he didn't sound optimistic.

I'd met Heaven, so I couldn't think of anything to encourage him. I let the subject drop.

Luke's dessert was a combination of pound cake, vanilla pudding, strawberries, and whipped cream. And it was indeed delicious.

"Can you write down the recipe?" I asked while finishing up my second helping. "I'll bet my mother would love to have it."

He moved to a computer in the corner of the room. "I'll print you off a copy."

Once I had the recipe in my purse, he started for the door. "Let's go look around Uncle Foster's house—unless you want more dessert."

"I want more," I assured him. "But I don't need more. So let's see if we can find out anything about your uncle's death."

We walked outside and crossed the dead grass interspersed with puddles of mud to Foster's house, which was an equally unimpressive dwelling a few yards away. But as with Luke's home, the interior of Foster's house was better than the outside indicated.

Luke read my mind and my body language again. "DHR comes by unexpectedly, so Uncle Foster had to keep it clean."

The reminder that we were there to solve a murder put a damper on my mood.

Luke gave me a quick tour, which I realized as we wandered around that he had not done at his own house. At the time, I assumed he was a private person. Later I wondered if he had something to hide. He also couldn't find the shoebox full of receipts and bills, even though he'd offered to show me at the Flying J.

Foster's living room was dominated by a large television and a wood-burning stove. The kitchen was small and outdated. Heaven's room was not pink and frilly like you'd expect for a seven-year-old girl. Instead it was stark with white walls and no curtains. Only cheap vinyl blinds covered the lone window. It was furnished with a scarred wooden dresser and an iron bed. The bed looked antique, and if given a good cleaning, it would be beautiful.

Luke noticed my interest in the bed and said, "My grandfather bought it for my grandmother when they got married. Nick's wife claimed it just like she did the china. But she left it behind when she ran out on Nick, and so it was passed down to Heaven for as long as she was here. It's like there's some kind of curse on Scoggins women that makes them unable to stay here more than a few years."

I smiled at his little joke but sensed that the dismal family history bothered him more than he let on. "Your grandmother died." I hoped he wouldn't ask how I knew this, because I really didn't want to divulge that Miss Eugenia and I had been gossiping about them. "So you can hardly hold her desertion against her."

Luke shrugged. "She still left . . . in the end."

I was spared from making a comment when he led the way into Foster's room, which was so barren that it made Heaven's stark décor seem overdone. We looked through the closet and under the bed and even in the poor man's drawers. But we didn't find anything.

"I'm sorry this trip was a waste of time," Luke said when we were finished.

"It definitely wasn't a waste of time," I assured him. "I got a delicious meal out of it."

He smiled. "That's true."

"And the fact that we didn't find anything supports our theory that there was no girlfriend."

"How?"

"Well, if he'd been meeting a woman, you'd think he'd have saved some little something—a movie ticket stub or matches from a restaurant or a postcard from a motel."

"Why?"

"Mementos to help you remember, to document the romance," I explained. "It's something people in love do."

He grinned. "I'll have to take your word on that."

I rolled my eyes. "Yeah, like I'm the expert."

"So do you still want to go see my father?"

"Is it too late?"

"There's a chance he'll be asleep when we get there," Luke admitted. "But that's a risk we'd take no matter what time of day we visited."

"Let's give it a try, then," I said.

We walked outside, and Luke was careful to lock up both houses before joining me by my truck. I pointed at the old Nova. "Your car?"

He grinned. "It used to be back when I was about ten. I had a good time driving around here."

I had to admit that being allowed the freedom to drive around in an old Nova sounded fun. Maybe being raised as a Scoggins hadn't been all bad. I transferred my gaze to the Torino. "Who owns this one?"

Luke looked over his shoulder. Then he said, "Uncle Foster. Somebody gave it to him in exchange for parts they couldn't pay for. He worked on it when he had time and finally got it running. But he wouldn't let anyone drive it. He kept it in a shed at the back of the property. Now that Uncle Foster's gone and I need a car, I've claimed it."

"It could be pretty valuable," I told him. "You should get my father to take a look at it. He could give you an estimate of what it's worth."

Luke smiled. "It actually belongs to my dad, I guess. So I won't be trying to sell it. I'm just using it for transportation until I leave for school." Another reference to his impending departure. "Should we take separate cars so you don't have to come back here?"

If Cade had asked this same question, I would have agreed immediately, but I enjoyed Luke's company, and I wasn't worried about his intentions. So I shook my head. "Let's just ride in my truck. I don't mind dropping you off afterward."

Luke gave the passenger door a hard yank and pulled it open. "Sounds good to me."

So we climbed into my truck and headed out of the salvage yard.

CHAPTER TEN

As we drove, Luke said, "Does your dad keep this truck running for you?"

"He does," I confirmed, "although I don't have many problems with it."

Luke rubbed his hand along the sun-damaged dashboard. "Yeah, they don't make 'em like this anymore."

We passed through Midway and then headed toward Albany. As we drove, we talked about my old truck and his uncle's old Torino. It was nice to be with someone who appreciated the value and beauty of things that were past their prime.

When we reached the nursing home, we parked near the front entrance. Luke waved to the lady at the information desk as we walked by and then passed through to the assisted living wing. Parnell's suite was at the end of the hall by a rear exit. Luke knocked once. There was no response, so he took a key from his pocket and unlocked the door.

It was quiet inside the suite, and I felt a little like a trespasser as we walked in. Luke closed the door behind us and crossed the small living space to the bedroom door. Unsure of what I should do, I stopped in the middle of the living room and watched as Luke entered his father's bedroom. Through the doorway I could see Parnell reclining on a hospital bed. He was either asleep or dead. I prayed for the first possibility.

"Dad." Luke moved to the side of the bed and shook Parnell's shoulder. "Dad!" he called a little louder.

Parnell startled awake, his eyes red-rimmed and frightened. "Who, what?! Oh, Luke. It's you."

"Yep, it's me," Luke confirmed. "And I've brought a visitor for you." He waved me to come closer.

I approached the bed with trepidation.

"Dad, this is Kennedy Killingsworth."

"Oh, hello." Parnell sat up a little and squinted his eyes in my direction. "You were at the viewing. Luke said you were a friend."

His resemblance to Foster, who was so recently dead under such unpleasant circumstances, was unnerving. "Yes, sir."

He ran pale, trembling fingers through his hair. "I wish I'd known you were coming so I could fix up a little."

"We should have called." I felt awful. Apparently I had forgotten all the manners my mother had spent so much time teaching me.

"We're only going to stay a few minutes," Luke interjected. "Kennedy just wanted to ask you a couple of questions about Uncle Foster."

Parnell shook his head. "I don't know what I'm going to do without my brother."

"I'm sorry for your loss, sir," I said awkwardly. I had been so intent on investigating the murder that I hadn't taken into consideration the fact that asking questions might be painful for Luke's dad.

"We had to postpone the funeral," Parnell said. "I can't remember why. But I wish we could just hurry and get poor old Foster laid to rest."

Now I felt guilty, since I knew exactly why the funeral had been postponed.

"Kennedy wants to know if Uncle Foster ever said or did anything that would make you think he had a girlfriend," Luke told him.

"Foster had a girlfriend?" Parnell repeated as if this was the first time he'd heard of it. "I didn't know."

Luke seemed exasperated.

"Do you remember your brother being gone overnight on weekends recently?" I forced myself to ask.

Parnell looked around the room. "No, since I've been in here, I don't know what goes on at home."

I smiled at him. "Thank you, Mr. Scoggins. You've been very helpful."

Parnell's vacant eyes widened. "I have?"

Luke frowned. "How are you feeling?"

"Tired," his father replied. "I'm always so tired. I think that new nurse is giving me too much medicine."

"I'll talk to the head nurse about it," Luke promised.

Parnell reached out and grabbed his son with one frail hand. "Can't you just take me home? I don't like it here."

"I'll see what I can do," Luke promised. Then he turned to me. "Is there anything else you want to ask him?"

I looked at the pitiful old man and shook my head.

Luke told his father to go back to sleep and then led me out of the room.

When we were in the hallway, he said, "I need to talk to the head nurse about my father. Do you mind waiting for a few minutes?"

"Of course not," I assured him. Then I stood by the wall while he walked down to a desk where two nurses were seated behind computer terminals.

He leaned forward and pressed his hands onto the desk as he consulted with the nurse in charge. With his crisp blue shirt and short, spiky haircut, he bore no resemblance to the pitiful little boy I'd known in Mrs. Springer's third grade. He was far from a helpless child now, and I hoped for the sake of the nursing staff that they weren't mistreating his father.

When he returned, he looked grim, and I asked, "What did they say?"

"There's not a new nurse here, and there's been no change in the amount of medicine Dad receives. They said he's just confused because of the Alzheimer's."

I was hesitant to state my opinion. After all, I barely knew Luke and didn't know his father at all. But as he opened the driver's-side door to my truck, I felt that I couldn't remain silent. Instead of climbing into the truck, I turned to face him. We were very close, and the moonlight was very romantic. I had to struggle to maintain my focus and knew my voice trembled as I said, "I think there's another possibility you should consider."

His eyes locked with mine, and I saw his strength and his sadness. His lips were full and looked impossibly soft. A breeze blew a lock of hair into my face, and Luke pushed it back into place. His finger left a little warm trail along my cheek, and I felt a surge of tenderness toward him.

He brought me back to reality by asking, "What is the other possibility?"

I cleared my throat to help me regain my composure. "It's possible that your father is telling the truth."

He took a step back, and I knew that his withdrawal from me was emotional as well as physical. I had overstepped the bounds of our newfound friendship, and now I would pay the price.

"But they don't have a new nurse here, especially one who is giving out extra medication," Luke reiterated. "The nurses looked at me like I was as crazy as my dad when I suggested it."

I persevered. "Whoever is giving your father extra medication might not be an employee here, but it wouldn't be too hard to slip in and pretend to be a nurse—to give a confused old man some drugs."

Luke considered this for a few seconds and finally nodded. "I guess that would explain his odd behavior over the past few weeks. But why would someone want to drug my dad?"

"If someone in Midway *killed* your uncle, they wouldn't hesitate to drug your father," I said gently.

Luke moved close again and whispered, "So you think this is still about the land sale?"

"We can't afford to ignore the possibility," I replied. "You should bring Cade or the sheriff out here to talk with your father. If he can describe the new nurse who he thinks gives him the extra drugs to them, they might be able to find the guilty party and question them."

"I guess I could talk to the sheriff," Luke said with a worried glance back at the nursing home.

I noticed that he didn't even consider consulting Cade.

"Maybe my dad's not safe there."

"Could you bring him home until this is all settled?"

Luke frowned. "I could, but the problem with that is that I'm leaving for school soon, and once I'm gone, there won't be anyone at home to care for him."

I saw the problem but didn't think it would be a terrible thing if his plans to leave were delayed. "Maybe we could mention it to Mark Iverson. He's an FBI agent in Haggerty, and he might be willing to talk to your father or even assign someone to protect him. He's going to have someone keep an eye on my apartment at night . . ."

I realized my mistake too late.

Luke's eyes narrowed. "Why does someone need to watch your apartment?"

I sighed. "Because someone followed me home from the Flying J last night," I admitted reluctantly. "It looked like a rental car, and by the time Cade got there, it had disappeared."

I watched as he processed this. Then he said, "And I presume this is related to the land deal too?"

"We don't know for sure," I hedged.

"But you weren't being followed before you started investigating my uncle's death?"

"No."

"Then I think it's safe to assume."

What could I say? "Probably. But Miss Eugenia seems to think it's a sign that we're on the right track. And Mark Iverson didn't discourage me from working on the case—he just offered to provide protection."

"I don't like it," Luke said finally. "It makes me feel like you're risking your safety for me and my family."

Nothing could be further from the truth, so I didn't have any problem with denying *this*. "My safety isn't at risk, and I'm doing this because I want to. Now climb in, and let's go. I need to make a stop in Haggerty before I take you home."

"Why do you need to go to Haggerty?" Luke asked as he settled into the seat beside me.

I couldn't lie. "Cade gave me copies of the letters that were supposedly written by your uncle's girlfriend. Miss Eugenia wants to see them. She hopes she can find a clue about the murder."

Luke frowned. "Can I read them?"

I glanced away from the road in front of me to give him an incredulous look. "Of course."

I pulled my Murder Book out of my purse and removed the copies. I handed them to Luke and put the notebook on the seat between us.

"What's this?" he asked when he saw the title I'd written on the notebook.

I shrugged. "It's where I've been writing notes about the investigation. But I named it that way just to aggravate Cade."

Luke nodded vaguely and settled down to read the letters. When he was finished, Luke put the copies in my notebook and said, "I didn't see any clues."

"Me either," I conceded, "but then, we aren't the murder experts."

When we arrived at Miss Eugenia's, I parked the truck at the curb and led the way up to the house. I knocked on the door and waited for a response. Nothing. I knocked again. And again.

Finally Luke said, "Maybe she's not home."

"Where would an eighty-year-old woman be at this time of night?"

"It's only nine," he pointed out. "She could have gone out to dinner or something."

"She has a sprained ankle," I told him. "The doctor said she can't put any weight on it."

He shrugged. "Maybe we could just put the letters in her mailbox."

I looked over at the Iversons' house. The lights were on in the kitchen, so I knew the family hadn't retired for the night. "Let's walk over and ask the neighbors." I started down the steps without waiting for him to respond. He followed me, and soon we were knocking on the Iversons' front door.

Kate Iverson opened the door in response to my knock, and instead of inviting us in, she stepped out onto the front porch. She was holding Baby Jake, and he was wearing blue and white–striped pajamas. He was sucking on one fat little fist and looked incredibly soft. I couldn't stop staring at him.

"Good evening, Kennedy," Kate greeted. "Who's your friend?"

I introduced Luke without taking my eyes off Baby Jake. "This is Luke Scoggins."

"Hey, Luke. I'm Kate." She extended her free hand, and he shook it.

"Nice to meet you."

"We're looking for Miss Eugenia," I told her.

"She's at Annabelle's house in Albany, under protest," Kate explained. "We didn't think it would be wise for her to stay alone, since she's not supposed to put any weight on that foot, and it was easier to move her than set up round-the-clock volunteers to sit with her. She said she was expecting a visit from you and left a message on your home phone."

I pulled my eyes from the blue-and-white bundle in her arms. "I forgot to check my messages." I looked sheepishly at Luke. Then I turned back to Kate. "I was bringing her these letters."

"You can leave them with me," Kate offered. "I'll see that she gets them first thing in the morning."

I gave the letters to Kate. "Thanks."

Kate tucked the copies of Foster's letters under her arm and moved back toward her front door. "I'd ask you to come in, but Mark's getting the kids to sleep, and if they find out we have company, it will be hopeless."

I tried to hide my disappointment. "I understand completely. Is Miss Eugenia coming home tomorrow?"

"First thing in the morning, I'm sure," Kate replied. "Annabelle will be more than happy to get rid of her."

"When you see her, if you'd ask her to call me?"

"I'll tell her," Kate promised. Then with a little wave, she stepped inside and closed the door.

As Luke and I walked back to my truck, he asked, "Is something wrong?"

"No," I answered, feeling silly. "It's just that I wanted to hold the baby."

His eyebrows rose. "Mrs. Iverson's baby?"

"Jake is a foster baby," I told him. "They're keeping him until an adoptive mother is found. I got to hold him the other day and, well, I don't know. I kind of bonded with him." I knew this sounded foolish and was prepared for ridicule.

But Luke just shrugged. "He looked cute."

I felt all the tension melt from my body and rewarded him with a smile. He was such an easy person to be with. I didn't have to constantly be on my guard. We climbed into the truck and headed back to Midway.

"Will you get mad if I make a suggestion?" Luke asked.

"As long as you don't join the rest of southern Georgia and suggest that I remarry Cade."

"I promise that I'll never make *that* suggestion."

I laughed. "Then go ahead."

"I hate the thought of you driving from the salvage yard back to your apartment alone—especially since you were followed last night."

"So what do you have in mind?"

"If you'd trust me with your truck, I could drop you off at your place and drive myself home. Then I could bring your truck back to you tomorrow morning."

I probably would have found the same type of offer coming from anyone else annoying—even offensive. But with Luke making the proposal, I saw the wisdom and was touched by his concern. And I did trust him with my truck. So I agreed.

Luke didn't act surprised when I parked my truck in front of the office at Midway Store and Save, and I had the feeling that he already knew where I lived.

"I collect rents for Mr. Sheffield," I explained just in case he hadn't also investigated my employment circumstances. "And I live in an apartment over the office."

He nodded. "Nice employee benefit."

I was about to give Luke his instructions regarding my truck when I noticed something odd. Staring up at the door to my apartment, I said, "I'm sure I left the outside light on when I left. I knew I would be late and didn't want to have to come home to a dark apartment."

"Maybe the bulb burned out," Luke said.

"Maybe," I repeated. But a feeling of dread washed over me, and I was fairly certain that there was a more threatening reason for the darkness. "Would you mind walking up with me—just to be sure it's okay?"

Luke's expression became very serious. "I will definitely go with you."

I leaned over and pulled Daddy's gun from the glove compartment. Luke seemed startled. "Is that loaded?"

"Yes, and I know how to use it."

He put his hand over mine and the gun. "Would you mind if I hold it? This may sound chauvinistic, but as a soldier, I feel better when I'm in charge of the firearms."

I was too affected by the feel of his hand on mine to object. So I nodded dumbly, and he slipped the revolver from my fingers. Then he opened the passenger door and waved for me to slide across and get out on that side as well.

"When we walk up, you stay behind me," he instructed.

I wasn't about to argue with a Marine in a combat situation, so I nodded. We climbed the wooden steps to the little stoop in front of the door. I was torn between hoping the murderer was there so Luke could catch him and praying that he wasn't.

As we stepped onto the small stoop at the top of the stairs, glass crunched under our feet. We looked up and saw that the bulb in the outdoor light fixture was broken.

"That explains the darkness," I said.

Then we noticed that the door was slightly ajar.

"Someone broke into my apartment!" I whispered.

Luke nodded. "Stay close to me."

I didn't even *want* to argue with that. So I grabbed a handful of the crisp blue shirt that covered his back and followed him into my apartment. Luke turned on the lights, and we looked around. Everything seemed the same as when I'd left it. We walked quickly through the tiny apartment. I was embarrassed by the dishes in my sink and my unmade bed, but Luke didn't seem to notice, and I liked him better than ever.

Once we were back in the living room, he lowered the gun. He locked the door and said, "Nobody's here."

I let go of his shirt. "No. And nothing seems to be missing."

"Maybe you just didn't close the door all the way when you left."

"I'm certain I did," I insisted. "I'm always cautious since I know the dangers of a woman living alone. But I was *extra* cautious today since I had been followed last night. And I definitely didn't break the bulb in the porch light."

Instead of arguing, Luke insisted that we call the sheriff, which was worse than arguing. I tried to dissuade him, saying that the agent Mark Iverson had assigned to watch my house would surely be along any moment, and involving the sheriff, or his deputy, was unnecessary. But I learned that evening that while Luke was pleasant and easy to get along with most of the time, he did have a stubborn streak.

Finally I gave in and called the sheriff's office, praying that it was Cade's night off. Naturally Cade answered the phone. I explained the situation, and he promised to be right over. We could hear the sirens almost immediately, and Cade arrived in record time. He took the steps two at a time and was soon in my small living room, which was now crowded to near capacity.

It was obvious that he was not happy to see Luke there. I made no explanations about Luke's presence but just restated the situation.

"Are you sure you closed the door all the way when you left this morning?"

"Of course I closed my door." I was much more insulted by him asking than I had been when Luke had suggested the same basic thing. "And I had locked it and turned on the porch light so I wouldn't have to come home to a dark house." I wanted badly to add "since I don't have a husband anymore," but I refrained—more for Luke's sake than Cade's.

"Can you tell if anything has been stolen?" Cade asked.

I shook my head. "I don't think anything is missing."

"Maybe it was Mr. Sheffield," Cade proposed. "I'm assuming he has a key?"

"He has a key," I confirmed. "But why would he come into my apartment when I'm not home and then fail to close the door behind him when he left? And why would he break the light?"

"Why would anyone leave the door open when they left?" Luke interjected. "Even an intruder? Unless they wanted you to know that they'd been here?"

Cade and I both turned to look at him. Then we looked at each other. "That's true," I said.

"He's got a point," Cade concurred.

This possibility was just marginally better than an armed invasion. "So someone broke the light and opened my door just to scare me?"

"Hoping to stop your investigation into my uncle's death," Luke guessed.

"Possible," was as far as Cade was willing to go.

Headlights flashed in my front window, and Luke walked over to check them out. "I think the FBI just arrived."

Cade headed for the door. "Wait inside while I go talk with him," he commanded us—as if he had the authority to prevent our departure should we choose to leave.

I rolled my eyes and then purposely disobeyed him by walking outside, but I only went as far as the front porch. Luke joined me there, and together we watched Cade trot across to the dark sedan parked a few feet behind my truck. Cade leaned down and consulted with the man behind the wheel for a few minutes.

When he returned, he scowled upon seeing me standing outside, but he didn't make an issue of it. "The agent said he would have been here sooner, but he was delayed by a train."

"Convenient how my stalker managed to come before the agent got here."

"Yeah, that's bad luck," Luke agreed.

"It makes me wonder if he knew an agent was coming and made certain to get here first."

Cade reached out and put his hand on my arm. "Whether we're dealing with a lucky criminal or someone with insider knowledge, one thing is certain: you can't stay here tonight."

I'd already thought the same thing to myself. If someone had a key to my apartment—or the ability to break in so easily—there was no way I would be able to close my eyes. Not even with an FBI agent parked in front. I was about to say this when Cade made a fatal mistake.

He added, "The only sensible thing for you to do is come with me and spend the night at home."

His casual comment made me furious. Did he think our divorce was just a temporary inconvenience that could be put aside whenever we felt like it?

I yanked away from him, and my voice trembled as I said, "*This* is my home, and I am not going to spend the night in the same house with you ever again." And when I said these words, I knew they were absolutely true. Our marriage was over, dead, murdered just like poor old Foster. The occasional fantasies I'd entertained in moments of weakness about things going back to how they used to be were no more than that. Fantasies.

But while I was having this epiphany, Cade's expression changed to a combination of anger and embarrassment. He glanced at Luke, and I knew he thought I was being unnecessarily rough on him to impress my guest. But he was wrong. I had just finally accepted the truth.

"Thank you for coming and checking things out," I told Cade. "But everything is fine now, and I'll be safe. You can go."

"I'll go when *I* think it's safe." He clenched his fists, and his face turned a dangerous shade of red. "At least let me take you to your parents' house."

"No, thank you," I replied. "If I decide to spend the night there, Luke can take me."

Cade hooked a finger toward Luke. "Why does he get to stay? You're not married to him either."

"That's why I won't be spending the night at his house," I said as patiently as I could. "And he gets to stay because I haven't asked *him* to leave."

Cade sent Luke a malicious look and then stomped down the stairs. When he reached the bottom, he called back up, "Don't forget that I'm coming by the library to get you tomorrow. We've got more interviews to do."

Actually, I had almost forgotten about that. Cade climbed into his squad car and left the storage compound with tires squealing and gravel flying. Even Cade's taillights looked angry as they disappeared into the darkness.

"Let's hope you don't need more assistance from the sheriff's department tonight," Luke murmured.

"Yes, let's hope."

I got a new light bulb and watched as Luke screwed it into the porch light. Then we walked inside, and I closed the door. I had never had a male guest in this personal space before, and I wasn't sure what to do with him now that he was here.

To break the awkward silence, Luke smiled and said, "So are we still going to church together on Sunday?"

I knew he was kidding—just making small talk—but I couldn't help thinking that there were worse ways to spend a Sunday morning than sitting beside Luke on a church bench.

I said, "Only if you want the sanctuary roof to cave in."

Luke's smile became a little strained. "Yeah, a Scoggins in church might be too much for the good Christian folks."

"Actually, your presence would probably thrill everyone since saving Scoggins souls has been on the preacher's to-do list for a long time. I'm the unrepentant sinner who would shake the church to its foundations, since I won't forgive Cade and take him back like a good little wife."

He smiled. "I'm sorry if I made things worse between you and Burrell."

"Things have been beyond repair since I saw him at the drive-in with Missy Lamar. And I'm the one who should apologize. I'm sorry you had to witness the death throes of my marriage."

We sat on the couch, and he said, "I haven't had a close personal relationship yet, but I can imagine it would be hard if one ended badly. The only advice I can give you is that the past is past, and there's nothing you can do about it."

I raised my eyebrow. "That's the best you can do?"

He nodded with a grin. "Regrets are a waste of time. Look forward and move on."

I couldn't argue with this, so I didn't reply. We sat quietly for a little while. Then he turned toward me with a serious expression.

"I hate to bring up a sore subject," he prefaced, "but you really shouldn't stay here alone tonight."

I sighed. "I know. I could go to my parents' house, but my mother will make a fuss." I couldn't control a little shudder. "I could call my sister Madison who lives in Albany. She'd let me spend the night at her house—but she's almost as bad as my mother when it comes to fussing. And besides, she has three fiendish children. I think I'd rather take my chances with your uncle's murderer."

He frowned. "That's not funny."

I was only half kidding. But I nodded. "I know."

Before I had to make a decision between my equally awful options, Mark Iverson knocked on the door.

When we let him in, he said, "My agent called to report the possible break-in at your apartment. Is everything okay here?"

"As far as we can tell," Luke answered for me. "Kennedy's trying to decide where she wants to spend the night, since it's not safe here."

Mark shook his head. "It'll be fine here. I'm going to spend the night in the office downstairs."

I saw the relief I felt reflected on Luke's face. "Thank you," I told Mark.

"I'm just sorry we didn't catch the intruder. If you'll unlock the door to the office, I'll get settled in there."

I unlocked the door that led down into the office, and Mark Iverson descended the steps.

Then Luke said, "It's getting late, so I guess I'd better go."

I was more disappointed by this than I would have expected. But I didn't argue. "Thanks for dinner and for letting me look around your uncle's house and . . . everything."

He smiled. "You're welcome."

We shared an awkward little moment. I didn't want him to go but knew he needed to. I sort of wanted him to kiss me, but it seemed too soon. Besides, he'd just witnessed an argument between me and my ex-husband. Like I said . . . awkward.

Finally he leaned down and kissed me on the cheek. "I'll have your truck back early in the morning so you won't be late for your date with Burrell." Then, with a smile on his face, he walked out onto the porch and down the steps.

I watched him drive off in my truck with my hand pressed against my cheek covering the spot where he'd kissed me.

CHAPTER ELEVEN

ON SATURDAY MORNING I WOKE up to the sound of knocking. I thought there was somebody at my front door and staggered through the living room to peer out the peep hole. But my front porch was vacant. Then the knocking came again, and I realized that someone was knocking on the door leading up from the office downstairs. Then I remembered that Mark Iverson had spent the night there. I hurried over and unlocked the door.

"I trust you slept well?" he asked.

"I slept great." I took in the circles under his eyes. "But you look terrible."

He gave me a weak smile. "It comes with the job."

"Are you headed back to Haggerty now?"

He nodded.

"Do you know if Miss Eugenia is home yet?"

"I happen to know that Annabelle dropped her off at my house fifteen minutes ago," he reported. "Which means my day is destined to be even worse than my night."

He didn't smile, so I wasn't sure if he was joking.

"Miss Eugenia is quite a character, and I can see how living next door to her might be a challenge," I ventured.

He sighed heavily. "You have no idea."

I wanted to laugh but controlled myself since Mark didn't seem amused. "Well, I need to talk to her, but I let Luke take my truck home with him last night. So can I catch a ride to Haggerty with you and have Luke pick me up there?"

"You're welcome to ride with me," Mark agreed, "if you can be ready soon."

"It'll just take me a few minutes," I promised.

"I'll be waiting in my car," he said. Then he trudged back down the steps to the office.

I called Luke while brushing my teeth. When he answered, he sounded groggy. "Did I wake you up?"

"No," he murmured. "The phone did."

I should have felt awkward talking to a man I barely knew while he was in bed and I was brushing my teeth. But I didn't. "Sorry."

"You did me a favor," he continued around a yawn. "You kept me from getting all soft and lazy."

These adjectives didn't describe Luke, and we both knew it, so I didn't bother to deny either self-accusation.

I rinsed my mouth and explained the situation. Luke listened quietly and agreed to pick me up in Haggerty in an hour.

After ending my call with Luke, I combed my hair and examined my limited wardrobe. Wishing that I'd had the foresight to bring the rest of the clothes Reagan had given me home instead of leaving them at the library, I picked out my least ragged-looking pair of jeans and the pink sweater I'd worn when I met Luke at the Flying J. Since that first non-date had been in the middle of the night, I hoped he wouldn't remember what I had worn.

I hated to keep Mark waiting any longer than absolutely necessary, so I grabbed my makeup bag and took it with me. During the short drive to Haggerty, I fixed my face, and Mark discussed safety procedures. A few days ago, the conversation would have been incomprehensible to me. But my life had changed so drastically that having the constant companionship of FBI agents didn't faze me.

When we arrived at the Iversons' house, Mark led me in through the back door. Emily and Charles ran to greet him, and Kate was only a few steps behind. In her arms was Baby Jake.

"Would you mind holding him while I get Mark some breakfast?" Kate asked me.

"I'd be happy to," I assured her.

We walked into the kitchen, where Miss Eugenia was ensconced in a chair by the table.

"Well, good morning," she said.

"Good morning." I sat beside her, and the baby was transferred into my waiting arms. Jake squirmed briefly and then settled against my chest with a contented little sigh. It was heaven.

Mark took a seat at the end of the table, and the other children sat on either side of him. While Kate put a plate of pancakes in front of him, the children began an interrogation.

"Where were you last night, Daddy?" Emily asked.

He poured some syrup on his pancakes. "I was in Midway."

"Did you go to a sleepover party?" Charles wanted to know. "Emily said you did."

"There was no party," Mark assured him.

Emily frowned. "Then why didn't you come home?"

"Your father was keeping Kennedy safe," Miss Eugenia answered for him.

"That might be overstating the facts," Mark murmured around a mouthful of pancake.

Emily and Charles both turned inquisitive eyes to me. "Are you dangerous?" Charles asked.

"He means are you in danger," Emily explained in behalf of her brother.

I nodded. "I knew what he meant."

"So are you?" Emily asked. "In danger?"

"We're not sure," I replied.

"But your father was watching her apartment all night—just in case," Miss Eugenia informed them with pride.

"You don't have to be scared," Emily told me. "My dad won't let anything happen to you."

"He certainly won't," Miss Eugenia agreed.

I smiled.

Mark rolled his eyes. "That's enough."

"Emily, why don't you and Charles go into the family room and watch cartoons for a little while?" Kate suggested.

The little girl didn't look happy about being sent away from the interesting adult conversation, but she climbed down from her chair and waved to her brother. "Come on, Charles."

Once the children were gone, Miss Eugenia demanded that I tell her all about my visit to Foster's house and the break-in at my apartment. I related all the pertinent information while watching Baby Jake sleep. I thought about including my suspicions that Parnell Scoggins was being drugged at the nursing home where he was currently residing but decided that I would be overstepping my knowledge and the bounds of my friendship with Luke by doing so. When I had finished my account, Miss Eugenia looked upset.

She turned to Mark. "I presume you've taken measures to ensure that Kennedy won't find her apartment broken into again?"

Mark nodded wearily. "I've got a combination of FBI agents and sheriff's deputies driving past her apartment regularly. Although the best safeguard would be to solve the mystery of Foster Scoggins's death."

"Well, one thing is for certain," Miss Eugenia said. "We now know that Foster did not commit suicide. If that was the case, we wouldn't have a murderer trying to discourage Kennedy from investigating."

"Actually, we don't *know* anything yet," Mark countered. "All we have are theories."

Miss Eugenia narrowed her eyes at him. "Well, then maybe it's time for the FBI to take a more aggressive role instead of making little halfhearted attempts to help the sheriff with his investigation and letting Kennedy and me do all the work."

I saw Mark's expression turn angry and stepped in to avoid an argument. "Cade said Sheriff Bonham is suspicious of the FBI. So if Mark muscles his way into the investigation, it might make the sheriff less cooperative and slow things down."

Miss Eugenia frowned. "Sheriff Bonham is impossible to bully. I've already tried. But I'm frustrated with the lack of progress on the case."

Mark nodded. "I would like to be more openly involved. But I talked to my supervisor about it last night, and while we all want to find the murderer—assuming there is one—what we don't want is to scare off a guilty party prematurely."

"Any ideas of who the guilty party is?" Miss Eugenia asked him.

Mark shrugged. "Like we pointed out before, many people stand to gain from Drake Langston's land-purchase deal." He turned to me. "And keep in mind that under these circumstances, you can't trust anyone. Even people who seem like friends might not be. If they had a lot to lose—and went to the trouble to kill Foster Scoggins—they won't hesitate to remove you if you become a serious problem."

Kate poured more orange juice into Mark's glass and then said, "It sounds to me like your murderer is pretty clever. They left Kennedy's door ajar but didn't steal anything or make a mess. With no proof of forced entry, the sheriff won't take it seriously. But it might be enough to scare her off."

I was impressed by Kate's observation and sobered by the thought that I really might be squaring off with not just a murderer, but a smart one.

"Cade said the autopsy results should be back on Monday," I said. "If they find that Foster was dead before he was electrocuted, that should get Sheriff Bonham's attention."

"Maybe," Mark murmured.

"Have you had any luck identifying Mary? The woman who supposedly sent Foster those love letters?"

"I haven't been able to locate her," Mark said. "But I have done some checking with motels in the Albany area. I sent out a picture of Foster, and two motels e-mailed back claiming that he had rented a room from them. The dates they gave me match up with the time period Foster was supposedly having a romance."

"Well, I'll be," Miss Eugenia whispered.

"Did the motel people have proof—like a credit card receipt or his signature?" Kate asked.

Mark shook his head. "They both said he paid cash and that the woman signed the register."

"Mary?" I guessed.

"Mary *Smith,*" he added.

"Was it the same woman both times?" Kate wanted to know.

"We can't be sure—neither one of them remembered enough about her to give a description," Mark replied. "He tended to stay in low-cost motels that didn't have much in the way of security equipment. But one of the places that contacted me has a camera in the lobby. Everyone who rents a room has to pass right by it on the way to the registration desk."

"So Foster and the woman would be on the security tape?"

Mark nodded. "The manager said he'd review the tape for the date in question and print me a copy of their picture. I'm not expecting it to be high quality, but it might give us a clue to the woman's identity."

I was thrilled. "That would be wonderful."

"Both of the confirmed outings Foster took with his girlfriend were on Saturdays—late at night. And it was back before Parnell went into the nursing home, so even though Foster was technically leaving Heaven alone for a few hours, Parnell and the live-in nurse were just a few feet away if Heaven needed anything. They checked in around midnight and checked out early the next morning, so that's why the family didn't know he'd left."

I frowned. "I'll ask Luke to locate Parnell's former nurse and ask her if she ever remembers hearing Foster leave during the night."

"Good idea," Mark approved.

"I just can't get over it," Miss Eugenia said. "I was so sure the girlfriend was fabricated by the murderer to distract us from what really happened."

Mark stood and carried his breakfast plate to the sink. "We all make mistakes."

"I'll have to see that to believe it. I'd like to see that picture when the motel manager sends it," I requested.

Mark nodded. "I'll get a copy to you."

The phone rang, and Kate answered it quickly before the annoying sound could disturb the sleeping baby. Then she held out the phone toward me. "It's for you."

Surprised, I shifted the baby, took the phone, and said, "Hello?"

It was Luke. "I'm here," he informed me.

"I'll be out in just a minute."

Reluctantly I returned Jake to his foster mother. Then I thanked Mark again for protecting me overnight. After admonishing him to get some sleep, I hurried outside where Luke and my truck were waiting. I was happy to see them both—and seeing them together was a particular pleasure. Seeing the FBI agent parked behind them brought me back to reality.

The agent got out of his car, and Luke got out of my truck. They both met me on the sidewalk in front of the Iversons' home. The agent introduced himself simply as Perry and showed us his credentials. He said he would be following me until eight o'clock that evening when another agent would replace him.

"Just go about your normal activities," Agent Perry encouraged. "I'll stay in the background and try not to draw attention. If you need me and don't see me, call this number." The agent handed me a card and got back in his car.

We strapped on seat belts, and I headed the truck back to Midway. As we drove along, Luke asked if I got to hold the baby while visiting the Iversons.

"I did." I held my right hand under his nose and said, "Smell."

He took several deep sniffs and then said, "It smells good."

"It smells like a baby," I corrected.

"If that's what babies smell like, I might want one—eventually."

I felt warm with pleasure and then silly. The fact that Luke might someday want a child didn't have anything to do with me. Cade had never had an interest in parenthood. Since I didn't think I wanted to be a mother, his attitude never bothered me. But Baby Jake had completely changed my perspective, and now I found that a man who liked children was particularly appealing to me.

Luke dragged my attention away from my baby dreams by asking, "So what did Miss Eugenia have to say about the murder case?"

I filled him in on everything—the most startling information being that according to two different sources, his uncle had been meeting a woman at Albany motels. "Miss Eugenia was particularly distressed by this," I told him, "since the murderer fabricating the girlfriend is central to her alternate death theory."

"Maybe the girlfriend *is* the murderer," Luke suggested. "She gained Uncle Foster's confidence by luring him to motels and then pushed him onto the high-voltage coils at the electrical relay plant."

I considered this. "Your uncle was a fairly large man. It's hard to imagine that a woman was able to push him to his death. Or drag him up the hill and throw him over after drugging him first."

Luke nodded in acknowledgment. "My uncle was not only big—he was strong. It's impossible for me to imagine *anyone* forcing or carrying him. I can pretty much guarantee you that he walked up that hill of his own free will."

"I'm glad Miss Eugenia didn't hear you say that," I said. "She's attached to the no-girlfriend part of her theory, but she's *really* attached to the idea that your uncle was dead when he fell onto those electrical coils."

"I'm just stating an opinion," Luke replied. "And on a more pleasant subject, would you let me buy you breakfast at the Flying J?"

I raised an eyebrow. "We're becoming regulars there."

He nodded. "The food is good and the service fast enough that eating breakfast there won't make you late opening the library."

"I'll take you up on breakfast. But the library won't be open today, so it doesn't really matter what time I get there."

"If you're not opening it, why are you going there at all?"

"I'm packing up books. Yesterday was the last day of operation at the current location. We'll be reopening in a couple of weeks at our new location—the old First National Bank building."

Luke whistled. "That's the nicest building in town—or it could be if somebody fixed all those broken windows."

"All fixed," I informed him. "You'll have to come and see what Drake and his construction crews have accomplished in just a few days."

At the mention of Drake's name, his enthusiasm dimmed. "Maybe I'll just wait until you're open for business and come check out a book."

I smiled, but some of the fun left the conversation as I thought of Foster Scoggins and Heaven checking out books on what was to be the last day of his life.

We ate a quick breakfast at the Flying J, and then I dropped Luke off at the salvage yard. He climbed out of the truck and walked around to my window. He leaned in and said, "When you're finished packing up the library, maybe we could go out to dinner."

"I can't let you feed me every meal," I said in a teasing tone that I hoped would take the sting out of my refusal. "And unfortunately I have a business dinner tonight."

"With Drake Langston?"

"I can't give you much credit for that guess," I said, determined to keep things light. "He's the only person I have business with."

He stepped back. "Well, call me when you get home, so I'll know you made it safely."

"I'll have FBI agents and sheriff's deputies driving by my apartment every hour on the hour," I reminded him.

"I know, but I'll still feel better when I've talked to you."

"I'll call," I promised.

I had already put the truck into reverse when I remembered about Parnell and his potentially dangerous situation at the nursing home. So I asked, "Did you talk to the sheriff about your father?"

Luke shook his head. "No, I'm just going to bring him home until things are settled."

My heart skipped a beat. Had he decided to stay in Midway? "What about school?"

"I've hired a live-in nurse to be with my dad while I'm gone. She's stayed with him before, so I know I can trust her to take good care of him."

I was disappointed even though I knew I had no right to be. And I really did want Luke to fulfill his dream. I just didn't want him to leave.

I arrived at the library a few minutes before the time I would normally open. There was no Miss Ida Jean standing impatiently on the porch, and the CLOSING notice I'd taped to the door was fluttering in the morning breeze. Even though we'd only been closed for a day, already it didn't look like a library to me anymore—just a couple of forlorn trailers without purpose.

After I unlocked the front door, I transferred the clothes Reagan had given me to the front seat of my truck. While waiting for Drake's moving crew, I went through my paperback section. I was depositing books that I didn't want to keep personally or transfer to the new library into a garbage bag when the mayor's wife, Francie, walked in.

She seemed annoyed by my presence. "I didn't expect anyone to be here. Drake told Terrance that you were moving out yesterday."

"We closed this library location yesterday," I corrected. "Today Drake's men are coming to pick up the books. They should be here in a little while."

Francie was still frowning, and I wanted badly to point out that the county library system had paid rent on the trailer through the end of the month, and I was perfectly within my rights to use the building until then. But of course I didn't.

Instead I told her, "I'll get out of your way as soon as I can."

Inexplicably, she shrugged and said, "No rush." Then she stood by the front door, fidgeting with the zipper of a hot pink jogging suit that looked new—if not flattering.

"Did you want a book or something?"

She shook her head. "No."

I didn't know what else to offer her, so I just continued tossing tattered paperbacks into the garbage bag.

Finally Francie said, "I guess I'll be going." But instead of reaching for the doorknob, she took a few steps closer to me.

I looked up expectantly.

She cleared her throat and said, "I'm not sure how to say this, but I think there's something you should know."

I prayed she wasn't going to tell me of another extramarital affair Cade had been involved in before our divorce that I was still blissfully unaware of.

Francie relieved me—temporarily—by saying, "I heard that somebody broke into your apartment last night."

"Well, my door was open, and the front porch lightbulb had been broken. But we don't know for sure that anyone actually went into the apartment. Nothing was stolen." Then a horrible thought occurred to me. If Francie Cook knew about the possible break-in, it was just a matter of time before my mother found out. I expressed my concern, and Francie waved a manicured hand.

"I only know about it because of Terrance's police scanner." She zipped and then unzipped her jacket. "I also know that you've been talking with people who had a lot to gain from Drake's land purchase deal and that you're suspicious about the way Foster Scoggins died."

Now my heart was pounding so loud I thought she could surely hear it. Was it possible that Francie knew something important about Foster Scoggins's death? Was I seriously about to solve our murder case?

"Well, because of Terrance's position as mayor of Midway, he's in a lot of meetings where future plans are discussed. And I think you should know that once the two housing developments are completed, Midway will have the necessary tax revenue to create its own police force—just like Haggerty. So instead of depending on the county sheriff's department, we'll have our own police chief and police officers."

"That sounds good," I said.

"Better for some people than for others," she said cryptically.

"Sheriff Bonham will benefit, since he'll be the new police chief?"

Francie nodded. "He has enough years to retire with the county, and then as police chief he'd be making a lot more than he did as sheriff—plus his retirement, not to mention the power and other perks."

"Are you saying that Sheriff Bonham had something to do with Foster Scoggins's death?"

"I'm just saying he has an interest in the land deal that you might not be aware of," Francie corrected me. "And Cade, too, for that matter. He stands to have a big salary increase once the switch takes place and when the sheriff retires in a few years, Cade will get his job as chief."

"I can't believe that either one of them would kill Foster."

Francie put a hand to her temple and rubbed. "I can't really believe it either. But Foster was so stubborn and, well, stupid. I can see how someone who had a lot to gain could have wanted to strangle him. Terrance said he had absolutely no reason for not selling. He just didn't want to."

It was a valid point, and it gave me a slightly different perspective on Foster's possible murder. Not that I thought there was justification—but I did feel a little more sympathetic toward the landowners whom Foster was thwarting.

"I wouldn't have said anything," Francie continued. "But when I heard about the break-in at your apartment, I realized how easy it would be for the sheriff or Cade to do that. And how if you disappeared, they wouldn't have to look very hard to find you, and it would just be one more unexplained tragedy in Midway."

I was speechless. On the surface her remarks seemed ridiculous. But Foster Scoggins was dead, and someone *had* followed me home from the Flying J and had broken my front porch light and opened my apartment door. I knew I couldn't afford to ignore anything. "I'm not sure what to think about all this."

She shrugged. "I thought you should know."

I felt an unexpected surge of gratitude toward the unattractive little woman. "Thanks."

She nodded in reply. Then she turned and hurried out the trailer door.

After Francie left, my mind was spinning. Could there be any truth to what she said? I immediately dismissed the idea of Cade as the guilty party. We'd already established that the murderer was clever, and Cade just isn't all that smart. (I'll use taking his old girlfriend to a drive-in in his hometown as evidence to back this up.) Besides, I didn't want to be the ex-wife of a murderer.

So I concentrated on the possibility that Sheriff Bonham had killed Foster. Who would be in a better position to cover up a murder than the sheriff himself? Maybe he wasn't really planning to kill Foster. Maybe he was just going to scare him—threaten him. But then Foster fell, and he had to come up with the cover-up. I *could* see Cade helping the sheriff cover up a tragic accident. Maybe that's why he had been so willing to help me with my investigation—to control the outcome. And maybe that's why the car that followed me disappeared right before he arrived. And why the Sheriff was resistant to the FBI's involvement.

I was so shaken by these unpleasant thoughts that when the trailer door opened, I let out a little scream. Sloan stepped in, looking startled. "Are you okay?" he asked. It only took him two strides to reach my side. He put one of his muscle-bound arms along my shoulders, serving to increase my heart rate.

"I'm fine," I lied. "You just surprised me."

He looked confused. "Drake told me to bring a crew over to pack up books and transfer them to the new library."

I gave him a shaky laugh. "I was expecting you—I just, well . . ." I gave up trying to explain and waved toward the bookshelves. "You can start anywhere."

He cupped a hand around my arm and said, "If you're sure you're okay?"

"I'm sure."

He didn't seem convinced, but he let his arm drop. He walked over to the door and summoned his moving crew. Three men entered the small space carrying boxes and huge rolls of packing tape. They set to work in an efficient, orderly fashion. I walked around, marking the boxes alphabetically so it would be easier to reshelve books in the new library.

I admired the way Sloan's muscles flexed as he lifted heavy boxes effortlessly. Then I remembered Luke's opinion that whoever murdered his uncle would have had to be very strong. Would Sloan have a reason to kill Foster? Did Drake ask him to do it? Or was I getting completely paranoid? Would I soon be suspecting Miss Ida Jean or my mother of murder?

I couldn't control a shiver, and Sloan must have noticed, because I felt his concerned gaze on me. I gave him the most reassuring smile I could muster and moved on to the next box in need of labeling.

A few minutes later, Sloan came over and pointed at the boxes I'd put in the corner that contained my personal collection. "What about these boxes?" he asked.

I explained that they were some of the first books I'd purchased and therefore had sentimental value. "I don't want them just mixed in with the other books at the new library."

"Do you have someplace to put them at home?"

I thought about my tiny apartment. "No, not really."

"Well, why don't you store them at the library?" he suggested. "You can keep them in a closet or something. But there's no point in cluttering up your place with them."

I didn't see why he cared, but I didn't have the energy to argue. So I nodded. "Fine. Take them."

Sloan and his men had just loaded the last box of books onto their truck when Cade arrived. He was holding a sack of food from Jack's and gave Sloan a suspicious look.

Sloan was not intimidated. "You need anything else, Miss Kennedy?" he asked.

I shook my head. "No, thanks for all your hard work."

He cut his eyes toward Cade. "You gonna be all right here?"

"I'll be fine," I assured him. "Thanks again."

With one last look at Cade, Sloan joined his moving crew and drove the truck toward town.

Once we were alone, Cade glanced around the empty space and said, "This place sure looks different."

I'd felt many things toward Cade over the years—attraction, love, disappointment, betrayal. But I'd never been afraid of him until today, thanks to Francie's veiled accusations. So I kept my eyes averted and murmured, "It's kind of sad."

He put the food on what used to be the circulation desk. "I brought lunch."

My conversation with Francie Cook and my subsequent suspicions about nearly everyone I knew had ruined my appetite, and I didn't think I would be able to swallow anything, but I nodded. "That was nice of you."

Cade unloaded the sack, which contained hamburgers, fries, and an assortment of freshly baked cookies. He ate his food hungrily while I pretended to chew a French fry. He kept looking at me, and I knew he thought I didn't want the food just because he was the one who'd bought it.

Finally he said, "If you eat, I won't tell people you went out to lunch with me."

I put the now-mangled French fry down. "It's not that. I'm just worried about the murder case," I told him honestly. "It's started to seem so much more real, and I guess I'm scared."

He balled up his hamburger wrapper and put it back into the Jack's bag. "I tried to tell you not to get involved. We'll quit asking questions about Foster, let his family bury him, and then you won't have anything to worry about."

This comment didn't help maintain the innocent status I was very anxious to give Cade. "Do you really want someone to get away with murder?" I demanded. "And do you really want to live here in Midway with a killer?"

"What I *really* want is for you to be safe," he replied testily.

"There's no guarantee that the guilty party would leave me alone if I dropped the whole thing right now," I pointed out.

"So you still want to go interview people?" he confirmed.

I nodded. "We've got to solve this case. That's the only way to put an end to it."

We cleaned up our lunch mess, and I locked the door behind us as we left—although this seemed a little silly since the trailers were now completely empty. Cade wanted me to ride in his squad car, and I didn't argue. We spent the rest of the afternoon talking to people who were part of the land sale. At each place we stopped, I hoped to find a suspect better than the ones I already had. But by the time we were heading back to the library to pick up my truck, we hadn't spoken with anyone who was remotely suspicious.

Cade was quiet as we drove, which was unusual. I knew him well enough to realize something was bothering him, and I also knew that he would tell me when he was ready. That moment came as we parked beside my truck in front of what used to be the Midway Library.

"I've got something to say," he began. "And I'll tell you from the start that you're not going to like it—but you're going to have to promise you'll listen if you want me to keep helping you with this case."

I nodded. "I'll listen."

"We've been going around talking with people who had an interest in Drake Langston's land deal. I still think Langston himself is the most likely candidate, but there's someone else we haven't mentioned who has quite a bit to gain."

"Who?"

"Luke Scoggins."

"Luke?" I repeated.

"I was talking to the sheriff, and he said the ownership of the salvage yard reverts to Parnell now that Foster is dead. But with the shape Parnell is in, Luke is running things. So once that land deal goes through, your good friend Luke will be swimming in cash. I figure that's how he plans to pay for that fancy education at Purdue."

"Luke didn't kill anyone," I said with certainty.

"Well, it seems mighty convenient that he's been gone for years, and then right as a land deal that could make the Scogginses rich is about to go up in smoke, Luke returns to Midway. A few days later, old Foster is dead, and Luke has all the money he could ever need."

In the course of all my questioning and investigating I hadn't really ever suspected Luke of any involvement in Foster's death. He'd helped me almost from the first. But looking at it from a different perspective, it could seem that he came back to Midway just for the money. The motive was strong enough. He openly admitted that he wasn't close to Foster and wouldn't grieve over his death. And maybe instead of wanting to help me, he was just monitoring my investigation—as I had suspected Cade of doing, especially after Francie Cook's tip.

The saddest part of all was that for the first time in my life, I had several attractive men showing interest in me at the same time, and now I had reason to be suspicious of them all. Which left me with few people I could trust, let alone date.

"Just be careful," Cade said.

"I will," I promised. I got out of his car, climbed into my truck, and headed back to my apartment so I could prepare for my dinner date with Drake Langston. One of the several murder suspects I was closely associated with.

CHAPTER TWELVE

WHEN I GOT HOME, I carried the clothes Reagan had given me inside. Then I took a quick shower. Once I was clean and my hair was styled, I called Miss Eugenia. After the customary small talk about her sprained ankle and my family, I got down to business.

"Cade and I spent all afternoon interviewing people involved in Drake's land deal," I told her. "And we didn't find anyone with excessive motive or real opportunity. However, while I was cleaning out the library this morning, Francie Cook came by and accused either Sheriff Bonham or Cade or both of killing Foster."

"And what evidence does she have against them?" Miss Eugenia asked.

"No evidence, but she is privy to some inside information and claims that once Drake gets his housing developments finished, Midway will be able to use part of the extra tax revenue to set up a city police department. She said Sheriff Bonham has already verbally accepted the job of police chief—contingent on the deal going through, of course."

"Of course," Miss Eugenia murmured.

"She said he'll make much more than he's making now with the sher-iff's department—and since he'll be able to retire from the county and start drawing retirement too . . . Well, Francie says he stands to make a lot of money—even though he doesn't have any land to sell."

"Do you think her information is accurate?"

"I can't say for sure, but I think so. She seemed concerned."

"And how does she think your ex-husband is involved?"

"Well, Francie said Cade will get a big pay raise too. And when Sheriff Bonham retires in a few years, Cade would become the new police chief."

"Making that big salary and running things the way he wants to without having to take orders from the county." It sounded even worse the way Miss Eugenia put it.

"Right."

"While this might qualify as a good motive, it isn't evidence, and it's hard to believe that either the sheriff or his deputy would kill old Foster over a better job."

I wanted to be relieved, but I couldn't allow myself to be . . . not yet, at least. "Unless they didn't mean to kill him. Maybe they were trying to intimidate him into selling, and somehow Foster died accidentally. Then they are just guilty of the cover-up."

"Now that is a reasonable possibility," she murmured.

"And there's more."

I could almost hear her anticipation. "Tell me."

I hated to, but I did. "When we were driving home, Cade pointed out that Luke has motive for the murders himself."

"Luke Scoggins?"

"Yes. We already knew that when Foster died, ownership of the salvage yard land went to his brother Parnell. What I didn't realize is that because of Parnell's physical condition, Luke has control of the land and the business and any proceeds from the future sale."

"I see."

"I don't know Luke well, but I've spent quite a bit of time with him lately, and I just don't think he would kill his uncle."

"He was trained in guns while in the military," Miss Eugenia said. "And he's probably been faced with the need to shoot people. So killing another person might not seem so bad to him. Especially if that person was an ornery old man who was ruining a perfectly good land deal for absolutely no reason."

"I hate this—being suspicious of everyone," I told her. "Investigating a murder isn't nearly as fun as I thought it would be."

Her cackle came through the telephone line. "That is the downside of murder investigations. You do have to suspect almost everyone."

"At what point do we start zeroing in on the killer instead of adding to our suspect list?" I asked.

Miss Eugenia laughed again. "Soon, I hope. But every case is different, and sometimes we just have to let things run their course. I'm curious about the ownership arrangement that the Scoggins brothers had. You remember my lawyer friend, Whit Owens?"

"I do."

"I think I might ask him to look into the legal end of things."

I hated the idea of investigating Luke, especially when he thought he was helping me investigate other people, but I couldn't deny that some of the circumstances surrounding his return to Midway were suspicious. So I agreed.

Miss Eugenia had me go over the suspect list and insisted on knowing everything that was said during each interview that Cade and I had conducted. I referred to my Murder Book and gave her succinct and detailed descriptions.

"It sounds like the preacher and his wife have a lot to gain from the land deal."

"They do," I confirmed. "But if I accused Brother Jackson and his wife of murder, you'd have another dead body on your hands, because my mother would kill me!"

Miss Eugenia really laughed at this. Apparently I was a regular riot.

"Don't accuse them of anything," she said when she got her laughter under control. "But if you can find an opportunity, talk to one or the other of them again. You'd be surprised what people will divulge in simple conversation—especially if they don't realize you suspect them."

"I did promise to go to church tomorrow with Luke," I said. "But I never meant to actually do it."

"You should!" Miss Eugenia hollered through the phone. "That's a perfect way to get more information from the Jacksons and Luke Scoggins."

"I hate to get my mother's hopes up," I hesitated. "If I go to church, she might think I'm changing my evil ways. And I'm *not* going to remarry Cade. Ever."

"Your mother would be glad to have you at church whatever your reasons are for being there."

I didn't really agree with this. If my mother found out I had lured Luke to church under false pretenses so I could spy on the Jacksons . . . I knew she'd be less than glad. But I didn't even try to argue with Miss Eugenia. "I'll call Luke and see if he's still interested in going to church with me. If he is, I'll do it."

"That's the spirit! Now aren't you going on a date with that dashing Drake Langston tonight?"

"The same Drake Langston who might be Foster's murderer?" I added. "Yes, I am."

"Call me when you get home to let me know what he says."

I promised to do so and ended our conversation. The phone didn't have time to get completely settled in the charger before it rang again. This time it was my mother. She wanted to hear about the afternoon I'd spent with Cade and what I was planning to wear to my dinner date with Drake. She was relieved when I told her Reagan had given me an outfit for the occasion. I finally got her to hang up by reminding her that Drake would be picking me up soon.

While I finished getting ready, I thought about Luke and what I was going to say when I called and asked him to come, of all places, to *church* with me the next day. I was just pulling on the only pair of black pumps I own—boring but hopefully elegant enough—when inspiration struck.

I quickly dialed Luke's number, hoping for the voice mail. But he picked up on the second ring.

"Hey, Kennedy," he said, so I knew he had caller ID.

"Hey," I replied in what I hoped was a casual, friendly, unsuspicious tone. "I was going to see if you were busy in the morning."

"You're addicted to Flying J food and want me to meet you there for breakfast?" He sounded pleased.

I laughed nervously. "I do want to meet you, but I was thinking more like the Midway Baptist Church. My parents attend the traditional services that start at ten o'clock."

"You seriously want to go to church? With me?"

"*Want* is such a strong word," I hedged. "But it would make my mother happy if I came, and I was thinking that while we're there, we might be able to talk with the preacher about finding some foster parents for Heaven so she doesn't have to stay in that juvenile prison."

"That's very kind of you," he said.

I felt like dirt. "So is that a yes?"

"Yes and no," he replied. "Yes, I'll go to church with you, but no, I won't meet you there. I'll pick you up at your apartment promptly at 9:45."

"I'll be waiting," I told him.

I hung up the phone just as I heard tires crunching gravel in the parking lot. I looked out my window to see Drake Langston's Lexus pulling to a stop beside my old truck. I grabbed my purse and hurried outside. After pausing to make sure the porch light was on and the door was closed and locked, I walked down the stairs to meet Drake.

* * *

Drake and I come from completely different worlds, and we didn't know each other well, so I expected the first part of our date to be a little awkward. But he didn't act like a rich guy, and from the moment I got into his car, I was completely at ease. We discussed the plans he had for Midway, which were beyond even the ambitious rumors I'd heard from my mother and Miss Ida Jean. He was so charming and genuine that before we arrived at the restaurant, I was convinced that he couldn't possibly have killed Foster Scoggins.

We ate at an exclusive steak house in Albany. The rolls were tiny but flaky and delicious. What they called a salad was really just a few tidbits of colorful vegetation artistically arranged on a white china plate. The steak was small but perfectly seasoned and so tender it almost melted in my mouth. And dessert was a French torte. (Heavenly.)

Since each course only took a few minutes to eat, there was plenty of time left over to discuss Drake's plans for the new library. Once we had exhausted that subject, Drake surprised me by directing the conversation toward himself.

He began by admitting that his family's wealth was more money than he could ever spend. "The fortune they passed down to me was earned at the expense of helpless children and immigrants in the early 1900s. When I learned our history . . . well, it wasn't a happy discovery, and for a few years I refused to associate myself with my family. I traveled around Europe with only a backpack and worked odd jobs to keep from starving. Finally I realized that I couldn't do anything to change the past. But what I could do was take the money my ancestors had given me and use it to help people. So that's what I do."

"And you do it very well," I said with sincerity.

He smiled. "Thank you. I know people speculate about my motives for these town renovations. But despite what they think, I really do want to improve the quality of life. It gives me great satisfaction to take something tired and hopeless and turn it into something useful and beautiful. And my personal reward is that in every town I remake, I ask them to name the library after my father."

"What was his name?"

"Willard Langston."

"So will that be the name of our new library?"

He nodded. "The mayor and town council have already approved it. The Willard Langston Memorial Library."

I had to smile. "Pretty soon you'll have libraries named after your father all over the country."

"That's my plan," he admitted. "Kind of a way to pay tribute to my dad and monitor my progress at the same time. It's not about the money. Sometimes I make a profit off of the projects—usually I just break even. But it's what gives my life meaning. It makes me feel like when I leave this earth, I'll leave something worthwhile behind—hope, a better future, beauty."

"So it looks like everything is going to work out with the land deal in Midway?"

"It looks that way."

I knew I couldn't pass up the opportunity to further my murder investigation. "I'm curious about something. Why do you make the land deals dependent on all prospective land sellers cooperating?"

"If I don't own all the land before I start, it leaves me open to too much liability later," he explained. "I might build a beautiful subdivision around a parcel someone doesn't want to sell to me, and then later they could sell to someone who wants to put in a strip mall or worse—a strip club . . ."

I laughed. "I see your point."

He told me about some of his previous projects and others he planned for the future. His voice was hypnotic, his sincerity irresistible, and his desire to leave an honorable legacy behind so noble. By this point, he had me completely under his spell. I felt honored that he would allow me this personal glimpse of himself.

As we drove back to my apartment, he turned the tables and asked questions about my life. Usually I'm resistant to any effort to make me share my feelings. But with Drake I was able to discuss my divorce and my family more honestly than I'd ever done before. He walked me up the stairs to my front door, and I was pleased to note that the porch light was still on and the door securely locked.

I unlocked the door and, although I was embarrassed by my meager living conditions, invited Drake inside.

He thanked me but shook his head. "I'd love to spend more time with you, but I need to get to my hotel and finish up a few things before tomorrow." He looked and sounded regretful. Then he gently kissed the back of my hand. It was an odd but wonderful experience that I doubt could ever be replicated.

I didn't know what to say, and fortunately he didn't seem to expect a response.

"I'll see you on Monday at the new library."

I nodded and watched him descend my stairs and climb back into his car. With a little wave, he was gone.

After Drake left, I felt dazed. He was such a presence that his absence seemed to leave a huge hole.

I kicked off the boring and uncomfortable pumps and then dug through Reagan's discards until I found a pink sundress that I could wear to church the next day. I ironed it, according to my mother's exacting standards.

Because dinner had been more attractive than filling, I got what was left of my mother's peach cobbler out of the refrigerator and had just settled down on the couch to eat it when there was a knock on my door.

I stood on my tiptoes to look through the peephole. I expected to see Cade, but instead I saw Luke Scoggins standing on my front porch. I opened the door.

"I was going to call you," I assured him.

"I'm sorry to be impatient," he replied. "But after you were followed and had your apartment vandalized . . . I just couldn't wait any longer to be sure you were okay."

I waved a hand from my head to my toes. "As you can see, I'm fine!"

Unlike Drake, who didn't have time to come in, Luke looked over my shoulder into my small living room in an obvious if silent plea. I pushed any concerns I had about him being a murderer to the back of my mind and stepped aside to let him in.

"Would you like some cobbler?" I pointed at the plate I had left on the coffee table. "I'll share."

"No, thanks."

"How about a Pepsi?"

He nodded. "I'll take you up on that. It's the best drink in the world."

You see why I didn't want to suspect him of murder? I got us each a Pepsi out of my refrigerator, and we sat on the couch and watched the local news in companionable silence. I've always thought that was the test of a good friendship. You can make small talk with just about anyone—but there are only a few people you can sit comfortably quiet with.

After the news ended, Luke stood. "It's getting late so I guess I'd better go."

I smiled. "We both have to get up early tomorrow for our church date."

I walked him to the door, and he turned to face me. I looked into his beautiful hazel eyes that I had never noticed in all the years we went to school together. Then my gaze dropped to the little lump in his nose where it had been broken and finally to his full lips—just as they began a slow, purposeful descent toward mine.

Our first kiss was sweet and undemanding. When it ended, I opened my eyes to see him watching me solemnly.

"I know that you couldn't ever be seriously interested in a Scoggins," he said.

I was too stunned to reply.

"I know this closeness we've developed is just temporary—because of your interest in my uncle's death," he continued. "And I probably shouldn't have kissed you . . . but I couldn't help myself."

"I'm not a pampered little princess anymore," I finally managed to say. "And you're definitely not a helpless little boy." I left out "dirty" and "neglected" on purpose, but I knew he was thinking it too. In an effort to distract him from old and painful memories, I put my hands behind his neck and pulled him close again. By the time our second kiss ended, I didn't care if he'd killed his uncle.

He seemed shaken, too, and gently disengaged my hands from behind his neck so he could put a little distance between us.

"You're still rebounding from a divorce, and I'm just back from a long stint in Iraq," he said as if I didn't already know these things. "So what we feel at this moment may not last."

"If you keep talking nonsense, you're going to force me to kiss you again!" I warned.

His laugh was a little shaky as he said, "Don't encourage me."

I laughed too. He was a man who knew the right thing to say.

"What I mean is—if there's any chance for you and me . . ." He twirled his finger in the small space that separated us. "I have to go to school, get my degree, and be . . . better."

I put a hand on his chest. "I like you the way you are."

He shook his head. "I'd never feel worthy to be with someone like you unless I improved myself."

I started to object again, but he interrupted. "I have to put as much distance between myself and the previous Scogginses as possible."

Using the hand I already had on his chest, I traced the pocket of his T-shirt. "You *want* to be with someone like me?" I whispered.

"Exactly like you," he replied with a quiver in his voice. "When the time is right. When Cade Burrell is a distant memory and I'm a self-made man."

I moved my fingers up to his lips. "That sounds like it could take a long time."

He caught my hand in his and pulled my fingers away from his mouth. "But the wait will be worth it."

It was clear that our possible romance was not going to go any further that night. I was mildly disappointed and at the same time wildly encouraged. Was it possible there was a meaningful relationship for me and Luke at some point in the future? Had I really found the man of my dreams in a salvage yard? Would my mother survive if I married a Scoggins?

At this point there was a knock on the door, and Luke opened it. An FBI agent, looking a little sheepish, was standing on my front porch. "Sorry if I'm interrupting," he said. "But I'm making my rounds, and when I saw your car, I had to be sure Miss Killingsworth was okay."

"You're not interrupting anything," I said a little too quickly.

"And I'm glad you're being thorough." Luke added. "It's time for me to go, anyway."

He saw the disappointment on my face and gave me a smile almost as sweet as the kisses we'd shared. "But I'll be here in the morning to pick you up for church."

I smiled back, and for the first time in my life I wanted to shout, "Hallelujah!"

* * *

The next morning while I was getting ready for church, I kept trying to think of the best way to present Luke to my mother. I considered and discarded several approaches—like the chance to save his soul (which I knew would appeal to my mother, but I wasn't sure she'd consider soul-saving worth sacrificing one of her children and her standing in the community).

I considered reminding her that there was a recent death in the Scoggins family and hope that she'd take pity on a grieving young man. (But that was a huge stretch since Luke openly admitted he hadn't been close to his uncle.) Finally inspiration struck. I would remind my mother of Luke's lonely childhood, his abandonment, and then I would tell her that he thought she was nice *and* a good mother. That should be enough to make her overlook, at least temporarily, the fact that Luke was a Scoggins.

I put on the sundress I had ironed for my return to church with Luke at my side. As I checked my closet for appropriate footwear, I came face-to-face with what most women already know—the more you improve your wardrobe, the more you see need for additional improvement. I had piles of new clothes—pants, shirts, jackets, and dresses. But now all my shoes looked old and shabby.

I was tempted to wear my only recent footwear purchase—the cute little black sandals I'd worn to Foster's viewing. But if I wore black shoes to church after Easter, it would put my mother in a bad mood, and that's the last place I wanted her to be when I started my learn-to-love-Luke campaign. So I settled for a pair of white flats that had seen better days but at least were not a breach of etiquette.

Luke arrived five minutes early wearing his funeral suit and looking magnificent. I didn't wait for him to knock but stepped out on the porch, and we stood there a little awkwardly for a few seconds. Last night we had kissed—twice—but he made it clear that he wasn't ready for a real relationship—at least not just yet. So I wasn't sure how friendly to be in my greeting.

He settled things by leaning down and giving me a quick kiss on the cheek. "Good morning," he said.

I smiled. "That remains to be seen."

We walked down the steps and spoke briefly with the FBI agent who would be following me for the day. Then Luke offered to drive and I accepted. On the way to Midway Baptist Church, we discussed how to handle our grand entrance. If we went in as soon as we arrived, we would have no choice but to speak to hundreds of curious congregation members as we made our way to my family's pew—which of course my mother had made sure was right in the front. Or we could wait in the car until just before the service began. This plan would mean no conversation—since everyone else would already be seated. But all eyes would be on us as we made our way to the front of the sanctuary.

Both choices were equally horrific to me, so I let Luke choose. He picked going in at the last moment. "I'm used to stares," he explained. "Polite small talk is much worse."

So once we got to the church, he parked the Torino in a quiet corner, and we waited until we heard the organ music change from prelude to the opening strains of "It Is Well with My Soul." We got out of the car and started toward the church.

As planned, the grounds and foyer were deserted. We were able to go straight through and into the sanctuary without saying a word to anyone. The long walk up the aisle, passing row after row of curious onlookers, was daunting. But I clung to Luke's arm, and finally we made it to the Killingsworth pew.

Fortunately my father was sitting on the edge. He saw us and stood to let us in without even raising an eyebrow. My mother paled slightly, but years of good manners prevented her from a more noticeable reaction. She scooted over and made room for us just as the choir began singing.

My mother waited until the choir's second number, a rousing version of "Stand Up, Stand Up for Jesus," when the entire congregation rose to their feet and joined in the singing, to lean over and hiss, "What are you doing?"

"I'm bringing a lost soul to church," I whispered back. "And you'd better be nice to him. He thinks you're the picture of Christian charity and the world's best mother all rolled into one."

This took her aback. "He said that?"

It was a loose translation, but I felt justified in nodding.

She processed this and then said, "Well, that's mighty sweet, although I'm far from perfect. But I do love the Lord and my children. And of course Luke is welcome to come to church with us anytime. And be sure to tell him he's invited to dinner afterwards."

Then something unexpected happened. I felt a sudden surge of love and gratitude toward my mother that I didn't know I possessed. She *had* tucked me in at night and made cute little sandwiches for my lunch and attended all my boring elementary school programs and sat through countless softball games even though sports are incomprehensible to her. She had ironed my clothes and helped me learn spelling words and taught me to be polite to cranky old ladies. She had been there with me every step of the way, and—whether I agreed with her or not—I knew that she always had my best interests at heart.

All my life I'd thought that what really mattered to my mother was keeping tarnish from our family name and maintaining her good standing in the community. But she was willing not only to tolerate Luke's presence at our family's pew, but also to welcome him there. And she had invited him to dinner afterward—regardless of the effect this might have on the social status she had worked her entire life to achieve.

Somehow my mother seemed to understand. She leaned over and whispered, "I love you, dear." The song ended, and we all sat back down.

As the preacher walked to the podium, I saw Luke watching me and whispered, "That song always gets to me."

He looked bewildered but didn't ask any questions.

"And my mother says you have to come over for Sunday dinner right after church."

I felt him stiffen and knew he was about to decline.

So I hurried to add, "Please! Your presence will keep her from itemizing my shortcomings throughout the meal."

His arm that was touching mine relaxed slightly, and although I could still sense reluctance, he nodded. "Okay. But just to save you from having to listen to that *long* list."

I cut my eyes toward him and feigned offense. "Thanks."

He smiled. "What are friends for?"

I felt the preacher's gaze on us frequently during his sermon, which I believe was about a Christian's duty to be optimistic, but I can't swear to it. When the choir began their last song, my mother whispered, "Would you like for me to find you and Luke a Sunday school class to attend, or do you want to wait at the house until we get there?"

A Sunday school class would require personal interaction—possibly with people who had made fun of Luke when we were all kids—and would therefore be uncomfortable for both of us. My mother probably suspected this and was giving us an easy way out. I took it gratefully.

"I think we'll just wait at the house. Is there anything I can do to help you get dinner ready?"

"If you'll peel the potatoes, we can eat sooner." Then she pointed to a side door. "After you speak with the preacher and tell him what a nice sermon he gave today, you can go out that way and avoid the crowds."

I shot her a look of gratitude. Then I took Luke by the hand and pulled him toward the preacher. With any luck, we could question Brother Jackson about Drake's land deal, ask if he knew anyone who would be willing to be Heaven's foster parents, and then get away before the other congregation members could start questioning *us*.

"Good morning, Kennedy," Brother Jackson said with a smile when we reached him. "May I say that it was a particular pleasure to see you with your parents on the Killingsworth pew during services today."

I responded with, "That was the best sermon I've heard lately."

His smiled widened, and I knew he was aware of the fact that I hadn't heard any sermons in over a year. "Coming from you, Kennedy, that is quite a compliment." Then he turned to Luke. "Mr. Scoggins, we're honored to have you here and hope you'll come and worship with us again soon."

"Thank you," Luke replied—polite but not what I'd call friendly.

"And we have a grief counselor to meet with people who have lost loved ones. I'd be glad to set you up an appointment."

"I'm doing fine," Luke said. "But my niece, Heaven, needs a foster home, and we were wondering if some of your church members might be willing to take her."

I felt bad that I hadn't been the one to pose this question—especially since it was the main reason I'd coerced Luke into coming.

Brother Jackson frowned. Obviously he'd met Heaven, and no doubt the child had made a lasting negative impression on him. "I will call an emergency meeting of our child outreach program," he promised despite any reservations he might have had. "Maybe we can locate some candidates."

"We'd appreciate that," I told the preacher, just like I was a member of the Scoggins family.

"Where can I reach you if I'm able to find someone?" he asked, looking from me to Luke as if unsure who to address.

"We'll be at my parents' house this afternoon," I answered. "We're headed there now—to give my mom a hand with dinner. If you don't reach us there, you can leave a message, and we'll get back with you."

The preacher nodded.

"Mother says you're planning a trip to the Holy Land," I ventured bravely, even though I could hear a crowd approaching from behind. "I know you and Miss Zelda must be so excited."

"It will be a great blessing in our lives to be able to walk where the Savior walked and improve our personal relationship with Him."

Surely someone who had killed to get their plane fare wouldn't want to go to Jerusalem to commune with the spirit of Jesus. I felt guilty for ever suspecting that Brother Jackson and Miss Zelda could have been involved in Foster's murder.

Brother Jackson glanced over my shoulder. "I need to speak to some other folks now, but I'll be in touch."

As we moved out through the side door, I realized that I had been holding Luke's hand during our entire conversation with the preacher. I wasn't sure this was sending the correct signals, but it was too late to fix that.

CHAPTER THIRTEEN

WHEN WE WALKED INTO THE house where generations of Killingsworths had lived, I saw Luke looking around in near awe. I tried to see my childhood home through his eyes. The old-fashioned architecture might seem charming to someone who hadn't spent years dealing with the constant upkeep. The well-used furniture, homemade curtains, and needlepoint throw pillows might seem homey. The zillion family pictures everywhere—on the walls, on tables, on shelves—might appeal to someone who wasn't in most of them.

"This is just like I expected it to be," he told me finally. "The perfect family home."

"My mom has to work constantly to maintain it. Something always needs to be repainted or refinished or replaced. Old houses are a pain."

"Old houses are full of history and memories. You should be glad you belong to something like this."

"I love my family, and I guess I love this house. But if I ever have a home of my own, I want it to be brand new. I'll gladly sacrifice history and character for doors that close and appliances that work."

He smiled. "Boring."

We settled at the counter in the kitchen with a big bowl of rinsed potatoes between us. I got out two paring knives, and while we peeled potatoes, I warned him about my sisters, who would certainly be coming to dinner.

"Do you remember Reagan and Madison from school?" I asked.

"I remember them. They were both beautiful and always being crowned queen of something."

"They're still beautiful," I conceded, "although their days of being crowned are in the past. Reagan is pretty normal. She married a guy from Macon named Chase, and they wisely decided to live there. It's close enough to visit here when they want to but far enough away to keep my mother out of their daily lives. They have a daughter named Dallas who is two, I think."

"You think her name is Dallas or you think she's two?"

"I know her name is Dallas, and I think she's two," I clarified. "My lack of detailed knowledge probably makes you think I'm a bad aunt. I'll admit that I haven't been all that into kids until lately."

"Until you met the little foster baby?"

A weight settled on my heart when Luke referred to Baby Jake in such a generic way. I wanted to insist that he be called by his name . . . but that was silly since "Jake" was just temporary. So I nodded. "Yes. The Iversons' foster baby changed everything for me. I know it doesn't make sense."

Luke shrugged. "It makes sense to me. You finally met the right baby."

I smiled and dragged my thoughts away from Jake. Then I cleared my throat and continued with the description of my family. "Reagan's husband doesn't always come to dinner with the family after church on Sundays. She says it's because he has to work, but I think he dislikes all the noise and confusion that's a part of any gathering including my oldest sister, Madison, and her family."

Luke put one neatly peeled potato into the bowl of water and picked up another one. "She has noisy kids?"

"She has little demons in human form."

He smiled, so I did too, although I wasn't really kidding. "Heaven is my niece," he reminded me. "So I doubt your sister's kids can impress me with their bad behavior."

I'd only spent a few minutes with Heaven, but I knew it was true. Luke was no stranger to ill-mannered children. "You'll be fine," I said with confidence. "Major is the oldest—he's six. Miles is four, and Maggie is two."

"You seem pretty confident about their ages," Luke teased.

"Madison has a baby every two years, so that makes it easy for me," I explained.

"And she made it even easier to remember their names by naming them all something that starts with M," he pointed out.

I hung my head. "My family has a sickness when it comes to naming children. It has to be done according to a theme."

"That sounds kind of cute."

"It's not. My grandparents named their children after plants. Mother's name is Iris. Her sisters are Lily and Rose. They have a brother named Forest."

"It could have been worse," Luke teased. "He could have been named Kudzu."

"Thank goodness they didn't have more kids," I muttered.

"Your parents were partial to U.S. presidents?"

"And Madison took the theme sickness a narcissistic step further by using only names that begin with the same letter as hers."

Luke smiled. "I wonder what Reagan will name her next child."

"Brooklyn wouldn't be too bad."

"There's always Atlanta or Chicago . . ."

I rolled my eyes. "Anyway, as bad as Madison's kids are, the one you really need to watch out for is Madison herself. She's the oldest sister and bosses everyone around. She's a pain under normal circumstances, but now that she's pregnant with demon number four, she thinks she can say anything and then blame it on hormones."

"I'll be careful around her," Luke promised. "Isn't she a Mormon now?"

Once again I was surprised by Luke's knowledge of our family. "Yes, she joined their church in Albany right before she married Jared. My mother was unhappy at first, but when she learned that Mormons believe in Jesus just like everybody else, she felt better. And when she found out that they encourage large families—which meant more grandchildren for her—she stopped complaining altogether. Besides—they were married, so what could she do?"

"Nothing to be done at that point."

I put a potato not quite as well-peeled as Luke's into the bowl. Then I frowned. "Do you have potato-peeling experience?"

"I peeled a few potatoes while I was in the Marines." He looked around the old kitchen. "But I've never enjoyed it so much before."

"Did you enjoy being in the Marines?"

"For the most part. I liked the structure—knowing what to expect. I didn't like the rules and lack of freedom. I liked feeling that I had purpose: helping to protect and defend the American way. I hated being in Iraq."

"What made you decide to leave the military?"

"I felt like I had done my duty and gained what I could from the Marines. It was time to move on."

"And get an education, now that you know you're smart?"

He grinned. "Yeah, that."

He put another perfectly peeled potato into the bowl. "So tell me about your parents."

"There's not much to tell," I replied. "My dad works for the post office and repairs old cars in his spare time. And my mom is a true homemaker—not just a housewife. She devotes all her time to this old house and her family—which sounds like torture to me, but she loves it. Seriously, she sings while she cleans."

His expression turned dreamy. "She cooks?"

"Constantly," I confirmed. "And she does everything the old-fashioned, hard way. For instance—today we're having fried chicken. Anyone else would have bought a bucket of KFC, but she spent hours soaking raw chicken parts in buttermilk and then rolled them in some secret concoction of flour and spices and finally fried them in a huge pot full of hot grease. Can you believe that?"

"I'll bet her fried chicken is delicious."

I nodded. "It is—as you'll soon find out. And it's not just cooking and cleaning—she beautifies. She can take an old Coke bottle and some dead flowers and make an attractive centerpiece. It's amazing."

"Your parents have been married for a long time, and they're still happy together?"

I had to think about this for a second. "I wouldn't call my parents' relationship *romantic*," I said finally. "But they do seem happy. My father likes to fix things, and my mother wants a lot of things fixed, so it works out. They started going steady in like the third grade and to my knowledge, their hearts never faltered."

"You look a lot like your mother," he observed, as Drake Langston had done a few days before.

"Thank you," I replied, "although I have more in common with my father. I curse when I clean, I can't even make edible microwave dinners, and if I put beautiful flowers in a nice vase, they look like something I threw toward the garbage can and missed."

Luke smiled. "I'm sure that's an exaggeration."

I raised an eyebrow. "I'll demonstrate my flower-arranging skills for you sometime and let you decide."

He leaned a little closer. "I'll look forward to that."

I tried to ignore my accelerated heart rate as I said, "I can fix things, though. Like last month when my carburetor was acting up. I got a book from a neighboring library—one that actually has a budget and can buy good books—and with a little help from an online repair forum, I fixed my truck. My mother was horrified, of course. She said it was bad enough that I drive an old pickup truck, but she was afraid if people saw me working under the hood—actually performing repairs—they might think I'm 'manly.'"

Before Luke could respond to this, my parents arrived from church. My mother joined the dinner preparations, and my father surprised me by sitting in a chair near the table. Usually on Sundays he changed out of his church clothes and went straight out to his workshop until time to eat. I realized that he was staying to make Luke feel more comfortable, and I smiled at him to show my gratitude.

Mother tied on an apron, efficiently diced the potatoes we'd peeled, and put them in a pot to boil. She assigned Luke and me to set the table while she reprised her Sunday school lesson for our benefit. The sermon summary ended when Reagan and Dallas arrived. Introductions were made, during which Reagan stared at Luke in bewilderment.

Finally she asked, "Are you related to the salvage yard Scogginses?"

He nodded. "I'm Parnell's son."

This didn't really seem to clarify things for Reagan. She just frowned and said, "Oh."

I never thought I'd actually be glad to see Madison, but since her entrance put a stop to this awkward exchange, I was thrilled when she walked in. And the news got better—her kids were sick so she'd left them home with Jared.

Madison didn't seem surprised by Luke's presence, and this meant that she and my mother had been talking about me, which I didn't like. But before I could dwell on this, Madison began itemizing the miseries associated with late pregnancy. I was afraid Luke would run for the door, but he didn't.

My mother placed the food in the center of the table and then instructed us to gather around. As was customary, we held hands for the saying of grace. I was pleasantly situated between Luke, whose hand was warm and a little rough, just like a man's should be, and Dallas, whose hand was warm and soft, just like a little girl's hand should be. For the first time in my life, I hated for a prayer to end.

We had just started serving our plates when the doorbell rang. Daddy went to answer it and a few seconds later returned with Brother Jackson by his side. My mother was a little flustered and very flattered when she saw the preacher.

"Oh, Brother Jackson!" she gasped. "What a wonderful surprise. Won't you sit down and eat with us?"

"It smells delicious, but I can't stay," the preacher declined politely. "I just need to speak with Kennedy and Luke for a minute."

I saw the curiosity on Mother's face and the wariness in Daddy's eyes. My sisters exchanged a speculative look.

Brother Jackson noticed as well and clarified. "It's regarding Luke's niece, Heaven."

"You can say whatever you need to in front of my family," I told him.

The preacher seemed hesitant, and when he delivered his news, I could understand why.

"With the help of our Child Outreach Committee, we contacted almost every member of our congregation today and asked if they'd be willing to take in Heaven, even temporarily, but . . . well . . . no one is available."

Luke smiled grimly. "Heaven's reputation preceded her."

"We do appreciate your help, though," I added lest the preacher feel we didn't think he put forth enough effort in Heaven's behalf.

"What about Heaven?" my mother asked.

Luke succinctly summarized the child's situation.

When he was finished, my mother asked, "Can't she stay with you, Luke? After all, you're her uncle."

Luke shook his head. "I tried, but the court said no. And anyway, I'm leaving for school soon."

"Well, that's a shame," my mother said.

"What about the Iversons?" I blurted without thinking. "They're already approved as foster parents."

"You really want to turn Heaven loose on that nice little family?" Luke asked.

I pictured Baby Jake and shook my head. "No. That probably wouldn't work." Then a thought occurred to me. I had some free time and, thanks to Madison, plenty of experience dealing with undisciplined children. "What do you have to do to be approved as a foster parent?"

"You fill out an application," Brother Jackson answered. "Then you meet with a DHR caseworker and submit to a home inspection."

I thought about my small apartment over the Midway Store and Save office. "What are the home requirements?"

"It varies depending on the age of the child," the preacher said. "Do you know someone who might qualify?"

"I was thinking of myself," I said. The stunned looks I received from my family were insulting, but I pressed on. "Eventually I would like to foster newborns, like Kate Iverson does. But if I go ahead and apply now, maybe I could keep Heaven for a few weeks until something more permanent can be found for her."

Luke looked uncomfortable, and my family members seemed incapable of speech.

Finally Brother Jackson broke the silence by saying, "It can take months to get approved. And before you accept responsibility for a troubled child, you might want to spend a little time with her and be sure you're really up to the duties of parenthood—even on a temporary basis." He turned to Luke. "Can Heaven leave the juvenile care facility for short periods of time?"

Luke nodded. "Heaven called yesterday and said she can leave on Sundays with an approved family member, which apparently I am. She wants to see my dad, so I figured I'd go get her this afternoon. We can visit my father, and then I can buy her an ice-cream cone or something."

The preacher addressed me. "Kennedy, you should go with Luke and get to know Heaven before you start filling out applications with DHR."

I had no objection to spending more of my afternoon with Luke, so I shrugged casually and said, "Okay."

"Then next week maybe the two of you can bring Heaven with you to our Sunday services." The preacher looked completely innocent, but I wondered if he was manipulating the situation to get us to church two weeks in a row.

"And she can come over here for Sunday dinner after church," my mother offered generously.

"That's very kind," Luke began in a tone that indicated he was going to decline.

"Please," Mother pleaded. "Let us help the poor little thing."

Heaven was not the helpless child my mother apparently envisioned, and I was about to point this out when Madison said, "Bring her! Major will enjoy having someone closer to his age to play with."

I was surprised by Madison's support of Heaven initially, but after some consideration I figured she was just jumping at the chance to have a child present at our weekly family gathering who was worse than her own.

My father put the subject to rest by saying, "There's plenty of time to decide all that." Then he stood beside my mother and shook hands with the preacher. "It was good of you to come by, Brother Jackson. Now we'll let you get home to your dinner."

The preacher gratefully took this opportunity to escape and moved toward the door. Mother trailed behind him and returned a few minutes later alone.

"That Brother Jackson is such a wonderful man," she said.

"He's a good one," my father agreed.

Madison turned her attention to me. "Were you serious about becoming a foster parent?"

"Nothing you could have said would have shocked me more," Reagan contributed.

My feelings were hurt, but I tried to hide it. "Why? You don't think I can take care of a child?"

"It's not that I don't think you can," Reagan said. "I just didn't think you'd *want* to."

"I didn't think you even liked kids," Madison concurred.

I ignored this chance to point out how Madison's unruly brood had contributed to my lack of interest in children and said simply, "I just want to help."

"That's very commendable of you, dear," Mother said. "Now let's eat."

I got the impression that she didn't take my interest in foster parenting seriously, and I would have pursued the subject if Luke hadn't been our dinner guest.

Once everyone was served and eating, my father asked about the changes that were being made to the old bank building to transform it into our new library. I cheered up considerably while discussing that pleasant topic.

When I finished the detailed description, Mother said, "I wonder what they're going to do with the trailers that have been housing the library."

"Francie said they are trying to find new renters," I reported. "She came by yesterday morning and showed me pictures of the new nose she wants to purchase."

Daddy looked up from his dinner. "I thought she already had one."

My sisters giggled, and even Luke smiled at the joke.

"Apparently she wants a surgically improved one," I replied.

"I've never seen anybody so obsessed with their appearance," my mother remarked.

I looked at my sisters, who, while naturally beautiful, were both very vain, with my mother not very far behind them. My father's eyes met mine briefly, and I knew he was thinking the same thing. But he didn't comment on the fact. Instead he turned to Luke and asked, "So you're headed off to college?"

When the subject of Luke's education had been exhausted, it was time for dessert. We moved out onto the back porch and ate homemade ice cream. After Luke had finished his second helping, my dad invited him to come out and see his workshop. Luke politely accepted, which left me with my mother and sisters. I tensed, waiting for them to start asking personal questions. But instead Reagan stood and lifted Dallas, who had fallen asleep, from the high chair.

"I might as well go check on Chase," she said. "Dallas can finish her nap on the way home and then be ready to play with her daddy."

"I hate for you to leave so soon," Mother protested. "You could put her in the baby bed in the guest room."

Reagan yawned. "I would if Chase had come with us, but I don't want him home alone on Sunday afternoon."

My mother offered a few more weak protests but finally hugged Reagan and the sleeping Dallas and watched as they walked to the driveway. It came as no surprise when Miss Ida Jean stepped around the corner, conveniently watering her lawn just while we were eating ice cream.

My mother spotted our neighbor and insisted that she join us. Miss Ida Jean made a show of not wanting to intrude, but eventually she allowed herself to be convinced. "I really shouldn't eat ice cream since I haven't had any dinner yet."

I looked away, refusing to play along with this embarrassingly obvious charade. But Mother kindly offered Miss Ida Jean some of the leftovers from our meal.

As Mother led Miss Ida Jean to the kitchen, she said to Madison and me, "I'm going to go and get Miss Ida Jean something to eat. Just sit out here and enjoy the nice weather and each other's company."

I didn't really want to listen to Madison discuss her ailments, but I *really* didn't want to be in the kitchen with Miss Ida Jean. I looked hopefully toward my father's workshop, but the men were nowhere in sight. "It's a beautiful day, and I don't get to spend much time with Madison anymore."

I saw the look of pleasure on my sister's face and felt guilty that my words weren't more sincere.

After a few minutes of awkward silence, I started searching for a topic of conversation. I came up with, "So what's wrong with your kids?"

Madison burst into tears. "They aren't sick," she admitted. "Major punched Emily Iverson during church today, and I was so mad that I told him he couldn't come over here."

Even for Major, hitting a girl was shocking, and I couldn't control a gasp. "Why did he punch Emily?"

"He said she was sitting in his chair."

Mormons have some peculiar religious procedures, so I had to ask, "Do children have assigned seats at your church?"

"Of course not." She put a hand up to rub her temples. "He just wanted to sit in a particular chair. It's his favorite. Emily knew he liked that chair, but she sat in it anyway. So he said that because she had eyes and teeth, he had the right to hit her. It makes no sense. Obviously I'm a terrible mother."

Guilt washed over me as I remembered the kicking incident from last week's Sunday dinner when I'd quoted the Bible about "an eye for an eye and a tooth for a tooth." No doubt that was where Major had gotten his justification for punching Emily Iverson. I knew I should admit at least partial responsibility for his bad behavior, but before I could, Madison had moved on.

"I was so upset," she told me. "I apologized to Kate over and over. She said it was okay, but I know she thinks Major is a monster."

I had suspicions myself, so I wasn't sure what to say here.

"Jared said I needed some time away from the kids. He told me to come over for Sunday dinner alone while he fed the kids a sandwich and put them down for naps." More tears welled up in her eyes and slipped over her cheeks. "He probably just wanted some time away from me. And who can blame him? Look at me!" She waved to encompass herself. "I'm a gross, swollen human incubator."

I thought that Madison was a very cute pregnant person, and I told her so. "Jared isn't trying to get away from you. He's trying to give you a break from Major. You know Jared loves you and wants to be with you."

I intended my words to reassure Madison, but they had the opposite effect. The tears increased until she was sobbing in earnest.

I stood. "I'm going to go get Mother."

She grabbed my arm. "No! I can't let Mother know any of this! Why do you think I'm talking to *you*?!"

That question had occurred to me several times since our conversation had begun, and I could come up with no reasonable answer. "When you're this upset, you need Mother."

"I'm not just upset—I'm scared. And Mother is the last person I want to tell."

"Tell what?"

She bit her lip. "I think I'm having marital problems."

Now I understood. Madison wanted to talk with someone who had experience in this department—and since she'd been with me at the drive-in . . . "You *think* you're having marital problems?"

"Well, Jared is never home anymore," Madison divulged.

This did raise a red flag of concern. "Where is he?"

"His job is very demanding," she said around a new wave of sniffles. "I was used to not seeing him much during the week. But lately he's been taking weekend shifts too. Sometimes the kids are asleep when he leaves in the morning and back in bed when he gets home at night—seven days a week."

Jared was a pharmacist and made pretty good money as far as I knew. However, they had just built a new house, and Madison was always trading in her car for the latest model, and her fingers were always manicured, her hair always highlighted, her clothes always stylish . . .

"Maybe he has to work that much to afford you!" I suggested.

The tears dried up, and Madison gave me a blank stare. "Do you really think that's it?"

"It's a good possibility."

Madison considered this. "I hope it's that simple," she whispered finally. "But why wouldn't he just tell me if I'm spending too much money?"

I shrugged. "He wants you to be happy."

She swiped at the tears on her cheeks. "I was afraid that Jared just didn't feel romantic about me anymore . . . since I'm always pregnant."

I held up a hand to stop her. "I cannot have this conversation. Your romantic relationship with Jared is private."

"If I can't talk to you, who will I talk to?"

"Talk to Jared."

"He won't understand."

"Then hire a shrink."

"You just told me I need to be less expensive!"

She had a point, but I contended, "A psychiatrist for you now would be cheaper in the long run. If you tell me personal stuff, eventually we'll both need a shrink."

Madison had to laugh, but a few more tears welled up in her eyes. "Sometimes I just feel totally . . . insufficient. There's so much to do with laundry and meals. I'm trying to potty-train Maggie and teach Miles his colors, and Major struggles with reading." She fixed me with a penetrating stare. "Do you think I have too many children?"

"I think you have a lot of children," I replied carefully. Then I pointed at her bulging midsection. "Or you will when this one is born. Is there a rule requiring Mormons to have a certain number of kids?"

Madison shook her head. "There's no rule."

The solution seemed simple to me. "If you're overwhelmed, just don't have any more children."

"But what about the ones I already have?"

"You *are* going to have to take care of them," I conceded.

"You might find this strange, but I'm not having all these children just for the fun of it. I believe it's what God wants me to do."

"Why does God want you to have a bunch of kids?" I was honestly curious.

"I believe that all of God's children deserve a chance to come to earth. There are lots of spirits waiting in heaven." She pointed up in case I'd forgotten where God lives. "They're waiting to come here. If I refuse them a place in my family, they might be born in a third-world country where they'll starve to death. And it will be my fault!"

"You can't invite all the babies left in heaven to your house."

She smiled. "Of course not. We're counseled by our leaders to have only as many children as we can physically, emotionally, and financially care for. What I'm trying to say is that I do love babies, but I also feel a sacred responsibility to bring children into this world."

I didn't exactly understand, but I felt her sincerity. And I was highly impressed that Madison, who up until this point I had considered to be one of the most self-absorbed people in the universe, actually cared about unborn children up in heaven. So I nodded.

"Have as many kids as you want—or think you should—but it would probably be okay if you took a little break, just to catch your breath and enjoy being not pregnant for a few months anyway."

She frowned. "I guess you could be right."

Emboldened by this less-than-glowing endorsement of my suggestion, I said, "And in the meantime you need some help. Maybe if you don't need a shrink, you could use the money you save to hire a nanny."

Madison gave me an almost shy look. "At dinner when you were talking about being a foster parent, I thought that if you wanted to get involved with kids, maybe you could start with mine. I think you'd like them if you got to know them."

I felt terrible. I had shirked my responsibilities as a sister and an aunt. Madison had needed me, and I hadn't been there for her. And the worst part was I really didn't like her children, and she knew it.

"I'll help you," I promised, knowing I was going to regret the words. "I'm going to come over to your house one day a week. I'll babysit or clean or whatever you want me to do—as long as you promise not to tell me how romantic Jared is."

Madison seemed delighted. "Really?"

I shrugged. "I'll have to wait and see what day I can have as my off day once the new library is up and running—then we'll make it official."

"Major has a field trip to the zoo coming up the week after the baby is supposed to be born. Would you go with him?"

I couldn't think of anything I would hate more, but I nodded bravely. "Sure." Even though there was a good chance I had—with these few words— ruined my life, I tried to take consolation from the fact that Madison looked so much happier.

"The teacher said he couldn't go unless a family member came along, so he thought he was going to miss it."

"I said I'd go, didn't I?" I repeated as Luke and my father finally emerged from the workroom. Luke didn't seem nervous or anxious to get away from Daddy, so I assumed that their man-time had gone well. And I don't know when I've been so happy to see anyone.

They walked over to join us, and Luke said, "I've got to go and get Heaven. Do you want to come?"

I nodded. "We'd better go tell my mother good-bye." I stood and hugged

Daddy. Then, as an afterthought, I hugged Madison too. She was so pleased I thought she was going to cry again.

My father stared at us suspiciously. "What's going on?"

I gave him my most innocent look. "Nothing. We've just enjoyed a little girl talk." Then I led Luke into the kitchen, where Miss Ida Jean was eating and my mother had things returned to perfect order.

Luke said to Mother, "I can't thank you enough for the delicious meal. But Kennedy and I need to go now."

I usually stayed longer on Sunday afternoons, and I knew my mother wouldn't appreciate an early departure. So to help Luke stay on her good side, I gave a fatalistic little shrug and said, "We want to follow Brother Jackson's advice and give Heaven some time outside of that children's facility."

My mother frowned, but she couldn't very well go against the preacher. "I guess you'd better go. I'll wrap up some chicken for you to take home."

I tried to discourage her, which I knew was a waste of time, and it was. While my mother filled various Tupperware containers with fried chicken and assorted side items, Miss Ida Jean asked, "You Luke Scoggins?"

He nodded. "Yes, ma'am."

"I thought you were in jail."

"No, ma'am. Just Iraq."

Miss Ida Jean turned to me. "I heard Madison's little boy Major kicked a girl in his Sunday school class today."

"He punched her," I corrected. Then I decided I didn't have to play by the rules anymore. After all, I was riding around town with a Scoggins. So I took a deep breath and added, "That's what she gets for sitting in his favorite chair."

Miss Ida Jean's eyes bugged, but before she could reply, Mother handed us the Tupperware, and I pulled Luke toward the door. Once we were outside, we hurried toward the Torino and climbed inside.

"Well," I said once we were settled. "That went better than I expected."

Luke started the car. "The conversation with Miss Ida Jean or the meal with your family?"

"Both," I replied.

Luke smiled. "Miss Ida Jean is a little spiteful, but I think your family is nice."

I strapped on my seat belt. "You'd better reserve judgment until next week when Madison's kids are there."

Luke didn't laugh. "Speaking of next week, I really don't think it's a good idea for me to bring Heaven to church or to your parents' house. I don't have much experience handling her, and, well, it could be a disaster."

"She should at least get a chance," I persisted. "If you bring her and she causes too much trouble, you can always leave."

"Maybe," he replied without conviction.

"It must be hard for her," I said. "Her parents have deserted her, she's been forced to leave her home, and she just lost the only person who loved her."

Luke considered this. "Uncle Foster wasn't a very demonstrative person, and Heaven certainly isn't very lovable, but for some reason they did seem to get along good together."

"What about your father? Isn't he close to Heaven?"

He shook his head. "My father has always been too sick to get involved with Heaven."

I took a deep breath and forced myself to ask, "And your brother?"

"Nick's not even sure he's Heaven's father. His wife is that kind."

I knew about that kind. "Did he have DNA tests done?"

"He was going to until Uncle Foster said he'd take care of Heaven. Nick went back to driving trucks, and the subject dropped. Now he may look into it again."

I didn't have much sympathy for Luke's brother. The time to dispute his claim to Heaven was when the child was first dropped off at the salvage yard. By allowing Foster to care for her for years, he had at least passively accepted the child as his own. To disclaim her at this point was, well, despicable. But because of Luke's relationship with Nick, I just said, "He should come back and have the blood tests done. Once he has the results, he can decide about his future and hers."

"I agree," Luke said. "But that's Nick's decision—not mine."

"What about the deserting ex-wife?" I asked. "Maybe she'll take Heaven."

"If she wanted Heaven, she wouldn't have left her," Luke pointed out. "And if she changed her mind, she's always known where to find her."

I felt bad for Heaven—a girl that nobody wanted. No wonder she was so hateful. "Maybe her mother loved her at least a little at first; otherwise why would she name her Heaven?"

Luke shrugged. "I don't know. Maybe that's where she thought she came from."

I narrowed my eyes at him. "But you don't?"

"The fact that she was sent to her particular parents casts the theory of a supreme being into serious doubt."

"Where else could she have come from?"

"Scientists have several explanations for our existence that don't have anything to do with God."

"Yeah, but no good explanations," I countered. "They say there was some big explosion in space and that all the molecules got mixed up and settled back to form the earth in layers. The top one just happens to be soil that grows stuff. Not to mention an atmosphere with gravity and air that supports both plant and animal life. Then more of the molecules formed into millions of different varieties of plants and birds and fish and bugs and cows and giraffes and perfect little babies with ears that hear and eyes that see and hands that can reach out and grab things." I wiggled my fingers as a visual aid. "I'm not even religious, and I can see how stupid that theory is."

"It does have a few holes," he said—whether he really agreed or just wanted to avoid an argument, I couldn't tell. "But the creation theory has a few weak points too—like how did anybody—even God—create the entire world, solar system, etc., in just six days."

"The creation theory does require a little faith," I agreed.

He smiled. "So do the others."

"Madison believes that there are literally people waiting in heaven to come down to earth as babies," I ventured, hoping that his reaction would help me figure out how I felt about the subject. "She says that the babies have to come down until all of God's children have been born, and if nice families won't have them, they have no choice but to go to countries where they will starve."

He considered this for a minute and then nodded. "I never thought of it that way, but I guess it's possible."

"What surprises me the most is that Madison has actual beliefs. I thought she just went to church with Jared because he's her husband."

"You don't have any religious beliefs?"

This was not the direction I had hoped our conversation would take. "I believe in God," I admitted reluctantly. "I'm not sure I believe in *religion.*"

Luke shrugged. "After seeing war up close, I'm not even sure I believe in God—so you're a step ahead of me."

I was almost glad that we had arrived at the juvenile care facility so that the conversation had to end.

CHAPTER FOURTEEN

HEAVEN'S NEW RESIDENCE WAS A grim, institutional building, and I felt a depression settle over me as we walked in. I didn't want to be inside and absolutely couldn't imagine having to live there. The woman at the information desk was on the phone, and we had to listen to a partial description of problems she was having with her landlord until she finally put her hand over the mouthpiece and acknowledged us with an impatient look.

Luke explained that he was there to check Heaven out for a couple of hours.

The woman sighed as though our presence was a huge inconvenience before telling whoever was on the other end of the line that she had to go. She disconnected her personal call and dialed another number. She relayed Luke's request to someone within the bowels of the facility. A few minutes later, Heaven descended a stairwell into the lobby. She was escorted by a no-nonsense woman wearing a uniform stretched to its limits.

Heaven was cleaner than she had been the last time I'd seen her. The blond hair was pulled away from her face in a tight ponytail. Her clothes were generic jeans and a plain green T-shirt. And the cut on her hand was bandaged with fresh medical gauze. She waved at Luke and gave me a probing look but didn't say anything. Nor did she seem particularly grateful to us for springing her—even temporarily—from her unpleasant accommodations.

Heaven's escort made Luke sign a liability form and reminded him that Heaven had to be returned by seven o'clock that evening. During the short walk back out to his car, Luke made conversation with his niece. Heaven answered in monosyllables. The only acknowledgment she gave of my presence was an occasional glare.

Once we were in the car, Luke and I in the front and Heaven in the back, Luke suggested that we go for ice cream. My stomach rebelled at the thought of more food, and I was saved from certain nausea when Heaven declined the offer.

"I just want to go see Grandfather," Heaven said.

I was touched by this comment, and my feelings toward Heaven became even more sympathetic. She seemed to sense this and turned to me before digging a finger up her nose. I interpreted this as a signal that I should keep my distance, so I looked away and did my best to control an instinctive shudder.

When we arrived at the salvage yard, Luke parked in front of his father's house. Heaven climbed out of the car and bounded across the grassless yard to Parnell's front door, where she commenced pounding on the weathered wood. The nurse answered the insistent knocking, and the child ran inside without waiting for an invitation.

Luke and I approached at a more sedate pace. He introduced me to Jenna, a pleasant-faced, stout woman, probably in her early forties. She hugged Luke affectionately as he asked how his father was feeling.

"He took a short morning nap, ate a good lunch, and is now watching television," Jenna reported. "I'm following the doctor's orders regarding medication dosage very carefully, and for the most part, he's been alert and lucid."

Luke frowned at this news, and I knew why. If Parnell was doing well now, with Jenna dispensing his medicine properly, then he probably had been overmedicated at the nursing home. The question was *who* had been slipping Parnell extra pills?

The nurse led us into the living room, and we found Parnell sitting in a recliner. Heaven was standing in front of him, talking in hushed tones. When we approached, she fell silent.

"I don't know about that, Heaven," Parnell said, his voice still weak in spite of the recent improvements to his health. "You'll have to ask Luke."

Slowly Heaven turned and fixed her uncle with a challenging stare.

"Did you want something?" Luke asked.

Heaven tilted her chin a little higher and said, "I want the keys so I can go home, just for a little while."

I felt a rush of sympathy for the child but turned away so she couldn't see.

"I think that would be fine," Luke replied. "Let me find the keys, and I'll take you over." He dug in the drawers in the kitchen and finally produced a set of keys. "We'll try these. One of them should work."

Heaven reached out and took the keys from Luke's hand. "I want to go by myself."

Before Luke could object, she was out the front door.

I moved to the window and watched the child cross the barren ground that separated the two houses. She hurried up the steps and tried several keys. Finally she found one that fit, and the door to Foster's house swung open. Without bothering to remove the keys from the lock, Heaven rushed inside.

I stared at the door and wondered what Heaven was doing. Was she walking around, touching the mementos from her childhood? Was she sitting in Foster's favorite chair? Had she cast herself onto the old iron bed that had belonged to her great-grandmother and dissolved into tears of frustration and grief? I felt like crying myself.

I sensed Luke behind me and turned to see him looking over my shoulder at Foster's house.

"I wish I could help her," he said.

I nodded. "I know."

Luke and I sat in the living room with Parnell while Jenna busied herself in the kitchen. Throughout the stilted conversation, Luke and I took turns alternately watching the clock and the front door.

Finally Luke leaned close to me and whispered, "Maybe you could go check on her."

I wasn't sure this was a good plan. "Heaven won't appreciate me catching her at a vulnerable moment."

"No," he agreed, "but she'd like it even less if I see her with her guard down."

I couldn't argue with that, so I went out the front door and walked over to Foster's house.

When I walked into the dim, silent house Heaven was not sitting in Foster's favorite chair or gazing lovingly at the tired but familiar décor. I glanced into Heaven's bedroom, but she wasn't sprawled across the bed crying her eyes out either. Nor was she in the kitchen. I was headed down the hall, thinking she must have locked herself in the bathroom, when Heaven walked out of Foster's bedroom. Her eyes were dry and her expression more determined than devastated. And she was holding a grocery bag tightly in her hands.

"What is that?" I asked, indicating the bag.

"I got some of my stuff," she explained. "Things Uncle Foster gave me."

I didn't think the folks at the juvenile facility would object to her having a few personal items. And since it seemed like Heaven was cracking open the door to amateur grief counseling, I decided to pursue that avenue. "The two of you were very close."

She nodded. "He told me everything. Like that someone was going to kill him if he didn't sell the salvage yard."

I stared at her in astonishment. Had I been overlooking the best source of information available about Foster Scoggins and his death? I needed a quick consultation with Miss Eugenia or Cade or Mark or even Sheriff Bonham to be sure I asked the right questions. But since this was impossible, I forged ahead as best I could. "Did he say *who* was going to kill him?"

She shook her head. "No, but he said he wasn't going to sell because this land had always been in the Scoggins family, and he was going to pass it down to me."

Suddenly Foster's refusal to sell his land became somewhat reasonable and even touching. He wanted to keep it for Heaven. Goodness knows the child needed something to look forward to.

"Foster must have loved you very much."

Heaven shrugged.

I licked my lips and then proceeded carefully. "Did Foster ever mention a girlfriend?"

Heaven shook her head. "He told me women were nothing but trouble, and he always said bad things about my mother and Uncle Parnell's wife."

Heaven didn't have a reputation for honesty, but looking into her eyes, wise beyond her years, I believed her. "Did you ever see any letters Foster got written on pink paper?"

She nodded. "I read one. It was mean."

I wasn't sure how well she could read, and so I asked, "Mean *how?*"

The shrug again. "Just some of the words were bad, and it didn't say love at the end."

My heart started to pound. This fit perfectly into Miss Eugenia's extortion-murder theory. Not that I expected Cade or Sheriff Bonham to consider Heaven a reliable witness, but this information gave me confidence to press on. "Can you tell me about that last day, after the two of you left the library?"

Heaven gave me a calculating look. "Are you a deputy?"

"No, but I'm trying to help the sheriff figure out who killed your uncle," I replied.

She considered this for a few seconds and then said, "Uncle Foster picked me up at school and we ran some errands. I told him about the paper on Abraham Lincoln, so he brought me to the library. After you wrote my paper, he bought me a king-size Coke and a hot dog at the Jiffy Mart for dinner. Then we went home. Luke was gone to Albany, and Uncle Foster said he had some business to take care of and would be back soon."

"He left you alone?"

"I wouldn't be scared," Heaven assured me. "But Grandfather's cleaning lady was there, so I stayed with her. A little while later Luke got home and showed me where you brought my report. Then the sheriff came to tell us Uncle Foster was dead." Her expression hardened. "And then Luke let him take me away."

I tried to think of something comforting to say, but before I came up with anything, Luke walked in.

"Are we leaving?" I asked.

"If you're ready," Luke confirmed.

I expected Heaven to object to such a hasty return to the juvenile facility, but she nodded. "I'm ready."

Luke and I exchanged a surprised yet relieved look over her head and then walked with her out to his car. He opened the front passenger door for me. While I was getting settled, he opened the back door for Heaven.

"What's in the bag?" he asked.

"Personal items," I answered for the child.

He leaned through my open window. "I presume you checked it for weapons?"

I felt certain he was kidding, so I shook my head. "No, but I'm sure the juvenile facility will."

"That's not going to do us much good between here and there," he murmured without a trace of humor. Once Heaven had secured her seat belt, he walked around the car and climbed in under the wheel.

We were mostly quiet on the drive back to Albany to drop off Heaven. I knew she was dreading her return to incarceration. Luke and I were dreading it too—and both felt guilty—but there was nothing anyone could do. At least not immediately.

When we got to the juvenile facility, Heaven reached in the bag on her lap and pulled out two small books. One was about goats and the other about gophers. "Can I turn these in to you?" she asked me. "I don't want no fine."

I accepted the books miserably. "Thanks."

Then Heaven climbed out of the car and walked toward the entrance bravely. She looked so small and helpless. My guilt knew no bounds.

With a sigh, Luke opened his door. "I'll be right back."

I felt like a coward waiting in the car but decided the best thing I could do to help Heaven was to solve the mystery of Foster's death. So I tucked the two little library books she had given me into the front pocket of my Murder Book and then used the time while I was waiting for Luke to write down the things Heaven had told me. When Luke returned, he had a scowl on his face.

"Did she cry?" I made myself ask.

"No," was the brief response.

I decided to leave it alone

Once we were driving again, I used the notes I had written to fill Luke in. I told him what Heaven had said about Foster being afraid for his life and the threatening letter she had read written on pink paper like the ones Foster received at the post office.

When I was finished, he pointed at my notebook and said, "You need to tell the sheriff all that."

"I will," I replied. "Not that I expect him to take Heaven's word seriously. But it's just one more indication that we should keep looking into your uncle's death."

"I agree."

"I asked Heaven about the night Foster died. She said they ran errands, and after their stop at the library he bought her a Coke and a hot dog for dinner."

Luke nodded again. "That was pretty much their regular routine."

As casually as possible I added, "She said you weren't at the salvage yard when they got home. That wasn't long after I dropped off Heaven's Abraham Lincoln paper. Do you remember where you were?"

He cut his eyes over at me, and his expression made it clear that he didn't think this was just a casual question. "I went into Albany to buy a laptop for school."

I made a note of this in my book. That night when I dropped off Heaven's paper, he'd been wearing greasy overalls—not what I'd expect him to have on if he was planning a computer-buying trip to Albany. "What kind did you buy?"

"I didn't buy one," he replied. "It was more of a recon mission."

This was a terrible alibi—pretty much impossible to confirm—but my mind wouldn't let me consider the possibility that when I saw Luke that night, he was about to go kill Foster. So I closed my book and put it in my purse. He drove into the parking lot of the Midway Store and Save complex and parked in front of my apartment—a fairly obvious indication that he hoped to be invited inside.

"Would you like to come in?" I asked.

"At least long enough to make sure you don't have any uninvited guests."

The door to my apartment was still securely locked, and things inside seemed to be just as I had left them. But I was in no hurry for Luke to leave, so I said, "Would you like some more of my mom's fried chicken?"

"I wouldn't mind," he accepted. "And a Pepsi if you have one."

We settled on my couch, nibbling cold fried chicken, which is better than the warm version in my opinion, and sipping Pepsi. If only we hadn't been feeling guilty about Heaven and wondering who killed Foster, the moment would have been perfect.

Finally I said, "You didn't seem too happy about the idea of me being a foster parent to Heaven."

"It's not that I don't think you would do a good job," he assured me quickly—a little too quickly—which made me believe that was exactly what he did think. "But Heaven is a difficult child—maybe even damaged by all the emotional upheaval in her life. She's a survivor and a loner, and I'm not sure anyone can win her trust—let alone her love." He looked around the room. "Besides, what little experience I've had with DHR makes me doubt that they'll let Heaven live here, especially with those steep stairs leading up to the front door. And I think you'd have to have at least two bedrooms."

There was nothing I could do about the stairs, so I said, "What if I let her have my room and I slept on the couch?"

"You can ask them, but I doubt it. And you'd have to arrange to be home when she gets off the school bus."

"I've always been able to set my own hours at the library," I said. Then I remembered that everything was changing for my job. "But once the new library opens, my schedule may be less flexible." I was discouraged for a few seconds, and then a thought occurred to me. "My mom only works at my uncle's dental office until noon, so she could keep Heaven until I get off work."

He shrugged. "Maybe."

"You don't think my mother could do it?"

"I'm not sure your mother wants to," he corrected. "She hasn't even met Heaven. The whole foster parent thing is your idea."

This stung a little. "I'm just trying to help."

"I know." His voice was kind but still firm. "But Heaven is not your responsibility—or your family's either."

"Whose then?"

"Mine, I guess. Since they won't let me take custody of her, I'll have to think of something else." He stood and carried the remnants of his dinner into my tiny kitchen. "I'd better get home."

I didn't want him to go, but I knew he had other things to do besides watch TV with me. So I nodded.

Luke smiled. "Keep your doors locked."

"Oh, you know I will!"

With a laugh he opened the door and stepped out on the porch. He waved but made no attempt to kiss me, even on the cheek. "See ya."

I was a little dejected after Luke left. It was silly to feel so attached to someone I barely knew, but I couldn't help it. I looked around my apartment, and all the faults Luke had pointed out seemed glaringly obvious. I wondered if I could move. Maybe there was a nice two-bedroom house for rent somewhere in Midway. And maybe the rent was something I could afford. I didn't know if Mr. Sheffield would still let me work for him at the Midway Store and Save if I didn't live on the premises. If not, I'd have to find another part-time job. Part-time jobs in Midway were scarce, and if I took a job that I couldn't do at home, it would mean less time with Heaven, too, with which the DHR was bound to take exception.

Finally I realized that there was only one reasonable way it would work. If I was seriously going to pursue the chance to be Heaven's foster mother, I would have to move back home with my own parents. Their house would pass any DHR scrutiny with flying colors. My mother would be there to watch Heaven when I was at work, and I wouldn't need any additional income to provide for her.

I studied the small private space that had allowed me my independence—from my parents and from Cade. Could I really give that up to help a little girl I barely knew? And why was I even considering it? Did I really care that much about Heaven or was I just trying to establish a tie with Luke?

My unpleasant thoughts were interrupted by the ringing of the telephone. I didn't want to answer it, but I did.

After I said hello, Miss Eugenia asked, "Are you watching the evening news on Channel 5?"

My eyes strayed of their own accord to the blank television screen. "No."

"Well, you should be!" she informed me. "Hurry!"

I walked over to the television (since it had been made before remotes were even dreamed of) and turned it on. Fortunately, Channel 5 was one of the three channels I was able to access, thanks to the analog converter box my mother purchased for me so I could get weather reports. A tiny dot of light started at the middle of the screen and then widened. Once I had a full picture, I gasped. Heaven Scoggins was sitting at the news desk between the two weekend anchors.

"For those of you just joining us," the anchor woman on the right with spiky blond hair (and identified in the information bubble as Hannah-Leigh Coley-Smith) said, "this is Heaven Scoggins, and she has walked to our studios from the Dougherty County Juvenile Care Facility nearly a mile away."

"So!" Miss Eugenia screeched through the phone line. "Do you see Heaven?"

"I see her, and I've got to go." I slammed the phone back into its charger and ran outside. Luke was just climbing into his car. He looked startled when he saw me on the porch and more so when I screamed, "Come back in here!" He turned pale as a ghost when I added, "Heaven is on TV."

Luke and I returned to my apartment in time to hear Heaven say, "Uncle Foster told me that he might get killed if he wouldn't sell the salvage yard so the town could build a bunch of houses."

"So you think your uncle was killed?" Anchor Hannah-Leigh's eyes were wide with excitement.

"Yeah, and the lady from the library thinks that too," Heaven confirmed. "She told me."

"The lady who runs the library in Midway?" Hannah-Leigh confirmed.

Heaven nodded. "Her name is Kennedy. I'm helping her find out who did it."

Afraid I might faint, I dropped onto the couch and stared at Heaven's angelic face magnified by the television screen.

"Is that why you came to our station today?" Hannah-Leigh asked. "So that you can make sure the person who murdered your great-uncle is brought to justice?"

Heaven shrugged. "Naw, I came because Foster said if anything happened to him, I was supposed to pull up the loose floorboards in his room and get out this blue book. He hid it there because he said nobody would see it there except spiders." Heaven held up a standard savings account passbook. It was a little worse for wear and obviously one of the items she had removed from Foster's house in the bag I didn't search.

Heaven continued. "He said not to trust nobody—even family. He said people would try to steal this book from me since I'm a kid. So he said to take it to a place where I could show a lot of people that it has my name on it. That's why I came here."

The camera shifted to Heaven's left and captured the image of the emaciated anchor wearing a bright red suit (identified across the bottom of the screen as Marlene Sutherland). Marlene gingerly took the blue book from Heaven. "Your uncle kept this passbook under the floor?"

Heaven bobbed her head affirmatively. "I was going to show my uncle Luke, but after he let them put me in the kid jail, I changed my mind. Then I thought maybe I could trust the library lady, Kennedy. But now I think she's Luke's girlfriend, so I guess Uncle Foster was right. I can't trust nobody."

"This other uncle of yours, Luke—he lives in Midway?" Hannah-Leigh inquired.

"Yeah."

"But he isn't your legal guardian?"

"Naw, he don't want me." Heaven pointed at the passbook. "I figured the best thing to do was like Uncle Foster said—show the book to a lot of people. We passed by the TV station when the sheriff was taking me to jail so I knew how to get here. When nobody was looking, I slipped out."

"Do you know what this is?" Hannah-Leigh asked, pointing at the passbook.

"Money," Heaven replied. "And Uncle Foster said he signed a paper at the bank saying whoever will be my parents gets to have it."

I was concentrating so hard on Heaven and wondering what she might say next that Luke had to shake my arm to get my attention. "Let's go."

I looked up and blinked. "Huh?"

He gestured at the TV. "We've got to get to Channel 5. Fast."

The phone started ringing, but I ignored it and followed Luke outside. As we descended the stairs, I heard my mother's strident voice leaving a message on the voice mail. "Kennedy! Is Luke Scoggins really your boyfriend?"

Apparently she had been watching the Channel 5 evening news too.

* * *

Luke drove so fast to Albany that I was terrified we'd either die in a fiery crash or—even worse—get pulled over by Cade.

I tried to calm him with, "You shouldn't be mad at Heaven. She's just a kid, and she's trying to follow your uncle's instructions."

"I've worked hard to prove that even though I'm a Scoggins, I can be respected and trusted." Luke was clutching the steering wheel of the Torino with a painful-looking grip, "And in less than a minute, Heaven's destroyed all my efforts."

I wanted to say this wasn't true, but since he *was* on my murder-suspect list, I couldn't in good conscience claim to trust him. So I just said, "I'm sorry."

He nodded and kept driving like a maniac.

We arrived at the Channel 5 studios safely (if not completely sound). Luke didn't take the time to come around and open my door like he usually did. Instead he turned off the car and ran toward the studio entrance, leaving me to get myself out of his car and trail after him.

By the time we got inside the building, the newscast was over, and Heaven was sitting in the lobby, surrounded by an assortment of Channel 5 employees. She was eating cookies and sipping from a little juice box. She smiled at us with false sweetness.

"Who are you?" Hannah-Leigh put a protective arm around Heaven.

Luke scowled at the anchorwoman. "I'm Heaven's uncle, and I'd like to know how you feel about being sued—since you put a minor on television without permission?"

Hannah-Leigh paled, so I assumed Luke had a legal leg to stand on.

A tall man with glasses moved into Luke's line of vision. "I'm Sam McLain, producer of the weekend newscast, and we didn't *put* her on television. She just wandered onto the set talking about escaping from an orphanage and her uncle being murdered and a passbook covered with spiderwebs. All we did was keep the cameras rolling."

"That's why you're in legal jeopardy," Luke replied. "And thanks for providing me with your name. Now I can put you in the lawsuit."

"It all happened so fast!" Sam claimed. "We meant no harm."

Luke didn't seem sympathetic. "You should have turned off the cameras when Heaven arrived."

The producer looked aghast. "We can't turn off the cameras in the middle of a live news broadcast! You shouldn't let your niece wander around Albany unsupervised!"

Luke's response was drowned out by the sound of sirens and squealing tires. A few seconds later, the room was crowded with people wearing a variety of uniforms. There were representatives from the Albany police department, two security guards who apparently worked for the television station, and a few sheriff deputies—including Cade. He shot me a look of accusation, as if I'd set the whole thing up to further my murder investigation. I lifted my hands to silently claim innocence. He turned away in disgust.

Before I could defend myself, a very upset woman wearing a badge that identified her as Trisha Spain, an assistant administrator for the Dougherty County Juvenile Care Facility, moved to the front of the crowd.

"Heaven!" Ms. Spain cried. "We've been looking all over for you!"

Heaven was unruffled. "I've been right here."

"How did she get away from you in the first place?" Luke demanded.

"Did somebody really kill her uncle?" Hannah-Leigh Coley-Smith wanted to know.

"What about the passbook?" Marlene, the painfully thin woman asked. "Is it for real? Does the kid really have almost half a million in cash?"

Ms. Spain ran a hand through her hair in a gesture of weariness. "I don't know, but if you'll give the passbook to me, we'll check to see if it is legitimate."

Hannah-Leigh narrowed her eyes at Ms. Spain, "We'll give you a copy, but the original is going to a family court judge for safekeeping, since Heaven's dead uncle was worried about someone cheating her out of her inheritance."

Ms. Spain looked insulted. "You are welcome to give the passbook to Judge Clements—he's the one who handles our cases." Then she spied Luke. She pointed a finger and said, "You're the other uncle!"

He nodded with reluctance. "I am."

Hannah-Leigh gave him a look of disdain. "It's terrible that the murdered man had to hide the passbook under the floor of his house just to keep you from stealing money from a helpless child!"

Luke ignored this and asked Ms. Spain again, "How did Heaven escape?"

"It was your fault," she accused him. "Our regulations require that you return children to the caseworker on their floor. You just left Heaven with the receptionist in the lobby, who didn't know Heaven and therefore trusted her to go upstairs by herself. And you see the result."

Luke took a step closer to the angry woman, and the tension in the room was almost tangible. "I can see that your facility is not as secure as it should be. Maybe we should get the cameras rolling again."

The producer, Sam, looked hopeful, but Hannah-Leigh Coley-Smith shook her head and hissed, "Don't you dare until you get written releases from everyone. I for one do *not* want to be sued!"

Chastised, Sam blended back into the crowd. I listened to Luke and Ms. Spain exchange a few more accusations. Behind me I heard the police arguing with the sheriff's deputies, trying to establish who had jurisdiction. Cade had moved up so that he was standing in my line of sight and kept sending me disappointed looks. Only Heaven seemed unperturbed. She sat quietly in the middle of the chaos she'd created like the calm eye of a hurricane.

I was watching the volatile scene with ever-increasing anxiety when the door of the television studio opened and Mark Iverson walked in. He elbowed his way through the rapidly growing throng, flashing his FBI credentials.

"Are you in charge?" Ms. Spain demanded when he reached the couch where Heaven was sitting. "Because Heaven Scoggins is a resident of the Dougherty County Juvenile Care Facility by court order, and I want her returned to my custody immediately."

"I don't want to go with her," Heaven said. "I hate it there."

Anchor Hannah-Leigh glared in Ms. Spain's direction, and I felt sure an exposé on the child facility would soon be in the works.

Heaven scanned the room, and her eyes stopped when they found me. Then she pointed a finger and said, "I want to go with the library lady."

I was horrified, knowing that I was going to have to decline and in the process explain all the deficits of my life and living conditions that made me ineligible to have a foster child.

I needn't have worried. Ms. Spain didn't even consider the child's suggestion. She turned on Heaven and fairly hissed, "It doesn't matter where you want to go. You've caused enough trouble, and you're coming with me." She reached forward and tried to grab Heaven, but Hannah-Leigh pulled the child out of Ms. Spain's reach.

"She has rights!" Hannah-Leigh cried with passion if not accuracy.

Then Mark surprised everyone by saying, "Actually, I think Heaven should go with Ms. Killingsworth."

I was speechless and could see my astonishment reflected on the faces of most everyone else in the room.

"But she's not an approved foster parent," Ms. Spain sputtered.

Mark shot a look over his shoulder at Sam McLain. "Thanks to Channel 5, Heaven's life is now in danger."

Producer Sam stepped back into the limelight and forced a nervous little laugh. "I think you're exaggerating the situation . . ."

"You just allowed Heaven to claim publicly on your newscast that Foster Scoggins was murdered and that she was helping Ms. Killingsworth solve the crime," Mark interrupted him. "Which places both Heaven and Ms. Killingsworth in danger."

The producer paled. "We didn't mean . . ."

"You didn't *think*," Mark corrected. "But it's too late to do anything about that now. The only thing we can do is take extreme safety measures."

I glanced at the subject of all this dire conversation. Heaven yawned—obviously terrified.

"I'm taking Heaven into protective custody," Mark said.

"This is most unusual," Ms. Spain insisted.

Mark frowned at the woman. "You are relieved of responsibility."

Ms. Spain's shoulders seemed to relax. "Well, as long as we won't be held accountable."

By now I thoroughly disliked Ms. Spain. I walked close to Mark and said, "Luke doesn't think my apartment will pass a DHR inspection."

"It may not be the perfect place to *raise* a child," Mark conceded, "but because it has such limited access, it's a great place to safeguard her temporarily. And we can use the office below as our headquarters." He turned to the law enforcement personnel, who had segregated themselves by department. "I'm going to need cooperation from the sheriff's department and the Albany City police. Please have some representatives at the Midway Store and Save in one hour for a strategy meeting."

There was nodding and a murmur of general agreement.

Then Mark looked at Heaven. "Please come with us."

I expected Heaven to argue, but she stood and walked over to me. "Okay."

I wasn't sure if Heaven really felt safe with me or if she just thought I'd be easy to escape from. But either way, she was a first grader (albeit an experienced one), and I was an adult. So I took her hand, and we followed Mark outside with Luke bringing up the rear. Cade walked with us but was careful to stay a few feet back to be sure everyone realized that he was with us in an official capacity only.

Mark insisted that Heaven and I ride with him in his FBI vehicle, and Luke drove behind us in the Torino. Cade followed him in his squad car. By the time our little parade reached my apartment, a crowd of Midway residents had gathered.

As we turned in, I saw Mayor Cook and Francie standing in the front row of onlookers and figured that they arrived first thanks to their police scanner. I saw Mr. Bateman, who ran the gas station out by the salvage yard, and a waitress from the Back Porch. Even Brother Jackson and Miss Zelda were there. I spotted Miss Ida Jean, and I was wondering who had given her a ride. Then I saw my parents, which answered this question.

"Kennedy!" my mother cried as I climbed out of Mark's car. "What in the world is going on?"

"Heaven sneaked out of the juvenile care facility," I explained. "Then she walked to the television station and . . . I guess you know the rest."

Daddy glanced at Heaven, who had jumped from the car and was already climbing the questionably safe stairs that led up to my apartment.

Miss Ida Jean stepped up and demanded, "So Foster Scoggins really was murdered?"

"That's the way it appears," I confirmed wearily as Luke joined us.

"Isn't that just like a Scoggins to go and get himself killed in a scandalous way," Miss Ida Jean murmured. Then she noticed Luke. "No offense."

"None taken," he assured her. He noticed Heaven on the stairs and called, "Heaven, get back over here before you break your neck."

Heaven turned to look at us, and as we watched, she climbed one more stair—just to be sure we knew she would do as she pleased. Then she turned and slowly descended the steps. When she reached us, she chose to stand beside my mother.

Brother Jackson and Miss Zelda walked over at this point. They extended additional condolences to Luke now that it appeared foul play had been involved in Foster's death. Luke thanked them, and then Brother Jackson offered to give Miss Ida Jean a ride home. I sent the preacher a look of gratitude, and he smiled.

"I'll see you Sunday," he told me, and I nodded in acceptance. I never expect to get something for nothing. Miss Ida Jean insisted that Daddy escort her to the Jacksons' car, which was parked near the road beside my mother's Buick.

The rest of us walked over to the entrance of the Midway Store and Save office, where Mr. Sheffield was pacing nervously while Mark and a couple other FBI agents searched the interior. Based on Mr. Sheffield's reaction to all the fuss, I figured I'd better be looking for a new part-time job and another place to live—soon.

During the FBI search of my apartment and Mr. Sheffield's office, my mother scolded me for not calling her personally to warn her about Heaven's embarrassing disclosures. My mother suspended this barrage when Daddy returned from taking Miss Ida Jean to the Jacksons' car, long enough to send him straight back to get a stack of Tupperware containers full of food from her trunk. I felt sorry for my father, but I couldn't be unhappy about the food, since now I had a child to feed and only Pepsis in the refrigerator.

Mark came out a few minutes later and gave us the all-clear. Then he informed Mr. Sheffield that the FBI would compensate him for the use of his property, which cheered up my employer/landlord considerably. So I quit worrying about being fired and watched as Mark assigned Cade to get rid of the onlookers who had gathered. Most of the townsfolk left at Cade's request, but Mayor Cook and his wife, Francie, insisted on speaking with me, and Mark agreed to let them come over.

"We were horrified when we saw Heaven on TV," Terrance said.

"Just horrified," Francie seconded. "We had no idea Foster was murdered."

"I hope Drake Langston won't decide to pull out of Midway." Terrance looked distressed. "This could be really bad for our town."

I smirked. "It wasn't too great for Foster either."

Apparently Francie thought I was kidding, since she flashed me a tight-skinned smile. "We just wanted to let you know that if Heaven needs anything, we'd be glad to help out."

I glanced at Luke, and he nodded. We had our first gold diggers.

"Thanks," Luke said. "We'll keep that in mind."

The Cooks looked reluctant to leave, but Mark had run out of patience. "Okay, folks." He waved his hand toward their car. "Time to go."

After the Cooks were gone, Mother took Heaven by the hand. She instructed my father to follow her with the food and then started up the steps to my apartment. I shuddered at the thought of my mother laying claim to my territory, but what could I do?

"Are you coming, Kennedy?" she asked over her shoulder.

"I'll be along in a minute."

Then just when I thought things couldn't get any worse, Miss Eugenia arrived, hobbling on crutches and accompanied by both her geriatric boyfriend and her unattractive little dog, Lady. The dog was obviously a good judge of character, because when she saw Heaven on my porch, she growled.

Mother called down a greeting to the newest visitors. "Won't y'all come in for some coffee?"

I cringed. There wasn't a speck of coffee in my apartment, and I wasn't in the mood to entertain.

"No, thank you, Iris!" Miss Eugenia hollered back. "We can only stay a minute. We just wanted to speak to Kennedy."

"Well, come again," Mother said. Then she led Heaven into the apartment, my father following them.

Once they were gone, Miss Eugenia limped over to stand beside me while Mr. Owens chased Lady. Miss Eugenia whispered, "What in the world is going on? You're not answering your phone, Mark's not answering his, and I've been trying to call the television station, but they aren't answering their phones either."

I succinctly described the events that had transpired since we saw Heaven doing her best to attract the murderer's attention on the Channel 5 News.

"Well," Miss Eugenia said, "if that's not the last word."

"It did come as quite a shock," I admitted. "But at least everyone is convinced that Foster was murdered. And Mark has taken Heaven into his protective custody."

"Does that mean you're taking over the case?" Miss Eugenia asked Mark.

"Not yet, but we're working on it," he replied.

"Then it might benefit you to know that Whit has spent a great deal of time investigating the Scogginses' financial setup," Miss Eugenia told Mark. "While it's true that Foster's part of the salvage yard goes to Parnell upon his death, this arrangement doesn't apply to other assets that Foster may have accumulated over the course of his life."

"Like the money in the passbook account?" I asked.

Mr. Owens walked up breathing heavily and carrying Lady. "Exactly like that."

"So it's legal to do that?" I wanted to be sure. "Give money to a minor?"

"She may not have access to the funds until she's older," Mr. Owens hedged, "but Foster Scoggins was certainly within his rights to give it to her."

"What I'd like to know is how did Foster accumulate that kind of money?" Miss Eugenia wondered aloud.

Luke shrugged. "The income at the salvage yard was steady, and the overhead was low. Uncle Foster never spent any money, so I'd say that the savings account represents what he earned in a lifetime."

"He did love Heaven," I whispered.

"I guess that explains why Foster wasn't in a hurry to sell the salvage yard to Drake Langston," Miss Eugenia said. "He had plenty of money."

"Besides, the salvage yard was Heaven's inheritance," I interjected.

Miss Eugenia had another thought. "I wonder if Foster gave Heaven the money partly to lure a guardian for her."

Luke frowned. "He knew that it was going to be hard to find parents for Heaven, and the money does make the job more attractive."

Mr. Owens nodded. "I predict that several willing guardians will come forward after Heaven's announcement on tonight's newscast."

"The Cooks already offered," I muttered.

"This case is really getting interesting," Miss Eugenia said.

"It may be interesting, but your involvement in it is over," Mark said firmly. Then he turned to look at me. "Yours too. It's gotten too dangerous for civilian investigators."

We both nodded, and he looked relieved. "Good. Now Whit, why don't you take Miss Eugenia home so she can get off that sprained ankle?"

Mr. Owens took Miss Eugenia by the arm. "I think that's a wise suggestion."

Miss Eugenia waved good-bye and encouraged me to come visit her. "I've enjoyed getting to know you," she said. "Just because we're not investigating a murder anymore doesn't mean we can't still be friends."

"I'll call you," I promised.

After Miss Eugenia and her boyfriend left, Mark waved to Cade, who was standing on the periphery, keeping his distance to make sure I didn't forget he was mad. Mark assigned him to lead the first security shift. Cade nodded at Mark, careful to keep his eyes from meeting mine. At first his resentful behavior had bothered me, but now I decided it was a good thing and ignored him back.

"The rest of us can go inside," Mark suggested and led the way into my apartment.

CHAPTER FIFTEEN

MOTHER HAD HEAVEN AT MY small kitchen table and was serving her leftovers from Sunday dinner. My father was standing at the front door with Mother's car keys in his hand.

I planted my feet to block his exit. "You're not leaving Mother here, are you?"

"He's just running to Wal-Mart for me," my mother hollered from the kitchen as if my father were incapable of answering for himself. Then she walked to the doorway where we could converse at a nearly normal tone of voice. "Heaven doesn't have pajamas or a change of clothes or a toothbrush or anything. I've called ahead and talked to the manager. A sales associate from the girls' department is collecting essentials to get us through, and your daddy is going to pick them up."

Only my mother would think it reasonable to call a Wal-Mart store and give their employees an assignment.

"Why don't I just get some of her things from Uncle Foster's house?" Luke offered.

Mother shook her head. "Wal-Mart is closer, and Heaven says most of her clothes are too small anyway. We can get a few things tonight, and tomorrow I'll call It's a Child's World in Haggerty. I'm sure they won't mind bringing over some things for Heaven to try on here—since we're under siege."

"We're not under siege," I corrected, but nobody paid any attention.

Mark said, "That should be fine."

"I'll call the owner, Mary Beth McLemore, right now and set it up." Mother took a step toward the phone and then remembered to mention, "I'm concerned about that cut on her hand too. Heaven said the juvenile facility's doctor rebandaged it, but I'd like to have our family physician take a look. He'd probably be willing to make a house call here at Kennedy's apartment under the circumstances."

"That would be my preference," Mark said. "Talk to him, and let me know what he says."

Mother waved at Daddy. "Hurry, Russell. I'm about to put Heaven in the bathtub and afterwards she's going to need the things from Wal-Mart."

Luke pulled out his wallet and said, "I'll pay for whatever Heaven needs."

My mother tried to object. "That's not necessary—"

Luke interrupted. "I insist."

"Let the man take care of his family, Iris," Daddy said.

My father rarely expressed an opinion, but when he did, we all knew better than to argue.

"Well, just wait until after we go shopping tomorrow," Mother said. "I'll add it all up and give you the final amount."

That seemed to suit everyone. Luke put away his wallet, Mother returned to the kitchen, and Daddy left for Wal-Mart. I invited Luke and Mark Iverson to be seated on my couch, and I took one of the chairs across from them.

Mother stepped to the kitchen doorway and offered us all something to eat, but everyone declined. "Well, if you're not hungry, I'll help Heaven get a bath."

Once she was gone, Luke said, "You should tell Mark about Heaven reading one of the pink letters."

"Foster's love letters?" Mark confirmed.

I nodded. "Yes, but she said it was a *mean* letter. I don't know how well she can read—"

"Probably well enough to know the difference between a mean letter and a love letter," Mark replied.

"I agree," I added. "So this seems to confirm our suspicions that the actual letters Foster was receiving were ones threatening him if he didn't sell his land."

"Which means the murderer switched them," Luke said.

"As part of the plan to convince people that Foster had a girlfriend and distract them from the odd circumstances surrounding the murder," I agreed. "And Heaven also says that Foster did not have a girlfriend."

Mark shrugged. "The only problem with that is Foster really did have a girlfriend—or at least he checked into a motel with a woman. The motel manager I told you about sent me a picture from his security camera yesterday. I faxed it to the sheriff's department here in Midway. Then I radioed Deputy Burrell and asked him to give you a copy."

"I haven't talked to Cade today," I said vaguely.

"And the desk clerk remembered that they were driving a green 1969 Torino."

"Not too many of them around," I remarked.

"I'm afraid I have more evidence to support the girlfriend theory," Luke said with an apologetic look in my direction. "Since my dad has been sick for several weeks, I decided I'd better check through Uncle Foster's box of important papers—to be sure we weren't about to have the electricity turned off or that the insurance on the cars hadn't lapsed."

Mark nodded in encouragement. "So did you find everything in order?"

"Yes," Luke replied. "The system is pretty maintenance-free. Most of the bills are automatically drafted from the business account, and the car insurance is paid in one annual premium in January of every year. So both Uncle Foster's truck and the Torino are fully covered."

I could tell that Mark was getting a little impatient with Luke's detailed account and tried to think of a way to hurry him along. "How does this relate to Foster's girlfriend?"

His cheeks turned red, and I knew I hadn't been subtle enough. "While I was looking at the policy statement I noticed something odd. The mileage listed for the Torino was just less than four thousand miles in January. But when I started driving it after Uncle Foster died, it had over six thousand miles. I couldn't believe he put all those miles on the Torino in a few months' time. He understood the importance of keeping mileage low to keep the car values high so he kept the Torino parked in the garage and never let anyone drive it."

"Apparently he was willing to put mileage on it in order to impress a lady," Mark said.

"I guess I'm going to have to rethink my whole theory," I murmured.

"So if there was a girlfriend, how does that affect the investigation?" Luke asked.

"Maybe not at all," Mark replied. "She may not have had anything to do with his murder."

I frowned. "Then why didn't she come forward after Foster died?"

"People were saying he committed suicide because of her," Mark pointed out. "She might have been afraid she'd be accused of wrongdoing if she came forward."

"What about the suicide note?" I asked in confusion.

Mark shrugged. "Either a good forgery or a note Foster had written for some other purpose."

"Or maybe he was coerced," I contributed.

"That's not likely," Luke said.

"I hate to mention this," I began, "but I think it's important for you to know we have reason to believe Luke's father may have been drugged while he was in the nursing home."

Mark looked shocked. "What?"

"He was fine a few weeks ago," I explained. "But then his condition worsened rapidly, and he had to be put in a nursing home. He claims that one of the nurses was giving him too much medicine, which made him confused. All of this coincides with Drake Langston's arrival in Midway."

"And his offer to buy the salvage yard," Mark added.

"Yes," I confirmed. "And now that Parnell is being cared for at home, his condition has improved dramatically."

"It's something that should be investigated," Mark said. Then he turned to Luke. "And in the meantime, your father needs to be watched closely. The last thing we want is another murder victim. And I'll ask my agents and the sheriff's department to include his house in their protective rounds."

I referred to my Murder Book. "I think it's time that I shared with you my conspiracy theory."

Mark raised an eyebrow. "You think there was more than one murderer?"

"Maybe a whole group of people," I confirmed.

"The land sellers?" Mark guessed.

"Not necessarily all fourteen of them—but it makes sense that some of them are involved. They had the biggest motive. And the more we learn about the circumstances surrounding Foster's death, the more I'm convinced that one person couldn't have handled it alone."

"Even just getting Uncle Foster up the hill by the power relay plant—drugged or not—seems to suggest at least two people working together," Luke said.

Mark nodded. "Go on."

"My feeling is that when Drake arrived and offered the people money for their land, everyone except Foster was excited. The money would make dreams come true for some, survival possible for others—like the Lebows, who are unemployed and on the verge of losing their house to foreclosure."

Mark nodded again, and I took this as at least partial agreement with my deductions.

"Everyone started spending the money or at least made plans on how they would spend the money. Brother Jackson and his wife are going to the Holy Land. Mr. Bateman is going to expand the convenience store at his gas station. Mrs. Castleberry is going to send her grandson to law school. And Mr. Lebow was going to take a course on how to install air conditioners so he'd be prepared for a new career if the tire plant doesn't reopen."

"Then they got word that Foster was refusing to sell," Luke provided, "possibly ending their dreams."

"It seems reasonable that some of the prospective sellers would meet together to discuss how they could convince Foster to change his mind," I hypothesized. "And maybe they even asked him to meet with them. No one has admitted to this yet, but I think that's what happened next."

"When friendly persuasion didn't work, they started sending threatening letters?" Mark asked.

I nodded. "I believe a few of them decided to take things a step further."

Mark raised an eyebrow. "Like an extreme splinter group from the main group of landowners?"

I took a deep breath. "I've known the people on this list all my life. They are good people who go to church and coach little league and collect for the March of Dimes. I hope that at first they were still trying to convince or coerce or even force Foster into selling his land. I don't believe they wanted to be murderers. But eventually I think they drugged Parnell and killed Foster."

"If we can identify at least one of the conspirators," Luke said, "we might be able to get them to testify against the others."

Mark nodded. "I'm hoping that my superiors will decide to take over this investigation, but until they do, I've got to work through Sheriff Bonham. I'll set up a meeting with him in the morning and propose that together we interview these fourteen people vigorously."

I had to ask, "Do you really think the landowners pose a danger to Heaven?"

"Not really," Mark replied. "I just used her safety as a way to keep her out of that children's jail and to recruit manpower from the Albany police and county sheriff's department. You're the one I'm worried about, and by keeping you and Heaven together, you benefit from all that added security."

Our conversation was interrupted at this sobering moment when my father returned with a large Wal-Mart sack. I left the men in the living room and carried the purchases to the bathroom door, where Mother was hovering. I gave the bag to her, and she checked to be sure all her purchases were there.

Apparently satisfied, she cracked open the door and passed in the new underwear and a pair of pink pajamas covered with hearts to Heaven. I was certain the child would refuse to put on those silly pajamas, but a few minutes later the bathroom door opened, and Heaven stepped out— squeaky clean and wearing the sissy night gear.

I watched Mother towel-dry Heaven's damp hair and brush it away from her face. Then she handed Heaven the new toothbrush and gave the child dental hygiene tips.

Once Heaven's teeth were as clean as the rest of her, Mother said, "Now it's time for bed."

I waited for a complaint, but Heaven followed my mother submissively into my bedroom.

Mother knelt beside my bed and instructed Heaven to do the same. Then my mother helped her to say the same prayer I'd recited every night of my childhood. Once that was done, Heaven climbed into my bed, and Mother tucked my covers under her chin.

Then Mother sat on the edge of the bed and sang the lullaby she used to sing to my sisters and me when we were little.

> *Sleep my child and peace attend thee,*
> *All through the night*
> *Guardian angels God will send thee,*
> *All through the night*
> *Soft the drowsy hours are creeping,*
> *Hill and dale in slumber sleeping*
> *I my loved ones' watch am keeping,*
> *All through the night.*

I'd always felt impatient during this lengthy bedtime ritual, but Heaven seemed to enjoy it. Mother continued to sing and stroke Heaven's forehead, and finally the child closed her eyes.

Mother stood and motioned for me to follow her out of the room. She left the door slightly ajar so we'd be able to hear Heaven if she called us. Then we joined the rest of the adults in my already crowded, tiny living room.

Mother moved to stand in front of the assemblage and said that the first order of business should be to move Heaven to her house. Her reason being, "I can care for her so much better there."

"But we can secure her better here," Mark said, kind but firm. "And safety is the most important consideration."

Even my mother couldn't argue with this. "I suppose you're right," she replied with a frown.

"You can arrange for her schoolwork to be brought here by a home-bound teacher," Mark suggested, "just until we're sure it's safe for her to go to school. Kennedy, either you or your mother will need to be here with Heaven at all times."

"I'll explain the situation to my brother and ask him to arrange for his wife to answer the phone at the dental office," Mother said. "That way I can come over every day and cook for Heaven and make sure she gets her schoolwork done while Kennedy is at the library."

My mother coming to my apartment every day was only marginally better than having to move back home, and I worked hard to control a groan of agony. I wanted to point out that no one had asked my mother to care for Heaven. But with the construction of the new library and the now-public investigation into Foster's death, I would have my hands full. Heaven seemed to like Mother, so I decided to leave it alone.

Luke stood. "I'd better head home."

Daddy rose from his seat on the couch. "It is getting late."

Mother glanced anxiously back toward my bedroom. "I hate to leave Heaven," she said. "After all, Kennedy has no experience with children."

"She'll be fine," I assured her, and I really was confident that she would be. I may not be an experienced mother, cook, or a good housekeeper, but a little dust and a few Pepsis wouldn't hurt the kid. Based on what I'd seen, I believed that Heaven could live off the land if necessary.

I walked outside with my guests as they made their collective exit. Cade was standing guard on the porch. I didn't like feeling grateful toward him, but I was. He scowled at me.

I waited until the others had gone down the stairs, and then I stepped close to Cade and demanded, "Why are you mad at me?"

"I'm disappointed," he corrected. "I can't believe you used that little girl to publicize your theory that Foster Scoggins was murdered. I didn't realize you would stoop so low."

"I didn't use Heaven—if anything, she used me!" I whispered in outrage. "And you're a fine one to talk about stooping *low*."

"Are you ever going to stop throwing that in my face?"

"Maybe, if I ever forget that image of you and Missy Lamar in the back of your Rodeo at the drive-in . . ."

Cade hung his head in defeat. "I'm sorry."

"I know."

The porch shuddered slightly, and we looked down to see Mark Iverson climbing up—fast.

"The preliminary autopsy results on Foster Scoggins are back," he told us breathlessly. "He had a drug called Versed in his system. It's a sedative that works almost instantly. It wasn't enough to kill him, but I think we can safely assume that Foster didn't jump onto those electrical coils under his own power."

I was thrilled and terrified at the same time. We'd uncovered a murder plot, and there was at least one killer in Midway.

"Based on that and Heaven's contention that Foster was afraid for his life," Mark continued, "the FBI has opened a file and is officially investigating his death as a murder."

"So where does that leave us?" Cade asked. "We have jurisdiction."

For some reason this question made me furious. "Until now you didn't *want* to investigate Foster's death! Now you're claiming jurisdiction?"

"The FBI is taking control of the case," Mark interrupted. "But we will continue to work with the sheriff's department and appreciate their cooperation."

"I'm sure Sheriff Bonham will help in any way he can," Cade said. "After all, we want to solve the case just like everybody else."

Mark smiled. "That's the attitude I like to see."

Cade hooked a thumb toward me. "Now that you're in charge, maybe you can convince Kennedy not to be too trusting of Luke Scoggins. She wouldn't listen to me."

"Do you have evidence against Luke?"

"As much evidence as we have against anybody in this investigation," Cade returned. "Who would benefit most if Foster died?" Cade answered his own question: "Luke. Who had access to both Parnell and Foster and could have given them drugs? Luke. Who would have known about Foster's secret girlfriend and been able to switch out the threatening letters with fake love letters without causing any suspicion? Luke. Who would Foster be trying to protect Heaven from by hiding the passbook to his savings account under the floorboard and telling her to show it to someone besides family if he died? Luke."

"Oh yeah, well Francie thinks *you* killed Foster!" I interrupted in a passionate attempt to defend Luke.

"Me!" Cade cried. "I didn't kill anybody!"

"Well, it can't be Luke," I insisted, even though all of Cade's accusations had at least some merit. Luke had been a hoodlum as a teenager. He had a police record. And I remembered those scratches I'd seen on his hands at the Flying J during our first non-date. Could those have been a result of throwing Foster onto the electrical coils?

Cade knew me well. He saw my uncertainty and pressed his advantage. "His whole life Luke has solved problems with violence. And now, thanks to the Marines, he's actually got killing *skills*."

"It's not fair to accuse him of things when he's not here to defend himself," I said stubbornly.

Cade smirked. "You're just too infatuated with him to see the truth."

Mark held up his hand to end the argument. "Luke is a suspect, but he's got a lot of company on that list. The FBI will investigate all of them." He turned to me. "And in the meantime, just be careful."

I nodded. I didn't like the idea of Luke being on the suspect list, but as long as he was one of many that the FBI was going to investigate thoroughly, I didn't mind too much.

"Is Kennedy still going to be working on the case now that the FBI is in charge?" Cade asked, and if I'd been close enough, I would have kicked him.

"Not officially," Mark replied. "But we'll keep her in the loop, and until the guilty part is behind bars, we'll have an agent following her wherever she goes."

It had been one thing to help the sheriff's department with a possible murder, but now I was unofficially helping the FBI with a real murder investigation. I stood a little straighter. "I'll be glad to do whatever I can."

Mark smiled. "I'm going to head home. Call if you need me."

I promised that I would as Mark left. Then I turned to Cade. "Mark said he faxed you a picture of Foster and his girlfriend and asked you to give me a copy."

Cade nodded. "It's in my car." He stomped downstairs and retrieved the picture. When he gave it to me, I was embarrassed that I'd made him go to the effort. It was probably the worst picture quality I'd ever seen. The lighting was terrible, and the angle was awkward. At a glance I knew the woman would never be identified from this picture since her face was turned completely away. But Foster was another matter. The camera had gotten a good profile shot of his face as he used one of his big hands to open the motel's door. So even though I didn't want to believe he had a girlfriend, it was hard to argue with proof in blurry black and white.

I went back inside my apartment and put the picture in my Murder Book. Then I tiptoed into my room and fumbled around in the dark for a pair of pajamas to keep from disturbing Heaven. Finally I gave up on the pajamas and settled for a pair of sweatpants and a T-shirt.

I changed out of the dress I'd been wearing since church and went to the kitchen. Thanks to my mother, there were numerous containers of food to choose from. I selected the potato salad and ate straight out of the Tupperware bowl while drinking a Pepsi and watching the news. The broadcast was dominated by reports about Foster's death and probable murder, the savings account full of money that apparently belonged to a seven-year-old, and the now-jeopardized land deal in Midway. But I noticed they were careful not to mention Heaven by name, so I assumed their legal department had made recommendations to protect their broadcasting license.

During the sports segment, Miss Eugenia called, wanting to know all that had gone on after she left.

"The FBI is taking over the case," I told her. "Mark is going to round up the potential land sellers and try to force some of them to admit to being part of a conspiracy to make Foster sell the salvage yard."

"That's good."

"Yes, but Luke stood to gain the most," I said. "And I can't bear to think that he was involved in his uncle's death."

"It's better to know the truth," Miss Eugenia advised. "Even if it hurts."

"I guess."

"And there are lots of suspects—so you don't need to start worrying about Luke getting convicted *yet.*"

This still didn't make me feel better. "I'm just glad Mark is taking over everything. He seems very meticulous and determined to find the murderer."

"He is. And now that Heaven is rich, it shouldn't be as hard to find parents for her," Miss Eugenia said with a chuckle. "That old Foster was pretty clever."

"Not clever enough to avoid getting killed," I pointed out.

"True," she agreed.

"Well, I'll let you go," I said around a yawn. "I'll come for a visit soon."

After I hung up the phone, I looked outside. Police officers and sheriff's deputies mingled around the parking lot of the Midway Store and Save. It was all dark and eerie, and I hate being afraid. When the phone rang, I almost jumped out of my skin. After a few calming breaths, I answered it.

"This is Agent Heflin of the FBI," the voice identified itself. "I've got a Mr. Sloan down here demanding to see you. We've searched him for weapons, and he's clean, but we won't send him up if you don't want to see him."

I walked to the door and opened it. A very unhappy Sloan was standing between the FBI agent and an Albany policeman. The construction worker was wearing one of his signature too-tight T-shirts—this time black—and a pair of jeans. His dark hair was loose on his shoulders and with his chiseled features he looked like he should be shirtless on the cover of a steamy romance novel.

For the first time since I saw Heaven on television, I wanted to laugh. "Send him on up," I told Agent Heflin.

After giving the agent a look of disdain, Sloan took the steps two at a time and was soon crowding the little stoop in front of my apartment.

"Are you okay?" he asked. "I saw you on the news."

"I'm fine." I saw Cade watching us, so I waved Sloan inside.

Sloan ducked under the doorframe, saying, "Drake was worried. Since he's in Cincinnati, he asked me to check on you."

I was flattered that Drake was concerned enough to send Sloan over. "Thank you for coming." I waved at my couch. "Have a seat."

He settled gingerly on the edge of my old couch. Then I offered him a Pepsi.

"No, thanks." He picked my Murder Book up from the coffee table and pulled out the picture of Foster I'd just received from Cade. "I didn't know you were looking into the salvage yard owner's death." Sloan's penetrating gaze was unreadable. "I guess you're more than just a pretty face."

I took the notebook and picture from him and returned them to the coffee table. Then I casually asked, "Why are you interested in Foster Scoggins's death?"

"I didn't even know the old guy," he said. "But the salvage yard land is crucial to this development project. If Drake can't buy it, we're going to have to pack up and move on to the next run-down town."

Sloan's words stirred a Midway loyalty that I didn't even know I had. "We were doing okay before Drake got here."

Sloan laughed. "Yeah, right."

Still annoyed but anxious to keep Sloan talking, I tried another tack. "I was surprised by how much time and money Drake has already put into the housing developments since the deal wasn't finalized yet."

Sloan shrugged his massive shoulders, and for the first time his muscular build seemed menacing instead of attractive. He was definitely strong enough to drag a drugged Foster Scoggins up the hill by the electrical relay plant and throw him onto the coils.

He interrupted these disturbing thoughts by further answering my question. "It's the way Drake operates. If he waited until every *t* was crossed and every *i* was dotted with these deals, it would take years to develop each town."

"So he's willing to risk losing money?" I clarified.

"If it doesn't work out, any money he's spent will become a nice tax write-off," Sloan explained. "But there have only been a couple of times in all the years I've worked for Drake where it didn't work out in the end."

"So you think there's still a chance the land deal will go through?"

"I think there's a good chance," Sloan confirmed with confidence. "The surviving brother didn't have a problem with selling the salvage yard back when his brother was alive to run it. Why would he want to hold on to it now that his brother is dead?"

This was sounding almost like a confession of murder, and I wanted to ask something that would make Sloan incriminate himself (and Drake). But before I came up with anything, he stood.

"It's late. I'd better go."

I followed him to the door. "Thanks for coming. It was nice of Drake to be concerned about me."

Sloan's smile widened. "Drake's a nice guy." When he reached the door he turned. "You free for lunch tomorrow?"

I shook my head. "I've got a busy day planned. I've got to meet the owners of the old library trailers at nine to turn over the keys and then check the progress at the new library, and then I need to get some groceries since Heaven is staying here . . ."

Sloan looked like he thought I was making excuses, but he nodded. "Some other time." Then he ducked out onto the front porch, and I felt the entire apartment vibrate as he descended the stairs.

I waited until I was sure he was gone. Then I got Mark Iverson's card out of my wallet. I figured he'd had time to get home but not enough time to go to bed. I dialed the home number, and when he answered, I listened for Baby Jake in the background without any luck.

"I'm sorry to bother you, but Sloan, a construction guy who works for Drake Langston, was just here. He said that they expect the land deal to go through since Parnell was okay with selling the salvage yard before Foster died."

"And he doesn't think that Parnell will be soured on the deal by his brother's murder?"

"He pointed out that Parnell can't run the salvage yard without Foster. So keeping the land makes no sense, especially when Drake is offering lots of money."

Mark sighed into the phone. "I guess."

"But Sloan said if the deal can't be worked out and they have to leave, it won't be a big deal. According to him, Drake always makes a significant financial investment in the towns he's refurbishing in the interest of time. Sloan said that's only happened a couple of times, and if it happens here, Drake will just use the loss as a tax write-off."

"That's probably true."

"I wanted to let you to know."

"And I appreciate the information," Mark said. "We'll catch whoever killed Foster. They won't get away with murder."

"That's good, but . . ." I paused. I really liked Drake and appreciated all he was doing to build the new library. But if there was a chance that he had killed Foster, I had to know.

"But what?" Mark prompted.

"Could you check the other towns where Drake has done major developments and see if anyone who didn't want to sell ended up dead?"

There was a brief silence, and then Mark said, "We're already in the process. I'll let you know if we find something."

I felt so relieved to have the FBI on my side. "Thanks," I nearly whispered. Then I ended the call and curled up on the couch. Before my eyes had time to close, Heaven called me from my bedroom. "Kennedy?"

I walked over and found her sitting up in bed. "Did you need me?"

Apparently she hadn't been asleep the whole time, since she asked, "Do you really think Luke killed Foster?"

"No," I told her honestly. I couldn't tell if she was worried about it or just curious.

"Me either," the child said, and I felt relieved. Then I felt stupid for taking comfort so easily. What did Heaven know? She was only in the first grade—for the second year in a row. "Try to go back to sleep," I encouraged her.

Heaven turned over and closed her eyes. I watched her for a few minutes. Then I double-checked the locks, climbed back onto the couch, and finally fell asleep.

CHAPTER SIXTEEN

I WAS AWAKENED THE NEXT morning by the sound of loud knocking. My eyes flew open in terror. Heaven was sitting on the far end of the couch by my feet. She had turned on the television, but the volume was so low I could barely hear it. Whether she was being courteous or just trying to keep me asleep so she'd have the TV to herself, I couldn't be sure.

"Someone's here," Heaven said as the pounding resumed.

I stood and staggered to the door. Through the peephole I saw my mother standing impatiently on the stoop.

"For heaven's sake, Kennedy," she said when I opened the door. "You sleep like the dead."

There was no sensible way to respond to such a silly remark, so I just stepped back to let her in and then closed the door behind her.

"Good morning, Heaven. I brought you buttermilk biscuits and home-made gravy for breakfast."

My mouth started to water. Maybe having my mother around wasn't going to be a completely bad thing.

We sat at the small kitchen table, and my mother distributed the meal. In addition to baking biscuits and making gravy, she had scrambled eggs, fried bacon, and made freshly squeezed orange juice. Heaven and I both ate ravenously while my mother outlined her plans for the day.

"First we're moving to my house," she announced.

I raised an eyebrow. "I presume you got permission from Agent Iverson?"

Mother nodded. "I talked to Heaven's principal. He is sending a home-bound teacher to give Heaven her assignments so she won't fall behind while she's not able to attend school because of this safety situation."

I refrained from pointing out that Heaven fell behind last year even when she *was* attending school and was making no effort to catch up.

Mother continued. "Dr. Hinton is going to make a house call, and the folks from It's a Child's World agreed to bring some things for Heaven to try on. When I explained to Agent Iverson that we just don't have enough room here for the teacher and the clothes and the doctor, he said we could move to my house for the day. He's sending some people with us for protection."

I was relieved to hear this.

"Can I get new shoes?" Heaven asked my mother. "Mine are too small."

"Of course we'll get you new shoes. Now finish eating," Mother encouraged Heaven and then turned to me. "What about you, Kennedy? Are you going to come with us to my house?"

Mother and Heaven both looked hopeful, but there are limits to my charity. "Sorry, I can't. I'm supposed to meet Francie at the old library at nine o'clock to turn over the keys. Then I need to go to the new library and see how things are progressing there . . ."

I glanced at my mother to gauge her reaction. She didn't seem to mind having me busy now that she had Heaven to care for. Some daughters would have been jealous of the attention she was showing Heaven, but I was relieved to have my mother's attention diverted elsewhere.

We finished our meal, and I rinsed the breakfast dishes while my mother helped Heaven get dressed for their day. When they reappeared, Heaven was wearing a coordinated shorts set. If not for the bone-deep cut on her hand and her unnaturally wise eyes, she'd have looked like any other kid. With police escort, they left in a hurry so they could make their appointment with the homebound teacher.

After savoring the peace and quiet for a few minutes, I got into the shower. While I was dressing for the day, the phone rang, and I answered it to find Luke on the other end of the line.

"Good morning," he said in that lazy drawl that made my heart pound.

I almost whimpered, *Please don't be a murderer.* Then I cleared my throat and said, "Good morning to you."

"The sheriff just called. Uncle Foster's autopsy is done, and they found traces of drugs in his system."

"That's what I heard," I replied.

"Oh." He sounded surprised.

"Mark Iverson told me." I was careful not to say exactly when Mark had given me this information since that would make Luke wonder why I didn't share it with him last night.

"How busy is your day?"

"I'm meeting Francie Cook at nine to give her the keys to the old library, and then I was planning to spend the rest of the morning at the new library. What do you need?"

"They've released Uncle Foster's body, so we're having the funeral at eleven o'clock this morning," he continued. "We're not announcing it—hoping to keep the press away—but Heaven will want to come, and I was hoping you'd bring her."

"Of course," I answered automatically. "I can work that in with no problem."

"I asked Brother Jackson to do the service since he's been so nice about Heaven," Luke continued. "We're just going to do a quick graveside service at the Midway Cemetery."

"I'll have Heaven there," I promised. Then I disconnected and called my mother to break the news that her plans for the day would have to be altered. I wasn't surprised that she already knew about the funeral. She had an amazing network. Apparently Brother Jackson had asked the Funeral Luncheon Committee of the Midway Baptist Church to provide a light lunch for the mourners after Foster's graveside service. So as a member of the FLC, my mother had been notified by the church secretary. She had then rescheduled the meeting with the homebound teacher and the doctor's visit before calling Mary Beth McLemore at It's a Child's World and arranging for her to add a couple of dresses appropriate for a funeral to the clothes she was bringing for Heaven to try on.

"I'll be by to get Heaven a little before eleven."

"There's no point in that," Mother replied. "Your father and I want to attend the funeral, so we'll just meet you at the cemetery at 10:45."

I knew for certain that my father did not want to attend anyone's funeral—especially Foster Scoggins's. But I also knew he'd do whatever my mother asked him to. So I said, "That sounds fine."

I hung up the phone and had just pulled off the comfortable jeans I'd planned to wear that day in preparation to don my black funeral dress when Miss Eugenia called.

"The FBI has released Foster's body," she informed me.

"I know. They're burying what's left of him at eleven o'clock this morning." Belatedly I remembered that Luke had asked me to keep this information to myself. "But don't repeat that. They don't want Channel 5 News at the funeral."

"I can certainly understand that," Miss Eugenia said. "I assume you're going?"

"Yes," I confirmed as I wriggled into my black dress. "I've got to go by the old library at nine to give the keys to Francie Cook. Then if I want to keep my job as head librarian, I've got to spend some time at the new one this morning. I have to get to the funeral and then—"

"Well, I can see you're busy," Miss Eugenia said, finally getting the hint. "I'll probably see you at the funeral."

I hung up, slipped on my cute black sandals, and hurried to the door. Since I was running late, I didn't take the time to actually speak to the officers milling around the Midway Store and Save. Instead I just waved as I passed by. I did share my schedule with the FBI agent who was assigned to follow me around all day. He nodded and started his government car while I climbed into my truck.

I pulled out of the parking lot with my escort close behind me. Figuring that I was safe from a speeding ticket since all the local law enforcement was on guard duty, I put the accelerator to the floor and zoomed toward the old library.

I was pleased when I arrived at three minutes after nine and found that Francie was not there yet. Saturday had been so rushed that I didn't get to say an adequate good-bye to the old space, and I was thankful for some time there alone. Out of habit I parked at the back of the small parking lot—a practice I followed to reserve the closer parking spots for patrons.

The FBI agent parked next to my truck and watched as I started toward the trailers that had once been the Midway Library. I had only taken a few steps when a horn honked. I looked around to see Sloan drive a big black truck into the small parking area. He parked and climbed out. While holding on to the open door, he said, "Since you can't go to lunch with me, I thought I'd ask you to breakfast."

He didn't seem threatening in the light of day—just gorgeous. So it was kind of fun to turn him down. "Sorry, but I've already eaten."

"You're breaking my heart," he claimed ridiculously.

I shook my head. "Save it for the big-city girls."

Sloan frowned, and for a moment I thought—impossible though it seemed—that I'd hurt his feelings. Then a strange expression, much like fear, crossed his handsome features.

I took a step toward him. "Sloan?"

"Kennedy!" he cried. Then he leaped across the distance that separated us and tackled me to the ground as the library trailers exploded into a blazing inferno. The sound of shattering glass and shredding metal was deafening. I wanted to cover my ears, but my hands were pinned under me. The heat from the nearby fire scorched my face, and Sloan's weight pressed my exposed skin into the gravel. My screams of pain and fear were swallowed by the all-consuming noise.

Footsteps rushed toward us, and soon a pair of black wingtips came into my limited view. "Are you okay?" the FBI agent asked. It sounded like he was whispering, but from his expression I knew it was more likely that he had yelled the question.

"Yes," I managed. "Except that my throat is raw from screaming, and I can't hear very well."

He didn't seem very concerned by these minor complaints. "Nothing broken?" he verified as he slid Sloan off me.

"No," I answered.

After checking Sloan's pulse, he lifted me gently and carried me across the street.

I craned my neck so I could keep my eyes on Sloan, who was lying ominously still in the old library's parking lot. "Is Sloan okay?"

The agent deposited me on a grassy area across the street. "He's alive," was the only information he gave me. Then he ran back for Sloan. I divided my attention between Sloan and the burning trailers. As the agent put Sloan on the grass beside me, I heard sirens in the distance.

A volunteer fire truck arrived first. In rural areas like ours, fire hydrants are few and far between. So they began dousing the blaze with water from the tanks mounted on the back of the truck.

One of the firefighters came over to check on us, and I directed him toward Sloan. I watched while he did a quick examination, and then I asked, "How is he?"

"His vital signs are good," the fireman replied. "He's got a bump on his forehead so it looks like he was just knocked unconscious."

I pointed at the smoldering remains of the old library. "What happened?"

"Gas," the fireman replied. "The furnace was on, but the pilot light was out."

Sloan started to stir, and the fireman urged him to hold still. "You might have a concussion," he said. "An ambulance is on the way to take you to the hospital so you can be checked out."

Sloan kept his head stationary, but his eyes moved frantically from side to side. "Kennedy!" he cried with a flattering amount of concern.

I leaned over into his line of sight. "I'm okay," I assured him. "Thanks to you."

Sloan's lips settled into an angry line. "Natural gas. I smelled it just before the trailers blew."

I frowned. "I don't understand why the gas was on. We haven't used the furnace for almost two months."

"Maybe it was a mistake," the fireman suggested.

Sloan shook his head, drawing a reproachful look from the fireman. "No, someone must have purposely turned it on."

"You really think so?" I asked in confusion.

"Yes, and if I hadn't gotten here when I did, it would have worked."

I didn't doubt him. My hands started to tremble, and I clasped them together. "The murderer?"

Sloan shrugged and winced. "Is there anyone else who would want to kill you?"

Before we could discuss what had happened further, the ambulance drove up with sirens screaming. Two paramedics jumped out and ran toward us. They stabilized Sloan's neck, loaded him onto a stretcher, and put him in the ambulance. As I watched them drive away, I struggled not to cry. Then Cade arrived, and I did cry. I even let him hug me despite the fact that he was a cheating, unfaithful jerk. I just couldn't help myself.

"It's okay," he said as he patted my back. His voice was shaky, and I wondered if he was going to cry too. "You're fine."

"Sloan thought someone was trying to *kill* me," I managed between sobs.

Cade's arms tightened around me. "Well, they didn't."

Mark arrived a few minutes later, and after making sure that I wasn't injured, he asked who knew that I was coming to the library that morning.

"Several people," I replied, trying to think. "I told Sloan and Luke and Cade and my family and Miss Eugenia." I looked up at him. "And there's no telling who they told."

He nodded. "We'll go on the assumption that everyone in the state of Georgia knew you were coming here."

"There's one person who knew for sure since she asked you to meet her," Cade pointed out. "Francie Cook . . . and I find it very strange that she's . . ." he checked his watch, "fifteen minutes late."

As if on cue, Francie pulled up at that moment. She parked her Escalade a safe distance from the carnage and ran over to join us. "What in the world happened?" she cried with convincing alarm.

I saw suspicion in Mark's expression as Cade responded.

"Someone blew up the library," Cade said harshly. "They meant to blow up Kennedy too. And I think that somebody was *you!*"

"Deputy Burrell." Mark's tone urged caution.

"Me?!" Francie screeched. "Why would I want to blow up my own trailers? I already had a tenant to rent them, and we need the money!"

This seemed like a trivial remark in the face of my near-death experience, but before I could complain, Cade said, "I'm sure you've got these trailers well insured and stand to make a pretty profit now that they are nothing but ashes!"

"Of course we have them insured," Francie told him. "Any responsible person has insurance on their property."

Cade gave her a menacing look. "Kennedy was getting a little too close to the truth, and you were desperate to keep anyone from knowing you murdered Foster. So you asked Kennedy to meet you here. You came early and turned on the gas so it would be ready to blow by the time she arrived. Then you waited from a safe distance for her to die!"

Francie looked furious. "That's ridiculous! I didn't have any reason to kill Foster Scoggins, and I certainly didn't try to kill Kennedy! I just knew she'd be late so I didn't rush to get here by nine."

"I am sometimes late," I said.

Cade ignored me and pointed an angry finger at Francie. "You did have a motive for killing Foster. The same motive you tried to pin on me—money. Drake Langston wants to build a bunch of houses in Midway, which would increase Terrance's salary. But Foster blocked the deal, which meant you'd be stuck here in this tired old town with no money to finance your endless plastic surgeries."

Francie's eyes bulged until I was afraid they might pop right out of her head. "How dare you!" she hissed. "You two-timing, sniveling skunk! I'll make sure you get fired, and then we'll see how arrogant you are!"

Mark stepped between them and gave Cade a stern look. "Control yourself, Deputy. You know this isn't the way to conduct an interrogation." He turned to the agent who had been following me at the time of the explosion and still looked a little shaken. "Take Mrs. Cook to our offices in Albany, and I'll question her as soon as I have time. Be sure she understands her rights." He glanced back at Francie. "You'll probably want to listen closely when he gets to the part about calling a lawyer."

Francie whimpered but didn't resist as the agent pulled her toward his car.

"Francie?" I whispered as I watched them leave. "Francie killed Foster Scoggins?"

"We don't know for sure," Mark hedged.

Cade grinned. "But it sure looks like we've solved the case."

"Francie never could have lifted Foster and thrown him over onto the electrical coils," I pointed out. "Even if he was drugged."

"No," Cade agreed. "Terrance must have helped her."

"Terrance?" I cried. "He might not be the brightest person, but murder?"

"It makes sense," Cade insisted. "They didn't have any land to sell to Drake, but they would both benefit if Terrance was mayor of a revitalized Midway with a bunch of taxpaying commuters living in the new subdivisions."

"It's worth looking into," Mark agreed reluctantly.

"It doesn't feel right to me," I said.

Mark pulled out his cell phone and stepped a few feet away where he could talk in relative privacy.

"You just don't want your first and only murder investigation to come to an end," Cade accused me good-naturedly.

There was some truth in this, but I did feel a little uneasy about the conclusions Cade had so quickly jumped to.

Mark rejoined us and said, "Whatever suspicions we might have, we can't go around throwing out accusations. We'll have to investigate first and then follow procedure."

"We'll keep our theories to ourselves," Cade pledged. Something about the way he included me in his promise made me uncomfortable. Then I realized that his arm was still around my shoulders. He was treating me like we were a couple, and I was not going down that road again—even if I did have a murderer after me.

I stepped out of his embrace and gave Mark my separate assurance that I would not tell anyone of our suspicions about Francie and the mayor until he'd had a chance to question them.

"I've got to get back to Albany and try to pry some answers out of the Cooks," Mark said to me. "But you absolutely cannot go anywhere alone."

Cade grinned like an idiot. "I'll take responsibility for Kennedy's safety. I'll be her bodyguard and follow her wherever she goes."

I gave Mark a tight smile. "While I appreciate Cade's offer, surely he could be better utilized investigating instead of following me around."

Cade's smile faded, and I knew I'd hurt his feelings. But it couldn't be helped.

Mark seemed to understand. "I could use Deputy Burrell to help me interrogate the Cooks since he knows them." He turned to Cade. "If you don't mind?"

Cade nodded stiffly.

"I've got a couple of guys I can put on Kennedy, and we'll add an Albany police officer to her security detail since they want to help and don't know the first thing about questioning people."

Cade looked mollified, and I was grateful to Mark for his tact.

I looked down at my torn dress and skinned knees. "I need to go home and clean up before the funeral. Can you take me?" I asked Cade. "And maybe Mark's guys can meet us at the cemetery?"

Mark nodded. "No problem."

I walked over to my truck and inspected it for damage.

He pointed to the back end of the truck that was listing dangerously to the left. "I think that tire is melted." Then he flecked off a piece of charred orange paint. "And you really need a new paint job."

I gritted my teeth. I'd always been so proud that my truck still had its original coat of paint. I reached out to pull a shard of broken glass from the truck's passenger window, which had blown out during the explosion.

"Could you call my dad and tell him what happened?" I requested. "Assure him that I'm fine, and ask him to break the news to Mother. I don't want to have to be the one to tell her. Then see if Daddy can have my truck towed to his workshop."

Pitifully anxious to do me a favor, Cade pulled out his cell phone. I was afraid if I heard my father's voice, I'd start crying again, so I walked over to Cade's squad car and waited until he'd completed his call.

"I talked to your dad, and he says he'll tell your mom," he reported.

"Thank you," I whispered fervently, as much to God as to Cade.

Then he opened the front passenger door and watched while I climbed in. I was already sore and could just imagine how much it was going to hurt to move the next day.

When we got back to my apartment, Cade made a big production of checking inside before he would allow me to go in. In a rare show of sensitivity, he stayed out on the porch after checking the interior, giving me a few minutes of much-needed peace and privacy. I stretched out on my bed and closed my eyes, letting my tears of fear and anger seep out.

At 10:15 I forced myself to get up and examine my reflection in the mirror. Thanks to the fire that destroyed the old library, my hair was slightly singed, and my face looked sunburned. Thanks to Sloan's protective tackle, my funeral dress was ripped and dirty. There wasn't much I could do about my hair except comb it. I put a new layer of makeup on my face, which helped to cover the heat damage. I pulled off my black dress and threw it into the garbage can. I washed my bloody knees and dabbed Neosporin on my numerous gravel-caused cuts. Then I covered them with flesh-colored Band-Aids.

I looked through the clothes Reagan had given me and found a navy blue suit. I put it on, knowing my mother would forgive me for not wearing black to the graveside service under the circumstances.

Once I was confident that I had done all within my power to improve my appearance, I walked into the living room and looked outside. Cade was standing on the steps, conferring with an Albany policeman who I assumed was going to be one of my bodyguards.

I didn't want to leave the safety of my little apartment. It was horrible knowing that someone had tried to kill me in earnest—that someone wanted to end my life. Someone wanted to make me draw my last breath, put me in a casket, and bury me in the Midway Cemetery.

Could that someone really be Francie Cook and the mayor? People I had known all my life?

The phone rang and startled me. It was my mother. She was so upset I could barely understand her—so I opened the door and handed the phone to Cade. I knew he would be able to reassure her better than I could.

He walked in a few minutes later and put the phone back on the charger. "Your mother is worried," he understated.

"I could tell."

"She wants you to stop investigating," he continued. "She doesn't want you to have anything else to do with Foster or his murder. She wants you to ride to the funeral with them and then stay in her sight for the rest of your life."

I tried to smile at the little joke. "I understand her concern," I replied. "But I'm not a child anymore. Tell her I'll meet them at the cemetery just like we planned."

He grinned. "I already did." He stepped forward and carefully wrapped his arms around me. "When I heard that call come over the radio . . ." he whispered, choking up and having to stop for a few seconds. "I know you don't believe it, but I really do love you, Kennedy."

I was scared and shaken and off balance. I wanted to be held and comforted and protected. I knew that Cade could offer me all of those things—temporarily at least. But utilizing all the emotional fortitude I possessed, I pushed away from him.

"I believe that you do love me," I told him.

I saw hope in his eyes. "The only thing I want in life is for us to be back together."

I decided it was time for a showdown. "What were you thinking when you went to that drive-in with Missy?"

His eyes clouded. This was not the direction he had hoped our conversation would take. "I don't know. I have no excuse except that I'd been drinking. We didn't mean to do anything wrong, but one thing led to—"

"You don't have to describe the things that happened. I *saw* them."

He stiffened. "I've said I'm sorry in every way I know how. It's time for you to forgive me."

"I do forgive you," I said, and surprisingly it was true. "I just don't trust you."

"That's not fair!" he complained. "You can't keep holding something against me when I'm sorry and I've promised not to do it again!"

"Okay," I said for argument's sake, "I'm going to ask you some questions, and I want you to answer honestly."

He nodded, a little wary but still hopeful.

"If you were out of town in, say, Atlanta or Savannah, far from here, and the risk of anyone seeing you . . ."

Cade frowned. "What do you mean by that?"

"Just listen," I insisted. "So you're far from home and you walk into a bar for a quick drink, and there sits Missy Lamar."

Cade started shaking his head. "I wouldn't sleep with her!"

I ignored the despair I felt at that remark. "Would you *speak* to her?"

This question seemed to annoy him. "Of course. Anything else would be rude."

"Then would you sit by her at the bar?"

He sighed. "Probably—just while I had my drink. That wouldn't be wrong."

"Would you buy her a drink?" I pressed.

Cade's expression was belligerent now. "Maybe. There's no crime in that—even for a married man."

I nodded. "And then one thing would lead to another, and the next thing you know, the two of you would be rolling around in the back of your Rodeo again."

He couldn't refute this, and we both knew it.

"You're just not meant to be a one-woman man, Cade. And I can't share my husband with any pretty girl who happens along. So we'll remain friends, and we'll remain divorced. That's really the best for both of us."

He looked so sad I was tempted to hug him, but I was afraid one thing would lead to another.

"You should start dating, Cade," I suggested. "If you're not comfortable dating one of the other girls around here, you could drive to Albany. Or look up one of those Christian dating services online. I'm really not trying to punish you anymore. I want you to be happy. But I'll never marry you again. I think I can trust you to be a good friend—but not my husband. I want this to be settled between us once and for all."

"You're sure?"

"Yes, I'm sorry."

"No, I'm sorry."

I smiled at him. I knew it was going to hurt the first time I saw him with another woman—or maybe every time I saw him with another woman—but I also knew this was for the best. Our time together was over. We both needed to move on separately.

"So since my truck has been charbroiled, can you give me a ride to Foster's funeral?"

Cade nodded and waved toward the door. "Ladies first."

Just as we parked at the cemetery, it started to rain. While Cade searched the trunk of his squad car for an umbrella, I looked at the small group of people huddled under a flimsy funeral home canopy which provided very limited protection from the weather. They all looked miserable, and it seemed that Foster's funeral was destined to be as sad as his life.

When my parents realized I had arrived, they came charging toward us. My mother was in the lead with Daddy trotting behind her, trying to keep an umbrella over her head. I opened the passenger door to greet them. Then my father held the umbrella over both of us while Mother gave me a fierce hug, her eyes searching me for injuries.

"Are you okay?" she cried. "When I heard about the explosion—well, I just couldn't believe it. Things like this don't happen in Midway."

"I'm fine," I assured her. "And bad things can happen anywhere." I pointed at the unmarked car that contained my security detail. "Don't worry, Mother. I've got two FBI agents to follow me around."

"The presence of an FBI agent didn't stop you from being almost blown up this morning!" Her bottom lip trembled, and tears filled her eyes. "It's just too much, Kennedy. I just can't bear it."

I was uncharacteristically moved with compassion. "The FBI is questioning two suspects right now," I said.

Both my parents looked significantly relieved. "It's over, then," my father said, and I didn't correct him.

"Oh, that's good." My mother dabbed her eyes with the edge of a starched, white handkerchief. She ran her hands down my arms one last time and then released me. "I guess we should rejoin the others so the funeral can proceed."

Cade gave up on the umbrella and came to stand beside us. "Are you sure you'll be okay?"

I nodded. "I'll be fine."

"Then I'll head on to Albany to assist the FBI," he said.

I waved and started walking with my parents toward the graveside. I saw that Luke had stepped out from under the shelter provided by the canopy and was watching my approach anxiously. Raindrops dotted the shoulders of his suit coat and sparkled in his short, spiky hair.

I smiled to reassure him, and some of the tension drained from his face. I was surprised that I could silently communicate so well with someone I'd known for such a short time.

We joined the people gathered around Foster's casket. Mark Iverson was there—whether to pay his respects or collect evidence, I didn't know. Miss Eugenia, leaning heavily on a cane, and her boyfriend, Mr. Owens, were also present.

"We heard about the fire at the old library," Miss Eugenia said carefully. "I'm glad you're okay."

I nodded. "I'm fine, thank you."

"Accidents do happen," Mark added, and I realized he didn't want everyone at the funeral to know the true details—especially not his nosy neighbor.

Parnell's wheelchair was parked near the casket. Heaven was beside him, looking like an angel in a white eyelet dress and matching ballet slippers. Her hair was pulled back with a white satin bow, and even the cut on her hand was taped with snowy white gauze.

"You look beautiful," I told her.

Heaven smiled, and my mother explained, "Heaven agreed to let me pick out the clothes she can wear to funerals, and she gets to pick the clothes she wears to school."

I raised my eyebrows. "It sounds like Heaven got the better end of that deal since she goes to school way more than she goes to funerals."

Heaven smiled again, and I knew she agreed with me.

"Keep in mind that I'll be choosing the stores where we shop for school clothes," Mother murmured, and I realized that she had outsmarted Heaven—something that probably didn't happen often.

Then Luke directed my attention toward a man and a thin, blond woman standing behind Parnell. He said, "I'd like you to meet my brother, Nick, and Heaven's mother, Shasta."

I can't say I was astonished to see them—but I was surprised. After all, Heaven had only announced her newfound wealth the day before.

"Nice to meet you," I lied. Then I couldn't help but add, "It's good that you were able to make it for the funeral after all."

Nick just nodded, but Shasta said, "Heaven needed us. Of course we came."

I wanted to point out that neither of them had made any plans to attend until they found out that Heaven's name was on a savings account full of money. But since I knew my mother would kill me, I kept this to myself.

Brother Jackson cleared his throat to remind us of the reason we were all assembled. I reluctantly left Luke with the rest of the Scoggins family and stood between my parents during the short and poignant service. I couldn't help thinking that Brother Jackson had finally gotten his chance to preach to Foster. Maybe it wasn't too late after all.

When the funeral was over, Brother Jackson insisted that everyone come to the church for a luncheon that had been prepared by the Funeral Luncheon Committee. My mother seconded this, saying she had made the spinach salad herself.

I wanted to decline, but Luke sent me a pleading glance, so I nodded. "I've got to check on things at the new library, but I guess I can spare a few minutes."

"We've all got to eat," Miss Eugenia said with a smile. "And I love Iris's spinach salad."

We stepped out from under the canopy and discovered that the rain had stopped. As we walked toward the cars, I saw Heaven up ahead, flanked by Nick and Shasta, and wondered how my mother felt about the sudden arrival of the prodigal parents.

When we got to the cars, I heard Shasta ask Heaven, "Do you want to come with us, Sugar?"

Mark Iverson stepped up and informed them, "Heaven is under FBI protection, and until we are certain she's in no danger, she has to be with either Kennedy or Mrs. Killingsworth at all times."

Shasta looked surprised and displeased. "But I want to spend some time with my little girl."

"We'll do our best to accommodate you, but Heaven's safety is our major concern." Mark didn't give Shasta a chance to argue. He turned to me and said, "I've got to head back to Albany and talk to some people."

I nodded to indicate that I understood he meant the Cooks.

"Will you and your mother accept responsibility for Heaven?" Mark asked.

"Of course," I said.

"Let's go eat." My mother held out her hand to Heaven. The child walked with my parents to their car.

Jenna, the nurse Luke had hired to care for Parnell, was sitting behind the wheel of an Altima, which I assumed belonged to her. She climbed out and helped Luke get his father into the car.

"We're going to the Baptist church for a short luncheon," I heard him tell her.

"Your father gets tired easily," she warned with her head close to his.

I knew it was ridiculous, but I felt a pang of jealousy. Jenna was several years older than Luke but pretty in an older, plump kind of way. And while I didn't think he was attracted to her, she was obviously fond of him.

"I know," he replied to Nurse Jenna. "We won't stay long. But it would be too rude not to even make an appearance after the church ladies have gone to so much trouble for us."

I was silently relieved. If there was anything the Scogginses could do to worsen their reputation in the community, it would be to bypass the funeral luncheon that the women of the Baptist church had thrown together out of the goodness of their hearts.

Jenna collapsed the wheelchair and stowed it in the trunk of the Altima. Watching her reminded me that Mark wanted to know if the nurse had ever noticed Foster leaving late at night when she was caring for Parnell, before his brief stay at the nursing home. I made a mental note to ask her that while we were at the funeral luncheon.

I climbed into the backseat of my mother's Buick beside Heaven. During the ride to the church, my mother quizzed me about the explosion at the library. I answered her as vaguely as possible—frequently cutting my eyes in Heaven's direction so they would think the child was the reason for my reluctance to give details. But my mother continued relentlessly, and by the time we reached the church, I was beginning to wish I hadn't gotten rid of Cade. Even if bringing him with me to the funeral would have given him the impression that I didn't really mean what I'd said about our time as a couple being over.

The luncheon was set up in the preacher's meeting room instead of the larger (and more logical) assembly hall. I assumed the luncheon committee ladies chose the smaller location to minimize the fact that Foster had few mourners.

Everyone, including Miss Eugenia, had their fill of spinach salad, ham and potato casserole, and Luke's recipe for strawberry shortcake in a bowl. It was an odd group, and there were a few uncomfortable silences, but for the most part Miss Eugenia and my mother kept the conversation going.

While the dishes were being cleared away, Luke made a point of walking around the room. He thanked everyone for coming and expressed appreciation to the ladies of the Funeral Luncheon Committee for providing the meal. I noticed that Parnell had dozed off in his wheelchair and that Nurse Jenna was not attending the luncheon.

I went out to look for the nurse and found her sitting in a little alcove just outside the preacher's meeting room.

"You missed a delicious lunch," I told her.

She smiled politely. "I have to be careful to maintain a professional distance from my clients. I'm like a member of the family because I'm around so much. But I'm *not* a member of the family, if you know what I mean."

"I think I do," I said. Then I shifted my weight from one foot to the other, nervously trying to think of a smooth segue into the question I wanted to ask for Mark. Finally I settled for, "I've been working with the sheriff's department, trying to answer some questions about Foster's death, and I was wondering . . . did you ever notice him leaving during the night—back before Parnell went into the nursing home?"

Jenna thought for a minute and then shook her head. "No, I don't think Foster ever left during the night—but my room was on the far side of the house, away from the place where they park their cars. So if he did leave, there's a good chance that I wouldn't have noticed."

"That's just something we were curious about." I took a step toward the preacher's meeting room. "You're sure you won't join us?"

"I'm sure," Nurse Jenna confirmed.

I walked back down the hall. After I turned the corner, so I was no longer in the nurse's sight and had not yet been detected by the participants of the funeral lunch, I took the time to jot Jenna's comments down in my Murder Book. Then I went in and saw Luke on the far side of the room. I was walking toward him when Miss Eugenia intercepted me.

"So what happened at the old library?" she hissed into my ear.

"It blew up," I replied softly.

"I know that!" Miss Eugenia replied. "My next-door neighbor, Polly Kirby, always keeps her television on, and she called to tell me about the explosion. Whit and I tried to drive by on our way to the funeral, but they have the roads blocked off."

"There's not much to see," I told her. "Just a pile of blackened rubble."

"I guess the real question is—*why* did it blow up?"

"They are pretty sure someone purposely turned on the gas furnace so that it would explode about the time I arrived there at nine to meet Francie Cook and give her the keys."

"Someone?" Miss Eugenia repeated.

"Well, Mark is questioning Francie and her husband, Terrance," I disclosed without thinking. Then I added, "But don't tell anyone."

"The mayor and his wife?" Miss Eugenia sounded surprised.

I nodded. "They didn't own any land that Drake wanted to buy, but Terrance's salary will increase if the housing developments are completed."

"That's a pretty weak motive for murder."

"Maybe there's more we don't know yet," I said.

Miss Eugenia shook her head. "It's just like those old mystery movies where the butler did it. Nobody ever would have guessed."

"It's not official yet," I warned. "Right now Mark's just asking questions, but he is doing it at his FBI office in Albany."

"That sounds pretty official. I won't say a word," Miss Eugenia promised, although I wasn't sure she could be trusted to keep a secret. Most old Southern women thrive on gossip. "Thank goodness you'd already gotten all the books out of the old library."

I thought of all the books I had lovingly collected over the years. "Thank goodness."

Luke appeared at my side as if he sensed my distress. He had Mr. Owens with him.

"My dad is exhausted, so Nick is taking him home," he said.

I glanced over and saw Nick, with Shasta close behind him, pushing Parnell's wheelchair toward the door.

Luke gave Miss Eugenia a meaningful glance. "So I guess the funeral lunch is over."

Mr. Owens took Miss Eugenia by the arm. "Time to get you off that bad ankle."

While allowing Mr. Owens to lead her out, she turned to me. "Call me later."

"I will," I promised.

After Miss Eugenia and her boyfriend left, I said to Luke, "I thought the funeral was nice."

"It was perfect," he agreed.

"I was surprised to see your brother and Heaven's mother."

He shrugged. "I called Nick and told him about the money that would be available to Heaven's foster parents. So I wasn't really surprised when he showed up with Shasta."

"They just want the money?"

"I prefer to think that they always wanted to be with Heaven but just couldn't manage it financially. Until now."

I had a very different opinion, but before I could share it, my parents joined us.

Mother expressed her certainty that Foster was now resting in peace and then said to me, "We're going to take Heaven by the dental office to have her teeth cleaned, and then we'll be headed to your apartment. Are you coming with us?"

I needed to make sure Sloan was okay, but I didn't want to mention him to my parents, since that would involve telling them that my life had been in more danger during the explosion than I had admitted up to this point.

"I was supposed to spend the morning at the new library, checking on paint colors and things like that," I reminded them. "I'd better go there now for at least a little while. However, I am temporarily without transportation so I'll need a ride."

"I'll be glad to take you to the new library," Luke offered, and I gave him a grateful smile.

My mother looked most unhappy. "I think you should stay with us until the FBI makes sure they've arrested the right people."

I knew I should correct her, since no one had been arrested at this point, but I couldn't bring myself to do it. I patted Luke's arm. "Luke is a Marine. He can protect me. And I'll have an FBI escort wherever I go, so don't worry."

Mother seemed only marginally relieved, but she didn't argue further. She took Heaven by the hand and instructed my father to follow her.

Daddy paused beside me long enough to whisper, "Be careful!"

I nodded. He kissed my cheek and then hurried after Mother.

Luke and I thanked Brother Jackson one last time and then followed my parents outside at a safe distance.

CHAPTER SEVENTEEN

I WAS MORE CONCERNED ABOUT Sloan's condition than I was about the progress at the library, and I hoped that someone there could give me information on his condition. During the drive, Luke made me go over every detail of the explosion. I accused him of acting like my mother, but he wasn't insulted.

Main Street was crowded with construction equipment, especially in front of the old bank building. So Luke parked the Torino two blocks away, and we walked along the partially replaced sidewalk to the library's front entrance.

The transformation inside the old First National Bank was incredible, and Luke was obviously impressed. In addition to the repaired glass and freshly painted walls, draperies were now hanging on the big windows, which gave the huge space color and warmth. The floors had been buffed and waxed to a satiny shimmer. The circulation desk was in place, and what seemed like miles of shelving were laid out, waiting to be assembled. Several new chairs and couches, still wrapped in plastic, were stacked in one corner. Miniature furniture, intended for the children's section, was in another.

To my surprise, Sloan himself was at the job site. He was standing on a scaffold, preparing to hang the Monet print that had been Drake's inspiration piece for the new library's décor above the circulation desk. The only evidence that he'd been involved in an explosion a few hours earlier was the Band-Aid on his forehead.

"Are you okay?" I called up to him.

He held out his hands and gave me a grin. "How do I *look*?"

I returned the smile. "You look great, but you've been through a traumatic experience. Aren't you afraid you'll have some lingering effect, get dizzy up there, and fall?"

He lowered the scaffold and hopped off. "Dizziness is for sissies," he declared ridiculously. Then he turned his attention toward Luke.

"Have the two of you met?" I asked.

They shook their heads in unison, so I made introductions. "Sloan was the one who tackled me at the old library this morning," I told Luke. "He probably saved my life."

Instead of congratulating Sloan, Luke said, "I find it amazing that you just happened to pull into the library parking lot right before the place blew up."

I gasped, and Sloan's expression hardened. "What are you saying?"

"I'm just marveling at your excellent timing," Luke returned.

Anxious to end this sudden and unexpected conflict, I pulled Luke toward the front door. "I'll check back later," I told Sloan. Then I waved to encompass the whole library. "This is looking fabulous!"

Once we were outside, I asked Luke why he was rude to Sloan. "He saved my life," I reiterated. "You should be nice to him."

"I'm telling you—his *amazing* rescue is suspicious."

"If he was trying to kill me, why would he arrive just in time to save me?"

"I don't know, but the guy seems shady to me. You need to be careful around him."

I laughed. "Now you're starting to sound like Cade."

Luke stopped and grabbed me by the arm. "There's nothing funny about this. You could have been killed this morning."

I found his concern flattering and his sudden anger frightening. I pulled my arm away and rubbed the sore spots where his fingers had been. "It was your protective attitude that I found amusing—not the destruction of the old library or the possible attempt on my life."

He ran his fingers through his short hair in a gesture of frustration. "I'm sorry. I just don't want you to be casual with your safety, and I really do think that Sloan character shouldn't be trusted."

"I'll be careful," I promised. But I wasn't ready to forgive him for grabbing my arm and yelling at me.

Once we were in the Torino, Luke turned it around and headed back toward my apartment. Then he said, "I really am sorry."

I nodded. "I know."

When we drove past the cemetery, Luke slowed down and asked, "Would you mind if I stop for a minute? I want to check on things."

I assumed he meant he wanted to be sure the grave had been filled in. "I don't mind."

I was mostly over being upset at him when we parked. Once we were standing beside the freshly turned earth that covered Foster's grave, I found it impossible to stay mad at him. After all, he'd been under a lot of pressure, and his uncle was dead and buried.

We arranged the flowers that had been provided by the funeral home at the top of the mound of dirt where Foster's headstone would eventually be. We stood back, and even though I'd only met Foster once while he was alive, I felt like sobbing.

"No one deserves to die like he did," Luke whispered.

I was glad I had forgiven him. "This is a nice place," I said. "He'll be able to rest here."

"I hope so."

"Lots of my family members are buried nearby."

"Where?"

We walked around, and I pointed out the graves of various ancestors. Finally we sat on a stone bench. We were quiet at first. Then we talked a little about Heaven and what the arrival of her parents might mean. Finally Luke asked, "How did you and Burrell get together?"

"It was kind of a fluke," I told him. "Cade is Reagan's age, and I think—even though he's never admitted it—he had a crush on her during high school. But she married Baxter while Cade was off playing football for Florida State. When he came home, I was the only available Killingsworth girl, so he asked me out."

"And it was love at first sight?"

"I didn't date much during high school, so I didn't have a lot of experience with boys." I felt I needed to preface the description I was about to give of my whirlwind romance with Cade. "I had two years at the junior college and was still living at home. He was so handsome and charming . . . I was head over heels in a matter of days. I knew he had a reputation as a ladies' man, but I thought love conquered all." I dragged my eyes up to meet his. "It doesn't."

He leaned down and kissed me softly. "You just married the wrong guy."

I forced a little laugh. "No argument there." I cleared my throat and said, "You don't seem to be a big fan of Cade's either."

All humor left his face. "He was one of the main reasons I left high school."

I felt sad and oddly responsible. "What happened?"

"He was always picking on people smaller and weaker than him to make himself look better. But until the tenth grade I'd always been too unimportant to attract his attention."

I winced. "What changed?"

"Football," he said grimly. "I hadn't ever played, but I was strong and quick. The junior varsity team needed a tight end, and the coach convinced me to try out for the position. I got it and learned to love the game. For the first time I had something in common with the other guys and felt like I kind of fit in. But Burrell put an end to that."

"How?" I forced myself to ask.

"It was his senior year and he was starting on the varsity team, but he made a point of coming to the JV practices. He criticized everything I did. I decided to take his attention as a challenge. If I could get good enough—he wouldn't have anything left to complain about."

"So did you—get good enough I mean?"

"Yeah, but I should have known that's no way to defeat a bully. When there was nothing about my performance to make fun of—he got personal. He started calling me names. Pretty soon everyone was calling me names and I didn't fit in anymore. So I decided I'd had enough and quit—football and school."

"I'm sorry Cade was so cruel to you," I told him.

"He's a jerk, but I was an idiot for letting him drive me away from school," Luke said. "If I could go back . . ."

"But we can't."

He leaned closer, and I think he was about to kiss me again, but then we heard someone approaching. We both turned and saw Cade walking through the grave markers toward us.

"Speak of the devil," Luke whispered.

"I've been looking for you," Cade said as though I owed him an apology.

"We've been right here," Luke replied in the tense tone he always used with Cade.

Ignoring Luke, Cade informed me, "Mark sent me to get you. We've thoroughly questioned both the Cooks, and based on their testimony, we got a search warrant for their house. We found some pink paper that matches the letters found in Foster's truck and a couple syringes full of Versed—the medication the autopsy identified in the body."

I gasped. "So they *did* kill Foster?"

Cade nodded. "It looks that way. And they tried to kill you too. In Francie's car we found the remote for a little device used to blow up the gas in the old library."

My throat started to ache, and I rubbed it absently.

"Francie and Terrance are going to be arraigned in a couple of hours," Cade continued. "But the reason I'm here is that Francie wants to talk with you."

I looked up in surprise. "Me?"

Cade shrugged. "She wasted her one phone call trying your apartment. Mark took pity on her and sent me to get you. Maybe she just wants to apologize. I don't know. But Mark asked me to bring you to the courthouse in Albany."

"I guess I'd better go, then." With an apologetic look at Luke, I stood. "I'll call you later."

He nodded. Then I followed Cade across the cemetery to his waiting squad car and climbed in for the ride to Albany.

* * *

I knew Cade was irritated—or worse—that I was still spending time with Luke. And I was mad at him for being such a creep in high school. So we rode in silence. When we reached the Dougherty County Courthouse, Cade pulled into one of the reserved officer parking spots in front and climbed out. He started up the stairs, leaving me to follow. Apparently as long as I maintained a friendship with Luke, he wasn't going to open doors for me.

He led the way through the main entrance, down a long hall, and into the criminal section—which up to this point I had never visited. There were several tables with chairs set up around the room. Several were occupied, presumably clients consulting with their lawyers. Cade walked straight to the far corner where Francie sat with a youngish, preppie man who was probably fresh out of law school. The lawyer was dozing, and Francie was chewing up her manicure.

When Francie saw me, she burst into tears. "This is a mistake!" she wailed. The combination of tears and mascara coursing over the surgically stretched skin on her thin cheeks was not a pretty sight. "I didn't kill Foster, and I certainly didn't blow up the library! I don't know how those syringes got into my house, and I've never even heard of a remote device that can make a spark and blow up gas!"

The lawyer jumped out of his seat, rubbing the sleep from his eyes. "Who are you?" he asked, interrupting Francie's tirade.

"My name is Kennedy Killingsworth," I told him.

The lawyer frowned. "The victim?"

This annoyed me. "Foster Scoggins was the victim."

Cade spoke to me for the first time since he "caught" me talking to Luke in the cemetery. "You were a victim in the library explosion—even though you didn't die."

"And I don't want you talking to my client," the lawyer added.

Francie flagrantly ignored her lawyer's advice. "I did send Foster threatening letters. Foster was a mean, selfish old man. We begged him to reconsider. We explained that people's lives and dreams and futures were at stake, but he wouldn't listen. Since he didn't care about his neighbors, we thought maybe he'd care about his own safety. So I wrote the stupid letters. But I didn't kill him! It must have been one of the others!"

I'll admit I felt sorry for her, even if I didn't exactly believe her. "So was there a group of landowners who met together to think of ways to make Foster sell?"

Francie nodded.

"And why didn't you tell us this in the beginning?" Cade demanded.

"I was glad Foster was dead," Francie said. "He deserved it, and I didn't want anyone to be punished for it."

"Well, you're going to tell us the name of every person in your little group. Now!" Cade said angrily.

Francie's expression changed from distraught to cagey. She turned and whispered something to her lawyer, and then he addressed us.

"Mrs. Cook will tell you everything she knows, but we want total immunity from prosecution."

"So much for all those claims of innocence," Cade muttered.

The lawyer ignored this. "My client will answer no more questions until we have a deal on the table."

Cade nodded. "I'll tell Agent Iverson." Then he turned to me. "Let's get out of here."

As I trotted along after Cade, I was torn between triumph (after all, my conspiracy theory had been correct) and horror (some of my neighbors in Midway were murderers).

Once we were back in the squad car, I listened quietly while Cade called Mark. "She wants a deal." There was a brief pause. "I don't know what she's got to offer, but she started negotiating when Kennedy asked her about a group of landowners conspiring to make Foster sell the salvage yard." Cade listened for a few more seconds and then closed his phone.

"So?" I prompted as he moved his car out into the Albany traffic.

He cut his eyes over at me. "What?"

"Is the FBI going to offer Francie a deal?"

He shrugged. "Probably. If Francie didn't kill Foster, it's better to let her go for her lesser crimes and catch the murderer."

I couldn't disagree with this.

A few minutes later, Mark called Cade back. Immunity from prosecution had been offered to Francie, and she was singing like a bird. She had named ten other Midway residents who were involved in the conspiracy to force Foster Scoggins to sell his land. Since one of them had, presumably, killed Foster, they were all being brought in for questioning.

"Who?" I asked Cade, and he relayed the question to Mark.

A few seconds later, he itemized the conspirators. The list consisted entirely of people I knew, including the Lebows and Mrs. Castleberry. I was grateful that Brother Jackson and Miss Zelda weren't part of the group.

"So there's no danger to me or Heaven anymore?"

"Once they round up all the group members, I guess not," Cade replied. "The FBI will question the suspects, get search warrants, and make arrests. Then the investigation will be over, and it will be in the hands of the justice system."

It was horrible, knowing that residents of Midway had killed one of their own. So my heart was heavy as Cade dropped me off at my apartment. I expected to find my mother and Heaven there—which ordinarily would be a bad thing, but I was sad and didn't really want to be alone. Instead I found the apartment empty and a note from my mother on the kitchen table requesting that I call her.

"Oh, Kennedy!" Mother answered the phone. "Mr. Owens, Miss Eugenia's boyfriend, petitioned the family court judge for us, and he has awarded your father and me temporary custody of Heaven. There will be a formal hearing in a few weeks where her parents can make their case, but in the meantime she'll be with us."

"That's good," I replied.

"And Agent Iverson said we could come home for good. We're on our way to the Sherwin Williams in Albany right now. I'm going to let Heaven pick out some paint, and then your daddy is going to fix up the guest room for her."

"That's nice of you." My mother has always been particular about home décor, and her willingness to allow Heaven to pick her own paint color was nothing short of miraculous.

"You're welcome to come with us," Mother invited. "We could get dinner in Albany and then have a painting party. You could even spend the night in your old room!"

I was a little bit afraid to stay by myself and even more concerned about losing my hard-earned independence. But mostly I hated painting. So I said, "Thanks for the offer, but I think I'll pass."

I regretted those brave words when it got dark. Even though I knew all the conspirators had been taken into custody, I still felt afraid. The only thing that kept me from running straight to my mother and the safety of her arms was the fact that getting home would require leaving the safety of my apartment.

I called Luke. Mark had already informed him about the new developments in the case, so we didn't have to go through all that again. He described how miserable things were at the salvage yard with both Nick and Shasta now in residence, and I commiserated.

"Is that going to be a temporary thing?" I asked.

"It's temporary for me," he replied. "I'm leaving in a couple of weeks. Then they can fight over Foster's money all they want."

The reminder that Luke would soon be gone further depressed me.

After we hung up, I double-checked the locks on my doors and looked out the window to make sure no one was lurking in the shadows. Somewhat reassured, I ate a dinner of delicious leftovers (thanks to my mother).

I was rinsing my dishes when Miss Eugenia called. She complained that she hadn't been able to get anything about Foster's murder out of Mark.

I felt that I owed her some kind of explanation, so I told her Francie had pretty much confessed to being involved as part of a Midway landowners conspiracy. "She's cut a deal with the FBI and has gotten immunity from prosecution by naming the others who were involved."

"Who were the others?"

"I'd better not say," I said reluctantly. "I'm sorry."

"I understand about confidentiality," Miss Eugenia assured me. "You must be pleased that your conspiracy theory was correct."

"Not as much as I thought I'd be," I admitted. "All I've managed to do is prove that Midway isn't the dull, sleepy town we all thought it was. Instead, it's a hotbed of criminals."

Miss Eugenia laughed. "Sometimes the truth hurts—but it's still the truth."

"I guess," I muttered.

After ending my call with Miss Eugenia, I had settled on the couch to watch television when there was a knock on my door. I nearly jumped out of my skin. Once I had my breathing under control, I peeked through the peephole and saw Sloan standing on the porch.

With a hand against my pounding heart, I let him in.

He ducked inside and asked, "Are you feeling okay?"

I nodded. "Sore, but that's my only complaint."

He touched the bandage on his head. "I'm good too. We were lucky."

I couldn't argue with him there.

"Drake heard about all the arrests, and he feels responsible."

"That's silly," I said. "It wasn't Drake's fault."

"If he hadn't chosen Midway for this development, none of this would have happened," Sloan said.

"If some of the people who live here weren't greedy with hidden criminal tendencies, nothing would have happened even when Drake started trying to buy up land."

He grinned. "I'll tell Drake that. It should make him feel better." Sloan touched a small gravel-laceration on my arm. "I'm sorry about the cuts and bruises."

My throat tightened with emotion. "You saved my life. I won't complain about a few cuts and bruises."

"I just can't stop thinking about what would have happened if I hadn't decided to go by and beg you for another date."

I shuddered. "I'm trying not to think about that. It's what we Southerners call borrowing trouble. And it seems we have plenty without looking for any more."

His fingers moved up to the singed ends of my hair. Then he leaned down and kissed me gently on the lips. I didn't kiss him back, but I didn't resist him either. I knew I didn't especially like Sloan and therefore knew I shouldn't allow him to kiss me. But I couldn't seem to muster the energy to stop him. Later I blamed the moment of weakness on the connection forged between us by sharing a near-death experience.

When the first kiss ended, he smiled. "That was nice." Then he put his arms around me and moved in to kiss me again. I put a hand on his chest to stop him.

"I'm sorry," I said, "but I can't do this."

"We're not really doing anything," Sloan pointed out. "Yet."

I disengaged myself from his embrace and walked to the window. While looking out, I tried to explain. "I'm a small-town girl with traditional values. I married young and was always faithful to my husband. Since my divorce, I haven't had an interest in men."

He kept his distance, allowing me my space. "How about now?"

I had to smile. "There is some interest," I admitted. "But I can't do casual relationships, and I have a feeling you can't do anything else."

He shrugged. "Everything doesn't have to be complicated."

"For me it has to be at least meaningful," I countered.

There was a knock on my door. Grateful for the interruption, I walked over and pulled it open. Cade was standing on my porch, scowling.

"How much longer is he going to be here?" Cade asked with a wave in Sloan's direction.

I had to work hard to control a laugh. "He's just leaving," I replied. Then I turned to Sloan and said, "Thank you so much for coming by to check on me. And please thank Mr. Langston too."

Sloan was a good sport. "I'll tell him. Come by the library tomorrow. We'll be ready to arrange furniture, and we'll need your input."

"I'll be there," I promised.

Cade stepped aside to let Sloan pass. The men eyed each other with open antagonism, and I held my breath until Sloan was safely down the steps. Then I turned to Cade. "What are you doing here? I thought Mark had called off the guards."

He shook his head. "I'm not here officially, but no matter what you say, I know you're scared. So I'm going to sit up here on the porch and keep an eye on things so you can sleep."

He knew me well. "Thank you."

He shrugged. "What are friends for?"

I was grateful that he was there and even more grateful that he wasn't attaching strings.

"See you in the morning," I told him. I went inside, locked the door, and fell into bed, exhausted.

* * *

I meant to sleep in the next morning, but the phone rang at seven, waking me up. It was Drake. He was back in town but only for the day, and he wanted me to meet him at the Back Porch for breakfast. I agreed to be there at eight.

When I tried to stand, my entire body screamed in protest. I hobbled to the kitchen and took some ibuprofen. I looked through the peephole on the door and discovered that Cade really had spent the night on my porch. He had borrowed a chair from Mr. Sheffield's office downstairs. He was sitting with his feet propped up on the railing sipping coffee from a Styrofoam cup. I pulled the door open and stuck my head out.

"I survived the night, so you should go home and get some rest."

He finished off his coffee, picked up the chair, and started for the steps.

"Cade!" I called.

He paused to look over his shoulder at me with bloodshot eyes.

"Thanks."

He nodded. "I owed you."

"Now I think we're even," I told him.

After Cade left, I called my mother and arranged to borrow her car for the day, since my truck was still in my father's workshop awaiting repairs. I took a shower and then with effort brushed my fire-singed hair. I put makeup on the peeling skin of my face and dressed in a lemon-yellow linen pantsuit that felt too dressy, so I knew my mother would think it was perfect for breakfast with Drake.

At eight-thirty my parents arrived in my mother's car, with Heaven in the backseat, to pick me up. I dropped them back off at their house—declining Mother's insistent invitation to come in and see Heaven's new purple room.

After Heaven and my mother had gone inside, Daddy leaned in through the open driver's side window and pointed at the glove compartment. "I moved my gun from your truck to your mother's car. After everything that's happened over the past few days, I'll feel better knowing you have it with you."

I nodded, accepting the wisdom of this. "How soon do you think you can have my truck drivable?"

He considered this question and then said, "Probably by tomorrow."

I kissed his cheek. "You're the best."

He pushed away from the car and waved. "You be careful."

I waved back and then drove to the Back Porch. I arrived five minutes early, and Drake was already there. He was as handsome as ever but looked more serious than usual in a dark suit and gray tie.

He greeted me with a kiss on the cheek, like we were old friends. "I've missed you," he said.

And I realized I'd missed him too. "So you're only here for the day," I forced myself to say around the lump in my throat.

He nodded. "The deal here is complete. Parnell signed the paperwork selling me the salvage yard last night, and certified checks are being delivered to all the landowners by courier this morning."

"What about the people the FBI are questioning about Foster's death?"

Drake frowned. "The only way to finalize the deal was to send out the checks. I'll leave it up to the courts to make sure the guilty party won't profit from their crime once the murderer is identified. But it's out of my hands."

"So why are you leaving?"

He smiled. "Once I have a project running smoothly, I move on and start the groundwork for another one. Hopefully the next town renovation won't be this stressful."

I nodded but couldn't get excited about Drake making improvements in another town, changing other people's lives—possibly for the worse.

We went to the breakfast buffet and picked up plates. I wanted to fill mine with comfort foods like eggs, bacon, and biscuits and gravy. But since I knew Drake was conscious of fat and cholesterol—I picked up a bagel, a carton of yogurt, and half a banana. Drake filled a bowl with Raisin Bran, topped it with a medley of fresh fruit, and then poured skim milk over the entire concoction.

We returned to our table and after we ate in silence for a few minutes he said, "I'm sorry about the explosion at the old library."

I swallowed a bite of bagel and replied, "I'm just glad Sloan was there to help."

"He's like that—maybe it's his Native American heritage that gives him a shamanist sixth sense. He's saved me from disaster many times."

"Will he be leaving too?" I tried not to sound too bereft.

"He'll stay for a while—at least until the library is finished. I have to make sure it's completed since it's inheriting my father's name." He reached across the table and covered one of my hands with one of his. "This may be a little sudden, and don't feel like you have to answer me immediately, but I could use someone like you in my organization."

I was completely stupefied. I opened my mouth to try and make a response, but he had rendered me speechless—which doesn't happen often.

"I have so many projects going at once, in various stages of completion," he explained. "And there are so many important decisions to be made continually—like the ones you've made about the library. You would have the chance to travel and make a difference in other towns like Midway."

It was an attractive offer, even though he was offering me a job and not a relationship. And I won't pretend that I wasn't tempted. But over the course of the investigation into Foster's murder, I'd bonded with Midway and couldn't imagine leaving—even to be with Drake. It was too much, too fast for a small-town girl like me.

So I shook my head. "Thanks, but I think I'll just stay here and run the Midway Library."

"The Willard Langston Memorial Library," he corrected, and we both smiled. "If you change your mind, the offer doesn't have an expiration date."

"I won't change my mind."

"Well, then maybe you'll come visit me sometime."

"Maybe."

When our meal ended, he paid our bill, walked me to my mother's car, and waved good-bye. Watching him climb into his Lexus and drive away was one of the saddest moments of my life.

Once Drake was gone, I walked the few blocks down Main Street to the new library. When I pushed open the doors of the old bank building, I was awestruck. The library was truly an inspiring sight. Most of the shelves had been assembled and installed. Boxes of new books were stacked along the aisles created by the shelving. But most amazing, twenty brand-new computers were arranged in two neat rows in what would now be our technology section.

Sloan walked over to greet me. "So what do you think?"

"It's wonderful."

He nodded. "Well, it will be by the end of the week when we finish up."

"You'll be finished by the end of the week?" I tried to be happy, but it was difficult knowing that when Sloan finished, he would be leaving.

"If not sooner," he confirmed.

"Are you Ms. Killingsworth?" a voice said from behind us.

I turned to find a tall woman who looked vaguely familiar. "Yes."

"I'm Valaida Price with the Dougherty County Library Board."

A knot of dread formed in my stomach. Ms. Price had probably come to personally deliver my pink slip. "It's nice to meet you," I lied.

"I wanted to stop by and check on the new location, and I have to say I'm pleasantly surprised. When this branch is completed, it will rival the new building in Haggerty. But I do need to discuss your lack of qualifications to be director."

It was like my dream come true mixed with my worst nightmare. "I know I don't have a library science degree—" I began.

"You can complete your undergraduate degree at any accredited four-year college," Ms. Price interrupted. "Then you can get your master of library science degree online through the University of Georgia. Funds have been set aside for this, and you have five years to complete your education. If at the end of five years you are still not qualified, you'll have to relinquish your job, and we'll hire a new director."

I sifted through all this information and asked, "So I still get to be the director—even though I'm not qualified?"

"The job is yours if you want it," Ms. Price confirmed. "It was a requirement from Mr. Langston."

Tears blurred my vision.

"But his influence only reaches so far," Ms. Price continued. "So I strongly encourage you to get qualified fast before someone tries to take this nice library away from you."

I was a little dazed, but I nodded. "I'll take care of it this afternoon."

"Because you will now have extra hours of operation, the county library system is increasing your salary. You'll also have the funds to hire two assistant librarians and six part-time employees." Ms. Price reached into her small briefcase and pulled out a piece of paper. "I've typed up the job descriptions for you and have posted them on our library website. They have to stay there for two weeks before you can start holding interviews."

"I've never interviewed before," I admitted.

"I'll be glad to come over and help you with the process this first time," she said. "My number is on the top of this page."

I took the paper from Ms. Price and read the words in amazement. In addition to running this wonderful library, I would have people working for me. "Thank you."

"Since it will be a few weeks before you have your own employees hired and trained, the director of the library's main branch in Albany has generously offered to loan you a couple of employees, and I recommend that you ask for volunteers from the community."

"I will," I promised.

Ms. Price took one more look around at what promised to be an incredible library. "Congratulations, Ms. Killingsworth. Things like this don't happen every day."

I wanted to say that things like this don't happen to me *ever*, but I decided that was none of her business.

After Ms. Price left, I took a detailed tour of the building, and Sloan updated me on everything that had been done and everything that still needed to be done—along with a timetable for when the unfinished items would be taken care of. I listened to his efficient accounting and marveled. All my life, things in Midway had happened at a torturously slow pace. Drake Langston had changed more than just the library—he'd put Midway into high gear.

The last stop on Sloan's tour was a door in the back by the staff break room. Sloan said, "The plans call for a section of offices in the atrium—whenever that gets built."

"*If* it gets built," I corrected, and he smiled.

"But for now this is all you've got." He opened the door and stepped back for me to enter.

The room was larger than I expected, with the same dark hardwood floors, high ceilings, and crown molding that were found in the rest of the building. The walls were painted light sage green—a color that was in our range but one we hadn't used in any other part of the library. The drapes that hung on the window were made from one of the coordinating fabrics I'd chosen. There was a wooden desk, substantial but not overpowering, and above the desk hung another Monet print—this one of a woman reading to a child.

I was overwhelmed. "I didn't even know this room existed."

Sloan smiled. "That's the way I wanted it. Your office was my own personal project." He pointed to a bookcase that ran the length of the wall under the window. "For your private collection."

This was so thoughtful I had to bite my bottom lip to keep from grinning like an idiot. My books would have a place of honor in the new library. "I can never thank you enough."

He walked over and gave me a little hug. "I don't want you to thank me—just like it."

I managed a little laugh. "I more than like it. This is my favorite room in the whole place."

Sloan seemed very pleased. "Then I'll consider my project a success."

It was strange. I'd distrusted Sloan at first, and by the time we got to be friends, he was leaving Midway. I'd trusted Cade immediately, and by the time I realized I shouldn't have, I'd wasted four years of my life.

I looked up at Sloan's amazingly blue eyes, his sleek black hair, and his prominent cheekbones. No doubt he left admiring women behind in every town he traveled to with Drake. I hated to be part of the crowd—but facts are facts.

"Hey, Sloan!" a voice called. "The computer guy is here!"

"We're getting *more* computers?" I asked in astonishment.

He smiled. "Naw, this guy has come to install software on the computers—including the circulation system that will help you account for all your new books. After he gets the software installed, he's going to train you—if you have time."

I couldn't really refuse, so I said, "I'll make time."

By one o'clock, I had been given a crash course on our new library system and had even scanned some books into our system. Sloan insisted that I personally shelve the first book—just so I could say I did. Then he advised me to hurry and hire some folks so I wouldn't have to shelve all the rest of them. When I told him I had to leave, he offered to buy me lunch.

"I really appreciate the offer, but I can't."

He raised an eyebrow. "What's the excuse this time?"

"I have to apply to college and make a trip to Haggerty and . . ."

He nodded in easy acceptance, just like he did every time I'd turned him down.

"But I do appreciate everything you've done and I am going to miss you," I added.

"I'll be coming back occasionally to check on the housing developments. The next time I'm in Midway, I'll be sure to stop by here and ask you out so you can turn me down."

I had to laugh. "I'll look forward to that."

After I left the library, I drove to Albany and met with an admissions specialist at the campus of Troy State University. She helped me fill out papers, request transcripts, and pick classes. She even called Ms. Price at the library and got the details about my "Drake Langston" scholarship. By the time I left, I was an enrolled student ready to begin classes in two weeks.

On my way home, I stopped by Haggerty. As I drove through the town square, I admired the new Haggerty Library, but I didn't feel the least bit envious. I parked by the curb in front of Miss Eugenia's white house surrounded by beautiful flowers, shrubs, and trees. Then I walked up and rang her front doorbell.

I heard Lady barking from inside, followed by slow-moving footsteps. Finally Miss Eugenia pulled open the door.

"Kennedy!" She looked delighted to see me. "What a pleasant surprise."

"I should have called," I began.

Miss Eugenia waved this aside. "Nonsense. Come in and I'll get you a piece of pound cake. Whit tried a new recipe and we're trying to get opinions on it."

I followed Miss Eugenia through her cluttered living room and into her equally cluttered kitchen. It was the kind of place where I could relax. Miss Eugenia cut a generous slice of cake and put it on a small plate. Then she placed it before me with a fork.

I took a bite and nodded. "It's good."

"I think so too," she said. "I'm a pound cake purist, and usually don't like any variation from the basic recipe. But I think the addition of cream cheese helps it stay moist and gives it a little extra flavor."

I agreed that the cream cheese was a clever ingredient. Then I said, "I just enrolled at Troy State. I start in two weeks."

Miss Eugenia beamed at me. "Wonderful! Why this sudden interest in furthering your education?"

"Drake Langston made the country library board agree to keep me on as director of the Midway branch even though I'm not qualified—with the stipulation that I have to get qualified within five years. He even set up a scholarship for me. So I'm getting started right away."

"That Drake Langston . . ." Miss Eugenia said in the reverent tone people always use when they say Drake's name.

"What about Drake Langston?" Mark Iverson asked as he walked in through the back door.

Miss Eugenia stood and returned to the cake on her counter. "Mark came home for lunch, and I told him to come over and try some of Whit's pound cake before he heads back to Albany."

She put a huge hunk of cake on a small plate and set it on the table.

Mark sat down at took a bite of cake. "This is okay," he said. "But I prefer Whit's usual recipe." Then he looked at me. "Now what were you saying about Drake Langston?"

Miss Eugenia answered before I could. "He arranged for Kennedy to keep her job as director of the Midway Library, and he's given her a scholarship so she can complete her education."

Mark didn't look as impressed by this as seemed reasonable.

"You don't like Drake, do you?" I asked him.

"It's nothing personal," Mark said. "But since he's been the center of an FBI investigation, I'm very suspicious of everything he does."

"The FBI is investigating *Drake*?" I confirmed in horrified surprise. "And you haven't mentioned that why?"

"I couldn't mention it," Mark said. "Until now—since my superiors are closing down the investigation. I think we should keep watching him, but they think we've spent enough time and money on him without result."

"That's why you were so anxious to help Kennedy with Foster's murder!" Miss Eugenia accused mildly. "You wanted to keep tabs on Drake Langston."

I waited for Mark to deny this, but he just shrugged. "Since Langston was a suspect, it stands to reason that I would want to be involved."

I felt a little betrayed, but before I could say so, Miss Eugenia asked, "What did Drake Langston do?"

Mark swallowed a bite of pound cake before responding. "We suspect him of defrauding the government in these town upgrade developments."

"By your use of the word *suspect*, I assume you don't have any actual evidence of illegal activity," I guessed.

"If we had evidence, we wouldn't be closing the investigation," Mark muttered. "He's very smart, and we can't figure out exactly how he's stealing from the government, but I'm convinced that he is."

Miss Eugenia looked almost as upset as I felt. "So he's not helping people?"

"He does help the towns he renovates," Mark conceded. "But he does it at the taxpayers' expense and skims money off the top. We figure just last year he cleared ten million with this scam."

"How does he do it?" I whispered, shaken.

"He picks towns that are backward and unsophisticated and grateful for help. Then he starts a bunch of big projects at once so the people in the town can't keep up with what grant is being filed for what and don't realize that only a fraction of what is awarded is actually spent on them."

"That's inexcusable," Miss Eugenia said.

"Yes, it is," Mark agreed.

I remembered all the things Drake had told me—all his lofty philan-
thropic claims—and felt sick. "He probably chose Midway because the
librarian was a loser with only two years of college, who was checking paperbacks out of a set of trailers to largely uneducated patrons."

Mark didn't exactly agree with me but said, "Midway met all of
Langston's criteria—small with unsophisticated leadership."

I wanted to cry. Drake chose us because he thought we were stupid.
He was a beautiful, perfect con man. I forced myself to ask, "But was he
involved in Foster's murder? Did he arrange it?" I added, thinking of Sloan,
"to keep from losing his investment in Midway?"

"I don't think so," Mark replied. "The way Langston operates, he was
never in any danger of losing money here. So there was no reason for him to
kill Foster." Mark stood and put his empty plate in the sink. Then he turned
to Miss Eugenia. "Thanks for the cake. I've got to get back to work."

I watched Mark leave, feeling more discouraged than I had been in a long
time.

"I'm sorry about Drake," Miss Eugenia said. "I know you liked him."

I wanted to point out that I wasn't the only misguided fool. All of
Dougherty County loved Drake. But instead I replied, "I do—did—like
him, and I'm sorry too . . . about everything. I'm sorry the Cooks and several
other Midway residents are in police custody; I'm sorry that Drake isn't what
he claims to be; I'm sorry Luke is about to go to college in Indiana; and I'm
sorry that I let you talk me into investigating Foster's murder."

"You don't mean that," Miss Eugenia said in a reproachful tone. "You
don't want anyone to get away with murder."

"I guess not."

"I understand," she said kindly. "The investigation is over, and you're
going through a sort of grief process."

"It sounds crazy—being sad that something so terrible is over."

"It's not crazy at all," Miss Eugenia replied. "And here's what I suggest
you do to make yourself feel better. Go home and get out your Murder
Book. Reread all the interviews and look at all the evidence you collected
one last time. Remember how hard you worked and how much you accomplished. Then put it away and move on. It's called closure."

"That's what I'll do." I stood, and after thanking Miss Eugenia for her
time and the cake, I walked out to my mother's car and headed toward
Midway and closure.

* * *

By the time I got to my apartment, Mother had left six messages on my answering machine, so I called her back. I assured her that I was fine and told her the good news about my return to college—all expenses paid. She was ecstatic.

"That Drake Langston is a marvel!"

I didn't have the heart to tell her that there was suspicion to the contrary. Fortunately she moved on to another subject quickly.

"Heaven's homebound teacher came today. It's not going to be easy, but I think we can pull her up to where she needs by the end of the year so she won't have to repeat first grade again."

I smiled, imagining the celebration that would take place among the first-grade teachers when this news was announced.

"Her parents came to visit this afternoon, and said they are thinking about remarrying."

I was scandalized. "That's just a shameless ploy to get to Foster's money."

Mother laughed. "Children need their parents, and if the money gives them incentive to be a family, maybe it's a good thing."

I didn't agree, but I didn't argue. Mother invited me to dinner, and I declined. I still had one last piece of fried chicken left over from Sunday and wanted to get the grieving process for my ended investigation started.

So I curled up on the couch, nibbled my chicken, and as I opened my Murder Book, I felt an unexpected tenderness toward Cade. Without his assistance, my investigation would never have taken place. I read through all the interview notes and wondered which one of the conspirators had actually given Foster that last push off the hill and onto the electrical coils.

I read the copies of the letters from "Mary" found in Foster's truck and his so-called "suicide note." Finally I took out the picture from the motel security camera. I studied it for a few seconds, changing the angle frequently to get a fresh point of view. I was about to return it to my Murder Book when something caught my eye. I moved into the kitchen where the light was better. My heart pounded as I stared at what I should have seen before. The killer had been right before my eyes the whole time.

Any regret or disappointment I felt was overwhelmed by my fury. I hate being tricked, and I'm equally opposed to having my emotions toyed with. So with my heart broken and my resolve firm, I walked outside. Then I got into my mother's Buick and started driving toward the salvage yard to confront the guilty party.

* * *

Even though the sun had set, I didn't have any trouble finding the turnoff to the salvage yard. The route had become almost familiar over the past few days. Rather than drive openly up to the house, I parked Mother's car under some trees on the side of the dirt road. After removing Daddy's gun from the glove compartment, I climbed out of the Buick and closed the door with just a tiny click. Then I started walking stealthily up toward the house.

I'd only gone a few feet before I started regretting my hasty departure from home. I should have taken the time to change into more comfortable shoes and darker clothes so that I wouldn't be easy to spot. I should have called Mark Iverson and told him my suspicions. I should have followed my mother's advice months ago and gotten a cell phone.

I was considering these mistakes and hoping that my entire visit wasn't doomed when I heard something behind me. It wasn't exactly a noise, more like an air disturbance. Before I could decide whether to turn and investigate or run as fast as my legs would carry me, a hand reached out and covered my mouth. Then a strong arm pulled me back with excessive force against a warm, hard chest.

I tried to scream, but the hand at my mouth prevented it. I tried to struggle, but the arm around my waist made that impossible. I raised the gun, knowing I wouldn't be able to get off a decent shot but hoping the mere presence of a weapon might intimidate my captor. It didn't. He just took the gun away. I craned my neck to see him, although I didn't need visual confirmation. I was already familiar with the arms that held me.

When our eyes met, I saw the wild, desperate look in his and whispered, "Oh, Luke."

CHAPTER EIGHTEEN

LUKE TUCKED DADDY'S GUN INTO the waistband of his pants and then dragged me under a tree a few feet away. He turned me to face him, and after indicating with a finger to his lips that I had to be quiet, he removed his hand from my mouth and whispered, "What are you doing here?"

I searched for a nice way to say it, but there wasn't one. Finally I settled for, "I have bad news." Then afraid that this wasn't going to adequately prepare him, I added, "Really bad news."

"You mean that my father killed my uncle?"

I was sorry he knew but relieved that I didn't have to be the one to tell him. I nodded. "Yes."

His restraining arms became an embrace. I slipped my arms under his so that I could hug him back. We stood there for a few minutes, lost in mutual misery. Then he gave me the silence signal again and led me back to my mother's car. Once we were seated inside, he asked, "How did you find out?"

"Miss Eugenia said I was grieving because my investigation was over," I told him. "She said I should go back through my Murder Book and kind of relive the accomplishment. But while I was looking at the picture taken by a motel security camera, I noticed something odd. When your uncle came in and filled out his library card application, I particularly noticed his hands. They were callused and scarred and, well, dirty. The hand I could see in the picture was smooth and white and very clean. A hand that had never worked on old cars at the salvage yard."

Luke nodded. "My dad's."

"The brothers looked a lot alike, but we all just assumed the man in the picture was Foster since he was wearing overalls and *standing*."

"Apparently my father has been faking his back injury for years." Luke sounded more sad than angry. "I knew when I saw the mileage on the Torino that something was wrong. Uncle Foster never would have driven it that much—even to impress a woman. But my father didn't care about the car."

"Who was the woman?"

"Jenna. The two of them have probably been carrying on together for years. Right under my nose, and I never suspected a thing until now."

"How did you find out?" I hated to ask but needed to know.

"I found some airline vouchers in my father's room this morning. Dad said Foster bought them—apparently with the intention of taking his girlfriend on a trip—and that he was going to cash them in. But Uncle Foster didn't know anything about the Internet, and the airline vouchers had been purchased online. I thought that was strange, but I never dreamed . . ."

"Of course you didn't," I said.

"Nick and Shasta needed a ride to the airport this evening. They're flying to California to pack up her stuff, and then they plan to move back here and live. We had just left when the Torino started making a weird noise. I pulled into Mr. Bateman's gas station and asked him to take a look. He said it was the carburetor and that I shouldn't drive it anymore until it could be repaired. He was headed to Albany, so he offered to take Nick and Shasta to the airport. He dropped me off at the end of the road on his way."

"So your father and the nurse weren't expecting you to be home so soon?"

"No, they thought they had at least an hour before I'd be back. When I got to the edge of the woods, I could see that the trunk of Jenna's car was open, and I can't even describe how I felt when Dad came walking out of the house carrying some suitcases. They were making use of the time they expected me to be gone to pack for the trip for which they undoubtedly bought the airline vouchers."

I was indignant in Luke's behalf. "Your father's not crippled at all?"

"He's not even weak or unhealthy." Luke laughed without humor. "I figure he pretended to be paralyzed at first to avoid serving his jail sentence. Later it was probably just a way to keep from having to work in the salvage yard. He sat around all day, played on his computer, and visited with Jenna. Then on weekends late at night, they would sneak out and go to Albany or another place where they could have fun without being recognized."

"And just to be safe, your father dressed up like Foster?" I said.

"Right."

"Did you confront them?"

Luke shook his head. "No. They didn't know I saw them, so I decided to walk back to the road where I could make a phone call without fear of being overheard."

"Who did you call?"

"I guess I should have called the sheriff's department since they are closer, but I was afraid I'd get Burrell, and I just couldn't admit to him that my father was a murderer."

I have never felt as completely sorry for another human being in my life as I did at that moment. Luke had tried to rise above his family, but they kept dragging him down. I reached over and touched his shoulder, but he didn't acknowledge the contact.

"So I called Mark Iverson. He's on his way from Albany and said not to do anything until he gets here." He sighed. "I hate to imagine what your parents will think when they hear about this."

I had a pretty good idea of what their reaction would be, but rather than further depress him by sharing my predictions, I said, "I wonder why they decided to leave now."

"Probably because Drake Langston's check was delivered by courier this morning."

I glanced toward the houses and could see lights glittering through the trees. "What if they leave before Mark gets here?"

Luke lifted a shoulder in a gesture of helplessness. "How can we stop them?"

If Parnell and Jenna made their escape, I was afraid they'd never be found. And after all we'd been through because of them, that was something I just couldn't allow to happen.

So I said something that makes me sound braver than I really am. "I think we should go up there. We don't have to confront them—we could just pretend like we don't know what they did and stall them until Mark gets here."

Luke turned to me, his expression mildly hopeful. "I guess we could do that."

"It's better than just waiting here and watching them escape," I encouraged myself as much as him.

We invested a few precious minutes in devising a general plan. I would drive my mother's car up to the house with Luke as my passenger. We'd tell Parnell and Jenna that I was coming to see Luke and found him walking on the side of the road. We would explain his car trouble and Mr. Bateman's kind offer to take Nick and Shasta to the airport. Then we'd say we were going to watch television together for a little while. It wasn't much, but it was the best we could do under the circumstances.

Luke untucked his T-shirt to cover Daddy's gun. I started the Buick and headed toward Parnell's house. Jenna was standing on the porch, holding a box when we pulled up. The light was insufficient for us to see her expression, but I could guess how she felt about our unexpected arrival. She quickly put the box down and went into the house while I parked my mother's car behind her Altima. By the time we followed her inside a couple minutes later, Parnell was sitting in his wheelchair, slumped forward as if he were dozing.

Jenna put a finger to her lips and said, "Shhhh! Your father is asleep."

This was highly unlikely since Luke had seen him loading the car a little while before, but neither of us contradicted her.

Using somewhat hushed tones, we gave her our planned story. And in the process we learned that we are both very bad liars.

"You've been gone for almost an hour," Jenna said to Luke with a frown. "Why did it take so long for you to walk here from Bateman's gas station?"

I wanted to tell Jenna she was just Parnell's nurse and didn't have any right to question Luke, but since we were trying to keep things friendly, I refrained.

I heard the tension in Luke's voice when he replied and knew he didn't appreciate Jenna's attitude either. "It took Mr. Bateman a while to figure out what was wrong with the Torino. So I didn't start walking immediately."

I was watching Jenna, trying to determine whether or not she believed Luke's explanation. So when Parnell, who was supposed to be asleep, spoke from behind me, I was startled.

"Why didn't you just call us, son?" Parnell asked. "Jenna would have run down to Bateman's and picked you up."

"That wasn't necessary," Luke said. "It's a short walk."

"And you didn't mention that you were having company tonight," Jenna added with a suspicious look in my direction.

"We hadn't planned my visit," I said, and I sounded stupid even to my own ears. "But if it's not a good time, I'll leave." I took a step toward the door, anxious to get away (and fervently regretting my suggestion that we try to stall them).

"No," Parnell said with a thoughtful expression. "I think it's best you stay." Then with casualness I found terrifying, he pushed the afghan off his lap and stood up.

From a standing position, his resemblance to Foster was even more pronounced—and he was much more menacing.

I was trying to think of a way to salvage our plan when Luke said, "So you did kill Uncle Foster?"

Jenna cursed under her breath. "They know!"

Parnell nodded. "I could tell from the minute they walked in with that crazy story."

I didn't like them acting like *we* were the liars. "Luke's car did break down, and I did give him a ride up to the house."

"But she came because she suspected that you killed your own *brother*," Luke said.

"For what it's worth, we didn't mean to kill him," Parnell claimed. "We had it all worked out so that no one would get hurt."

"Worked out how?" Luke asked.

"We faked a kidnapping to force Foster to sell." Jenna sounded tired. "It was all his fault that it didn't work, the hateful miser."

Parnell regained our attention by saying, "I faked my physical decline so that I could be admitted to the nursing home."

Luke pressed his lips into a hard, bitter line. "That way no one would suspect you when Uncle Foster died?"

Parnell shrugged. "Actually it was just to keep Foster from monitoring my activities. That night I sneaked out through the exit by my room, and Jenna called Foster—claiming that she had kidnapped me. She told him to meet her behind the electrical plant and sign the land sale papers. She said if he didn't come, she'd kill me."

"And Foster came?" Luke asked.

"Yes," Parnell confirmed. "But even to save my life he wouldn't sign the papers."

"The stupid old man!" Jenna cried. When I looked at her, I saw that she was now holding a gun. I touched Luke's arm, and he glanced in her direction. I felt him stiffen. The presence of a gun changed everything.

"Instead of signing, he tried to overpower Jenna," Parnell told us.

"Fortunately I had the foresight to bring a syringe full of a medication that induces almost instant unconsciousness," Jenna said, her face twisted into a cruel expression. "Parnell was holding it under his afghan."

"I had no choice but to stab Foster in the back with the syringe," Parnell said. "But I didn't want to hurt him, so I only pushed it halfway in. When he started to fall, Jenna grabbed for him, but he was too heavy. He went over the hill—right onto the electrical coils. It was an accident."

I wanted to believe Parnell, mostly because he was Luke's father. But Jenna didn't look very innocent, so I asked, "After Foster fell onto the electrical coils, you made up the whole suicide scenario?"

Parnell nodded. "Yes, exactly. I'd been signing things for Foster for years with his permission. So I wrote out that suicide note and put it in his truck."

"What about the love letters?" I asked suspiciously. "You conveniently had them written and ready to switch with the threatening letters Francie Cook had written to Foster on *pink* paper?"

Parnell said, "What?"

"The love letters the sheriff's department found in Foster's car. Since he didn't have a girlfriend—and since Francie Cook admits to sending him threatening letters on pink paper—someone had to have written the love letters and then swapped them for the ones Francie sent. And that had to have been done without leaving any fingerprints."

"And in the dark," Luke pointed out. "Since half of Midway was without power after Uncle Foster fell on the coils."

"It sounds to me like at least one of you planned for Foster to die that night—regardless of whether or not he signed the papers," I said.

Parnell looked at the nurse. "Jenna?"

"Shut up, Parnell," she said. "Don't say another word. We've wasted enough time on this." Turning to Luke and me, she waved toward the couch with her gun. "Both of you sit down."

"Are you going to kill us too?" Luke asked as we sat down. "Like you did Foster?"

"No," Parnell replied. Then he sent Jenna a worried look. "Please, we can't kill them."

"We don't need to *kill* them," she replied impatiently. "We'll just tie them up and leave them here. By the time anyone finds them, the check for the salvage yard will have cleared the bank, and we'll be out of the country."

Parnell looked almost as relieved as I felt.

"Search them for weapons and cell phones," Jenna instructed.

I watched with disappointment as Parnell collected Luke's phone and Daddy's gun.

"Check to be sure it's loaded," she told him.

Parnell opened the gun and nodded. "It is."

"Then hold it on them while I go find some rope." Jenna skirted us and started down the hallway. After taking a few steps, she turned back to add, "And while I'm gone, remember that if they tell their little story to the police, you'll spend what's left of your life in prison instead of on a foreign beach. So if they move, shoot them." With one final glare in our direction, Jenna left the room.

Parnell looked unhappy but determined, and the gun he had pointed at us didn't waver. Luke angled himself so that he was shielding me as much as possible. I could tell by the tension in his body that he was preparing to make a move while we temporarily had Parnell outnumbered two to one. If he could disarm his father, when Jenna returned with the rope, Luke would be the one holding the gun.

Luke stood and motioned for me to do the same. I didn't even hesitate. Then together we faced our captor.

"Don't make me shoot you, son," Parnell nearly begged.

Luke hesitated, as if considering the request. Then, without warning, he shoved the couch forward. It caught Parnell in the legs, toppling him backward. Luke grabbed my hand, and we ran through the front door into the dark night.

"What now?" I asked as Luke pulled me across the porch.

"We've got to get out of here quick," he answered breathlessly. "I want my father and Jenna brought to justice, but mostly I want us to *live*!"

I didn't argue, although I hated the thought of that evil duo lounging on a foreign beach with Drake's money. We made it to the car, and Luke was reaching for the handle on the driver's side door when a bullet shattered the window. I froze, staring in horror at the damage. If Parnell and Jenna didn't kill us, my mother probably would.

Luke snapped me out of my mental paralysis by yelling, "Kennedy!" just as a second bullet penetrated the pearly gray surface of the Buick's hood.

I grabbed his shirt and let him lead me around a pile of crumbling bricks, past a stack of frayed tractor tires to the old Nova he'd driven as a boy. He pushed me behind it and whispered, "We can't escape, but Mark should be here any minute. All we have to do is avoid getting shot until then."

A bullet passed easily through the Nova's corroded chassis and embedded itself in a patch of sundried dirt to our left.

"Well, we can't wait *here* without getting shot!"

Luke looked around and then motioned toward a structure a few yards away. "We'll move to that shed."

The "shed" he referred to was more like a few pieces of metal leaning against each other, and in order to reach its limited protection, we'd have to be in the open for several dangerous seconds. I gave him an incredulous look. "We might as well just surrender!"

"We can do it. I'm a soldier, remember?"

He was experienced in battle, and since I didn't have a better idea, I deferred to his superior skill in matters involving enemy fire. "Okay."

He took my hand, and we crept awkwardly to what was left of the Nova's front bumper. Bullets continued to pass over our heads at regular intervals.

"When I give the signal, you run as fast as you can to the shed," he told me. "I'll be right behind you."

I looked at the little building that seemed impossibly far away. The chances of us making it there unharmed weren't good. But another bullet barely missed us, and I knew there wasn't any choice. To go was risky, but to stay was death.

More terrified than I'd ever been in my life, I said, "Kiss me for luck."

I thought he was going to refuse, but after a short deliberation he put his hand behind my head, pulled my face close and pressed his lips to mine in a quick, hard kiss. Then he said, "Go!" and shoved me toward the shed. I didn't realize his intentions until it was too late.

Instead of moving straight for the shed, he veered right—drawing the attention and the gunfire away from me. Despite the insanely dangerous nature of his plan, it worked. I dove behind the shed, and a few seconds later he landed on top of me. The bullets continued but didn't pierce the thick metal. For a time, at least, we were safe.

I carefully peeked at the porch, where Jenna and Parnell were standing. "How long do you think we have before they walk over and shoot us?"

Luke frowned. "Not long."

"So what are we going to do?"

"The way I see it, we have two choices—besides just waiting here to get shot."

I waved this aside. "That's not an option."

"We could run for the woods," Luke continued, "which is what I think they expect us to do."

I nodded. "Or . . ."

"Or we can do something they won't expect."

I didn't like the sound of this but forced myself to ask, "What won't they expect?"

"For us to circle back to your mother's Buick and drive it out of here."

I was appalled. "Of course they won't suspect that! It's suicide!"

"Surprise is one of a soldier's best weapons," he insisted as another bullet pinged against the metal behind us. "I don't think my father will actually shoot us, and Jenna is going to have to reload soon. That's when I'll make my move."

I narrowed my eyes at him. "Don't you mean *our* move?"

"I can move faster on my own."

I clutched his arm. "You can't leave me here!"

"Once I get the car, I'll come back by here and let you jump in. So you'll have to be ready."

I shook my head. "It's too risky. I'd rather we die together than for you to die trying to save me!"

Luke laughed grimly. "Well, I wouldn't!"

There was a short lull in the bullet barrage so Luke looked around the shed toward the porch. "She's reloading," he reported. "Here's my chance."

"If you get killed, I'll never forgive you!" I threatened with tears stinging my eyes.

"I won't get killed," he promised. Then he rolled into a crouch and left the protection provided by the shed.

When his departure was not immediately accompanied by gunfire, I felt a little encouraged. So I leaned forward until I could see Luke and monitor his progress.

He moved with stealth and surprising speed to the Buick. Jenna and Parnell were standing close together on the porch and didn't notice his return. Keeping the car between him and the armed couple, Luke moved along the side to the passenger door. I held my breath as he reached up and grabbed the handle. He lifted it slowly and opened it so quietly that Jenna and Parnell didn't seem to hear a thing. Unfortunately the interior light came on when the door opened, and everyone saw that.

Jenna popped the chamber of her gun closed, swung it around toward my mother's Buick, and opened fire again. I ducked instinctively, so I couldn't see what was happening. But I heard a tire blow, more glass break, and finally a soft moan.

I knew Luke had been hit, and all sense of self-preservation evaporated. I moved out into the open and crawled toward him. He was slumped against the car door, and in the moonlight I could see an ominous dark stain spreading on the fabric of his T-shirt sleeve.

When he realized I was coming, he tried to wave me back, but I ignored him. As I reached his side, I heard footsteps and guessed, correctly, that Jenna was moving in for the kill. I leaned across Luke to protect him as much as possible just as she rounded the front of my mother's ruined car with Parnell right behind her. She looked furious.

"Take care of them!" she commanded Parnell.

Luke's father cowered before her. "Where's the rope?"

"It's too late for that now," she informed him. "Thanks to your incompetence, you'll have to kill them."

Parnell shook his head. "No."

Jenna fixed him with a penetrating gaze. "I took care of your stingy brother. This time it's your turn."

"I can't!" Parnell insisted desperately.

"You can and you will." She brought the gun in her hands up and pointed it at him. "Because if you don't kill them, I'll kill you."

"After all I've done for you?" Parnell whispered.

Jenna laughed. "In a heartbeat."

Parnell was visibly upset, and I was beginning to hope that he'd realized the error of his ways (and regretted his felonious partnership with Jenna). But gradually his shoulders slumped in compliance, and he said, "I guess I don't have a choice."

Then I watched in horror as Parnell aimed my father's gun at Luke.

Luke made no effort to defend himself. He just stared up at his father with heart-wrenching resignation.

I saw several emotions cross Parnell's face. Sadness, despair, fear. And all I could do was look on helplessly as his finger found the trigger and pulled. But at the very last second, he jerked the gun, and the bullet tore into Jenna, not Luke. For a few seconds Jenna stared at the dark red spot on her chest in confusion. The gun dropped from her hand, and she crumpled into a heap beside the bullet-ridden Buick.

I turned back to Luke, expecting to see the same relief I felt reflected on his face. However, Luke looked anything but calm. Clutching his wounded shoulder, he struggled to his feet as Parnell turned the gun and pointed it at his own heart.

"Don't do it, Dad!" Luke yelled.

"I'm sorry," Parnell whispered. Then he pulled the trigger again.

The shot echoed through the still night, and I screamed as Parnell collapsed onto Luke. In his injured state, Luke couldn't support the extra weight, so both men fell to the ground. Luke was pinned underneath his father and didn't answer me when I called his name. I tried to pull Parnell off of Luke, but he was too heavy. Desperate, I was headed into the house to call 911 when I heard the sound of vehicles approaching fast.

Seconds later, Mark's inconspicuous FBI sedan burst through the trees with Cade's squad car close behind. After bringing their respective vehicles to simultaneous screeching halts, both men climbed out and ran toward me.

"Are you okay?" they called in unison.

I waved their concern aside. "I'm fine, but I'm not sure about Luke. I can't get him out from under his father!"

Mark and Cade combined their efforts to shift Parnell's body. Luke's eyes were closed, and he was covered with blood. It was too much, and for the first time in my life I fainted.

* * *

I woke up with a pounding headache to the sound of sirens in the distance. I was lying on the ground, and my head was resting against Luke's thigh. At first I was confused by the odd circumstances. Then the memories came rushing back, and I turned to Luke with a little whimper.

His back was leaning against my mother's Buick. His eyes were closed, and he looked pale, but his chest was rising in a steady rhythm, so I knew he was alive. The bottom half of his T-shirt had been ripped off and tied around his right arm. The makeshift bandage appeared to be successfully staunching the flow of blood from his bullet wound.

I could hear Cade and Mark talking nearby, although I couldn't make out their words. And the sirens were getting closer and painfully louder. I put a hand on Luke's good arm, and he opened his eyes.

"Try and hold still," he urged me. "Mark said your head hit your mother's car when you fainted so you might have a concussion."

I reached up and gingerly touched the lump on my temple. "That explains my headache."

The ground around us trembled as the ambulances arrived, and soon the salvage yard was teeming with people. Mark brought a paramedic over to check on us, and when he saw that I was awake, he said, "Did you have a nice nap?"

I did my best to smile. "I've had better."

Some of the tension left Mark's face. "How do you feel?"

"Fine," I replied. "Luke's the one who got shot."

"It's just a scratch," Luke said, trying to minimize his injury.

"I'll be the judge of that," the paramedic said as he knelt beside Luke and placed his medical kit on the ground.

Luke put a restraining hand on my shoulder so I couldn't sit up. "Check Kennedy first," he told the paramedic. "I won't let her move until you do."

The paramedic looked annoyed, but he examined the bump on my head. After flashing a light in my eyes and testing my reflexes, he finally said, "I don't want to take any chances with a head injury. We'll get you to the hospital where they can do a proper examination." He used his radio to call for a stretcher.

I felt like crying. "I don't want to leave Luke."

The paramedic cut off Luke's blood-encrusted shirtsleeve to expose a nasty "scratch" about three inches long. "Don't worry," he said grimly. "Your friend here is coming to the hospital with you."

"Is it bad?" I asked.

"He's lost a good bit of blood, and he'll definitely need a few stitches," the paramedic replied, "and maybe a tetanus shot." The paramedic sprayed Luke's wound with something that smelled antiseptic and covered it with gauze. Then he said, "That should hold you until we can get you to the hospital."

My stretcher arrived, and the paramedics strapped me on and loaded me into the back of the ambulance. During this process I lost track of Luke, but

I didn't worry since I thought we were riding to the hospital together. But when the paramedic climbed in and the ambulance doors were slammed shut, I realized Luke wasn't coming with me. The ambulance began to move, and I'd never felt so alone in my life.

The paramedic misunderstood the reason for my distress. He gave me an encouraging smile and said, "Don't worry. We'll be at the hospital soon."

* * *

At the emergency room I was examined and then informed that an entire battery of tests and procedures would have to be done to make sure the bump on my head wasn't serious. The required tests included a CT scan, and they advised me to stay awake until they could be sure I was okay, even though I felt like I just wanted to sleep forever—I was so tired and disoriented.

I vaguely remember being loaded into Mark's car once I was given a clean bill of health. I fell instantly asleep. But when I finally woke up, I was lying on my bed in my old room at my parents' house, and my mother was hovering over me.

"She's awake!" Mother cried. Seconds later my father's face joined hers.

Feeling groggy and a little ill, I pushed myself up on one elbow and tried to think. "Parnell killed Jenna and then shot himself," I said slowly. "And they both killed Foster."

"That's what we heard," Daddy confirmed.

"Luke!" I cried. "He was shot too!"

Mother put a restraining hand on my shoulder. "Be still, dear!"

She didn't have to insist. With my head swimming, I leaned back on my pillows and asked, "Is Luke okay?"

"He's got a few stitches in his arm but he says he's not in pain."

"He's been waiting in the living room for you to wake up," Mother added with a smile.

"A fine young man," Daddy decreed to my astonishment.

My mother continued. "I can't believe that Luke is even related to Parnell. Shooting his nurse was scandalous, but killing his own brother is too much, even for a Scoggins!"

"Parnell claimed that killing Foster was an accident, and he only shot Jenna to protect Luke," I told them. "I guess Jenna and Parnell are both dead?"

"The nurse is dead," Daddy confirmed. "But Luke's father is still alive. He had surgery last night, and from what I hear, they expect him to recover completely. At least physically."

"I bet he won't be able to avoid jail this time," I muttered. "In spite of his injuries."

My father nodded. "I bet you're right."

"Mark and Luke both feel terrible that you were exposed to so much danger," Mother said.

This annoyed me. "I went to the salvage yard of my own accord, and they weren't responsible for what happened once I got there."

"Well, they feel bad just the same," Mother insisted.

I didn't want to argue, so I turned to the window, where bright sunlight was streaming in. "I slept all through the night?"

Mother smiled. "Like a baby. It was so nice to have you home again."

I didn't want my mother to forget that I was a responsible adult, so I sat up with more determination this time. I was still a little woozy, but Daddy helped me stand.

"You said Luke is in the living room?"

Mother pushed the hair from my face the way she used to when I was a child. "I'll go let him know you're awake."

"I'll tell him myself." I grasped Daddy's arm and walked with him into the living room. But when we got there, Luke was nowhere in sight. Cade, however, looked right at home sitting on my parents' couch.

"Where's Luke?" I demanded

Cade shrugged. "As soon as he heard that you were awake, he said he had to go."

I walked over to the window and looked out, but there was no sign of the Torino. "Did he say when he was coming back?"

Cade shook his head. "No."

Mother frowned. "Why in the world would he wait all night and then leave as soon as you're able to see him?"

Of course I knew the answer. Once again Luke's family had humiliated him, and he couldn't face me.

From Cade's expression, I was pretty sure he knew too.

I hated to be rude, but I was worried. So I told Cade, "Excuse me, I need to make a phone call." Then I picked up the phone and dialed Luke's cell number. He didn't answer. I called the salvage yard. There was no answer there either.

When I put the phone down, Cade said, "You were right about the whole murder thing. Foster was definitely murdered and by his own brother. And Parnell wasn't even handicapped! For years he's been fooling everybody with that wheelchair." This seemed to bother Cade almost as much as the murder.

I touched the sore lump on my temple. "I think Jenna was the mastermind behind the whole murder plot. Parnell is weak and lazy, but not really criminal."

"He has to take a lot of the responsibility," Cade insisted. "But exactly how much will be up to the courts to decide."

I wasn't going to waste any more of my limited energy defending Parnell. "What about the Cooks?"

"The FBI released them, and Terrance checked Francie into the hospital for psychiatric evaluations."

"Because she sent Foster those threatening letters?" I asked.

"Mostly because she blew up the old library and almost killed you," Cade corrected.

I gasped. "It *was* Francie who turned on the gas in the furnace?"

"Yeah," Cade confirmed. "She was afraid if you kept digging, you'd find out she wrote the letters. She swears she wasn't trying to hurt you, but . . ."

"And to think that just a few days ago I was envious of Francie because she's so thin," Mother whispered.

"Francie is obviously not right." Cade shook his head. "It's a shame."

"Fortunately no one was hurt when she blew up the old library," Daddy pointed out. "And she's getting the help she needs."

"Of course Terrance will probably have to resign as mayor," Cade said. "The town won't want him to represent us after what Francie has done."

"I guess not," I agreed, although it didn't seem fair. "What about the other landowners?"

"Mark's leaving it up to Sheriff Bonham to decide whether to press any charges," Cade said.

"Then that's the end of it," I predicted. "The sheriff doesn't like to stir up trouble."

"There's been a lot of that around here lately, so I can't really blame him," Daddy said.

"And even if the landowners don't get investigated, they've still been punished," Cade added.

I raised an eyebrow. "How?"

"The land deal is off," Cade reported. "Because of the murder, Drake Langston canceled payment on all the checks and pulled his crews out of town."

This was not unexpected, but it still made me sad. Without Drake, Midway would never achieve its modern potential. "So the preacher and Miss Zelda aren't going to the holy land?"

Cade shook his head. "And the Lebows will lose their home to foreclosure, and Mrs. Castleberry's grandson will have to find another way to pay for law school."

I sighed. "There will be no new houses built for taxpaying families to move into."

"And the church won't be getting a new family center," Mother said woefully.

"What about the library?" I asked.

Cade gave me an anxious glance. "I don't know, since the old one blew up and Drake Langston left without finishing the new one."

I sighed. "Well, I guess I'd better find out. Then I need to go to Haggerty and talk to Miss Eugenia and hold a baby." Belatedly I realized that my mother's car was ruined, thanks to me. "Oh, Mother. I'm so sorry about your Buick!"

She smiled. "I'm just thankful you're okay. Besides, Daddy called our insurance agent, and he said we're covered. We're going to go pick out a new car this afternoon."

I was immensely relieved.

Then Daddy cheered me up even more by saying, "I've got your truck drivable. It looks pretty bad—but it will get you where you need to go."

I gave him a hug. "Thanks, Daddy."

Mother started frowning. "I don't think Kennedy should drive yet."

"I don't have a concussion," I reminded her.

Mother wasn't deterred. "But you were given a sedative."

"That was hours ago."

"Kennedy knows whether she's alert enough to drive," Daddy said. But Mother still didn't look happy.

In an effort to reassure her, I said, "And I'll take a shower—so that should completely wake me up."

"And I'll follow behind her just in case," Cade offered.

"Well, I guess it'll be okay, then," Mother finally said—as *if* she could stop me once my mind was made up.

I took a shower and changed into a pair of jeans and a T-shirt that I found hanging in the closet of Reagan's old room. While drying my hair I was again reminded that I needed to get the singed ends trimmed. I helped myself to a new toothbrush from the stash Mother pilfers from the abundant supply at Uncle Forest's dental office. Then I searched through the assortment of makeup in the bathroom drawers and was able to do a respectable job of covering the peeling skin on my cheeks and the lump on my temple.

By the time I walked out to rejoin my parents and Cade, I felt like my normal self.

"Oh, you look beautiful!" Mother exclaimed. This, of course, was a total exaggeration, but that's to be expected from your mother—especially if you've just survived two near-death experiences.

I saw the look of admiration in Cade's eyes and smiled. He wasn't completely unbiased either.

I used my parents' phone to try Luke's numbers one last time but still got no answer. We all walked outside. My truck was parked in the driveway, and Miss Ida Jean was watering her lawn just a few feet away.

She rushed over when she saw us and shrieked, "Kennedy! I heard that you were involved in a shooting!"

"I'm fine, Miss Ida Jean," I reassured her.

"And Parnell Scoggins never was paralyzed, and he killed both his nurse and his own *brother!*"

I didn't want to get into a lengthy conversation with Miss Ida Jean but felt I had to say a little something in Parnell's behalf. "There were extenuating circumstances."

Miss Ida Jean didn't seem to even hear me. "I can't believe that those Scogginses have been allowed to live here in Midway for all these years, causing trouble and giving our town a bad name!"

I didn't think Midway had a bad name, and if it did, the Scogginses couldn't be held totally responsible. "The whole family isn't bad," I said. "You've met Luke. He fought for our country in Iraq, and soon he'll be going to engineering school in Indiana."

This gave Miss Ida Jean pause—but only for a second. "Well, I remember that Luke Scoggins when he was a teenager. He was a troublemaker and spent some time in jail."

That was it. I'd had it. Ignoring the fact that my mother was standing a few feet away, I looked straight into Miss Ida Jeans eyes and said, "Speaking of jail, how's your son Robby doing down at the state penitentiary?"

I heard a collective gasp from my parents and Cade. But Miss Ida Jean's reaction to my remark was not what I expected. Tears filled her eyes (this part I expected), and she grabbed my arm with one of her clawlike hands. "He's good," she said. "Thank you for asking. Nobody ever does. I can't remember the last time someone said his name."

I glanced back at my mother, and since she didn't look like she was going to kill me, I told Miss Ida Jean, "People feel a little awkward about mentioning Robby because he's in jail."

"Do they think I've forgotten where he is and that by saying his name they'll bring back a bad memory?"

I had to laugh. "Sometimes it's hard to know what to say."

This seemed to confuse her more. "I can always think of something to say."

I waved and started for my truck. "I've got to go, Miss Ida Jean. I'll see you next time I come to visit my parents unless you're through watering your lawn."

"I don't want the grass to die," she called after me.

I didn't think my mother was mad at me, but it seemed wise to leave quickly just in case. So I climbed into my truck, turned the key (which my father had thoughtfully left in the ignition), and backed down the driveway. I headed for downtown Midway with Cade right behind me.

CHAPTER NINETEEN

Main Street in Midway had been lacking for as long as I could remember. But there's something about unfinished repairs that makes a place look even worse. All the dump trucks and other heavy equipment that had been blocking traffic in Midway for weeks were gone. And when I saw the partially replaced sidewalks, piles of debris, and abandoned supplies, I wanted to cry. Before Drake's renovation, the downtown area had been shabby and neglected. But now it looked rejected and completely hopeless.

I parked in front of what was supposed to be the new library. Cade pulled in beside me.

"I can take it from here," I told him as I climbed out of my truck. "I'm fine."

He ignored this and joined me on the sidewalk. Once there, he shuffled from one foot to the other.

Finally I asked, "What's wrong, Cade?"

"I got you something," he said. His uncharacteristic discomfort was alarming. "Please say you'll keep it—even though it's from me."

"What is it?" I demanded, expecting a reengagement ring or a poem professing his undying love or something else equally horrible. I was immensely relieved when he placed a small, black cell phone in my hand.

"I put you on my account, but they said you can change it over to your own name whenever you want."

I looked down at the little phone. It was something I'd wanted and needed for a long time. And now, strangely, Cade was the one to provide it. "I don't know what to say."

"Just say you'll answer when I call," he requested.

I nodded. "Thanks, Cade. For everything."

"Thank you for being my friend, in spite of everything," he replied.

I was afraid that I'd dissolve into a puddle of sentimentality if I stayed there one more minute. So I tucked the phone into the pocket of my sister's jeans and hurried to the library's entrance.

I was surprised to find the door unlocked and even more surprised to find the old bank building full of people. Mr. Bateman was unpacking DVDs with the assistance of Brother Jackson. My part-time employer and landlord, Mr. Sheffield, was screwing bulbs into light fixtures. Mayor Cook was there, fresh from FBI custody, helping Miss Mabel Osgood and a group of teenagers arrange books in the fiction section.

"These are some of my senior English students," Miss Mabel explained. "I thought shelving books might give them a better appreciation for the written word."

I doubted this, but I smiled. "Thanks," I told the kids.

Several women from the Midway Baptist Church were dusting and sweeping and arranging furniture. They all called out greetings, and I waved in response.

"Everyone wants to help," Cade said from behind me.

I remembered the slogan Drake had come up with to attract young families to what we thought would be a newly renovated town. "In Midway we really do care about the education of our children!" I loosely quoted with pride.

"In Midway we really do care about each other," Cade added.

"You got a delivery a few minutes ago," Miss Mabel said with a wink. "Flowers."

"We told the florist guy to put them in your office," Mr. Bateman added.

"Which is surprisingly the only room in the library that is completely finished," Cade added while raising an eyebrow, and I had a feeling that he knew my office was a gift from Sloan.

I walked to the back of the library and opened the door to my office. On the desk was a beautiful arrangement of flowers.

"I wonder who sent those," Cade murmured from behind me.

"They are from Drake Langston." The card read simply, *The offer still stands. Drake*

I was staring at the words when Mayor Cook knocked on the open door. Looking uncertain, he said, "I don't know how to apologize."

"You don't need to. A lot of terrible things have happened in Midway over the past few days, but a lot of good things have happened too. We need to put the bad behind us and look toward the future."

He seemed greatly relieved. "I'm glad you feel that way. And speaking of the future, with the help of our volunteers, we hope to have the library finished and ready for business by the first of April."

"But without Drake . . . how will we purchase this building?" I waved to encompass the old bank.

"He signed it over to the city of Midway," the mayor said. When I heard those words, I knew in my heart that Drake was not a criminal. He might not be completely honest—but then, who is?

"Before you start feeling too grateful," Terrance Cook interrupted, "keep in mind that he got the place for a fraction of its original value and covered that with government grants."

I smiled. "I'm just glad he got it."

Mayor Cook smiled back. "Me too. Drake also left us all these books, and more are on the way. We've got the computers from Microsoft and fancy furniture picked out by an interior designer from Atlanta, and who knows—someday we may even have an atrium!"

I laughed. "It doesn't hurt to dream big!"

When Cade and I walked out of the library, I felt prouder to be a citizen of Midway than I ever had in my life. As I stepped over a pile of rubble, I said, "Maybe once the library's done, everyone will pitch in and finish these sidewalks."

He grinned. "It doesn't hurt to dream big."

I laughed again. I liked this new relationship I was developing with Cade. No pressure to go on dates or remarry—just friends.

"I have a favor to ask you," I told him.

"Anything," he promised dangerously.

"I need to talk with Luke, but Parnell took his phone last night, and, well, I'm not sure if he got it back."

"He's got it," Cade said. "I gave it to him myself."

This was not good news, but I pressed on. "Well, then he's not answering my calls so do you think you could locate him?"

"Not answering the phone isn't a crime," Cade pointed out.

"I don't want you to arrest him," I clarified. "Just *find* him. As a favor for a friend."

Cade turned and stared at the horizon for a few seconds before asking, "Do you love him?"

I answered honestly. "I don't know. Maybe."

I saw his shoulders slump, but he said, "I'll see what I can do."

"Thanks."

He nodded without looking at me.

"Now I'm headed to Haggerty for a quick visit with Miss Eugenia, but I don't need an escort."

He turned to face me, and I could tell he didn't like the idea. But he didn't try to stop me the way he would have a few days ago. "Be careful. You may still have some lingering effects from that sedative."

"I'll be careful," I promised. "And if I run into trouble, I can call you on my new cell phone."

He grinned. "That's true. And I'll let you know if I find out anything about Luke."

* * *

When I arrived in Haggerty I decided not to leave an encounter with Baby Jake to chance again. So instead of going straight to Miss Eugenia's house, I veered left and walked up to the Iversons' front door. My intention was to use Major's assault on Emily (and my need to apologize on behalf of my ill-behaved nephew) as an excuse for the unexpected visit.

When Kate opened the door in response to my knock, she had the baby wrapped tightly in a blanket and nestled in the crook of her arm. "Come in!" she invited. "If you're looking for Miss Eugenia, she's here."

"I am looking for Miss Eugenia," I replied as I stepped into the entryway. "But I also wanted to talk to you and apologize for Major's inexcusable behavior on Sunday."

"It's okay," Kate said, but I could tell that Madison was right. Kate was just being polite.

"No, it's not! Major is out of control, and the others will be just like him if something doesn't change. I've blamed Madison's strange views for retarding her discipline, but after talking to my sister on Sunday, I realize that I have some responsibility too. Instead of criticizing them and their parenting skills, I should be helping them."

"I believe you're right!" Kate said over her shoulder as she led me down the hall. "I think a little attention from you would do wonders for Madison and her children."

When we entered the kitchen, I saw Miss Eugenia seated in a chair by the table, looking out the big window at Emily and Charles, who were playing on the swing set in the Iversons' backyard.

"You've got company!" Kate announced.

Miss Eugenia smiled. "I was hoping you'd stop by."

Kate walked over to stand by the window where she could see her children. "She's been *dying* to get a firsthand account of the shoot-out at the salvage yard."

I winced at her choice of words as I sat in the chair beside Miss Eugenia. Then I gave them a succinct description of all that had transpired the night before. I summed it up by telling Miss Eugenia, "So you were ultimately responsible for solving the crime, since you suggested that I go home and look back through my Murder Book."

Miss Eugenia shook her head. "No, you're the one who deserves all the credit. I just gave you a little guidance."

Kate smiled. "Miss Eugenia is *always* willing to share her knowledge."

"When you get to be my age, knowledge is about all you have," Miss Eugenia replied.

Kate winked at me. "I told the kids I'd push them on the swing. Would you like to hold the baby while I'm outside?"

I nodded. "I'd love to."

Kate transferred the little bundle into my waiting arms. She pulled back the blanket to reveal pale, chubby cheeks and red fuzzy hair.

I stared speechlessly.

"Isn't she cute?" Kate asked. "We're calling her Karen."

"Where's Jake?" I finally managed.

"His adoptive mother took custody of him yesterday."

I stared at the new baby—stunned with grief. "You mean Baby Jake is gone—*forever*?"

Kate looked puzzled. "I thought I explained that we don't keep the babies for long."

It was ridiculous to feel so bereft about a baby I'd only seen twice, but I couldn't help it. I was devastated. "I didn't think he'd be gone so soon."

Kate could tell I was upset but obviously didn't know why and seemed unsure about how to answer me. Finally she said, "Some stay longer than others. Things worked out pretty quickly for Jake. And that's a good thing. We want them to get settled with their new family as soon as possible."

"New family," I repeated bleakly.

"Go swing Emily and Charles," Miss Eugenia told Kate. "Kennedy will be fine."

With one last concerned look in my direction, Kate hurried outside to play with her children.

I dragged my eyes up to meet Miss Eugenia's. "Obviously I'm not cut out to be a foster parent."

"It's not for everyone," she agreed. "But it works great for Kate. She has two children of her own who don't leave. The babies come, and they name them using their alphabetically consecutive system. They bathe them and dress them and play with them and love them. Then that baby moves on and a new baby comes."

"How do they keep from getting attached?"

"There have been a few times when Kate cried over a departure," Miss Eugenia told me. "But she's been doing this for a while and is more used to it. And I think you're right—you're not cut out to be a foster parent. At least not yet. You need to get your own life in order first."

I groaned. "In that case I'll never be a foster parent."

She laughed. "Your life isn't so bad. Now give me a report on all the fascinating men who want to date you."

"Well," I began with a sigh, "that seemingly endless pool dried up fast. Drake is gone—renovating another town and defrauding the United States government of more taxpayer dollars. Sloan is assisting him."

"I thought you didn't like Sloan."

"He grew on me," I admitted. "But even though I enjoyed his company and really enjoyed looking at him, I don't want to have his children, wash his clothes, or sit in a rocking chair beside him as we grow old."

Miss Eugenia waved her hand dismissively. "Then he's not the man for you."

"No," I murmured, trying to forget the feel of Sloan's warm lips against mine.

"What about Luke Scoggins?" Miss Eugenia asked. "The two of you seemed pretty close."

"Luke has been embarrassed, once again, by his family. So he's gone off somewhere and won't answer my phone calls."

"He'll get over it," Miss Eugenia predicted.

"I hope so," I said with more conviction than I felt. "I've asked Cade to try and find him for me."

"Which brings us to the last man on your once long list of suitors," Miss Eugenia pointed out.

"Cade and I had a nice, long talk—actually several long talks—and I think he finally understands that we will never get back together. We've agreed to be friends, and he's stopped asking me out. I think he might start dating the receptionist at the sheriff's department."

"Sincere?"

"Her name is Serene, but yes, that's her."

"I've met her a few times. She's cute."

I nodded. "I'm glad he's finally accepted the need to move on, but it was kind of nice knowing he was there just in case."

Miss Eugenia frowned. "Just in case what?"

"In case I can't do any better."

"Better than a faithless two-timer?" Miss Eugenia exclaimed. "Of course you can."

I felt a little relieved. Maybe I hadn't doomed myself to a life of lonely misery. "Drake did offer me a job traveling around with him. Maybe we could have lived happily together with all that money, fixing up towns."

"And pocketing ill-gotten gains," Miss Eugenia contributed.

I ignored this. "But I decided to stay in Midway and get my education and try to run the new library if the town volunteers ever get it finished."

Miss Eugenia cackled. "They'll get it finished, and I think you made the right decision. But you should keep Drake's phone number—just in case."

I was surprised by this advice. "In case what?"

She shrugged. "You never know. And don't be in such a hurry to start a serious relationship. You're so young." She sounded a little wistful. "You have plenty of time. No need to rush things."

Since I'd been kissed by three men in the past week and enjoyed every one of them, I figured she was right. So I said, "I won't."

It started to drizzle, forcing Kate and the children inside. Kate sent the children to wash their hands while she began making sandwiches. "Will you stay for lunch?" she invited me.

I shook my head. "No, I need to go. But thank you." I looked down at Baby Karen. She wasn't as adorable as Baby Jake, but she was kind of cute. And she was definitely warm and soft. So I pressed a kiss on her fat little cheek. Then I passed her over to Miss Eugenia.

"I guess Kate told you that my nephew Major punched Emily on Sunday," I said after the baby transfer was complete.

"Kate didn't tell me," Miss Eugenia said, "but Emily did. I told her next time to punch him back."

"And I told her to do no such thing!" Kate called from the counter, where she had slices of bread spread out. "Violence is not the way to settle differences."

"Hopefully it won't be an issue again," I said. "It may kill me, but I'm going to try to help Madison and Jared with their evil brood."

Miss Eugenia laughed. "It won't kill you, but it won't be easy. Those children are in serious need of a firm hand."

"Well, I've got two of those!"

"What you should do is come to church with Madison on Sundays," Miss Eugenia suggested. "I've been going with Kate and Mark for years—just to sit with the children, since Mormons believe that the entire congregation should run around doing things during their services instead of sitting quietly and listening to a well-paid preacher."

"Everyone doesn't run around," Kate contradicted from her position by the counter. "I play the organ, and Mark has to sit on the stand. Therefore we are very grateful to Miss Eugenia for making the huge sacrifice of coming with us to church every Sunday."

I thought I detected a trace of sarcasm, but Miss Eugenia didn't seem to notice.

"And most families do sit together—if not always quietly—during our meetings," Kate added.

"Madison's children are never quiet—even though both parents are sitting with them," Miss Eugenia said. "So your presence would be a blessing to us all!"

I knew my mother and Brother Jackson were expecting me at the Midway Baptist Church. But if I went to Sunday services with Madison, I'd be helping my sister *and* attending church (killing two birds with one stone—so to speak). And as long as I was in church, even a Mormon one, I didn't see how my mother or the preacher could complain. "Maybe I will."

As I left the Iversons' home, I pulled out my new cell phone and used it to call Cade.

"Why haven't you been answering your cell phone?" he demanded in the way friends can talk to each other. "I've called twenty times!"

"Sorry!" And I really was. "I'm not used to having a phone and forgot to turn it on. Did you find Luke?"

"Sort of," Cade replied with mild annoyance. "Your dad said he came by their place a little while ago and dropped off the Torino. He's headed to Indiana early, and he wants you to keep it for him until he gets back."

Among old car lovers, this was practically the same as going steady. My heart was pounding as I asked, "What else did he say?"

There was a little pause, as if Cade was reluctant to tell me, then he said, "Nothing, but he left your parents' house in a taxi headed for the airport in Albany."

If I hurried, there was a chance I would catch him before his flight left. So I thanked Cade and closed my cute little cell phone. Then I climbed into my old truck, stuck the key in the ignition, turned it, and listened to the ominous silence. I wanted to cry. How could my old truck let me down at such an important moment?

When I ran back up to the Iversons' house, I was fighting frustration. Kate opened the door, and I told her, "My truck won't start, and I need to get to the airport immediately! Luke is leaving, but if I hurry, I might catch him. Can I get one of you to pull your car around so we can jump-start my engine?"

Kate walked over to the round table in the center of the room and pulled some keys out of her purse. "We don't have time for that. Take my van to the airport. We'll worry about your truck when you get back."

I was stunned by the generous offer. But I was desperate, so rather than argue I just said, "Are you sure?"

She nodded. "Good luck."

I gave her a grateful smile and ran back out her front door.

* * *

I arrived at the Albany airport in near-record time and miraculously found a good parking spot. I hurried inside, searching frantically as I rushed from one end of the terminal to the other. I found Luke standing in the security line, which was fortunately quite long but which unfortunately provided us with no privacy. He was facing away from me, and his profile looked sad and lonely.

I wanted to run up and hug him but knew this would be inappropriate (based on the undefined nature of our relationship) and foolish (since I didn't want to hurt his injured arm). So I just ducked under one of the ropes that created a huge maze for the prospective passengers to walk through. Apologizing to those I was breaking in front of, I made my way to Luke's side. His eyes widened with surprise when he saw me.

I decided to try a humorous approach. "You didn't hold my family against me, so I won't hold yours against you."

He shook his head. "That's not even close to a fair bargain." His eyes skimmed me, and then he asked, "Are you feeling okay?"

"I'm fine. How about you?"

He glanced down at his shoulder. "It's just a scratch and much less than I deserve. I should never have let you talk me into stalling Jenna and my father."

"That was a bad idea," I admitted. "But like I said, I'm fine."

He nodded. "It's over anyway."

I wasn't sure what to say, so I settled for, "I'm sorry about . . . everything."

He shrugged like he didn't care, but I could see the pain in his eyes.

I knew I was trespassing the lines of friendship again, but I had to tell him how I felt. "Your father has made a lot of bad choices in his life, but he loves you. He proved that last night when he sacrificed everything for you."

"I'm grateful that he didn't kill me," Luke acknowledged. "And I guess I even appreciate that he sacrificed a life as a fugitive on foreign beaches for me. But one big act of bravery doesn't make up for a lifetime of neglect. I can't stop thinking about all the time we could have spent together, all the ball games he missed and school programs he didn't attend. What good is it to love someone if you only show them once in a lifetime?"

"Your life isn't over yet, and neither is his," I reminded him gently. "Maybe the two of you can still work out a relationship of some kind."

"Maybe."

The line moved forward, and I walked along beside him. When we stopped again, I said, "I heard you've left the Torino in my care."

"I was afraid if I left it at the salvage yard, Nick and Shasta would sell it."

"I won't sell it," I promised, "but is there a limit to how many miles I can drive it?"

He gave me half a smile. "No, I trust you."

I raised an eyebrow. "Do you?"

He nodded.

"Then why are you leaving me?"

He regarded me with a solemn expression. "I need to put some distance between myself and Midway."

"In a few days, your father and the shoot-out at the salvage yard will be old news," I predicted optimistically.

"It may take a little longer than that." He stepped closer and put his mouth close to my ear. "I want to be the kind of man you deserve, but I'm not there yet. Can you be patient?"

My heart was pounding so hard I was sure he could hear it. "Yes," I managed. "Besides, I'm going to be busy getting my degree and running the Midway Library. I probably won't even notice you're gone."

This earned me a whole smile. "If you'll get a cell phone, I can call so you don't forget me."

"Actually," I pulled the little phone out of my pocket, "I have one, but I don't know how to work it yet. Can you program your number in?"

He put his carry-on bag on the floor by his feet and entered his number into my phone book. Then he put my number into his.

"There," I said when he was finished. "Now we're connected."

We were reaching the point where passengers had to show their boarding pass, and since I didn't have one, I knew I was going to have to leave the line. "Midway's going to be so boring without you," I whispered.

He smiled and put both his hands behind my head. Then he kissed me as thoroughly as I've ever been kissed in my life. When he pulled away, I was dizzy (which I partially blamed on the sedative I'd received at the hospital the night before).

The other passengers around us cheered, and I wanted to beg Luke to stay. But I knew he needed to go. So I did what I had to do. I ducked under the ropes and moved into the crowd of people watching the departing travelers. I blinked back the tears until he passed through security. He turned and waved before continuing down the ramp to the gates. Once he was out of sight, I let the tears fall.

"Everything will be okay," the lady standing beside me said in an attempt to comfort me.

My new cell phone beeped, and I looked down to see a text message appearing in the small screen. "I miss you already."

And I knew it was true. One way or another, everything was going to be fine.

* * *

So in a matter of hours I went from a woman with four fascinating men constantly asking me out to a woman alone in an airport. But I'd solved a murder case and enrolled in college and helped to design a new library for Midway. Not bad for the unluckiest girl in the dullest place on earth.

RECIPES

Miss Ida Jean's Cheese Ball
(perfect for care packages to the state penitentiary)

2 eight-ounce packages of cream cheese (softened)
1 package Hidden Valley Ranch Salad Dressing Mix
1/2 cup black pepper

Combine cream cheese with Hidden Valley mix using an electric mixer. Clean the beaters off well. Form into a ball. Pour pepper onto a plate or cutting board. Place cheese ball in pepper and roll until completely covered. Store in the refrigerator until time to serve. Serve with crackers of your choice.

Back Porch Specialty Layered Dip
(not recommended for the fat and cholesterol conscious)

1 can refried beans
1/4 cup sour cream
1/4 cup mayonnaise
2 Tbsp taco seasoning
3 mashed (ripe) avocados and 1 tsp lemon juice (mixed together)
2 cups shredded Colby Jack cheese
1 large tomato, diced
1 can medium pitted olives, sliced

Spread refried beans on a platter. Mix sour cream, mayonnaise, and taco seasoning together and then spread it as the next layer. Spread avocado as next layer. Sprinkle diced tomatoes. Cover with cheese. Top with sliced olives. Serve with tortilla chips.

Funeral Committee Fruit Punch
(perfect for an unexpected funeral luncheon)

1 pkg Kool-Aid lemonade
2 cups sugar
1 quart water
1 gallon freezer bag
1 large can pineapple juice
1 two-liter bottle of ginger ale

Mix Kool-Aid, sugar, and water. Pour into freezer bag (be sure to get all the sugar into bag) and freeze for at least 2 days. A few hours before serving, put pineapple juice and ginger ale into freezer until it is a little slushy. Remove bag of Kool-Aid mixture from the freezer about 30 minutes before serving. Mash bag until Kool-Aid mixture is slushy. Put in punch bowl. Add can of pineapple juice and bottle of ginger ale. Stir and serve.

Iris's Famous Spinach Salad
(perfect under any circumstances)

1 lb fresh spinach
1 eleven-ounce can mandarin oranges (drained)
1 medium purple onion (thickly sliced and separated into rings)

Remove stems from spinach, wash leaves, and pat them dry. Tear leaves into bite-sized pieces. Combine spinach, oranges, and onions. Toss with Tangy Orange Vinaigrette Dressing (below). Serve immediately.

Tangy Orange Vinaigrette Dressing

1 1/2 tsp grated orange rind
1 1/2 tsp Dijon mustard
1/2 tsp minced garlic
1/4 tsp hot sauce
1/4 cup cider vinegar
1/2 cup vegetable oil

Use food processor or blender. Add first five ingredients and pulse until well blended. Add oil and mix until well blended.

Killingsworth's Homemade Chocolate Ice Cream
(perfect for Sunday dinner dessert)

1 large carton Cool Whip
1/2 gallon chocolate milk (whole, not reduced fat)
2 cans sweetened condensed milk

Mix ingredients together. Pour into an ice-cream freezer and prepare according to manufacturer's instructions.

Salvage Yard Strawberry Shortcake
(perfect for impressing a date)

Pound cake (homemade or store-bought)
1 large box vanilla instant pudding mix
3 cups milk
1 eight-ounce carton of sour cream
1 large carton Cool Whip
3 cups strawberries
1/4 cup sugar

Slice strawberries. Add sugar and a little water. Stir and refrigerate. Mix pudding according to package directions. Stir in sour cream and half of the Cool Whip. Break the cake into bite-sized pieces. Line bottom of a punch bowl with a third of the cake pieces. Top with a third of the strawberries. Pour a third of the pudding mixture on top of strawberries. Repeat layers twice and then top with remaining Cool Whip.

BETSY BRANNON GREEN currently lives in Bessemer, Alabama, which is a suburb of Birmingham. She has been married to her husband, Butch, for thirty wonderful years, and they have eight children, one daughter-in-law, three sons-in-law, and four grandchildren. She loves to read—when she can find the time—and watch sporting events, especially if they involve her children. Although born in Salt Lake City, Betsy has spent most of her life in the South. Her writing and her life have been strongly influenced by the town of Headland, Alabama, and the many generous and gracious people who live there. Her first book, *Hearts in Hiding,* was published in 2001, followed by *Never Look Back* (2002), *Until Proven Guilty* (2002), *Don't Close Your Eyes* (2003), *Above Suspicion* (2003), *Foul Play* (2004), *Silenced* (2004), *Copycat* (2005), *Poison* (2005), *Double Cross* (2006), *Christmas in Haggerty* (2006), *Backtrack* (2007), *Hazardous Duty* (2007), *Above and Beyond* (2008), *The Spirit of Christmas* (2008), and *Code of Honor* (2009).